"Been writing crime too long in this town to think otherwise, Babe. Sometimes I get lousy ideas about big trouble. Sure, I bet next month's rent that all these two-bit jokers in masks take orders from Dregovich. What for? Only lonely men and fools lean into stiff wind."

Masks, Mayhem and Murder

Another tale of Red Maguire,
crime-solving ace reporter

BOOK 2

Kevin S. Giles

BookLocker

Print ISBN: 978-1-64719-582-3
Ebook ISBN: 978-1-64719-583-0

Published by BookLocker.com, Inc., St. Petersburg, Florida.

The characters and events in this book are fictitious. Any similarity to real persons, living or dead, is coincidental and not intended by the author.

Library of Congress Cataloging in Publication Data
Giles, Kevin S.
MASKS, MAYHEM AND MURDER by Kevin S. Giles
Library of Congress Control Number: 2021907871

Printed on acid-free paper.

kevinsgiles.com 2021

First Edition

To our fantastic seven:
Haylie, Kazin, Kimberly, Seanna,
Liam, Kyleigh and Kayde

~ 1 ~

'Pay up or ...'

Pink morning light fell over the dark city as Kieran "Red" Maguire walked into the *Bugle* city room. He found the newspaper's obituary writer, Calvin Claggett, hammering the keys on his ancient Remington typewriter. Maguire brushed snow off his brown overcoat and fedora and hung them on a hook near the door. He squared his broad shoulders and ran his fingers through thick red hair.

"How's she go, Cal? Legendary Butte stiff writer snag another cold one?"

"That's staff writer to you, Maguire, you damn Irish mick. Show some respect in this family's time of need, will you?"

"So what's got you burning the Remington, Cal?"

"Bodies stacking up faster than I can put them to bed, Maguire. You know how it goes in Butte during the holidays. Half the city gets caught up in the Christmas rush. The funeral homes get the rest."

Maguire pointed to the paper in Claggett's typewriter. "Who's the poor soul crushed under the weight of your prose this morning?"

Claggett lit a butt from an overfilled ashtray. "Another wop from Meaderville. I knew her husband back when the Forever More paid him to haul bodies to the basement embalming room. He told me stories. His old lady was cold as ice and that's before she was dead."

1

"Now she gets the distinction of her charmed life being commemorated at the hand of the *Bugle's* finest obituary reporter?"

"Something like that, Maguire. I'm busy. Go write your own damn story."

Claggett bent over his typewriter to resume his writing. Maguire went to his cluttered desk near the window. The *Bugle* city room filled the third floor of the Hirbour Block in uptown Butte. He looked down on lighted Christmas wreaths draped on light poles. Decorations twinkled in the snow. Soon 1955 would arrive. He would be happy to see 1954 go.

Except for Claggett's typing, the city room at that early hour was mostly quiet. The only other person present was Clyde Stoffleman, the *Bugle* editor, who seemingly never went home. He had seen the underbelly of life and survived it. Stoffleman never talked about war except to acknowledge he had helped kill Nazis in the Battle of the Bulge. The nasty scar across his face told the rest of the story. Maguire figured Stoffleman had good reason to harbor secrets and left him alone.

Stoffleman shouted across the room. "Maguire! You got a murder or two to report for tomorrow's paper? Not coasting on your laurels, are you, boy?" Then, for good measure, "Do I need to start looking for a new crime reporter?"

Maguire smiled. "Wait a day or so, boss. I'll see what Ferndale has turned up."

Stoffleman straightened his green eye shade. Maguire rarely saw him without it. A black strap encircled Stoffleman's balding head to hold it in place. He kept a pencil or two tucked under the strap.

The old editor waved Maguire away and turned his attention to Claggett. "You planning to put that obituary to rest any time this century, Calvin?" He laughed at his joke, a familiar and overused one, before turning back to a competitor newspaper he was reading. The *Bugle* was an independent paper unlike the Company mouthpieces. Stoffleman made sure the *Bugle* ate the others for breakfast.

Maguire allowed himself a quick glance at the desk where Nancy Addleston had worked. He had known her as Mary Miller, society reporter. For Maguire, the holiday joy on Butte's uptown streets failed to disguise a terrible summer and fall. He sat down and reached into the breast pocket inside his suit jacket for the familiar bundle of envelopes that a rubber band held together. Mary's note was there, among them, her red lipstick kiss still bright on the page.

With the note before him, Maguire dialed a number at the Butte Police Department. A growly voice came on the line. "Ferndale."

"How's she go, Duke? It's Maguire, looking for news."

"Hell, I know it's you. Don't sweet-talk me, newsboy. I ain't had my coffee yet. Chief started chewing on me the minute I walked in. Wants me prying into every damn crime in Butte, which you know ain't no short list. You'd think being a shot-up cop would earn a guy a little respect in this town."

"Give him time, Duke. You came back on the job what, a month ago? The chief's worried nothing got done while you were recuperating on the couch watching Jack Benny and George Burns."

"Recuperating, hell," Ferndale growled. "He's got thirty other cops to look into our bad business. Now here's what I've got to say about that ...."

Maguire held the phone away from his ear and reached for Mary's note as Ferndale ranted. "Thanks for being there for me last night," it read. He held it in front of him.

"Maguire, you there?"

"I'm listening, detective. You deserve better."

"Damn right. Now, about that news, not that I feel any affection for keeping the *Bugle* afloat with sensational crime stories. Remember that robbery I investigated a while back on the Continental Divide? At the bar in Elk Park?"

"Sure do. Strange one as I recall. The perp tore the owner's dress into strips to tie her up. Lots of drama for fifty bucks and change."

"I've got a feeling there's more to it, Maguire. Meet me over at the Silver Star coffee shop in an hour. Bring your notebook. Don't get too jacked about it. This ain't your sensational yellow journalism about a series of murders like we saw last summer. It's just, well, suspicious."

"No sensational murders, Duke? Claggett waded hip-deep in bodies this morning."

"Probably feeling warm all over about it too. Long as I've known Claggett, which has been my entire police career, he gets his jollies writing about dead people. Today I don't have the kind he writes about. Sorry about that, Maguire. See you at the Silver Star."

Ferndale hung up. Maguire put the black receiver back in its cradle. Whatever news Ferndale had to offer better be good. Stoffleman's demand for a story for the morning paper was no idle request. The editor gave Maguire three weeks of vacation after his stories about the summer Purple Rose murders. Maguire, like Ferndale, had never taken much time away from the job. Thoughts about Mary had consumed every mile of the lonely drive to California. How unbearable to see the ocean without her. Worse yet to know the woman he loved, if only for a short time, wasn't Mary but a stranger named Nancy. The ocean was new to him. Unceasing waves calmed a man who wrote about murder for a living. He thought about going with Mary to a sandy beach. Mary, in a yellow bathing suit, her shapely legs stretched and tanning under a tropical sun. Mary, before she was Nancy.

As Maguire pulled his overcoat back on, preparing to head to the Silver Star, Ted Ketchul strolled into the city room. Unlike his co-workers at the *Bugle* who dressed in business suits, Ketchul wore black trousers, plaid shirts, and work boots. As the *Bugle's* labor reporter, he covered miners on the Hill.

"Morning, Maguire," Ketchul said in his irking manner of looking past people when he spoke.

"Got any crime news for me, Ted?"

"Only crimes being committed today are coming from Company offices, as usual. Read about it in my story tomorrow, Maguire."

Maguire donned his fedora, overcoat and a pair of gloves and headed down the stairs to the street. Shoppers carrying packages crowded the sidewalk. An old man in a Santa cap stood outside a department store ringing a bell. A few men holding beer bottles loitered outside the M & M bar down the street. They shouted insults at passing motorists.

An aroma of fresh donuts and hot coffee hit Maguire when he entered the Silver Star. Ferndale waited in a back booth. The old detective reached out to shake Maguire's hand. He flinched from the gunshot wound in his left shoulder.

"Still hurting, Duke? You come back to work too soon?"

Ferndale grunted. "Nurses practically threw me out of the hospital after twisting my arm this way and that until I couldn't take it anymore and threw some cuss words their way. Never get shot, Maguire. First comes the bullet, then the damn sadistic therapy, then sitting around feeling sorry for yourself. One's as bad as the other. I ain't felt this bad since I got decked in that light heavyweight bout back in '22. Mind you, I never lost a fight after that. At least that I admit."

"Until Nancy Addleston shot you."

"Ain't that the sum of it, Maguire?"

A waitress wearing a robin's-egg blue uniform dress came to the booth. Maguire ordered black coffee and a donut with strawberry frosting. She wrote a ticket and left. Ferndale waited until she walked out of hearing distance.

"About the robbery in Elk Park. You already know Henry Fenton was in on it. Too bad Nancy Addleston silenced him for good. I think he might have made a useful informant until she put a bullet in him. Anyway, you wrote about Fenton and another man holding up the bar that night. Now we suspect the identity of the other robber. He's a miner at the Anselmo."

Just then the smiling waitress returned with Maguire's breakfast. Ferndale rolled his eyes as she flirted with Maguire. "Name's Simone, honey. New to Butte. Do you come to the Silver Star often? If you'd like to keep track, I work mornings, Monday through Saturday."

Maguire looked her over. "Where did you come from, Simone? I should drop in for coffee more often."

"Moved over from Deer Lodge a while back, honey. Been waitressing all my life." Simone touched Maguire's head. "I just love red hair. My mama gave me some Irish blood. Her name was Colleen Callaghan. Tip me more than a nickel, now, handsome, and you might see me tomorrow."

With that, Simone was gone.

Ferndale smirked. "What is this, a junior high dance? How about we talk about robbery, lover boy? You want a story or not?"

"Sorry. You have a suspect?"

Ferndale leaned over the table. "Name is Mack Gibbons. Hard case is what I hear. Likes to tie people up, call them names, make threats, that kind of thing. I plan to arrest him when he comes off shift at the Anselmo. Come along if you want."

"Sure, but what's the rest of the story? You told me on the phone that something doesn't add up."

Ferndale massaged his injured left shoulder with scarred fingers. Suddenly he looked older than his sixty-four years.

"Muscles stiffen in cold weather. Anyhow, this Gibbons character likes to mouth off when he drinks beer over at Babe McGraw's bar. He ain't no clear thinker, as you will see, but he said enough that Babe and a few others think Gibbons got himself in more trouble than this here one robbery. His name ring a bell?"

"Nope. Should it?"

"Beats the hell out of me. What I'm telling you is that while Gibbons gets drunk and crows about his crimes, maybe a few of them true, some of our business owners are finding hand-written threats in their mail."

"What kind of threats?"

Ferndale reached in his pocket. "Got one here. Take a look."

Maguire took the folded scrap of dirty paper. The crude handwriting read, "Pay up or we rob your joint. No dicks or else."

"I don't understand, Duke. How does somebody who receives this note know what it means? Pay how much to what people for what? This reads like a dime novel."

"That's the mystery, ain't it? Babe McGraw found this note on the floor behind the bar after she closed the other night. She had a hundred men and half a dozen women bellied up to that bar. Any one of them might have left the note." Ferndale took a deep drink from his coffee cup and signaled Simone for more. "You're curious, ain't ya? Hold on."

Simone swung by with a steaming carafe. When she finished pouring, she blew Maguire a kiss and sauntered away, smiling.

Ferndale smirked. "Evidently she don't know anything about your miserable history as a lover, Maguire. Sure as hell wish I didn't."

"How about if we keep that news out of the *Bugle*," Maguire cracked.

"So as I was saying, when Babe found this note she figured on more to come. I told her it looks like a classic case of extortion. Oldest trick for milking business owners I know. Threaten 'em, scare 'em, rough 'em up, force them into paying a so-called protection fee to back off. Seen some of this in Butte over the years but it's more like how the mob runs rackets in the big cities. Now I got to wonder if Babe's note, combined with similar verbal threats to business owners and that Elk Park robbery, adds up to a mile-high pile of trouble. You know, the Butte kind."

"Babe worried?"

"You kidding? She runs a bar full of miners fresh off shift wanting to wash the dust out of their throats. You've seen these men. She gets some of the worst. Tells me Mack Gibbons shows up every night. Babe takes matters into her own hands. Nothing scares that doll."

"You still romancing Babe?"

"Hell, that was over years ago. Except now and then."

"Tell me again when she hung the 'Duke' nickname on you?"

"Never tire of hearing it, huh? I was in her bar one night when a punk tried to rattle me over some grievance he had with cops. Came in swinging. I knocked him to the floor with a punch square to the face. Joker laid moaning. Babe poured beer on his head. When he tried to stand, she hit him so hard he slept for a week. Then she started riding me as Duke Ferndale. Of course, she made sure a couple dozen people in the bar heard."

"I can't think of a better title for a Butte light heavyweight boxing champ. How many fights did you win, anyway?"

"Fifty-two in the ring if you're keeping count. Off the books, a couple dozen. You know how she goes, helping the bar boys uptown understand who's boss. In this town, a couple punches to the face sometimes makes a better impression than a trip to jail."

"Your boxing credentials must warm Babe all over."

"Long time ago, Maguire. Titles make no difference to Babe but she does enjoy fighting. Anyhow, print what you want from what I said about the robbery. I ran it up the flagpole to the chief. He agreed it's a good idea to get the word out."

"So let me get this straight. You think this Gibbons character has something to do with scaring business owners? That he writes these notes?"

Ferndale shrugged. "Cops work on hunches. That is, unless real evidence stares us in the face."

"All you have on Gibbons is suspicion?"

"So far, Maguire, but he's a talker. He can't resist spilling the beans. If he's connected to these threats, he'll brag about it to anybody who cares to listen. Thing is, if he committed the Elk Park robbery with a gun and gets away with it, he's in the frame of mind that an old dick like me will never catch on to what he does next."

"Isn't robbery different from extortion?"

"Think about it, Maguire. The motive in both crimes is the same. The criminal wants to steal jingle. We call it jingle, most people call it money. You wonder why I think Gibbons is involved? Forget the method of the crime for a minute. Look at the result. Give me a little help in the *Bugle* if you can."

"Seems sketchy but I see what you're driving at, Duke. Think Babe will talk with me about it?"

"Ever hear of Babe holding back an opinion?"

Ferndale looked at his watch. "Time to head to the Anselmo to round up Gibbons. Word is, he comes topside at the noon whistle. You coming along?"

Maguire followed Ferndale out of the coffee shop. Simone waved goodbye. Hardly glamor girl material, thin with streaks of premature gray in her brown hair, but Maguire felt his heart leap. He walked back to the booth to leave a dollar tip.

Ferndale took no chances at the Anselmo. Two prowl cars with two cops each followed his battered sedan to the mine gate. They stood near the chippy hoist, waiting for the whistle, and when the cage opened Ferndale seized a wiry little man with sleeves rolled above his elbows and cuffed him. Falling snow gathered on his bare arms.

Other miners stopped and watched. Some shouted threats at Ferndale. He and one of the other cops wrestled Gibbons, his face grimy from smoke and dust, over to a black and white.

"Ain't nobody messes with Cracker!" he shouted, invoking his Butte nickname. "I'm union, hear me? Mess with one of us, you mess with all of us."

Several blackened miners edged toward the cops. Ferndale stuffed Gibbons in the back seat and slammed the door.

"Time to get the hell out of here, Maguire. Got a feeling what comes won't be no picnic."

Gibbons, an ornery little cuss, argued and fought all the way to the jail. Handcuffed, he head-butted Ferndale's injured left shoulder as the cops wrestled him into a cell. Ferndale groaned at the pain before he knocked Gibbons cold with a smashing right hook.

"Let him sleep that one off!" Ferndale yelled. His angry voice echoed off the concrete walls.

Maguire stood back from Ferndale's explosion of violence. "Easy there, Duke. Judge will wonder how the defendant got a shiner and broken nose."

"Who the hell cares?" Ferndale retorted. He slammed the cell door and locked it. Maguire smiled. Seeing Duke at his best would make good copy in the *Bugle*.

That night, a union lawyer sprung Gibbons from jail. They came to court the next morning to plead not guilty. The judge fined Gibbons for disorderly conduct. He also dismissed the robbery charges for insufficient evidence. When the lawyer alleged police violence, pointing at his client's smashed and swollen nose, the judge laughed and ordered them out of the courtroom.

By noon, Gibbons was back at work, bragging to his buddies half a mile underground that when he caught Ferndale alone, he would work him over until he cried for his mama.

~ 2 ~

'Tragic story, Arnie'

Back at the *Bugle*, Clyde Stoffleman greeted the news of a robbery ring in Butte with predictable cynicism. "About time you found a crime story fit to print, Maguire. I figured I needed to retire you to the society pages to write stories about party favors and engagements. We have an opening, you know."

The editor cut deep. Maguire still endured nightmares over ending the Purple Rose Murders. His eyewitness story about lovely Mary Miller, society reporter, who became Nancy Addleston, killer, hit the big time. *Associated Press* and *United Press International* and all the big national papers ran the story under his full byline, Kieran "Red" Maguire, just as he asked. Stoffleman negotiated agreements that other news agencies run the story in its entirety or not at all. Not that any of them needed persuading. Stoffleman wrote an editor's note explaining how Maguire wrote the full story looking at Nancy's body, still warm after she plugged herself square in the chest. It was a sensational tale, too sad and salacious for even buttoned-up conservative news agencies to ignore.

The story ran first in the *Bugle*. Stoffleman read Maguire's typed copy with trembling fingers. The gruff editor put down the story and cried. He ran upstairs to show it to the Old Man, the publisher who owned the *Bugle*, who ordered an *Extra* to hit the streets. By mid-afternoon, newsboys barked from every street corner in uptown Butte with the startling headlines held aloft:

Purple Rose Killer Revealed

Butte's Greatest Murder Mystery Solved

Every bar patron in uptown Butte read the *Extra* that day. Maggie O'Keefe reported from Mercury Street that after a newsboy brought papers to the Windsor, customers lost their interest in her girls. Everyone convened in the parlor to talk about the story.

The press, two floors beneath the city room, kicked out *Bugles* until, as the ink-stained foreman described, it became "blistering hot" and blew a circuit.

City room telephones rang into the night. Other than Maguire's, the busiest was the phone belonging to the society reporter everyone in the city room had known as Mary Miller.

"Macabre curiosity," is what Stoffleman made of it. "They're probably expecting her to answer. You know, a voice from the grave, that kind of thing. Never underestimate the public's desire to know every last grimy detail, which of course we aspire to print for them in exchange for their hard-earned dimes."

Maguire loved the woman he knew as Mary. It was a short romance, one that teased him with its promise but left him abruptly, much as his mother had done when he was a young boy. After Mary shot herself, Maguire refused to let his emotion creep into the task before him. He sat at the typewriter and wrote the story of Nancy Addleston. He wrote furiously to suppress an irrational fear that she would awaken and confront him again. She lay slumped against the wall in the dreary abandoned warehouse. His urgent tapping on the keys echoed in the rafters of the empty building. He wrote everything he ever knew, and suspected, about Mary. An hour later he finished.

A flurry of activity followed. Maguire raced outside. He drove his Pontiac up Butte Hill to the *Bugle* where he handed his story to Clyde Stoffleman. The editor read the opening lines aloud, his hands shaking, his voice cracking, his emotion showing. He slumped into his chair and reached for the telephone to summon Police Chief Donald Morse. "Maguire blew the Purple Roses case wide open," Stoffleman barked. "He's got gunshots, a dead perp, even motive. I kid you not, chief. My boy has it all!" Minutes later, Maguire caught a ride with the chief and a parade of cops back to the dark abandoned warehouse. He led them up the stairs to Nancy's lifeless body. The gun she used to kill all those people, and herself, reposed against her right thigh, barrel up. Blood leaked from a small hole above her heart. Her hands, turning blue, lay palms up as if appealing for forgiveness. One eye remained partly open. The room felt heavy with death and the odor of gunpowder. Five other cops crowded around the chief, who removed his hat and bowed his head. "She's the one?" he said quietly to Maguire.

"All along it turns out," Maguire said. He struck a match on the wall to light a cigarette. Then he leaned against it, shoulder first, feet crossed at the ankles, hands thrust into the pockets of his dark suit. He pushed his fedora back. A hush fell over the room. The chief watched the crime reporter study the scene before him. He saw a tear glisten on Maguire's cheek. "I loved her," Maguire admitted. His face hardened. "Read about it in the *Bugle* and weep."

The chief touched Maguire's shoulder with manicured fingers. "I know loss, Red. You saw it firsthand. My daughter …," he offered, and then, "You saw her shoot herself?"

Maguire blew a ring of smoke and nodded. "Right in front of me, chief. She looked me in the eye first."

"Why didn't you call us right away instead of writing a story, Red?"

Maguire shrugged. "The *Bugle* butters my bread."

Arnie Petrovich came with a hearse. At the Forever More Funeral Home, Maguire carried Nancy's pale body to a basement table where Arnie would decorate her for burial. The stooping undertaker, reeking of formaldehyde, probed at her wound with cracked fingers. "Suicide, Maguire? Shame, all this. She knew where to place the bullet to end it. When I had her father in here all those many years ago, he was in far worse shape, all beaten to hell. In any case, dead is dead, no doubt about it."

"Tragic story from start to sudden conclusion, Arnie." Maguire lingered. At that moment he felt no sadness for the scene before him and wondered why. He felt nothing at all at witnessing death by gun. He leaned a broad shoulder against the wall, crossed one leg over the other, and took a deep breath audible enough that Arnie turned to see his blank stare.

"Maybe you want to stay for this, Red? I got another cold one in the other room that comes first because his funeral is tomorrow. Family wants open casket. They will hate what they see. I work miracles with face paint. Trouble is, a falling beam clobbered him in a tunnel at the Lexington mine. Want to see what that does to a man?"

"No, Arnie. I won't stay for her, either." Maguire bent to look at Nancy in her eternal sleep. Her blond hair framed her face. Unlike when he had known her as Mary, she wore no makeup. He touched her cold hand. He kissed her forehead. Pretty even in death.

"Suit yourself, Red. She was a beauty, all right. You knew her."

"Yes, that too," Maguire said.

"Does she have a family? If not, she's headed for a pauper's grave over at the city cemetery."

"No, Arnie, not that. I will pay. Bury her next to her father. Nobody knows. Nothing to gain by wrenching further public outrage over her sad life. Put her away quietly. I'll cover your costs."

"People will want to know, Maguire. You, more than anyone, know that."

Maguire felt for the letters in his pocket. He squeezed his eyes shut.

"We won't tell them, Arnie."

Two days later Maguire visited the fresh grave. He thought of Nancy's victims, dwelling in similar circumstances underground. "Mary, I loved you, but what Nancy did was so terribly wrong," he whispered over the broken soil.

He walked to his Pontiac and headed west to California. That was in September. Back on the job in October, Maguire struggled with his newfound fame. People came to the *Bugle* city room asking for his autograph. He sent them away. He spent evenings alone in his room at the Logan Hotel drinking beer and struggling with something called "vertical hold" on the television. He fell into fitful slumbers where Nancy's stricken face appeared. Always, she held the revolver to her chest an instant before she pulled the trigger.

Some afternoons Maguire went to visit Ferndale. Infection from his gunshot wound slowed the old detective's return to the police force. His doctor kept him in bed at Silver Bow Hospital for three weeks until Ferndale put on his clothes one morning and walked out. A cop on patrol found Ferndale walking along the road, coatless in a sleet storm, his left arm in a sling. He spent another three weeks convalescing at home. He asked Maguire to bring him whiskey. When Ferndale drank, he told stories about romancing Babe on the seat of her pickup truck. "Caught her reaching for my stick shift," he grinned, embellishing the story a bit more each time he told it.

One day Chief Morse arrived at the house, catching Ferndale in a rare sober moment. "Get your coat on, detective. You have work to do." That was that. Ferndale climbed off the couch, strapped on his gun, and resumed his twelve-hour days like he had never left.

Maguire wrote a *Bugle* story about Ferndale's return to the police department. It began: "The battered hero detective finds serious crime wherever he looks. Punched in the jaw, thrown to the pavement, shot in the shoulder, and ignored more death threats than any cop in Butte. Harold Ferndale, known as 'Duke' among Mining City denizens for his boxing skills, is back on the job."

Ferndale appreciated the story but confided to Maguire he had tired of chasing thugs and killers. "Getting shot hurts like hell," he said.

***

A few days before Christmas in 1954, Maguire reported in the *Bugle* that Ferndale again arrested Cracker Gibbons on suspicion of robbery. The detective admitted privately to Maguire that the arrest was another shot in the dark. "Make him worry that we know something he don't," Ferndale said. For publication, Ferndale spoke of Gibbons as "an uptown drunk who does bidding for union influences and none of it good." The quote appeared two paragraphs below Maguire's byline.

He sat at his typewriter in the city room when he noticed Ted Ketchul pacing in front of him. Ketchul held the morning paper in front of him like it was poison.

"Something bothering you, Ted?"

"It's your latest story, Red. You imply somebody on the Hill is running a racket with the business types. Are you accusing miners and unions? I'm not hearing any of that."

"Not implying, Ted. My information comes from Duke Ferndale over at the cop shop. I'm reporting the story as you well know."

"Don't talk down to me, Maguire. It's the general tone, isn't it? Accusation without verification. Why didn't you talk to me about it first? Did you forget labor is my beat?"

Maguire squinted at Ketchul, who twitched like a prowling cat.

"Did you forget crime is mine, Ted? What makes you think miners don't commit crimes? With ten thousand miners on the Hill there's a good chance of it."

"There's nothing to it," Ketchul said, looking somewhat subdued. Maguire knew little about Ketchul. They had worked together for nine years. Ketchul, like Stoffleman, was a war combat veteran. He had survived the Japanese bombing of Pearl Harbor. Ketchul said little about his experience aboard the USS Nevada. Maguire knew him as a daring but secretive reporter who wrote stories about mine safety and labor negotiations. Ketchul rarely reported news about trouble between miners. Stoffleman, having experienced combat himself, said Ketchul had seen enough heartbreak at Pearl Harbor to last a lifetime.

Ketchul crumpled up the paper, tossed it at Maguire, and stormed out of the city room. A few desks away, Claggett watched the exchange. He pulled himself into a standing position, which for Claggett meant stooped. Forty years of writing obituaries shaped him that way, as did his second job helping Arnie Petrovich embalm bodies at the Forever More.

Claggett shuffled over to Maguire. He offered a pack of Old Golds. "Care for a smoke, Red?" he asked in his raspy voice.

"Appreciated," Maguire said, reaching for a cigarette.

"Don't let him get to you. Ketchul, he had a hard life. People think I'm blind to struggles with the living, preoccupied with the dead as I am. Nobody dies without baggage. Ketchul fights demons like everyone else. He hides it but it eats at him. We hope whatever worry burns him inside might extinguish someday. Give him time."

Maguire blew a cloud of blue smoke. "I never figured you for a philosopher, stiff writer."

Claggett cracked a rare smile. "Staff writer, which you well know. You and me, Maguire, we have something in common. We both know where the bodies are buried in this town."

He knows, Maguire thought. He knows about Nancy.

Claggett returned to his typewriter. What irony that he will pen obituaries until he dies, Maguire thought to himself.

Maguire began writing the news about Gibbons' latest quick exit from jail when his phone rang. It was Ferndale.

"Meet me at the Valley View service station," he said. "We have another robbery and this one's worse."

~ 3 ~

'Well, hell. Red Maguire'

Maguire arrived at the gas station just as an Irish cop he knew as Jimmy Regan heaved his broad figure out of a black and white.

"If it ain't Red Maguire, Butte's ace crime reporter," Regan greeted him.

"Morning, Jimmy. Shouldn't you be home in bed at this hour?"

"I got promoted off graveyard shift after twenty-six years. Who would have thought?"

"Congratulations, Jimmy. Hope the new job doesn't go arseways on you."

"No worse than before, me Irish mate."

"I hear you boys might have some news for me."

"Let's go inside to find out. Ferndale's here already. You can figure he ain't none too happy when a man trying to make an honest living gets jumped."

Maguire followed Jimmy past the gas pumps and a trail of blood in the snow. Ferndale stood inside the door of the tiny office. A younger man in a soiled brown uniform that said "Dick" above his pocket knelt over an older man wearing the same uniform. The younger man held a greasy rag to the older man's bleeding head.

Ferndale turned to Maguire and Regan. "Harry here is the owner," Ferndale said of the injured man. "Two men jacked him for twelve bucks and change in the register. Then they crowned him with the butt of a gun. One tall, one short. Harry says they hid their faces with Halloween masks."

"One was a pirate and the other a mean cat," Harry said. He moaned and pointed to the door. "Dick here, my son, he was tuning a motor in the back so didn't hear nothin'. After they clubbed me, I followed those thugs outside in hopes of getting a license plate number, but they disappeared. I worked in this neighborhood since before the war. Never had a lick of trouble until today."

Maguire looked down at the trail of blood. "Red Maguire from the *Bugle*, Harry. Did they say anything to you?"

"The short guy, he tells me I need protection from people like him. Fifty bucks a month. I'd go broke paying those men off."

Ferndale reached to the floor to pick up a framed photograph under cracked glass. It showed a younger Harry with a woman and a boy.

"That's my family. My wife and son. The bastards. Dick practically grew up in that shop back there, fixing cars." Harry reached for the photograph. Ferndale handed it to him.

"Jimmy, take this man over to the hospital, will you? He'll need stitches."

Dick spoke. "I'll take him if you think it's safe to leave the station unattended. My mother will want to meet us there."

"They won't be coming back, at least not today," Ferndale said. He pulled open his coat to reach for a pencil. Maguire saw that Ferndale no longer wore his police revolver in a shoulder holster but on his hip. Ferndale was feeling more pain from that gunshot than he would let on.

"Here's my phone number at the department," he told Dick, scrawling it on a scrap of paper from Harry's desk.

After Dick left with his father for the hospital, Ferndale reached into the window to turn the "closed" sign outward. He took off his hat and ran a hand over his bald head.

"We'll dust for prints but you know, the perps probably wore gloves. Harry don't remember. Made a mess, didn't they? Drawers pulled out, furniture knocked over, general trashing of the place. This ain't no robbery and it ain't no kids getting their jollies with vandalism. Ain't none of this making sense. What do you think, Maguire?"

Maguire tipped up his fedora and crossed his arms. He closed his eyes for a moment as the cops watched him. "Seems to me, detective, that we've got a bigger crime going on here. If they wanted to scare Harry into paying them off, why try to kill him? Perps in the other robberies tied up their victims. Maybe these men today intended to do that until they saw Harry's son working in the back? Or the perp who hit Harry was a hot-headed type who thinks it's funny to beat up an old man who works for a living? And why wear little kids' Halloween masks? Got a feeling those perps are trying to hide something more than a simple robbery."

"Red's got a point, boss, even if he is a damn mick," Regan said.

"You're both damn micks, Jimmy. Everywhere I turn in this town I stumble over you Irish. Been doing it for years. Now, find some clues."

Maguire pulled a notebook out of his coat and began jotting details. "What I'm not understanding, Duke, is how these guys plan to collect money from business owners without being caught."

Ferndale, bent over to look closely at the cash register, took his time to respond. "What I know about extortion, Maguire, is that it takes time to unfold. Criminals make threats without a plan until somebody with a bigger brain comes along to plot it out for them."

Jimmy eyed Maguire's notebook and laughed. "You writing another story, Red? Any chance it will be better than all the others?"

"This is what passes for daytime police humor, Jimmy? I hear the chief has an opening on night shift."

Ferndale straightened. "Regan, if you hope to make detective someday go find neighbors who saw or heard anything, will you? And Maguire?"

"I'm out of your way, Duke. I figure I'll go find out what Babe McGraw can tell me."

"Stay on her good side, for chrissakes. She worked over a drunk but good last night. Who's telling if she's calmed down to her usual good-natured self."

Maguire pointed his Pontiac up Montana Avenue to Park Street. He drove east to the Finn Town neighborhood. It was late afternoon. The neon sign at Babe's Bar, on the corner, glowed in the fading daylight. Babe would be hustling drinks behind the bar. It was advisable to pay up, drink up, and pay up again. Babe hated freeloaders.

Maguire stepped through a battered wooden door into the bar, gloomy from shadows and cigarette smoke. A few miners sat on round stools at the bar. One of them coughed into a dirty handkerchief. Maguire went to the end of the bar where Babe stacked warm cans of Great Falls Select into a cooler. She saw Maguire and wiped wet hands on her bib overalls.

"Well, hell. Red Maguire right here in my bar. Closest thing to a celebrity in Butte. I gotta know, right from the horse's mouth, was that crazy woman going to shoot you?"

"Pour me a beer. I'll tell you about it."

Maguire took note of the legend before him. Husky shoulders, thick arms. She looked shorter than barroom gossip about her would suggest. Eyes, gray and kind, seemed out of sorts with the general growl on her face. Her lips curled as she spoke. Maguire thought of an angry dog eager to bite. Babe's belligerent stocky swagger agreed with her reputation in Butte.

Babe pushed a tall can of Rainer in front of Maguire. She punched two triangle-sized holes in the top of it with a church key she took from her shirt pocket. "On the house but I won't make no habit of it," she said. Maguire noticed three fingers missing on her left hand. She saw him looking.

"Ever chopped kindling wood, Maguire? Now, what you want to know?"

"So you read my story about Nancy Addleston?"

"Me and everyone else who has two eyeballs. Well, was she?"

"Going to shoot me? Yes, until she turned the gun on herself. I was as good as dead. I'll never know why she changed her mind."

"Hell of a story, Maguire. Beats anything I got going here."

Maguire took a sip. "Safe to bring up Ferndale's name?"

"Got no current beef with him. Another day might get you a different answer. You wanna know about the threat?"

"Hoping to quote you for my next story, if you're willing."

Babe slid her remaining fingers, five on her right hand and only her thumb and forefinger on the other, under the straps on her bib overalls. "Don't make no difference to me. Any man who comes in here thinking he'll deprive me of my livelihood will find his sorry Butte ass kicked from here to Sunday."

"I've no doubt," Maguire said.

"So here's the deal. First, I get the note on the bar, then I find one on the windshield of my pickup out back. All about somebody wanting jingle they didn't earn. My money. Ain't got no idea how much they want, or how they plan to take it, but they ain't taking it from me without a fight. Put that in your story. Babe McGraw don't take guff off no one, least the puny whiners who can't face me like a man."

Maguire told her about the attack on Harry at the Valley View station.

"Someone comes swinging at me, they better buy good dental insurance. Swept up my share of teeth in here, fair number I extracted myself."

"Ferndale tells me you had a go-around last night."

"Clumsy fool tried to fight me at closing time. Swung a beer bottle at my head when I pushed him to the door. Kneed him in the groin hard enough that he'll be clutching himself into next year." She held up a bruised right fist. "My uppercut to his nose was to remind him who's boss in my bar. Ain't nobody telling me how to run my affairs."

Maguire managed a grin. "You scare me, Babe."

"Naw, you don't strike me as a man who scares easily. What are you, 200 pounds and six feet?"

"On the button on the first count and three inches more on the second."

"Ever had anybody mess up your pretty face?"

"When I was a kid in Dublin Gulch after my old man and I moved from Chicago. Nowadays I prefer to talk my way out of fights. Too many people want a piece of me."

"Don't get none too comfortable, Maguire. Them thugs running around trying to scare honest business owners will come looking for you after a few more of your newspaper stories."

"Been there before, Babe."

She turned and hollered down the bar. "You lunkheads get your money on the bar for more beer or get the hell out. I run a paying establishment here."

She turned back to Maguire. "I hear loose talk in here every night. Tongues flap like window shades after a few drinks. These miners come off shift full of scuttlebutt they hear underground. They joke about these threats and robberies. Say they come from a union."

Maguire nearly spit out a mouthful of beer. "A union? We're talking hundreds of men. Maybe thousands."

"I doubt they're all dirty. Probably a few dozen, but they're organized."

"Which union, Babe?"

"Turns your crank, huh, Maguire? The biggest. Local 1235. Tough crowd run by Rusie Dregovich. He don't come in my place but the men who do fear him. If you put that in your paper, Maguire, watch your back."

"This Mack Gibbons, Babe, what's his connection?"

"Hold on." Babe went to pour beer for the three miners. He heard coins tinkle on the bar. "Not my best customers," she told Maguire when she came back. "Lay-ins, scared of a hard day's work so they come here looking for sympathy and pass a few coins. It's jingle, I guess, but damned little of it. They hang around until first shift comes off the Hill, which is any minute now, and then skulk out of here. Know I put up a Christmas tree once? It got trampled in a brawl."

"Gibbons, Babe?"

"Oh yeah. That idiot? Works for Dregovich on the same crew at the Anselmo. Dregovich, he's shift foreman. Cracker drives a tram hauling ore on the half-mile level. Little man who gets drunk and claims he kills people for fun. Dumber than a pump handle."

Babe watched Maguire take notes. "If you're quoting me in the *Bugle*, print my full name will you, Ruby McGraw?"

"All of Butte knows you as Babe."

"A girl has to maintain her dignity, Maguire."

Snow fell as Maguire left Babe's Bar. Miners came walking alone and in twos down the icy dark streets, drifting toward the bar. Some carried lunch pails. Maguire drove back to the *Bugle* city room. Stoffleman waited to pounce.

"You nail the goods on this service station robbery, Maguire, or do I have to read about it in the Company papers? I've been chasing reporters around all day except for Claggett, who churned out four obituaries."

"Claggett never leaves the city room, boss. He writes about people who can't run away from him. No chasing to be done. But yes, I have the story."

"I heard that, Maguire," Claggett yelled across the long room. He continued typing, violently, his head down.

Maguire told Stoffleman about what Babe McGraw had told him.

"The union angle adds a significant new dimension to the story, all right." Stoffleman gripped his eyeshade and moved it slightly left and right. It was a signal, Maguire knew, that he was thinking. "You don't know if this union business is true?"

"Not yet. I need to find someone to verify it on the record. Ketchul, is he around?"

"Gone home," Stoffleman said. "We'll talk with him in the morning."

Maguire wrote his story about the Valley View station robbery and assault. Before handing it over to Stoffleman for editing he called Ferndale.

"Anything new on this afternoon's event, Duke? If not, I'm heading home for the night."

"Cool your heels, Maguire. Things just got more interesting. Those fools hiding behind Halloween masks like little kids out trick or treating are now murder suspects. Harry went downhill fast at the hospital. Turns out the clubbing he took caused bleeding on the brain. He died five minutes ago."

~ 4 ~

'Beaten to a pulp'

A knock came at Maguire's door around dawn as he slept. Few people knew where he lived. His room on the second floor of the Logan Hotel was anything but auspicious. Maguire threw the blankets aside. He pulled on his pants and a shirt and reached under his mattress. Revolver in hand, he crept to the door that opened into a long hallway.

"Who's there?" The knock came again. Then came a distressed woman's voice.

"Maguire? That you? Babe McGraw, open up, dammit."

He swung the door open. She buckled against the wall in the dim light of the hallway. Blood dripped from her lip. Babe peered at Maguire through blackened eyes. A rip in her plaid shirt exposed a swollen bruised shoulder under her bib overalls.

Maguire reached for her hand, the one with fingers. He led her to one of the two chrome chairs near the stove. When she saw his gun, she nodded her approval.

"Wise to take precautions, Maguire. Wish I had. I won't be winning no beauty contests anytime soon."

Maguire reached for a towel, wet it under the faucet, and wiped blood from Babe's face. She pinched the towel with her thumb and remaining finger on her left hand and pressed it against her cheeks.

"How come you missed your thumb in that wood chopping accident?"

"Because I was careful when I swung that axe."

"Tell me who beat you up, Babe. You look like you went a few rounds in the ring with Ferndale. Without gloves."

Babe winced from the pain. "That old duffer would look worse. Got aspirin?" While Maguire rummaged through the cupboard, Babe laid it out for him.

"Do my books after closing. Done it that way for years. Do the books, mop the bar, check inventory, that kind of thing. Sitting at the bar counting money about an hour ago when I hear the back door open. I know I locked it after taking a few hundred empty beer bottles out to the alley. I look up to see somebody in a mask. This damn fool thinks he's Porky Pig. Know what, Maguire? He holds a copy of the *Bugle*, pointing to your front-page headline about the robberies."

"What did he say?"

"That's the crazy thing. Not a damn thing. Spooky, I tell you, being stared at by a damn sissy acting like a cartoon character. I tell him to get the hell out of my bar. He stands there holding the paper. Three more men in Halloween masks walk in. They come toward me at the bar. I start throwing punches. Ain't nobody messes with Babe. One of them clubbed me in the eye. I took harder punches from miners but not from four at once. They knock me to the floor and kick me a few times. I see them scooping my money into a paper sack. They robbed me and left, Maguire. I pulled myself onto a bar stool and found this."

She took a scrap of paper from her pocket. "Pay for protection," it read in scrawled pencil.

Maguire looked it over. "Did you call police?"

"Don't trust cops. Maybe Ferndale when I feel like it. Everyone in this town knows a dirty cop. I wouldn't be surprised if some of them are in on this."

"Do you think they came after you because I quoted you in the *Bugle*?"

"Who knows? Them fools tried to intimidate me once already. Nobody muzzles Babe McGraw."

"You need medical attention, Babe. I'll drive you."

"Bring your gun, Maguire. You never know who is prowling these lonely streets before this town wakes up."

Maguire phoned Ferndale from the hospital. The cranky old cop swore his displeasure at being called at home before the sun was up. Maguire smiled into the receiver until Ferndale finished his rant.

"It's Babe McGraw, Duke. Beaten to a pulp by four trick or treaters. Right in her bar after closing time. She got a few licks in. They ran with her cash."

Ferndale cursed anew into the phone. He still had a thing for Babe, that much was clear to Maguire.

"Tell her I'll be right over. We need to get on the record with this attack. How bad is she hurt?"

"Been knocked around. Bruised and cut. Flat on her back in the ER taking stitches and not too happy about it. She's also mad enough to take on those thugs for another round when she finds out who they are."

"She'll be fine then. I've never known Babe to back down after a beating."

When Ferndale arrived at the hospital, Maguire went back to the Logan Hotel to shave. Half the building was vacant. Maguire knew of three other tenants on his floor. They were old and stayed indoors. At least from his room, at the front of the hotel, he could see the street below.

Maguire turned the key in the lock. The door, unlatched, pushed open. He peered cautiously into the gloomy rooms. Someone had cased the joint. Mattress overturned and thrown to the floor. Drawers pulled out, chairs overturned, clothes pulled from their hangars and tossed aside.

Feeling a sudden panic, Maguire sorted through the heap until he found the clothes he had worn a day earlier. He felt a wave of relief when his fingers touched his love letters, still intact in the wax paper wrapping, undisturbed.

Maguire dressed in a clean shirt and cinched a blue tie around his neck. He pulled on a pair of rubber snow boots. The snub-nosed .38 Special, a gift from Ferndale some years ago, fit snugly into one of Maguire's coat pockets. He slipped the letters into the other.

This time he locked the door. Somebody had followed Babe McGraw to the Logan and broke in after they left for the hospital. The lobby of the old hotel had a counter where a desk clerk once checked lodgers into their rooms. Nobody had worked there for years. "Criminals and bums, a home to everybody," Maguire said to himself. He stepped outside where he stood under the blinking neon sign and put a match to a cigarette. Wind off the Hill blew a stench of oil and grease from the mines. The Logan loomed over East Granite Street a half dozen blocks from the *Bugle*. Maguire pulled his overcoat tight to his throat and walked to the newspaper. He passed a few shopkeepers shoveling sidewalks but despite their efforts he waded through deep snow most of the way. At the *Bugle*, Stoffleman hovered over his desk, his green eye shade firmly affixed. The editor rarely slept. After the war, in a rare moment of confession, he told Maguire that every time he closed his eyes, he saw dead German civilians hanging from light poles as the Allies nudged closer to Berlin. "Nazis killed them, Maguire, cruel beasts that they were. Still, that image haunts me as symbolic of lives I personally took in combat." He never talked of it again.

Maguire shook snow off his fedora and pulled off his rubber boots. He hung his overcoat on a hook on the wall.

"No question about a white Christmas this year, boss."

Stoffleman lifted his shattered face. Cold weather made the scar that ran along his jaw more obvious. He was in a surly mood. "Meanwhile, we have people who can't tell one holiday from the next, running around scaring the daylights out of people with masks."

"Clearly not everybody caught the spirit of the Christmas season."

"Hell of a scoop this morning, my boy. Nobody else reported that old Harry died. None of the Company papers, no broadcast."

Maguire told Stoffleman about the attack on Babe McGraw.

"I stopped for a beer in Ruby's place once," Stoffleman said. "Apparently I lingered too long with the first glass. She told me to buy another one or she would clean my clock but good."

"Circumstantial evidence shows she wasn't kidding," Maguire said.

"Does she know who jumped her, besides Porky Pig?"

"The cat showed up again. She saw a skeleton mask. They were measuring her for a coffin from the sounds of it."

Ted Ketchul walked into the city room. He seemed agitated. The labor reporter's muscled arms swung as if sawing logs in a lumber camp. His brown crewcut, although grayed at the temples, gave him an air of youth. "Far from flamboyant but unfailingly accurate in his reporting," is how Stoffleman described him. Stoffleman, typically hard on all of his reporters, cut some slack with Ketchul because of his war experience.

"Morning, Ted. Time to huddle. First, a cuppa." Stoffleman went to the coffee urn in the corner. He would drink from it all day. Coffee thick as motor oil. After Maguire drank a cup one morning, at Stoffleman's insistence, he stayed awake all night.

Ketchul swiveled in his chair as Maguire retold the story of Babe McGraw's beating. He also described the ransacking of his room. Ketchul tucked a pencil behind his ear. That was a signal to everyone in the city room that he was on the clock. He listened respectfully to Stoffleman's request that he confirm whether the men behind the masks were union members.

"If you wish, sir. I can tell you right now I heard nothing of the sort. I told Red yesterday there's nothing to it. I spend hours every day with these men. They complain about bad bosses and low pay and fear of dying in the hole."

"Which you document extensively in your stories," Stoffleman acknowledged.

Ketchul reached for the pencil and spun it around in his fingers. "It's hardly news that any crime committed in Butte would be committed by miners given the sheer numbers of them. I take the clowns behind these masks for rogues. Even if they are miners, there's no way they would have the backing of an entire union of hundreds of men."

Maguire knew what was coming. Stoffleman disliked his judgment questioned.

"Put that way, Ted, I must be two brain cells short of an idiot for suggesting we look into the union angle," Stoffleman said. "Pitch in with Maguire today to find the tentacles on this monster. No cause to debate the theoreticals. Do the reporting first. Then we'll talk."

Accustomed to taking orders, Ketchul rose to his feet. "I hear you loud and clear, sir. For the record, I want to say that these working men of Butte, they're the real story."

"Which you capably established in a thousand stories over the years, Ted. Carry on."

Stoffleman walked back to his desk, coffee mug in hand.

"People get hurt over stories like this," Ketchul whispered to Maguire.

"They already have," Maguire whispered back. "What about Gibbons? Does he speak for the unions?"

"Cracker doesn't speak for anyone but himself. That man is a lowlife who stirs trouble over what he fails to understand. In straight talk, Cracker doesn't know his ass from a hole in the ground, pun intended."

"So the unions will condemn his criminal behavior?"

"Where are you going with this, Maguire?"

"I'm thinking if the unions don't condemn him, there's more to the story."

Maguire and Ketchul argued over the story until Ketchul threw up his hands. "I don't report to you, Maguire."

"Then go about it your own way, Ted. Going up the Hill today?"

"As I always do. Want me to blow the working men a kiss from you?"

Maguire ignored the insult. "How well do you know a union leader named Rusie Dregovich?"

Ketchul stiffened. "Everyone knows Rusie Dregovich. You read my stories. Most powerful man on the Hill. Nothing happens without his say-so."

"Then maybe he'll tell you about the robberies," Maguire said. He caught the dark look in Ketchul's eyes as he walked away.

Maguire sat down at his typewriter. Letters had worn off the keys. The loose carriage rattled when he typed. Stoffleman, tired of reading faint script, reminded him daily to replace the ribbon. Maguire wrote stories on the old typewriter for a couple of decades. It had belonged to Peter Sullivan, the crime reporter who preceded him. Maguire had a soft heart for sentimentality. He reached inside his coat pocket to touch the small bundle of letters. Touching them before writing a story had become a ritual.

The one personal note he ever received from his mother was there. It was written when he was a boy, before she disappeared without saying goodbye, before he and his father moved to Montana and settled in Butte. Only after she left, a week later, did he find the note in his bedroom. It had fallen on the floor behind his pillow. He knew the words by heart.

"Dear Kieran. Lord knows how you got stuck with a mother like me. I suppose I ain't done much good for this world except for you. When I get sad and crying I think of your smiling face and the tears go away. You are a light. You give me hope. Sorry for the hurt I caused. I don't want to ruin you so I'm going away. Believe me when I say this is the most loving thing I can do for you. Love Mother."

Lily Maguire had kept her word. She disappeared from her son's life. He hoped to find her someday in Chicago where he last saw her. He hoped.

Maguire settled his fingertips on the worn keys and began writing his story about Babe's beating. He had asked her, at the hospital, if a news story about it would scare her. "Go ahead and tell it," she muttered through swollen lips as a doctor stitched a gash below her eye. "Anybody gets on their hind legs about it, tell 'em nobody messes with Babe and gets away with it. Those miners know what happens when they cross me."

Maguire smiled at Babe's sassy defiance. He finished his story and headed to the Silver Star to see Simone.

~ 5 ~

'Butte's prettiest woman'

Maguire took the back booth where he had met Ferndale a day earlier. Customers at the counter, drinking coffee from white ceramic cups, held copies of the *Bugle*. From his vantage point, Maguire watched them reading his front-page story.

"Look at this!" crowed a man in a business suit. He nudged a customer in gray coveralls next to him and stabbed at the paper. "Says here those robbers with the Halloween masks killed Harry Dalton. Old Harry, I can't believe it. I've bought my gas at the Valley View for thirty years." The man continued reading, his expression suggesting his disbelief at the turn of events.

"Coffee, handsome?" A white apron entered Maguire's line of vision, followed by a lime green uniform. He looked up to see Simone smiling down at him. "You came alone today, I see. You're the man behind the byline in the *Bugle* is what I hear."

Maguire shrugged. "People know me."

Simone held a steaming glass coffee pot. "Here, let me fix you up, *Bugle* boy." She winked at him as she poured the coffee.

"Do you charm all the customers like this?"

Simone leaned close, scent of perfume and odor of bacon grease wafting over him. Ringlets fell over her forehead. She had a year or two on Maguire. She had known a hard life, most of it on her feet, most of it wearing a path in the linoleum in one diner or another.

"Truth is, Mr. Red Maguire, the owners of this fine establishment don't like the help flirting with customers. My husband doesn't like it either."

Maguire, feeling disappointed, glanced at her hands. "I don't see you wearing a ring, Simone."

"Waitresses don't wear wedding rings, handsome. My god, you're gorgeous." She puckered her lips in a kiss. Then she was gone, pouring coffee at the counter, as Maguire turned in the booth to watch her with new interest.

Suddenly another woman caught Maguire's attention. She emerged from a booth with an elegance out of character with working class Butte, bearing evidence of a city much different from what it was. Maguire took note with his newsman's eyes as he always did. Bobbed reddish-brown hair shimmering in the morning light from the cafe's front window. Glittering earrings. Facial features screaming a stunning likeness of Hollywood goddess Jane Russell. Lipstick matching a long red coat that covered all but the bottom few inches of a black dress. Nails painted red. Slender long fingers brushing strands of that gorgeous hair from her cheeks. She walked like a woman who knew her business.

Maguire watched, captivated, until their eyes locked. The woman looked away to reach for her purse. Then she walked toward him. A hush fell over the Silver Star.

Maguire knew of Irene Rossini by reputation. She owned the most fashionable jewelry store in Butte. Only at this moment had he seen her in person. She moved with the poise of a dancer. Heads pivoted at the counter. Maguire looked into Irene's brown eyes. She smiled with perfect white teeth. "Good morning, Mr. Maguire."

She slid a small green envelope across the table, slowly, until he reached for it. She nodded and left the cafe.

Maguire watched her go. Simone came with the coffee pot.

"I'll never have a chance with you now lover boy," she said mournfully. She stole a glance at the envelope as she refilled his coffee cup.

"Thanks, Simone. I don't know her."

"I imagine you'll find a way," she said before walking away, her lips in a pout.

Maguire found a folded sheet of stationery inside the unsealed envelope. Under a letterhead that said, "Rossini's Fine Jewelry," written elegantly in ink, was this: "Mr. Maguire, please contact me by telephone (don't come to my store) as I wish to attend to a matter that's come to my attention. Butte Exchange 14-992. Honey."

Maguire read Irene's note six times. What did she want? Why was she calling him Honey? He replayed their brief meeting in his mind. He had never seen her except in advertisements in the *Bugle* when she was reigning queen of the Butte Snowball winter festival. The grainy newspaper image failed to do justice to her beauty. She was a belle in the midst of Butte's grimy backdrop.

He held her note, unsure what to do next, until sliding it into his pocket next to the bundle of letters. It belonged with the rest.

Maguire tipped Simone before pulling on his overcoat. He waved goodbye at her across the room. She acknowledged him but with little enthusiasm.

Outside, with Christmas Eve a week away, shoppers crowded the snowy sidewalks. Many people carried packages. Maguire remembered the meager Christmases before his father Sean died in the mine accident. Each November they drove to the woods above Walkerville in search of a tree small enough to fit inside their shack in Dublin Gulch. The neighborhood, squeezed between the

Kelley and Steward mines, lacked joy. The row of houses went dark early on winter nights. On Christmas Eve, Sean and Red each drank a glass of Irish whiskey and went to bed. Santa never came to the Maguire house in those days. It was a sad place any day, worse on holidays. When Aggie Walsh came into their lives, becoming Red's surrogate mother, she chastened Sean for giving a boy the drink.

When Maguire walked into the *Bugle*, he heard his phone ringing across the room. He picked up to hear a gravelly threatening voice.

"We's knows that you butts into other people's business for a living, Maguire. Take up another line of work or be sorry." A click followed five seconds of silence except for a mine whistle Maguire heard in the background.

He looked up to see Stoffleman standing at his desk. "Nice story you wrote about the attack on the bar owner but let's agree it's old news by tomorrow. How about you find something new to freshen the story?"

Maguire shrugged. "Have I ever let you down, boss?"

"Not recently, Maguire, although I can think of a few instances during your skirt-chasing escapades over the years. But it's not the past that concerns me. Ever since you hit the big time with the story about Nancy Addleston, I hear people describing you as the 'legendary Red Maguire.' Who is that? The Irish teenage punk I took off the streets to whom I taught some of everything I know? That Red Maguire? The Red Maguire who will never let me down because he wants my job running this paper someday? That one?"

"Ah, boss, I'm not going anywhere. Does that excite you or disappoint you?"

Stoffleman put his hand on Maguire's shoulder, a rare show of affection. "I figured the big papers in Chicago would come for you after you wrote that sensational story. I will say this only this once, because unlike you I'm hardly a sucker for sentimentality. Not only are you my best reporter but you are like a son to me. Tell me if they succeed in prying you out of Butte."

Stoffleman turned away. Maguire saw him wipe away a tear. The editor had a heart after all.

Mail arrived at the *Bugle* in bundles after Maguire revealed the Purple Rose Killer. When he returned from his California vacation, he found his desk heaped with envelopes. Most of them came from people who wanted to discuss theories about her motivations. Others expressed their sympathy. A few came from editors in Chicago and Minneapolis telling of their interest in hiring Maguire to cover crime. He found the offers tempting at first. Eventually he ignored them. He had lived in Butte most of his life. His childhood memories of Chicago, tainted with his mother's drinking and prowling, lacked sentimentality.

Maguire reached for Irene's note. He read it three times before dialing her number.

"Rossini's," came a purring voice.

"I'm calling for Miss Rossini, please."

"Speaking."

"Miss Rossini, this is Red Maguire at the *Bugle*."

"Can I call you back in a moment? I'm helping a customer."

His phone rang a few moments later.

"Hello, Mr. Maguire. I suppose you wonder why a woman you don't know handed you a note in the coffee shop. A bit forward, perhaps?"

Maguire felt warm all over. "I was hoping so," he admitted.

"What did you think I wanted, Mr. Maguire?"

"Did you call me honey for a reason?"

Irene laughed. "No, you misunderstood me. Honey is my nickname."

Maguire squeezed the phone receiver. It was good Irene couldn't see his disappointed face.

"I feel like a fool, which is becoming more and more of a habit," he said.

"Don't apologize," she said. "It should have occurred to me. May I call you Red?"

"You may call me anytime. Sorry. That was a pathetic joke."

Irene laughed into the phone. "Another come-on from a *Bugle* reporter. Day and night, when is it going to stop? It seems to me, Red, that we're both apologizing when instead we need to get to the point."

"Which is, Miss Rossini?"

"Please call me Honey. If my nickname makes you uncomfortable, call me Irene until you know me better. Now, I read your stories about the robberies. If you want further proof you are on the right track, I can tell you something strange is going on in this town. I hear talk but, for me, it gets worse. I've received threats in my store."

"What kind of threats?"

"Two anonymous warnings sent through the post office. Will you come over to look at them? Come at five o'clock after I close to customers. Can you do that, Red?"

"Yes, but don't open your door to anyone who looks suspicious."

"Other than you, Red?"

"I must say, Irene, that you have a way about you."

"A skill long practiced by any woman wanting to succeed in Butte," Irene said, signing off and hanging up.

Maguire reached for the bundle in his pocket. He unwrapped the wax paper, added Irene's note, and folded it all back together while whispering to himself. "What a cheap heel I am thinking Butte's prettiest woman would flirt with a hopeless scribe like me," he muttered, looking around to see if anyone heard him. At that moment, Ketchul walked into the city room.

Maguire eased back in his chair as the stocky labor reporter pulled off a red hat with ear flaps and unbuckled a knee-high pair of rubber boots. Ketchul, outwardly annoyed, made a show of slapping a notebook down on his desk.

Maguire tried the personal approach. "Is Santa coming to the Ketchul house? I imagine your two little boys can't wait."

"Santa always comes to our house," Ketchul replied, sounding huffy. "Why do you care about it anyway? You ever celebrated Christmas, Maguire?"

The question stung. Maguire thought of his lost mother.

"Easy, Ted," Maguire said. "I was being friendly."

Ketchul fumed. "Think you've known somebody who's worked next to you for what, ten years or more...." His voice trailed off.

Stoffleman walked up, fidgeting with the buttons on a red cardigan, a rare display of color for the editor. "My sister in Maine made it for me," he said, feeling a need to offer an explanation. Absentmindedly he ran a hand over the wicked scar on his face.

Maguire cracked a smile. "We've never seen you wear anything but white shirts, boss. This is a banner day."

Ketchul said nothing.

Stoffleman studied his two reporters. He sensed the tension between them.

"Tell me, Ted, what are you hearing about union involvement in these robberies?"

Stoffleman leaned against the corner of Ketchul's desk. He pushed back the sleeves on his cardigan as a signal that he wanted to get down to business.

"None of that checks out, boss. I interviewed at least a dozen sources on the Hill. Reliable, well-placed people. Not one of them knows of any such thing. There's no evidence these crimes are being organized by unions."

"So it's Mack Gibbons and a few other go-it-alone men running the show?"

"I found no evidence to think otherwise."

Maguire rose out of his chair. Ketchul's explanation seemed too convenient, too rushed. Ketchul was a bulldog on big stories, especially in demanding information from Company spokesmen in the big offices up the street. Ketchul, Maguire knew, didn't back down from anyone.

Maguire reached over to Claggett's desk where he bummed an Old Golds cigarette from the hunched obituary writer. Claggett, preoccupied with writing about Butte's latest death, barely noticed.

"Do you think they're bluffing, Ted?" Maguire asked as he set flame to a match.

"If I did I would have said so, Maguire." Ketchul's eyes smoldered.

"Seems to me you arrived at your conclusion awfully fast. There's what, ten thousand miners on the Hill? What about Rusie Dregovich? What did he say about it?"

Ketchul's face reddened. Stoffleman raised his hands, palms down, in a gesture to calm the reporters.

"What are you implying, Maguire? You telling me how to run my beat? Trying to take it over? Why don't you take care of your own house? Everyone in Butte knew you were romancing the Purple Rose Killer. Maybe if you had kept your pants zipped you would have saved a life or two."

Maguire stepped toward Ketchul, who stood to face him. "Take it back, Ketchul. You knew how it went down. How about we talk about you? Tell us what you're hiding about these miners. Quit covering for them. Spill it, will you?"

Ketchul shot his fist out in a vicious hook, clubbing Maguire on the jaw. Maguire stumbled backwards from the weight of Ketchul's strength. Stoffleman jumped between the men to hold them apart. Several seconds passed with nothing said. Claggett stopped typing to watch.

Maguire, rubbing his face, reached to the tile floor for his smoldering cigarette and returned to his desk. Stoffleman pushed Ketchul, fight gone out of him, to a meeting room across the hall. Stoffleman hated fist fights in the city room. Ketchul would hear about it.

Claggett shuffled over. "Nice of you to give Ted a break, your reputation for brawling considered, Red."

"You have a long memory, Calvin. I was a kid in the gulch. I last threw a punch when I was eighteen. Well, maybe a few since."

"What changed you?" Claggett asked.

"Coming to work at the *Bugle*, ironically. Having a purpose in my miserable life. Now I get walloped in the city room. I feel like I got hit with an axe handle."

"I never figured Ted to go mean against one of his own, Maguire. Still waters run deep."

Claggett looked at his watch. "Well, having knocked out two obits this morning, I'm now taking a well-deserved break. Agnes awaits at the Dumas. Want to walk down with me, Maguire? Hooking up with a girl on Mercury Street might do you some good."

"Calvin, you know I don't do business at the parlor houses. The *Bugle* doesn't pay enough."

"Agnes, she's there for me once a week. Sort of like going for a haircut. Better see a doctor about that face, Maguire."

Claggett left the city room. Maguire considered looking at himself in the mirror down the hall in the men's room. Going to see Irene Rossini seemed like a better idea. As he left the *Bugle*, clomping down the creaking wooden stairs to the sidewalk, Stoffleman's voice echoed from above. How ironic,

Maguire thought, Stoffleman taking the lumberjack-like Ketchul to the woodshed.

~ 6 ~

'I sell emotion'

Irene's store, on Park Street, glimmered in the twilight. "Rossini's Fine Jewelry," said the neon sign that hung above the sidewalk. It was written in blue script that resembled a woman's accomplished penmanship. Neon light reflected on the windows. The spent day blended into night.

Maguire tried the glass door, found it locked, and knocked. Irene emerged from a back room. She sashayed toward him. He could tell it came naturally to her. Maguire imagined her appearance alone sold jewelry. What a contrast with the tough and brawling Babe McGraw, Maguire thought, the two sides of Butte.

When Irene swung open the door her eyes landed on Maguire's discolored jaw.

"Shall I guess that not everybody in Butte loves Red Maguire, crime-fighting *Bugle* reporter?"

"That's a fair assumption," Maguire said.

Irene locked the door behind him. "Tell me what happened, Red. You have a bruise the size of western Montana on your face."

She pointed to a mirror mounted on a display cabinet full of rings and necklaces. Maguire tipped the mirror to see a purple splotch that ran from chin to neck along his jaw. He gingerly probed the swelling with his fingertips. As Irene hung up his overcoat, Maguire told of his argument with Ted Ketchul.

"I know him by reputation but frankly, Red, my clientele isn't miners but the people who earn money off mining. There are two distinct groups in this town, do you agree?"

"I do. Sure enough so would Ted," Maguire said. He looked around the store. Three glass chandeliers cast soft light on the black and white tiles. Watches studded with diamonds gleamed under glass. In the corner, two wing chairs sat on either side of a tall potted plant that, considering its exotic appearance, Irene had imported to Butte. Maguire noted, casually, a stack of Hollywood fashion magazines on a small table between the chairs.

"First time in my store, Red?"

"Never had reason to come before," he said, brushing his hand along the modest bundle in his suit jacket as he had a habit to do.

"No woman in your life, then?" Irene blushed.

"I'd guess you say that to every man who comes through that door."

"Or some variation of it, Red. I sell jewelry but I also sell emotion. Everybody has somebody tugging at their heart."

Maguire wanted to ask Irene who tugged at hers but thought better of it. He was seeing her in his professional capacity as a crime reporter, after all.

"You had letters to show me?" he said to her, more abruptly than he intended. She was so lovely that he felt nervous in her presence.

"Take a seat," she said, motioning to the wing chairs. As Maguire sat, she went to the back room. She returned with two white envelopes that she handed to him. "The first one came a week ago. I received the second one yesterday."

Maguire looked at them front and back. Both were postmarked in Butte. Neither had a return address. Inside each envelope was a short crude message scrawled in pencil.

The handwriting resembled what Babe McGraw had found behind her bar.

The first note said this: "Soon you will make sure no harm come to your jewlry store." Maguire noted the spelling errors. "Go to cops and you got truble."

He looked at the second note. "Pity something wuld happen to those nice earrings girly. $100 every month. We say where. Pay up stay safe."

"Whew," Maguire said. "Any idea who sent them?"

Irene lit a cigarette and took a deep drag from it. She blew a circle of blue smoke.

"I wish I did. I have no experience in dealing with extortion. It's apparent to me that the author of these notes can barely read and write. Is the clue useful to you? I regarded the notes as clumsy attempts to scare me until I read your story this morning about the beating Harry took over at the Valley View. He's done a lot of good for his customers."

"You haven't gone to police?"

"For that very reason. Look, I've run a respectable jewelry business in this town since the war. After a burglary in the early years I fortified the back door and installed a safe that dynamite won't budge. I had one attempted armed robbery in all these years. Lucky, I suppose. I expect some trouble running a high-risk business in a belligerent city full of troublemakers. So yes, I am accustomed to summoning police and they oblige. This time I'm not so sure that it's in my best interests to notify them."

Maguire leaned toward her. She looked again at the bruise on his face.

"Paying a ransom for so-called protection against thugs isn't in your best interests, Irene."

"I'm not the only business owner closing my shop early during the holiday shopping season. I should be open until eight o'clock. I keep the largest inventory of any jewelry store in Butte. After I lock up, I clear the merchandise from the display case to the safe in the back room. It's crazy to worry about robbery while I'm here, with sidewalks full of people, but that's how it is."

"You know of other uptown business owners being threatened?"

"Up and down the street. Some go to police, some refuse. Leo, who owns the shoe store up the street, is one. Betty at the dress shop is another. Earl down at the body shop on Galena is another."

Irene snuffed out the remains of her cigarette in an ashtray. "I rarely smoke. Silly, isn't it? Nerves, I guess." She looked at him with her caramel brown eyes. "Tell me what I should do, Red. I know that being quoted in the *Bugle* will make things worse for me. Promise me you'll go easy?"

Maguire reached for one of the magazines. "Glamour," said the cover title above a headline that promised "100 Christmas Gifts $1 to $5." Maguire noted that the laughing woman shown on the cover, dressed in a white terrycloth bathrobe, resembled Irene Rossini enough that they could be twins.

"How did you know me at the coffee shop, Irene?"

"My friends call me Honey. They call me anytime." She smiled.

"The joke never gets old," Maguire said. "Honey. If I call you by that in public, people will think you and I have something. Who gave you that nickname anyway?"

"My neighbor in Meaderville when I was a little girl. She said my hair was the color of honey. 'Honey!' she would yell when I pedaled past on my bike. Martha was kind to me. She bought me my first dress."

"What about your mother?"

"She died from influenza when I was eleven. Daddy said the hospital tried to save her. He raised me the best he could.

It was Martha who acquainted me with becoming a lady."
Irene smoothed her shiny hair with slender fingers and
smiled. Maguire felt outmatched. Irene oozed high-society
Butte.

"She did well, I must say."

"What about you, Red? How did your nickname come
about? You couldn't have gone wrong by sticking to the
dignity of Kieran."

"So you know my given name from my byline in the
Bugle. Nobody called me Kieran except my mother. I haven't
seen her since I was eight."

When Irene started to ask why, Maguire held up a hand
to stop her.

"Some other time. It's a long story and a painful one. Most
people refer to me by my last name, although it's refreshing
to hear my nickname once in a while."

She pointed to his head. "Ah, yes, the source of my
nickname is obvious. It came from my father, whose name
was Sean. Natural nickname, I guess, for redheads. Honey, I
imagine, was harder to catch on?"

"Are you calling me Honey, Red?"

Maguire, flustered, held up *Glamour*. "Some might say,
'What's a girl like you doing in a town like this?' Care to
comment?"

"Do you plan to include everything I say in your story,
Red?" Irene looked at him with her unsettling gaze, her chin
high. She lit another cigarette, filtered, and put it to her red
lips. Maguire realized he was staring.

"Of course not, no. Sorry to pry. That's not why I'm here."

Irene studied Maguire. "I read everything you wrote
about the Purple Rose Killer. How terrible. Your stories
reflected the demeanor of a private eye. I also sensed a broken
heart."

"Good compliment for a crime reporter on the first count," Maguire said, dropping the magazine back on the table. "Not so much on the second. Maybe I let too much of myself into the story." He absentmindedly reached into his suit pocket for his .38 Special, which he placed on the stack of magazines. Irene showed no surprise.

"Tell me you don't plan to shoot up my glass display case, even accidentally, Red." She watched him with an expression of mischief.

"Don't know why I did that," said Maguire, flustered. "I never put a bullet in the chamber. The detective over at the police department gave me this gun. You might know him, Harold Ferndale?"

"Everybody in Butte knows Duke," she said.

"He told me I might shoot myself before I use it in self-defense. Words to live by no doubt."

"And yet you carry it in your suit jacket like a smoking pipe?"

Maguire put the revolver away. "Just today," he told her, offering details of Babe's beating and a warning from Ferndale to watch his back.

"Now you are scaring me, Red. I can't fight off attackers with bare fists the way Babe McGraw does." She looked nervously toward the front window. Suddenly she flinched. Maguire followed her gaze to the sidewalk. A man wearing a mask stared back at them.

Maguire jumped to his feet, reaching for the revolver as he did so. The masked man bolted as Red ran to the front of the store.

"My god! What the hell was that?" Irene gasped. She jumped from the chair, fright replacing her poise.

Maguire ran outside. He raised the gun to shoulder height with his thumb on the hammer. Shoppers passing in the falling snow shrunk from him. He looked both ways on the street. The masked man was gone.

Maguire returned to the store, locking the door behind him.

"Where's your phone?" he said to Irene. She pointed to the black receiver on a shelf behind the display cabinet. Maguire dialed Ferndale's number. The detective barked a greeting into the phone. Maguire gave him the particulars.

"I'll come right over, Maguire. Keep the weapon handy. Now that they know you're armed they might feel inclined to respond in kind."

Irene edged away from the front window. She brushed a hand over her eyes.

"Nobody will scare me away from my own store," she said, lacking conviction. She began removing silver watches and rings from the display case. Maguire helped her.

"You are insured?"

"As much as I can afford. Fortunately I'm good at making sales because this inventory doesn't come cheap."

The safe, tall as Maguire and twice as wide, was set into a concrete wall. When they finished moving the jewelry, Irene closed the heavy door and turned a key. Then she twirled the combination lock.

"Like a bank, Red."

Ferndale arrived with two uniformed officers. "Irene," he nodded, acknowledging her. One officer waited near the front door, watching the sidewalk. The other went to the back door to make sure it was barred and locked.

"Detective Ferndale. Good thing Mr. Maguire was here interviewing me when Porky Pig showed up. They warned me not to notify police."

"Better us than dead," Ferndale said. She showed him the two letters she had received in the mail. Ferndale nodded as he read them.

"Standard issue. Handwriting resembles the others. Fits a pattern, all right."

"Which is?" Irene looked concerned.

"Which is to put the bite on business owners until they pay a ransom. In the police world we call it extortion. Paying criminals don't make the problem go away. They want one hundred dollars from you. Steep and more than we see with some others. These criminals apparently think you can afford it. Two months from now they would want twenty-five dollars more and another twenty-five after that. Protection rackets show no mercy. They make money off fear and bodily harm. Sorry to scare you with this cop talk."

"Who are these criminals, detective?"

"We have suspicions, Miss Rossini." Ferndale turned to the uniformed officers, now standing behind him.

"You boys check out back and next door. See what you can find."

Ferndale turned to Maguire. "How much of this you planning to put in the *Bugle*? Seems to me that between nursing Babe McGraw and defending Miss Rossini, you've got yourself in pretty deep."

"I can't ignore this evening's turn of events, Duke. News is news."

"Don't do anything to hurt her," Ferndale said.

Maguire leaned on the glass display case. He caught Irene frowning and stood away from it. "You ever known me to do otherwise?"

"Can't say when," Ferndale said. In the presence of her elegance, the old cop looked beaten and worn. Maguire knew different.

"Better that you lay low for a while until we find the perps and get them in custody," he told her.

Irene, now sitting in a wing chair, crossed her legs. Maguire found himself staring, approvingly. "I can't close my doors in the middle of Christmas shopping season, Detective Ferndale. I need the income to operate my store. It hurts business to compound threats of extortion with a closed sign. And yes, I understand the consequences."

Ferndale nodded. "I guess we can't close every store in Butte. Expect to see extra patrols. Maybe Maguire can swing by for another interview. Cross your fingers that he knows how to use that piece he carries around."

The uniformed cops came back inside. They stomped snow off their boots on a rug near the front door. One of them held the Porky Pig mask.

"Found it in a trash can out back," the older cop said. He handed it to Ferndale. It was a child's Halloween mask, made of thin rigid plastic, with eyeholes and an elastic band for wearing.

"Same mask the Valley View robber wore. Harry was close enough to his assailant to snap it right off his face. Too bad he never got the chance."

Ferndale pointed at Maguire's face. "Nasty bruise, Maguire. Run into yet another reader who don't like what you put in the *Bugle*? Or did you make a pass at Miss Rossini?" Ferndale laughed.

Irene blushed. Maguire privately thanked Ferndale for his insinuation. Each man understood the other's failures with romance despite being twenty-five years apart in age.

"Nothing more than a family disagreement over at the *Bugle*. I've had worse," Maguire said of his swollen jaw.

"I like a newsman who can take a punch," Ferndale said. "Now, can you see Miss Rossini home? Meanwhile, Miss Rossini, I'm taking your letters as evidence."

Maguire felt for the weight of the revolver in his pocket. "I'll make sure nobody gets to her."

"If a clown jumps you, Maguire, make sure you shoot at the big red nose." Ferndale and the uniforms, howling at the bad joke, left the store.

"That's what passes for police humor, Irene."

"Call me Honey. I told you, Red."

"Let me take you home, Honey."

"Are you calling me Honey, Red?"

Maguire grinned at the warmth he felt.

~ 7 ~

'Suffering sells big'

Maguire left Irene Rossini with her neighbor, Martha, after persuading her to turn on lights in her own house. "If anybody comes prowling, they'll think you're home and won't go looking further," he told her. They stood in the snow. Large flakes sprinkled on them under the yellow street globe.

"I'm glad you came to see me tonight, Red. I look forward to your story in the *Bugle* in the morning. Don't ask me why I thought to involve you instead of police. Maybe because you are a man of reputation. I admire fame."

Maguire hoped he hid his blush. "I, in turn, admire your compliment but I'm a mere byline in the *Bugle*. You are something more, Honey. Do you know that you resemble Jane Russell?"

She laughed. "Everyone I meet says so. I've heard it for years. Purely a coincidence, I assure you."

Maguire watched Irene go inside Martha's house. They lived in the Italian neighborhood of Meaderville. The nearby Berkeley Pit, which the Anaconda Company intended to replace underground mining, had gained in size, nibbling at Meaderville with early hints of a voracious appetite. Someday, he suspected, the Rossini house and all of Meaderville would disappear.

Back at the *Bugle* city room, Ketchul's desk sat empty. Stoffleman, the editor who never slept, stepped close to inspect Maguire's face.

"I've seen uglier but can't remember when. He came at you like a jackhammer. I don't condone fighting in the city room but admit I'm surprised you didn't strike back, Maguire. I know you're no stranger to throwing punches."

Maguire shrugged. "It's Christmas."

He told Stoffleman about the incident at Rossini's Fine Jewelry. The editor took off his black-rimmed glasses to rub his eyes.

"It's one thing for these thugs to rough up the owner of a bar where miners gather. Going after Irene Rossini is a different matter. She commands influence in this town. Hard to believe a few rogue miners thought this up. No, there's more to it. Somebody behind the curtain, so to speak."

"Yet Ketchul rules out the unions. What do you make of that, boss?"

"I've never had a reason to doubt Ted's judgment despite his behavior today. I admit to being skeptical. Push on the labor angle, Maguire. Ted will hate you for it. Do it anyway."

"Let's hope he doesn't mess up the other side of my pretty face."

"Not in here he won't unless he looks forward to hunting for a job. I gave him hell for hitting you. I hope he went home to regret his behavior instead of drinking away his fury in a bar. You planning to file a complaint?"

Maguire shrugged. "Maybe I deserved it. These grown men wearing masks have me on edge. The case is taking on a life on its own much like those Purple Rose Murders. The only conclusion I've reached is that this is how we do it in Butte. Wish I had a better answer."

"It's sitting there for you to solve if police don't do it first," Stoffleman said. "Make sure you stay on top of this one. I don't want to read any scoops in the Company papers."

Maguire finished his latest story, combining the Babe McGraw and Irene Rossini incidents into further proof that uncooperative business owners who deny "protection" were being hit with robberies and other threats.

"Anonymous thugs who confront Butte business owners in a wave of robberies beat a well-known bar operator early Tuesday in an attack inside her Finn Town establishment.

"At least three men wearing masks viciously punched Ruby McGraw to the floor after closing time at Babe's Bar, 540 East Granite Street. As usual, McGraw gave a fair accounting of herself, landing a fist to bone more than once, but she told the Bugle the assailants came at her swinging, from all sides.

"McGraw was taken to Silver Bow Hospital for facial injuries and damage to her ribs and shoulders. 'Them boys have a fight on their hands when I get out of this hospital bed,' McGraw told the Bugle. 'Nobody pushes Babe around.' She remains in the hospital under care of doctors who cautioned her not to start fighting anytime soon.

"Hours later, after dusk, a man disguised as Porky Pig, the cartoon character, menaced prominent Butte citizen and business owner, Irene Rossini, through the front window of her store. A Bugle reporter, interviewing Miss Rossini at the time, witnessed the incident.

"She received two threatening handwritten letters demanding she pay for 'protection,' a pattern consistent with previous occurrences including the beating death of Valley View gas station owner Harry Dalton.

"Police now are investigating numerous reports of threats to business owners. Detective Harold Ferndale advised the people committing these felonious acts that they can expect trouble. 'When

we catch these damn fools we'll come down on them like a ton of mining slag,' Ferndale said."

Red Maguire wrote forty-three more paragraphs on his Remington typewriter before he quit. He detailed the incidents with Babe and Irene, included more comments from Ferndale and Chief Morse, and even managed a useless quote from Mayor Ticklenberg: "I fully anticipate forthcoming arrests from our capable police department."

It was late evening before he handed over his story to Stoffleman. The old editor muttered from somewhere under his green eyeshade, "Took you long enough, Maguire. Dreaming about that pretty jewelry store owner, no doubt?"

"Sorry, boss. Maybe."

"Next time you decide to take the slow train to Chicago, remember there's this thing in newspapers called a press run. We have deadlines for reporters to finish stories so we can start the press on time. Savvy?"

"I've heard this every day for twenty years, boss."

"That tell you anything, Maguire?"

Stoffleman put his pencil to Maguire's story, crossing out words and adding others. He waved the pencil like a maestro conducting a symphony. He was fond of saying, "It's my job to bring this tripe up to publishable standards." Stoffleman's scrutiny fell on every reporter in the *Bugle* city room. "Real hard-ass, ain't he?" Ferndale said to Maguire one day, a rare compliment from a man with a matching outlook on life. "True," Maguire told him, "the Old Man upstairs owns the joint but Stoffleman runs it."

Maguire waited at his desk while Stoffleman edited his story. The editor finally waved his arm, signaling Maguire that he was free to go home to the Logan Hotel. The story would go downstairs to compositors who would set the type. The press would come alive at midnight, roaring into production with twenty thousand copies of Maguire's front-page story. It would hit doorsteps and news racks by dawn.

Maguire drove up the hill to the Logan. The neon sign below his window blinked orange in the moonlight. "The Loga," it said, the final letter unlighted. The former hotel, if never fashionable, at least booked rooms for travelers in its day. Now, musty curtains hung faded and torn at the lobby's front windows. At least twice a week Maguire found drunks sleeping on the leather couches where men in business suits once read their morning newspapers.

He climbed the creaking wooden stairs to his room and locked the door behind him. He had seen his home in better shape. Intruders who ransacked the place wanted him to back off the story. Newsmen who covered crime knew well how the underworld worked. Criminals hated scrutiny in the papers. Maguire wiped the last of Babe's blood from the linoleum. He decided to check on her in the morning. Ferndale said she would stay at the hospital for a couple of days because of her head injury. Pity her attackers when she got loose.

Something was off with Ketchul. The labor reporter acted like a man in trouble. Maguire had seen it before. News reporters lived on the edge of their emotions. While people read the morning paper in the safety of their kitchens, reporters waded into the fray to report the news, often talking to warring parties who sometimes committed violence to get their way. Maybe Ted had covered the labor beat too long. Maybe it was getting to him. Maybe someone threatened him to stay away from the story.

Maguire inspected his bruised face in the mirror. It was ugly, all right. Irene Rossini had seen the purple evidence of a fight, yet she stood her ground. His new story, when the *Bugle* hit doorsteps in the morning, would put more heat on her. What worried him was that someone might attack her. Look what happened to Babe McGraw.

He propped a chair under the doorknob before going to bed. He put his revolver on the night table. Maguire hoped for a good night's sleep. It might be the last for a while.

In the morning he headed to the police department. He met Ferndale coming out of his office, a red Christmas ribbon dangling from the pistol grip on his hip.

"Did Santa Claus come early to the Ferndale residence?" Maguire asked, pointing to the ribbon.

Ferndale looked down. "Now ain't that sweet? If you got to know, Maguire, I wrapped a present for Babe seeing that she's spending Christmas Eve all banged up in the hospital."

"I can see the *Bugle* headline now. 'Butte flatfoot and aging boxer has a soft spot in his heart after all.' "

"You pull a stunt like that and your nose will be mashed worse than mine."

"Where you headed, Duke?"

"Down the hall. Chief wants to chew on me about the robbery investigation. Haul your sorry ass along if you want. Chief won't mind. He likes the show."

Unlike the dumpy Ferndale, dressed in a twenty-year-old suit, Chief Donald Morse wore a crisp blue uniform. Tall, like Ferndale. Brown hair turning gray. Trimmed moustache. Eyes like steel. Morse was a longtime member of the Butte force. Twice he was shot on duty. Maguire wrote the story about the second shooting. It left Morse with a permanent limp in his right leg.

"Morning, Maguire. If you want news, I don't have any. That is, not unless Ferndale can tell me something I didn't already read in the *Bugle*."

"Morning, Chief. You don't mind if I sit in?"

"Not at all. You've been privy to everything that goes on here for as long as I can remember. I guess I'm not surprised how many of our secrets I read in your paper." Morse shot a look at Ferndale.

"Take a seat, gentlemen. The mayor's coming to join us. These masked robberies have him worked up. Ferndale, I propose you give him some cause to simmer down."

The men sat quietly as Morse shuffled papers on his desk. Two pink teddy bears permanently inhabited one corner of it. They had belonged to the chief's daughter, Shirley, who died in a car accident when she was fourteen. Maguire covered that story. Her mother was driving her to school one morning when a '39 Ford barreled through a stop sign. Donald Morse, on patrol that day, arrived at the scene minutes later. Maguire and a *Bugle* photographer found Morse sitting in the street cradling his dead daughter as his wife stood beside him, screaming in disbelief. Maguire wept as he wrote the story.

As Maguire recalled that tragedy, Mayor Fred Ticklenberg puffed his way down the hall toward them, laboring over a cane he didn't need.

"Enter the boss," Maguire said.

Ticklenberg charged into the chief's office with an obvious purpose in mind. He took a position near the chief's desk like a sentry, daring all who felt inclined to pass.

"What the hell is the *Bugle* doing here?" the mayor said, sounding less than friendly about it.

Morse looked unruffled. "Fred, we all know Maguire has got himself in deep on this matter. There's no pretending we have any secrets because he'll find them out anyhow, one way or another."

Ticklenberg glanced at Maguire before turning to hang his hat and overcoat on hooks on the wall. "It's bad for the city's image, that's what it is. Now the *Bugle* goes blaring bad news about these idiots in masks. I heard plenty from the boys at Rotary Club yesterday. A few of them wanted to kick my butt up the hill to Walkerville. 'What kind of town you run here?'

they say to me. 'Get a lid on this mess right now. All this crime is bad for business,' they say. Maguire, none of us doubt your credentials but, once again, you carry things much too far with your graphic chronicles of people's suffering. Nobody wants to read that."

Maguire, feeling indignant, felt obliged to defend his newspaper's honor. "To the contrary, mayor, everyone wants to read that. Suffering sells big in Butte."

Mayor Ticklenberg stopped to catch his breath. "And you, Detective Ferndale, what are you doing about this latest crime wave?"

Ferndale bristled. "Mayor, I report to the chief."

The mayor snorted. "Well, Maguire, do you have anything else to say? It's nobody's business what goes on inside our city police department. If we let every Tom, Dick and Harry in here, why, criminals would run wild in Butte."

Maguire straightened in his chair. He tipped his fedora back and reached to straighten his tie. "Mayor, my editor at the *Bugle* says news enlightens the community. You know Clyde Stoffleman. Stop by if you want an earful. Crimes in Butte happen all by themselves without help from the *Bugle*. My stories, however, help solve them."

The room fell silent as the mayor pondered this.

"That argumentative Stoffleman and I differ," the mayor said. "The *Bugle* surely ruins our chances for prosperity by telling the world Butte is a city of robbers, gamblers and whores."

"Isn't it?" Maguire said, his voice flat.

The mayor continued with his rant. "And another thing. You have no right to expose Irene Rossini, one of our most prominent and respectable citizens, to public ridicule. Queen of the Butte SnowBall three years running. Chaired the Uptown Improvement Committee. Do you know that lady attracted some of the finest entertainment in the Pacific northwest to Butte's theaters? There she was in this morning's *Bugle*, hung out to dry like a common street urchin."

"Miss Rossini called me, Mayor Ticklenberg. She asked that I write about the trouble at her store."

"Aw!" the mayor said, waving his hand dismissively at Maguire.

The chief motioned to a chair beside the coat rack. The mayor, his anger expended, took it. "I've been mayor for six terms. People ask me why my hair is silver. I presume you gentlemen understand how difficult it is leading a city in a positive direction under these circumstances. Tell me, how bad is it?"

"Bad enough and worsening by the day," Morse conceded. He nodded to Ferndale.

"It ain't a pretty picture," the old detective said. He shifted in his chair, wincing at the stiffness in his left shoulder. "In addition to the beating at the Valley View gas station, which is now a murder investigation, we have robberies and threats at businesses all over town. Fast as we respond to one, we have another pop up. I doubt these perps have the brains to act on their own. They make crude work of it. Somebody is organizing it. Their first tactic is to scare business owners through threats and robberies. Once word gets around Butte, fear takes over. They will scare people to the point they pay up without asking questions. Them perps come for the money next. That's how these rackets work."

The mayor stood to pull on his overcoat. "You police boys had better clean up and fast. We can't have criminals running this town. And you, Maguire, do this city a favor for a change. Expose the thugs behind this enterprise without hurting decent citizens. Tell that to Clyde Stoffleman."

The angry mayor stormed out of police headquarters. Maguire, Ferndale, and Chief Morris watched him go.

"Hotheaded old fart," Ferndale said.

The chief leaned back in his chair. It creaked in protest. "He's not wrong, Ferndale. Preaching to the choir is all. The mayor takes lip from everybody in Butte. His job must be hell."

Sensing the meeting was ended, Ferndale stood, as did Maguire. "You're accommodating today, chief."

"I know how my bread is buttered, Ferndale. The mayor hired me, remember? Now, what about this Mack Gibbons character? What's he been doing since the judge gave him a free pass? That lowlife lacks the smarts to figure out a protection racket but he's plenty capable of running errands for the big boys. He still working at the Anselmo?"

"Drives an underground tram is what we're told. Gibbons surrounds himself with an unsavory bunch of bare knucklers. Babe McGraw thinks he has a hand in these threats. Dumber than a rock, Gibbons is, but he's anybody's definition of trouble."

"Take another run at him, Ferndale. Gibbons isn't the brains behind these shakedowns of our business owners but he's stupid enough to brag. A rube like him might lead us to the big fish if you can find him in a talkative mood."

"We'll head back to the Anselmo," Ferndale said.

The chief straightened his badge. Nothing about him was out of place. "Don't go alone, Duke. Take Jimmy Regan and a few other officers big enough to throw some weight."

Ferndale smirked. "You think I'm too damn old to handle a few dozen miners, chief?"

"There was a day in your boxing glory days, Ferndale, when it wouldn't cross my mind. Take Maguire too. I want our policing of this case on the record." The chief dismissed them with a wave of his hand.

In the hallway, Maguire raised a fist to Ferndale's face. "Sounds like you better sharpen your boxing skills, you old pug, just in case."

Ferndale brushed Maguire's hand away without blinking. "I'd practice on you, Maguire, but somebody already did. Maybe it's you who needs the work. Confronting miners at the Anselmo ain't the same as beating up neighborhood kids in Dublin Gulch."

"When are you heading to the Anselmo?"

"This afternoon when Gibbons comes off shift. We could probably catch him in some dive after work, but I want to see who lines up behind him at the mine. After your story hit the streets this morning, if Gibbons or any of his buddies are going around with those masks, you can bet they won't be as hospitable as last time."

~ 8 ~

'Poor lovesick fool'

Down at the Silver Star, more customers than usual chattered over their coffee about Babe McGraw and Irene Rossini. When Maguire walked in, people whispered and pointed under the bright fluorescent lights. Several of them held copies of the *Bugle*. Simone waved from behind the counter where she served a line of customers. They had claimed every stool. Maguire waved back and took a seat in the one remaining empty booth. Quick as a flash, Simone appeared at his side with a glass pot full of steaming coffee. She took her time pouring it.

"Everyone in here knows you, handsome. They say you're a famous person, don't you know? Managing to interview Babe McGraw and Irene Rossini in one day. What talent."

"News to me, Simone. The fame part, I mean."

Simone leaned in close. "When I saw Miss Rossini come up to you yesterday, I thought to myself, 'Simone, you'll never have a chance with him now.' You want to give me reason to think otherwise, sweetie?"

"You told me you were married, Simone. How about that?"

"This is a coffee shop, Red. We are as open here as bars and confessionals. Besides, this is Butte. I might be new around here but I hear everybody's secrets. Believe me, I can tell you who lost money gambling and who is climbing into bed with who. Get my drift?"

"So everybody knows everybody's business. Is that it?"

Simone lowered her voice to a whisper. "I got divorced a few years ago, Red. He hated me caring for my disabled brother. Combat veteran, not right in the head after the war. I tell customers here in the Silver Star that I'm a married woman to avoid unwelcome company, if you know what I mean."

Maguire poured sugar into his coffee. "I like it sweet," he said to explain, and then, "I'm talking about the sugar, Simone."

She whispered, "So am I, Red. I'm all about sugar. You know, you're not only famous, I give you credit for being smarter than you look. Even with that beat-up face, and don't worry, I won't ask." Simone smiled and sashayed away. Men sitting at the counter whistled in appreciation.

"Maybe she'll write me a letter," Maguire muttered to himself. He patted the thin bulge of paper he kept in the pocket of his suit coat. He had to admit it was a humble collection, hardly fitting for a tall red-haired man with decent looks. He was nearly forty years old. Maguire knew something of psychology, if only from practical experience. His mother's disappearance when he was a boy had something to do with his failure to find love. Maguire also knew that the other culprit was his job at the newspaper. It stole his life years ago.

Maguire left the Silver Star after a parting wink and smile from Simone. He walked two blocks south to Rossini's Fine Jewelry, where he found Irene unlocking the front door well past the nine o'clock opening advertised in the window. She was a head-turner in her red dress and sparkling necklace. "Good morning, Red. Did you come to pay me a social call? Or do you see me as the subject of tomorrow's story as well?" She smiled broadly.

"I came to make sure my story didn't do you any harm, Honey."

"Do you always make personal visits to confirm the wellbeing of all your sources, Red?"

"Hardly," he said, returning her smile. "Lately I've got too many to count and most of them not as agreeable as you."

"Then I'll take your visit as a compliment," she said, flipping over the "closed" sign in the window. "Open for business, even if a bit late. Should I put the coffee on, Red? Or did your girlfriend over at the Silver Star take care of that?"

"She's not my girlfriend, Honey. Her husband would object, for one thing."

"That woman made it known she's got her eyes on you. Every customer in there has heard her say so."

"You know this how?"

"Like you, I've got my sources, Red."

"And what are your sources telling you about these perps hiding behind masks?"

Irene rested her elbows on the display case and folded her hands. Jewels sparkled on either side of her adorable figure. There was nothing artificial about her, Maguire could see. No need to fake Hollywood beauty. She came by it naturally without knowing it.

"What I hear is that people are scared enough to pay up, no questions asked. The police can't be everywhere. Sooner or later somebody else will wind up like Babe McGraw or worse yet, Harry Dalton. Fear has taken over, Red. What worries me is that this fear will chase my customers away. That's why I called you in the first place. I want it known that Irene Rossini stands against intimidation in Butte. Like Jane Russell said, 'Publicity can be terrible, but only if you don't have any.' "

Maguire shrugged. "Some people run at the first sign of trouble. Others make a stand. Sounds like you stand in the second category. You can take care of yourself, but have you got someone to help? A husband? A boyfriend?"

"Are you asking for the *Bugle*, Red, or is this a personal inquiry?"

"Call me a concerned citizen."

"I had a husband. His name was Frank. Not Rossini. That's my maiden name. Frank froze to death in Korea after a sniper shot him. It was below zero in that sector. His Army friends found him with bullets in both shoulders and frost on his face. We were married only a few months when he went to war. I never saw him again. Your newspaper reported his death. Maybe you remember? Calvin Claggett wrote a long obituary about Frank Mills being the best skater in East Butte before the war killed him. I loved Frank but hardly knew him. As for a boyfriend, not lately. Maybe I'm not over losing Frank, or maybe I haven't found the right man to keep me in furs and fairytales. Now you know the summary of my romantic past, Red Maguire, but not for print."

"Not for print, Irene Rossini. My advice is that you close up and go home before dark. Better yet, to Martha's house."

"Aren't you sweet? Detective Ferndale said he would send an officer to keep watch while I close up. If you want to save me from bad men, feel free to stop by anytime. Call me Honey, remember?" Irene leaned over to kiss Maguire on the cheek. "Now go find another story for that hungry newspaper of yours. I have jewelry to sell."

Maguire stepped onto the sidewalk with the scent of Irene's rose perfume lingering in his nostrils. He looked back inside. Honey waved at him from behind the display case. He waved back, nearly knocking over an elderly woman on the sidewalk as he turned to leave.

"Poor lovesick fool," Maguire said to himself.

He found the *Bugle* city room quiet except for Claggett, two lighted cigarettes dangling from his lips, banging out his latest obituary on his battered typewriter. The pace would pick up later in the afternoon when more reporters began writing stories. Stoffleman stood at a window, drinking coffee and staying at the city's rough edges. The editor had an uncanny ability to sense someone's presence even when not looking.

"You know, Maguire, I've been thinking," he said without turning from the window. "How did that robbery suspect, Mack Gibbons, get off with a slap on his pathetic little wrist? We have a union lawyer doing his bidding and a judge eager to oblige. Why would anyone with some prominence in this town want to help a runt like Gibbons? Corruption is no stranger to Butte, that's for sure, but are we headed back to the days when every judge on the bench is bought off?"

Maguire squinted out the window to the Flats below Butte Hill. He was a head taller than Stoffleman and at least thirty pounds heavier. Maguire knew he was no match for Stoffleman intellectually. The editor possessed a photographic memory, Maguire was sure of it. His entire mission amounted to documenting facts in the *Bugle*. He rarely mentioned his personal life. Maguire figured it amounted to nothing anyway.

"Boss, you're thinking what the chief is thinking. If Gibbons is going around scaring our business owners, somebody is standing behind him telling him what to do."

"A metaphor for those Halloween masks, Maguire? They might cover more faces than anybody originally suspected?"

"Someone with influence and money, boss."

Stoffleman looked satisfied. "Get on it, Red. We could use a strong story on tomorrow's front page."

Maguire motioned toward Ketchul's empty desk with an inquisitive expression. "Don't ask," Stoffleman snapped. "Ted didn't come in and didn't bother to call. I'm going to presume he's either covering one of the locals on the hill or he's working the robbery story like I told him to do. I hope both."

Maguire walked across the hall to Luverne at the switchboard. She brightened at seeing him. "There you are, Red, delicious hunk of manhood. Your story this morning got tongues wagging. I've got at least a dozen people wanting you to call them back to talk about the ways of the world." She handed him a stack of yellow notes. "Then we have the other kind of nuisance. This same man has called for you three or four times. No manners, rude as hell. Refuses to leave a message either. I told him, honeybunch, get your ass off the phone unless you talk nice to old Luverne. He told me to go take a leap off one of them mine gallows frames."

"Sorry, Luverne, you sexy bohunk, you deserve better." Maguire blew her a kiss. "If the mug calls in the next hour, ring him through."

Luverne stuck out her tongue at Maguire and went back to work pulling plugs out of the panel and reslotting them. At the *Bugle*, telephone calls came all day and into the night.

Maguire made notes at his desk, thinking of calling Ferndale, when his phone rang. "Red Maguire, *Bugle* city room!" he barked. A growling man's voice blared through the receiver.

"What business ya got putting lies in the paper, Maguire? Masks and protection rackets? Ya gotta be kidding. Stop now or figure on a beating that will mess up that pretty boy Irish mug of youse and send ya on a free ride to the Forever More. Hear me loud and clear?"

A click came on the line before Maguire had a chance to respond. "There we have it, the predictable death threat!" he hollered across the room to Stoffleman. "Caller says he's going to mash my face."

"Ketchul already did that, Maguire. Tell the bonehead caller to come back with something original." Stoffleman and two of the night editors sitting with him laughed up a storm.

Claggett raised his head in a rare show of interest. "They're not laughing with you, Maguire, they're laughing at you."

"Thanks, Calvin, for that worldly insight. Meanwhile, I'm on my way to a story." He stood and pulled on his overcoat and fedora.

"Don't get beat up again," Claggett advised, watching him leave the city room.

~ 9 ~

'Don't blame Cracker'

Maguire walked to the police department where he met Harold Ferndale sliding a shotgun onto the back seat of his sedan. "About time, Maguire. We're headed to the party at the Anselmo. Figured you couldn't be bothered, your eyes all aglow with romance at Miss Rossini's jewelry store for a start."

"She's a source for the *Bugle*, Duke."

"Source my butt. How long have I known you, Maguire? You been chasing skirts since you were knee-high to a grasshopper. Too bad you never caught any."

Maguire put a hand on the fender of the sedan. "Someone turning your crank, Duke? Looks to me like your usual sour mood got worse since the pleasant chat we had with the mayor this morning. You're also packing an arsenal."

He watched as Ferndale slid handguns into either pocket of his overcoat, buttoned to his throat. Snow covered the brim of his fedora.

"Storm coming in," Ferndale said, peering at the sky. "More than one kind. A few boys from the union local 1235 came off the hill for an unscheduled visit with the chief after you were there this morning. Got heated is what I hear. The chief called Mayor Ticklenberg over from his office. Imagine having to deal with the mayor twice in one morning. Anyway, the union boys warned the chief to back off from accusing the union of committing crimes in Butte. The chief told them straight out, if the union is straight-up lawful they ain't got no reason to worry about us questioning Mack Gibbons at the Anselmo this afternoon. They saw no humor in that. Gibbons is union, those boys said. Mess with one, mess with all. So we got us a ball game. Chief tells me to expect half the union waiting for us. Having the benefit of old-timer wisdom, I tell him, why bother cruising for a fight? We'll catch up to Gibbons at an uptown dive tonight where we can pull him outside for questioning clean and simple. Chief says no, says we can't have the union thinking they can push around the police department. So here we go."

"The 1235, that's Rusie Dregovich's outfit?"

"The very one. Most powerful union on the Hill. He wasn't present in this delegation of upstanding citizens but the chief says they were doing his bidding, all right. The four who dropped in are known brawlers around Butte. Dangerous men, Maguire, sent to make an impression. Chief don't scare. Not since he lost his little girl and his wife shot herself over it. Chief wants heads rolling over this mess. No embarrassment if you decide to sit this one out. For the time being, the union's beef is with police, not the *Bugle*."

Maguire patted the revolver in his pocket. "Not anymore, Duke. An hour ago some rube threatened to reassign me to the Forever More."

"Keep that shooter under wraps, Maguire. This ain't your gunfight. If bullets start flying duck behind my car. You can write a story about the whole damn thing if you survive."

As they were talking, three prowl cars arrived. So did an unmarked sedan with three men inside. They were dressed in suits and overcoats. Maguire recognized them as cops. It was a good bet they packed even more hardware in their car than Ferndale did in his. Maguire climbed into the passenger seat of Ferndale's car. The old detective led the parade out of the parking lot.

"Don't be grabbing for that shotgun, Maguire. Got a live one in the chamber. Here's what we're doing. I ain't arresting anyone unless they give us cause. We will drive into the yard. The other unmarked car stays at the entrance. Uniforms in the black and whites stay out of sight down the street unless we need them. Jimmy Regan's in charge of those boys. I ain't got a worry. If trouble starts Jimmy will come full throttle."

Ferndale pounded his fist on the dashboard. "Damn heater. Ain't had an ounce of hot air in this car except for myself. I could kick some sorry ass right about now."

"Merry Christmas," Maguire replied.

The gates to the Anselmo stood open and mired in piles of dirty snow. A few men worked in the timber yard. They stopped to watch from blackened faces as Ferndale pulled his car to a stop near the chippy hoist. Dozens of men, the afternoon shift, stood holding their lunch buckets in the bleak light around the entrance. They would load and disappear after the day shift cleared the hoist.

"They know why we're here," Ferndale said. "Watch yourself. We'll be standing here like a couple of fools without a pot to piss in when that hoist starts coughing up angry miners. Gibbons might be the least of our worries."

Maguire pulled out his pencil and his notebook. "Hell of a quote for tomorrow's story, Duke."

"You'll get better," Ferndale growled.

The Anselmo gallows frame was even more imposing than it appeared from down the hill. It towered over the mine yard like a stern father. Maguire wondered how Ferndale planned to make himself heard over the groaning of machinery.

"Here it comes," Ferndale said, pointing to the chippy hoist. A mighty cable bounced and tensed above them, pulling a cage from deep underground. When it stopped and the doors opened, six grimy men emerged.

"There he is," Maguire said, pointing to Gibbons in the middle of the pack.

"And looky there, Dregovich right beside him," Ferndale said. "This oughta be fun." He threw the car door open.

Dregovich and his men waited for Ferndale. Gibbons slid behind Dregovich. Ferndale stopped ten feet from them. Maguire stood off to the side, close enough to hear but not wanting the miners to think he was choosing sides. Ferndale looked small as he approached the mob. He was taller than average, pushing six feet, but Dregovich loomed five or six inches over him. Dregovich, Maguire noticed, walked with a limp. Maguire remembered the story Ted Ketchul wrote about Dregovich working on the thousand-foot level when timbers collapsed in a drift, shattering his leg. He freed himself before dragging two other miners from the rubble. "He's the toughest man on the Hill, bar none," one of those miners said in Ketchul's story. Nobody in Butte doubted it. Soon afterwards, Dregovich took charge of the union by a near-unanimous vote.

The big man stood before Ferndale dressed in a floppy cap and overalls long enough to fit Paul Bunyan. Maguire thought he resembled a villain on the cover of a pulp fiction magazine. His coiled arms resembled the knotty steel cables littering the ground. He had big red ears and brooding dark eyes that gave the appearance of a scheming giant. Maguire had never seen a more fearsome man.

"I've come to talk to Mack Gibbons," Ferndale said, looking past Dregovich to the small wiry miner behind him.

"What ya want with Cracker?" Dregovich demanded in a booming voice.

"Police," Ferndale said, showing his badge. "Five minutes or so with Mr. Gibbons."

"Cain't no one tell this Cracker how to do his business," Gibbons yelled.

Maguire penciled the comment into his notebook. Ferndale stood calmly, gripping the hidden guns in each coat pocket. Maguire wondered what the cops hoped to achieve. The police department had no use for intimidation, including from a labor union, but Maguire hoped the chief's pride wouldn't come at Ferndale's expense. He was a much older man than the miners who stood before him. He stood staring back at them like when he was a boxer waiting for a fight to start. Maguire glanced toward the mine entrance. The three cops waited in their idling unmarked car for the first sign of trouble. White exhaust swirled in the cold air.

"Five minutes with Mr. Gibbons," Ferndale repeated. "Mr. Dregovich, you're welcome to join us."

The big man laughed. "Welcome, copper? I own this here mine yard. Ya mess with the union, ya mess with Rusie."

Ferndale stood his ground. "Ain't nobody messing with nobody. Is Gibbons scared of me? That why he's hiding behind you?"

Dregovich moved aside and pushed Gibbons in front of him. "He look scared to you, Ferndale? Yeah, we know who you are. Old prune of a flailer well past his prime is who. Youse boxing days disappeared with youse hair." Dregovich turned toward Maguire. "What business ya have here, newsie? Nosing around in our business again? Fancy clothes ya wearin' there, bub. How 'bout we muddy them up for ya? Some of my boys here inclined for excitement."

Maguire stood his ground. Some of the miners edged toward him. He figured on decking the first two with his fists. The others would swarm him. His fingers ran over the revolver in his pocket. He spun the cylinder in hopes of putting a live round in front of the hammer. Ferndale's advice to keep the barrel empty for safety seemed less sensible. Maguire heard Ferndale's voice, calm and firm, sounding more diplomatic than when it came from a bar stool.

"No point in violence, Mr. Dregovich. We have a legal right to question Mr. Gibbons. Don't make this something it ain't."

Heads turned as a car entered the Anselmo yard. Not a police sedan but a spanking new green station wagon, a family car, with a luggage rack. Maguire recognized *Bugle* labor reporter Ted Ketchul at the wheel. Ketchul parked and stepped out of his car wearing a parka and tall boots. He looked at the miners facing Ferndale and Maguire and shook his head. Without speaking a word he walked through the mud and slush to Dregovich and whispered in the big man's ear. Dregovich nodded and whispered back. Maguire strained to hear what was being said.

Ketchul turned toward Ferndale. "Rusie says you can talk to Gibbons. Rusie and two of his union officers here will sit in. So will I and so will Maguire over there. Rusie wants the *Bugle* represented."

"So do I," Ferndale said. He cast a questioning look in Maguire's direction before adding, "I'm calling a few of my boys up so we're on equal terms." Without waiting for agreement from Dregovich, he motioned to the idling car at the gate. It moved forward and stopped next to Ferndale's sedan. Maguire recognized the cops as Toby Muldoon and men he knew only as Bartlett and Miller. Ferndale posted Miller to watch over both cars, presumably to secure the shotguns inside, as the black and whites rolled into view at the gate. Some of the miners cussed at them. Wind whipped loose snow through the machinery. The cables overhead kept grinding.

Ketchul remained beside Dregovich. Maguire thought his fellow *Bugle* reporter might be trying to calm the union leader's temper. "We'll go to the union office," Dregovich bellowed in his big voice. He motioned to the crowd of miners standing behind him. "Ya men stay here. Keep an eye on these here dicks. We 'a going to have a word."

Ketchul fell behind the parade to wait for Maguire. "Sorry about the lick to your face, Maguire."

Maguire ran his hand over his sore jaw. "Felt more like an axe handle, Ted. If you've got a beef with me why don't you say so?"

"I did," Ketchul said.

"You look mighty cozy with Dregovich, although I do appreciate the help. I have no idea what Ferndale had in mind. Neither did he, evidently."

"No more cozy with him than you are with Ferndale and the other cops. Some people in this town think you're one of them."

"Knock it off, Ted. I'm not a cop and you're not a miner. Newsmen know where to draw the line. I know I do. Don't you?"

"Knock it off yourself, Maguire. Good thing I came along, or you and Ferndale would be getting the shaft by now, if you know what I mean."

They followed the procession into a long clapboard shack near the hoist house. At the far end it had a raised platform facing at least a hundred wooden chairs. A banner above the platform read, "United We Bargain, Divided We Beg." Below those words, in smaller letters, read: "Butte Miners Local 1235." It was a bleak meeting hall, drafty and worn, reeking of working men. Hardly any daylight filtered through the dusty windows. A skinny graying man fed wood into a blazing cast iron stove with his good arm. Half of the other was missing.

Dregovich walked to the platform. He motioned to Gibbons to sit beside him. The other union officers did the same. The men glared at Ferndale, a tribunal looking upon the accused, as the two other cops stood below them.

"This ain't no union meeting," Ferndale growled.

"Hell it ain't," Dregovich replied. "My boys made it clear to youse boss with the fancy buttons to leave the union out of his trouble. Now ya show up at our mine like ya got no lick of sense. I consent to ya asking questions because we have us a law-abiding local but when I say no more, we end it. I call this here meeting to order. Now get on with it."

Gibbons bounced on his chair. "Tell him, Rusie!"

"Shut it, Cracker," Dregovich warned him. Gibbons fell silent. The little man's greasy brown mop hung over birdlike eyes that flitted from his union boss to the cop standing before them. His mashed nose aimed sharply to the left. Maguire took note of the man's cocky lopsided leer, frozen to fit a beer glass, and recalled Babe McGraw saying how Cracker guzzled until she kicked him out at closing time. The drunker he became the louder he boasted of killing men who dared to cross him. Some men, he bragged, he killed with his thumb. "That twerp's got a mouth on him all right, and he's a wiry little combustible cuss, but he ain't got enough brains to avoid getting pounded outside the bar every week or so," Babe had related. "I don't know if trouble finds Cracker or Cracker finds trouble. Makes up wild stories nobody believes. Truth is, other people pull his strings. Whatever somebody bigger than him tells him to do, he does."

Maguire leaned against the wall, off to the side, figuring he could watch his back that way. Ketchul sat in the front row facing Dregovich, looking unconcerned. Maguire watched men shift nervously as they listened. Dregovich reigned over the room like a king. He might open the doors to a flood of angry miners. Ferndale, no stranger to confrontations, ignored the danger. The detective stood unruffled before the union men. Maguire imagined Ferndale as a prosecutor in a courtroom.

"Mr. Gibbons," Ferndale began, "you like to get around the bars in uptown Butte at night?"

Gibbons looked at Dregovich, who nodded. "Me and all the boys from the Hill. So what?"

"Which bars?"

"Been to most one time or another." Gibbons rolled a cigarette while he talked, brushing bits of tobacco from his soiled pants. "Babe's in the east, Leo's in the west, Atlantic and M & M in the middle. Ain't nobody who don't get a visit from Cracker now and again."

"So you know the business district better than anybody?" Ferndale asked. "That's what I hear. When you want to know how this town is run, go ask Cracker."

"Nobody knows his way around Butte better than Cracker," the little man replied. He clenched the cigarette between two brown teeth and scratched a match along the wooden chair. He put the flame to the cigarette and tipped back, his mood swelling to the task, seeming quite pleased with his sudden elevation of authority.

Maguire caught a grimace of recognition flashing over Dregovich's face. The union boss suddenly understood the trap Ferndale was setting.

"Ain't it true nothing gets done without Cracker?" Ferndale said.

"You hear that right, copper. Cracker knows what end is up."

"Cracker cracks the whip, so to speak?"

"I ain't never seen a man I ain't needed to straighten out," Gibbons said.

"Including Rusie Dregovich?"

Gibbons nearly jumped out of his shirt. "No, no, not Rusie. I got no beef with Rusie."

Dregovich raised his hand. He looked wary. "Where ya going with this, copper?"

"Getting to know Cracker, Mr. Dregovich. Seems like a friendly fellow, don't you think?" Ferndale motioned to the mine yard outside. "I imagine Cracker is an important man here at the Anselmo?"

"All the boys know it," Gibbons bragged. "This mine ain't nothing but a chain of missing links without Cracker. We dig in that hole down there until I tell them boys, knock off five for a smoke. Everybody listens to Cracker."

"Even Rusie Dregovich?"

Gibbons flinched. "Quit trying to turn me inside out with the boss. Rusie tells me somethin' needs doin', I'm his man."

"You take orders from Mr. Dregovich?"

"Ain't nobody up here who don't take orders from Rusie."

Ferndale paused. Maguire sensed a change in the detective's interrogation. "But you're saying when you're out in the bars, everybody knows Cracker?"

Gibbons puffed up. "I'm saying. Ain't nothin' that escapes Cracker."

"Cracker knows everything that goes on?"

"Ain't I said so three or four times?"

Ferndale smiled. He had cornered Gibbons. Dregovich knew it too. Everyone knew it but Cracker Gibbons. "Then you can tell me the names of these men going around uptown who wear Halloween masks to scare people, right? Are these the same men leaving threatening notes demanding money from business owners?"

Maguire marveled at Ferndale's interrogation skills. He had underestimated the old crank. Maguire penciled the conversation into his notebook. He had a great story for the morning *Bugle*. Dregovich appeared ready to explode. Ferndale noticed and moved back a few steps.

"He don't know nothin' about that, copper," Dregovich said.

"Let Gibbons answer for himself, Dregovich."

For the moment, Dregovich backed off. Maguire could see the giant's discomfort. He must regret the turn of events, Maguire thought. Dregovich held one big raw fist inside the other, as if restraining himself from charging Ferndale.

"Don't blame Cracker for them masks. Cracker ain't got a notion about them Porky Pig masks."

Ferndale smiled again. "Who said anything about Porky Pig?"

Gibbons looked confused. He glanced at Dregovich, who shook his head. The big union boss rose to his feet. "This here interview is done for, Ferndale. Ya coppers take your stupid questions and git off my mine or we help ya along. My boys outside lose patience when they come off shift hungry and have to stand around because the police say so. Take that newsie over there with ya," Dregovich said, nodding to Maguire. "He ain't wrote an honest thing about this union. His daddy was a union miner, we give him that, but he ain't learned nothin' from him."

Maguire backed out of the long room with Ferndale and the other two cops. Ketchul stayed seated a few feet from Dregovich. As Maguire stepped outside, he glimpsed Ketchul whispering to the union boss again. Dregovich, red faced and agitated, pushed Ketchul away.

Ferndale led a retreat through the mob of miners. At least thirty of them crowded outside the door. A few of them spat in Ferndale's direction. Maguire followed the cops. Someone shoved Maguire from behind. He stumbled. A miner holding a pickaxe kicked mud and slush onto Maguire's suit pants. Back at the cars, the cop named Miller looked worried.

"I thought they were going to rush me," he told Ferndale. "Odds of fifty to one didn't calm my nerves any, even with Jimmy Regan and his boys watching my back from down at the gate."

Ferndale looked back at the mob, which had stopped a few dozen feet away. "Damn fool idea I had to bring a loaded shotgun to the party. Thanks, Miller, for keeping them away from my car."

A frozen snowball sailed past Ferndale's head. Another hit Miller in the shoulder. Maguire ducked yet another. The men jumped into their cars. Snowballs, hard and heavy, slammed into the hoods and fenders. A big one cracked Ferndale's windshield as he started the motor.

"The chief's paying for that," Ferndale said. "Let's get the hell out of here."

He pulled out of the hail of fire but only after another hard snowball knocked out a taillight. Ferndale drove onto Excelsior Avenue past a grinning Jimmy Regan, who sat at the wheel of his prowl car.

"I won't hear the end of this from Jimmy," Ferndale said. "He knows these men. He knows what they're capable of doing when they get riled."

Maguire shifted in the seat to ease the pain between his shoulder blades. He was sure he had been hit with a closed fist. "You get life insurance on this job, Duke?"

"No point in it if I wind up dead anyway," Ferndale said. He reached into his coat pocket to retrieve one of the .38s. He dropped it on the seat. "Take this. Newer than the rusty old peashooter you itch to put to good use. Don't tell nobody where you got it. Chief don't like me giving out our guns to civilians, even if it's you."

"What happens next, Duke?"

"Don't put this in your next story, background only. Our night prowlers will arrest that idiot Cracker coming or going from one of the bars. Drunk and disorderly, some charge like that. No need to make it up. He's got a lot more to tell but I need to work on him away from Dregovich and those other Anselmo boys. Cracker as much as admitted being the fool behind the Porky Pig mask. That puts him at Miss Rossini's store. He was one of the four men who jumped Babe, too, unless someone borrowed his mask for that caper. Babe gets wind of what we heard just now and Butte will see another case of vigilante justice."

"How would she do it, fists or a gun?"

"Same to Babe either way. Whatever's handy. I saw her work over a man with a whiskey bottle. She clubbed him with it and then rearranged his face with the jagged edges. Ain't a pretty picture in anybody's book."

"Did she go to jail for that?"

"Naw, the judge made her promise to quit fighting and let her go. That very night she coldcocked another miner on grounds still undetermined. If she gets her hands on Cracker Gibbons I might have a murder case on my hands."

"You can't pin the Elk Park robbery on him?"

"We showed the owners his mugshot but no luck. No usable prints either. I've had cops tailing him whenever he's not in jail. So far, no luck catching him wearing the mask. Hangs around like rotten garbage, don't he? Stinks worse if you have no place to dump it."

Maguire rubbed his hands together under a feeble breath of warm air coming from the heater. "What else did you see back there in the union hall anyway?"

"Our man Cracker revealed he runs favors for Dregovich. Now the big man knows I know it. He knows you know it too, so keep that piece handy."

Ferndale stopped in front of the *Bugle* offices. "Break this story open, Maguire. The best damn crime reporter in Montana ought to find a way. Ain't that what Stoffleman would tell you?"

"To the word," Maguire said.

"What's Ketchul doing kissing up to Dregovich? They having a love affair? He goes and socks you in the jaw over this union thing and then shows up at the Anselmo like he's a card-carrying member."

"Ted tells me he's only covering his labor beat like I cover crime."

"You kiss my ear like he did to Dregovich and I'll crown you."

"I figured," Maguire said. He pocketed his new weapon and stepped out of the car.

"Maguire? Get to the bottom of this. Hurry up before somebody else gets hurt. These racketeering hoods don't play games. When they come for the jingle, I guess soon, they'll crack skulls to let people know they mean business. Speaking of cracking skulls, wish me luck when I go check on Babe. She might be fighting the nurses by now."

"Detective, you should marry that gal."

"No such criminal intent," Ferndale said, gunning the motor for good measure.

Maguire watched Ferndale drive away. He has guts, Maguire thought. The crafty old detective, in a single afternoon, managed to put both Mack Gibbons and Rusie Dregovich on notice. Maguire would tell the story in the morning *Bugle*, sparing no details except what Ferndale told him on background. By dawn, all of Butte would learn of growing police interest in Union Local 1235.

~ 10 ~

'I've been worse'

Clyde Stoffleman clapped his hands when he finished reading Maguire's account of Ferndale's confrontation with the miners. "Fine reporting, Maguire. Your story will light a few torches in the streets tomorrow."

"Hopefully not in the hands of anybody inclined to set fire to the *Bugle*," Maguire said. "I've grown fond of the old place."

Stoffleman looked unimpressed. "Save your typewriter if they do. You owe me a million more stories before you sleep. No coasting when there's news to report."

"You expect trouble, boss?"

"I never discount the possibility of it, Maguire, but as you know, our brand of journalism doesn't bow to threats. Our first consideration is getting the story and getting it right. We've published this newspaper in this building for what, forty years? The Hirbour Block was built in 1901 as a place of distinction. We plan to keep it that way. Still, be careful out there, Maguire. It's your byline on this story, not mine, and that thug Dregovich and his playthings now can recognize you on the street."

Maguire went to his overcoat, hanging on the wall, and pulled the .38 Special out of his pocket. He handed the gun to Stoffleman, who looked it over with the same scrutiny he gave Maguire's stories. Stoffleman handed it back.

"Keep this piece close at hand, Maguire, until this thing blows over. Take it from someone who knows, if somebody shoots at you, they're not playing games. Shoot back like you mean it. Otherwise you're dead."

"The war, boss, did you ...?"

"I don't talk about that," Stoffleman interrupted.

"Boss? It's Christmas Eve. You got plans?"

"Only to put out the morning paper before Santa starts parking on rooftops, Maguire. You?"

Maguire pulled on his fedora. "Nothing that I know of. Didn't give it much thought, I suppose."

"That makes two of us," Stoffleman said.

Maguire said good night to Stoffleman and four other men who congregated around him under a pool of yellow light, all of them assembling stories before the press started its midnight rumble in the basement. The night men had a fraternity of their own, united in common purpose on a tight schedule, working long after most people went to bed. A city room late at night was a lonely place.

He descended the long wooden staircase to the street. It was cold and his breath came in clouds. Uptown Butte was aglow with Christmas lights. Wreaths shaped like snowflakes adorned light poles and store fronts. Maguire thought of the snowballs the miners threw. They had compressed slush and ice into hard missiles. A blow to the head would knock a man cold. Maguire walked past an idling car, parked at the Copper Penny Bar, with four men inside. He climbed into his own car farther up the street. He watched in the mirror as the men headed into the Copper Penny.

He pulled into his usual parking spot at the Logan Hotel and went upstairs. He found Sal, a frail relic of a man who lived at the back of the hotel, pushing his broom down the dreary hallway. Sal used to brag he was from Italy. That was before he lost his mind. These days he pushed his broom for hours at a time, sweeping imaginary dust, remembering nothing that happened even in the past ten minutes.

"Busy place," he called to Maguire. "Some men with a key came to that door you're opening. Who lives there, do you know? They kept knocking. Real hard. Wake up the dead, I told them. I said they should use their key to open it. Busy place. Can hardly keep up with the cleaning around here."

"How many men, Sal?"

The man stopped sweeping. "Who's Sal?"

"How many men?"

"I counted three. I said quit banging, use your key. They said them bad words and went away."

"How long ago were they here?"

"Was who here?"

Maguire dismissed the old man with a wave of his hand and went into his room. Nothing disturbed. This time they planned to do more than ransack my place. Maguire took off his suit jacket. He loosened his tie and rolled up the sleeves on his white shirt. He turned on his coffee percolator. When it began bubbling into the little glass dome on top, he poured himself a cup. Drinking coffee late at night wasn't his habit. His nerves were shot. He didn't have a drop of liquor in the place. Maguire drank heavily during his early years at the *Bugle*. He rarely came to work without a hangover. All the *Bugle* reporters drank on the job in those days. Claggett kept a bottle in his desk. Antonio Vanzetti plowed through five or six bars after work, ordering the hard stuff at each stop. Even Ketchul put down several mugs of beer at lunch. When his kids came along, he stopped drinking altogether and condemned his *Bugle* colleagues for failing to do the same.

Snow fell again in Butte. The Logan Hotel stood precisely at a mile above sea level. If a foot of snow fell at the Logan, it might be six inches deeper a few blocks up the hill. Maguire went to the window above the orange neon sign. The grimy old mining city, decorated in its white holiday coat, resembled a Christmas Eve wonderland. Snow hid the city's dark alleys and broken buildings and black dust that settled over it all.

Maguire had no good memories of Christmas. Each year the holiday came and went as something to survive. He knew he was a lonely man like Stoffleman and Ferndale and Claggett and other people in his life. He thought fleetingly of Simone at the coffee shop but more passionately of Irene Rossini. "Call me Honey," she had told him. He tried to picture her next to her Christmas tree as soft candlelight illuminated her beauty. Maguire pressed against the window glass to look east toward the bright lights of Meaderville. Honey was there somewhere, hopefully safe.

Suddenly the window exploded in a shower of glass. Maguire flinched and grabbed for the frame. He hung halfway out the window. As he pulled himself back inside, he felt his skin tear on a shard stuck in the frame. Confused, Maguire looked outside at the sidewalk a few dozen feet below him. Had he leaned too heavily on the glass? A movement caught his eye. He saw a black sedan parked across the street. Saw a flash of light. Heard a roar. The second bullet came so close to his head he could feel its heat. Maguire dropped to the floor. He reached for the piece Ferndale had given him. He raised above the window frame and took aim. He felt the recoil in his palm as he fired off two rounds at the man on the street. The car raced off.

Maguire fell back on the floor. Blood pulsed from his left arm. A ragged cut stretched from the back of his hand to his elbow. Blood and coffee had splashed on his white shirt. The cup he had been holding lay in pieces on the tile floor. Someone pounded on his door.

"Red? Red, you okay? Red?" Maguire recognized the women's voice as Myrtle from next door. She lived with her husband Buck. He was a retired miner who spent most of his days coughing from black lung. Maguire eased his grip on the .38 and opened the door to find Myrtle in a frayed yellow housecoat. She held a dish towel. "Red, what happened? We heard shots. Buck says to me, 'Somebody shooting up Red's place again.' I think we have a bullet hole in our bedroom wall. Oh, you're hurt, Red!" She pointed to the blood.

"I've been worse, Myrtle. Sorry for the trouble." He heard sirens.

"Buck called the police, Red. We thought you were dead in here. On Christmas Eve, of all times." She shook her head, adorned with curlers, in disapproval. "Men who come shooting up a person's home on Christmas can't be Christian, now can they? Me and Buck, we been reading your stories in the *Bugle* about these masks and trouble with the business owners. You think them folks done this? One of them criminals?"

"Fair guess, Myrtle. I doubt he'll come back after the fuss around here."

Myrtle wrapped her towel around Maguire's arm as two prowl cars screamed to a stop on the snowy street below. Their emergency lights flickered through the shattered window. Two cops thumped up the old staircase with their weapons drawn. One of them was Toby Muldoon from the afternoon visit to the Anselmo.

"What the hell happened here, Maguire? When we got dispatched to the Logan, I knew this was bigger than some drunk capping a few outside a bar. I figured we was headed to trouble after that deal at the mine today. This is shaping up as the busiest Christmas I ever had the misfortune of working."

Maguire gave the cops a rundown of the course of events.

"So it was a gunfight on Granite Street then? He shot at you, you shot at him?"

"That's the summary of it," Maguire said.

Muldoon looked over the damage in Maguire's room. The other cop, a beefy short man named Banes, headed back outside to look for clues. Myrtle pointed to the reddening towel on Maguire's arm. "You probably oughta keep a supply of these on hand, Red, or stop newspapering."

He grimaced. "The first idea seems more likely."

Banes came back a few minutes later. "You winged the shooter," he told Maguire. "I found blood in the snow beside tire tracks. You get lucky with that piece or what?"

Maguire, feeling dizzy, flopped into the overstuffed chair where he did his reading. "Lucky any way you cut it," he said. Cold night air and swirls of snow blew through the shattered window.

"You need a medic," Muldoon said. "Banes, get Maguire over to the hospital. I'll take a look at the bullet hole in this lady's room. Oh, and Maguire, there's more. Couple of prowl cars went to the *Bugle* on a report of a beating. Might be a bar fight. Bad enough that dispatch called Ferndale out of bed. Can you imagine rousting that grouchy old crank to show up on scene in his night clothes? Duke might throw a few punches if anybody gives him lip."

"That nickname stuck on Ferndale since his glory days in organized boxing," Maguire said, reciting a line from one of his new stories.

"Me and some of the older boys in blue remember those days well," Muldoon said. "Hell, I've been working with Duke since the stock market took a tumble in '29. That very day was my first and probably my worst. I spent my entire shift outside the banks trying to hold back screaming mobs wanting to withdraw their jingle. No respect for cops, I tell ya. A couple of mugs ripped my uniform shirt off my back."

Maguire pulled the shade over the shattered window. With his knees, he pushed his small table against the bottom of the shade to hold it in place. "That will have to do until the owner of this place gets me new glass," he said.

Banes looked puzzled. "Why not move someplace where people can't shoot at you from the street? This ain't the first trouble that's come knocking for you at the Logan."

Maguire swept his hand around the room. "And leave this dump? Sure, no fresh paint for fifty years and the water runs brown but it's home. Besides, what would I do without Myrtle looking out for me?"

She smiled at the compliment.

"Here, Maguire." Muldoon held out the .38 that Maguire had fired twice. "Looks suspiciously like police issue, but who's counting?" He handed the gun to Maguire. "Better keep this within reach given the intense interest in your yellow journalism lately."

Maguire hugged Myrtle, taking care not to bloody her housecoat. "Merry Christmas to you and Buck," he told her before heading with Banes to Silver Bow Hospital.

'You shot back?'

Kieran Maguire's earliest memory of Christmas involved a red wooden rocking horse Santa Claus left beside the tree. It was near dawn when Kieran jumped out of bed. He raced into the living room of his family's little house on Chicago's south side. His parents, Sean and Lily, came smiling when they heard Kieran's shouts of surprise. His mother hugged him, sharing in his joy, while his father took a picture of the two of them with his Brownie camera. The Great War in Europe was finished. Money was tight after Sean lost his job when the bullet factory closed but he had a knack for making things with his hands. Little Kieran rode his new rocking horse like the cowboys did in picture books his mother read to him.

Long after his given name became forgotten to most everyone but him, Red Maguire tried to remember what had become of that wooden horse. It was as hazy as his memories of his mother. He kept the cracked and faded picture in a shoebox under his bed at the Logan. His mother's smile warmed the room. She looked happy in a rare instance when she was sober. Maguire remembered the ugly times, too, when the drink stole her life. She ran off with that laughing sailor and Sean soon divorced her. The photograph under Kieran's bed remained his only visual reminder, a good one, of his mother.

At Silver Bow Hospital, Maguire waited for a doctor in the emergency room. Banes wished him well and left. Butte needed its police on the streets. Nurses had put up a

Christmas tree. Beside it sat a tiny rocking horse. Not red like Kieran's, but blue. Not big enough for even a small boy to ride but it sat there, beckoning, a happy sight to anyone but Maguire. He turned away.

A nurse wearing a crisp white cap called Maguire to an examination room at the far end of the hall. She pulled the privacy curtain and unwrapped the bloody towel Myrtle had tied on his arm.

"Oh, my, Mr. Maguire, this is deep," she said. Her name tag said, "Peach." Her reddish blond hair shimmered a light orange, a combination Maguire figured arrived at her nickname. "My guess is the doctor will want to stitch this laceration. How did it happen?"

"I collided with a broken window. That's the short of it, I guess."

"We'll have to clean the glass out of the wound. This is going to sting."

"I've heard that before," Maguire said playfully. "Sorry you have to work on a patient like me on Christmas Eve, Peach."

"A darn handsome one, too, Mr..."

"Red," he interrupted.

"I can see why," Peach said, looking at him. "We have something in common then, don't we?" Maguire jumped when she touched the wound. "I know, Red. Hold on. You nicked an artery. You would be running a couple of quarts low if the glass had cut any deeper."

They heard moaning in the room next door. A man in considerable pain. Maguire cocked his head to listen.

"Get used to it. It's the emergency room, sweet stuff. He took a terrible beating uptown. Came by ambulance before you got here. Dr. Hansen is in there with him now. He'll come see you when he's done."

The moaning came again, sounding ghostly over the tiled floor, followed by a feeble, "Help me."

Maguire jumped to his feet. "I know that voice," he said.

Then another voice called his name. Ferndale pulled the curtain aside. "Sorry, Peach," he said, showing the nurse his badge. "Official business as usual. I need to speak to this man privately."

Peach nodded and wrapped gauze around Maguire's torn arm. "That's only temporary. Please make this quick, Detective Ferndale. We've got a bleeder here."

When she was gone, Ferndale bent over Maguire. "It's Stoffleman, Red. Beaten to a pulp. Some goons from the Copper Penny jumped him as he walked out of the *Bugle* tonight. Got a few licks in before they knocked off those thick glasses. Doubt he saw a thing after that. Pounded about as bad as a man can get without being dead. Tried to get details out of him but he's looney as hell at the moment. Blows to the head will do that. Ask me how I know."

Maguire winced at the news. "I saw those men when I left the *Bugle*. Four mugs looking for trouble? Why Stoffleman? I could see why somebody came after me because of my bylined stories, but why him?" He looked down at the bandage soaked with blood.

"That's what we'll find out. Night for trouble for sure. Muldoon told me about the gunfight at the Logan. My figuring is you came close to giving old Arnie your business over at the Forever More. Good thing you managed to shoot straight. Our boys are looking for anyone with an unreported gunshot wound. Hope to find out if you hit that mug fair and square or nicked him. How a damn mick like you managed a shot like that on a dark street from a second-story window leaves me shaking my head, that's what."

"Duke, Irene Rossini..."

"Not a worry, Maguire. We posted an officer outside her house this evening. With you and Stoffleman and Babe McGraw all taking up space in this hospital, we got to cut down on future occupancy."

Maguire felt faint. "Hell of a quote, if only I had my notebook. Speaking of that, I've got to see Stoffleman." He tried to stand up but fell back on the cot.

"Leave Stoffleman alone. Got problems you can't fix right now. You got a bleeder, all right. Look at that damn arm. Peach!"

The nurse came running. "We called a second doctor. Dr. Hansen has his hands full next door. He's taking his patient to surgery."

"It's okay," Ferndale said to Peach. "Maguire knows it's Stoffleman. He going to make it?"

Peach looked noncommittal. "Dr. Hansen is doing the best he can, detective."

"Clyde Stoffleman fought in Germany," Maguire said, as if the battered editor's war service mattered at that moment. It testified, he thought, to the man's toughness. Stoffleman's moaning faded as nurses wheeled him down the hallway to the operating room.

Peach gave Maguire a sedative. He awoke on his back in the dark. His arm throbbed. Uncertain where he was, he called out. Peach hurried into the room. When she opened the door a shaft of light fell across Maguire. He saw his arm bandaged from wrist to elbow.

"It's Christmas morning," Peach said cheerfully. "I was hoping you would come around before I go off shift. How are you feeling, Red?"

Maguire managed a smile. "Worse than when I came in, I think."

"Dr. Hovic went to work on you right away after we called him in. You've got enough stitches to join the Butte

Sewing Club. He said you'll live. That glass cut even deeper than I thought, and I thought it was bad enough."

Maguire watched as the trim nurse worked over him. She was about his age, pushing forty, smelling of peppermint. She bounced around the room like a rubber ball, reaching and mending and pulling supplies out of cabinets all at once, smiling like she never knew hard luck.

"I suppose you're married, Peach?"

"I suppose I am, Red."

"Just my luck in this two-bit town." He watched her slender fingers clasp his right wrist, the uninjured one, to check his pulse.

"Haven't seen him in three years, Red. He went off to find a fortune and never came back. I guess I'm not married after all. Not that I care to worry about it working these night shifts. Maybe I should go to the courthouse someday and sign papers."

Maguire shifted on the crinkly paper on the exam table. "What's your hurry anyway? You must see plenty of lonely men in this hospital."

"Nurses aren't supposed to consort with patients, you know. Being that it's Christmas, here's a secret souvenir from your stay here." She doodled on a sheet of paper and handed it to him. She had drawn a heart with "Peach + Red" written inside. "Don't tell anybody," she whispered. "It's a reminder of the night you spent with Peach and yes, you can find me here most nights."

Peach kissed Red on his cheek. "Consider that your discharge," she whispered, and left the room. Maguire, feeling woozy, slipped her note into his coat pocket and pulled his coat over his bloodied shirt. He went to a telephone in the lobby to call for a taxi. Ten minutes later, he walked into the *Bugle* city room, dark and empty. He flipped on the lights. It felt odd without Stoffleman there in his green eye shade. Stoffleman never missed a day in the city room, even on holidays. Maguire thought about writing a story, felt weak, and canned the idea. Tomorrow's paper would get printed without him. Hard to imagine how.

Maguire struggled the five blocks to the Logan Hotel. Few cars moved in uptown Butte. Stores were dark. He thought of Honey and cut a detour past her jewelry shop. Locked, no lights. At the Logan, he opened his room to find snow on the floor. Wind had torn the shade from its roller. The shade lay in a heap on the floor. Cold air rushed through the window. The old coil radiator beneath it popped and crackled trying to bring a semblance of warmth to the room. Maguire pulled a blanket from his bed to wrap around him. He sat on his bed and pulled out Peach's note and kissed it before adding it to the humble collection of letters he carried in his pocket. What a miserable lonely man, Maguire.

There he sat, shivering, watching dawn creep over the city. He fell asleep for a few hours before his telephone jolted him awake. Figuring it was another death threat, he ignored it until the fourth ring. He heard Honey Rossini's voice.

"Oh, Red! Detective Ferndale just told me what happened last night. Somebody shot at you? And you shot back? And you're hurt?" She waited for verification.

"All true," Maguire confirmed.

"You're coming over here right now," Honey said.

"I'm not much for driving this morning. Of course I'm not much for freezing, either." He told her about the window.

She asked for his address. "Good thing I could find your number, Red. Watch for me in ten minutes. And Red?"

"Yes, Honey?"

"Merry Christmas."

Maguire waited outside the Logan for Honey. Snow swirled in the cloudy sky. It felt warmer on the street than in his windblown room. He had washed spatters of blood from his face and changed into clean clothes. His hair, forever thick, barely needed a comb. He pulled his left sleeve down to hide most of the bandage. The .38 felt heavy in his right coat pocket. Ferndale had asked him at the hospital how many shots he fired at the gunman on the street and handed him two fresh bullets. Fully loaded, Maguire stepped across the street to where he last saw the gunman. Fresh snow covered any evidence of tire tracks and blood. Maguire turned to look upwards at his room. He could see how the gunman had a clear view of him standing at the window, one of two in his room. The orange glow from the neon hotel sign would have illuminated him from the front, the ceiling light in his room from the back.

"How did he miss?" Maguire asked aloud.

Honey arrived in a gleaming new Chevrolet Bel Air. Red front and side panels. White roof, trunk and back fenders. She had tied a red scarf around her neck.

"Business is good?" Maguire cracked. He was feeling more comfortable with this beauty of SnowBall fame.

"A jewelry store owner can't go around in a junker, now can she?" Honey smiled back. "It's almost 1955, after all. If you follow business news, something other than crime, you might know that Chevrolet has declared war on Ford with these sporty new models. A sweet-talking car salesman on the Flats talked me into parting with seventeen hundred big ones. Does this Bel Air look good on me, Red?"

Maguire looked her over. His eyes lingered more than he intended. "What doesn't? Anybody who takes a picture of you with this car, they'll sell a million of them."

Honey tossed her auburn hair and smiled. "More flattery I hope I never read in the *Bugle*."

Maguire settled onto the cushioned seat. He shook from fatigue and the chill that had settled over him. Honey reached to the dashboard where she flipped the fan switch higher.

Maguire felt a wave of hot air wash over him. She swung the Chevy around in the empty street and headed east.

"Little Italy, here we come. Meaderville puts up the best Christmas lights in Butte, bar none. Did you know about that, Red? I served on the neighborhood decorations committee for six years running. This is a bleak city, all right, but we do our best to brighten the holidays. The miners hang colored lights on the gallows frames at the Leonard and Minnie Healy to give Meaderville more sparkle."

Maguire fought the urge to fall asleep. The night's events weighed heavily on him. "I worry, you know. Even after Ferndale told me he posted a prowl car outside your house, I worried."

Honey smiled. "Are such gushes of concern shared by all newsmen? Or do you treat me different from everyone else?"

"That's a trick question, Honey, and you know it."

She improvised a tone of *Gone With the Wind* fake indignation. "Why, Red Maguire, I don't have the faintest idea what you're talking about."

"You should be in the movies, Honey."

"Compliments like that will get you everywhere," she said, her cheerful voice calming him.

They followed East Park Street farther up the hill to Meaderville. At the entrance to a strip of businesses, a painting of Santa landing on rooftops greeted them with the words, "Merry Christmas." Just as Honey described, green and red lights adorned the neighborhood, easing the hard lines of industrial disruption on all sides.

"I love Meaderville, Red."

"Not as much as you would love Hollywood, I suspect. Or maybe anywhere else that isn't all dug up."

"I've got dreams, Red. Truth is, I fear I would fail anywhere else. I'm a Butte girl through and through. We grow up here to understand that. I know you do."

"It's been said," Maguire replied in a weak voice.

"What am I thinking, Red? You're hurt. When did you last eat?"

"Not sure, Honey. I still feel dizzy, from losing blood, no doubt." She stopped in front of a broad building bustling with business. "Rocky Mountain Cafe," the sign said.

Honey pushed the shift lever into park. "Open every Christmas, Red. Biggest steaks in America, made possible by the famous Teddy Traparish. A food reviewer from back east said his steaks come seven inches thick and half an acre wide. Let me buy you one."

Maguire found out the reviewer's metaphor hit close to the mark. The steak hung over his oversized plate. He ate like the hungry man he was, surrounded by a conversational din that sounded mostly Italian. Honey Rossini nibbled at a pasta dish across the white tablecloth from him as he demolished the steak. He felt renewed when he finished. He wanted to talk with her about the night's trouble, but the restaurant was full of listening ears. He leaned across the table, grimacing from pressure on his throbbing arm.

"Can we talk?" he asked her. She insisted on paying the bill. They worked through the tables to the front door. Most of the patrons knew Honey and exchanged holiday greetings with her before staring at him. Falling snow muffled sounds of passing cars and draped the broken landscape in a fresh white coat. Honey took Maguire's hand and walked him to her Chevy. She drove to her house a few blocks away.

"The officer outside my house left at dawn," she said. "Detective Ferndale said he would send another one at nightfall for as long as it takes. I couldn't stay next door with Martha because she left on the bus to spend Christmas with her son in Anaconda. She wanted to stay home because of me but I talked her out of it. I didn't want to drag her any deeper into this mess."

On the porch of Honey's house, Maguire held up his bandaged arm, signaling for her to wait. He slipped his right hand into his coat pocket to grip the .38. She unlocked the door. He pushed it open and kicked off his snow boots on the rug with his gun raised. He looked in all the rooms, including her bedroom, feeling like an intruder himself for having seen her nightclothes hanging from a peg on the wall. He went to the kitchen where he found the back door locked. He saw no tracks in the snow. The Minnie Healy gallows frame loomed over her neighborhood. Mining noise fell over her house.

"Nobody brought gifts of bad business this morning," he told Honey, who shivered on the front porch. He waved her inside.

Maguire eased onto the couch while Honey brewed coffee in the kitchen. Her house was clean and orderly. A Christmas tree at the front window glittered with tinsel and shiny blue ornaments. She had no presents beneath it. A black and white framed photograph on a table beside the couch showed a man and woman with a young girl standing between them. The man wore a suit, the woman a flowered dress and a drooping hat, no doubt fashionable at the time. The girl held a purse in one hand. She clenched a Bible to her bosom with the other. The three of them stood in front of the very house where Irene lived. He knew without asking that he was seeing a young Irene Rossini and her parents.

"It was Easter when I was seven," said Honey, noticing from the kitchen. "We had just come home from church services. My father asked our neighbor to take our picture. We hunted for colored eggs in the yard. My mother fixed a ham dinner. It was one of the happiest days of my life. I never had a brother or sister, you see. I have these memories of my little family branded in my brain."

"You said your mother died young. Your father?"

"Gone, too, Red, years ago. I don't want to talk about it, not today, not when we've dealing with all this other unhappiness infringing on Christmas."

Honey came into the room carrying a tray with two steaming cups. She looked every bit as elegant in her home as when he saw her for the first time in the Silver Star. She wore the same red dress. Maguire decided it was her best color. He had seen the heads turn when they walked into the Rocky Mountain Cafe. Men stared at her adoringly, their women with visible expressions of envy. Some of the well-dressed patrons glanced disapprovingly at Maguire, evidently questioning his scruffy appearance if not his credentials for escorting her. Irene "Honey" Rossini was Meaderville's resident darling, Maguire decided, but she also reigned over all of Butte. A walking, talking magazine cover in appearance, a mystery for solving in romance. Encouraged by the reaction around him, he suddenly felt a desire to know her better.

"Honey, can I ask you a question?"

She laughed, showing white teeth. "Is it fair to presume this is the first time in your life you asked for permission?"

"You have a point. Are you waiting for someone from Hollywood to discover you?"

"Charming, Red, but you misunderstand me. The only time I acted was at Butte High School in the stage play *You Can't Take It With You*. I had the role of Alice Sycamore. Are you familiar with that one? Really, Red, it's a classic."

"Heard of it, yes. Familiar, no. I spent my years at Boys Central playing basketball. But why do I misunderstand you?"

"Because I only dream about Hollywood. Don't all women dream of being in the movies? Of dressing up and being famous? At least I do."

"You're so pretty, Honey. Perhaps they will discover you."

Honey laughed again. "That doesn't happen in real life, Red. But thanks for the compliment. Now, tell me what happened last night?"

She sipped coffee, her eyes on him, as Maguire told her about the shootout, about Stoffleman's beating and feeble cries at the hospital, about Ferndale's new declaration of war against lawlessness in the city. He also described encountering Rusie Dregovich and the union men at the Anselmo.

"It will get worse," Maguire said. "Ferndale tells me the crooks will come for the money next."

"And like I'm hearing, fearful business owners will pay up?" Honey asked.

"That's the pattern in these crimes, Ferndale says."

Honey looked at Maguire with inquiring eyes. "Change of subject. Do you observe Christmas, Red? Excuse me for saying so but you seem all alone."

Maguire smiled. "Is it customary to ask the *Bugle* crime reporter about his personal life in the midst of one of the biggest stories of his career?"

"So you pay attention to what I say after all, Red Maguire. You have a reputation in Butte as a voice for victims, a legend of the dark alleys, a handsome newsie who belongs on the cover of pulp fiction magazines. Famous up and down the winding streets of the Mining City. Do you know that about yourself, Red? Do you hear the talk? Everyone in this town looks for your bylines. Don't let it go to your head."

Maguire shrugged. "I'm paid to write the news. I don't know about the rest."

"How do you get all those interesting stories, anyway?"

"By knowing people, Honey. There's no other way."

"I read your story about the Purple Rose Killer shooting herself right in front of you. She killed people even as she worked with you at the *Bugle*?"

"It appears I don't know some people as well as I should."

"May I share an observation, Red? For a man who prints stories about everyone else for a living, you reveal little about yourself. I suspect every woman you meet tells you this. How can I know your life's story by what I read in the pages of a newspaper? Ever been married, Red? In love, even?"

Maguire shifted uncomfortably on the couch. Probing comments from women made him nervous. Even after romancing Mary Miller, or Nancy Addleston as she turned out, he felt like a schoolboy in Honey Rossini's presence. She was known around Butte for possessing strong confidence, now on full display, and he began to understand why she commanded influence.

"I'll make you a deal," Maguire said, exhaustion clouding his mind. "On a day other than today I'll tell you my story if you'll tell me yours. I need to find a story for tomorrow's *Bugle*. Nobody remembers a day when Clyde Stoffleman missed a day of work in the city room. The men who jumped him cared less if he lived or died. I've got to find a way, got to write about the attack on Stoffleman, got to..."

Maguire awoke to find a pillow under his head and a pink blanket pulled to his chin. On the phonograph, turned down low, Bing Crosby crooned *White Christmas*. Shadows fell across the room. Honey swayed in a rocking chair, reading a book under a swag lamp. She lifted her head when he stirred. Soft light fell across her face. Maguire thought she looked more beautiful than ever, but sad.

"You've been out like a dead man for two hours, Red. I can't imagine why."

Maguire straightened, reaching instinctively for the .38 in his pocket. It was missing. Honey caught his sudden worry.

"On the table beside you," she said. "I saw the grip sticking out of your pocket. I was concerned it might go off."

"I'm sorry to scare you, Honey."

"Do you always carry that weapon, Red?"

"Only when I need it. This seems as good a time as any."

A knock came at the front door. Maguire reached for the gun. "Detective Ferndale, Miss Rossini!" came a voice. She swung open the door to let him inside. Ferndale looked over at Maguire, the blanket across his lap.

"Pretty in pink, Maguire. Figured I would find you here with your room at the Logan cold as an igloo. Your shooter turned up. Missed a turn and hit an abandoned house. Fair guess he lost his way on the road nursing a smashed kneecap. Your bullet, Maguire. Bet that hurt like hell. Night patrol says he whined like a little girl when they cuffed him."

Maguire set the .38 back on the table. "I'd never shot a man," he said.

"Nobody does until the first time, Maguire. Good thing you returned fire, or you'd be cold as ice and buck naked on the embalming table. We think the shooter slipped on the ice when he fired at you. That's why he missed. Both rounds came within a mick's nickel from taking you down. Something else you should know. The shooter ain't local. He had Chicago ID on him."

"I can't get away from the place," Maguire said. Honey listened, transfixed.

Ferndale declined an offer from Honey to stay awhile. "Stoffleman is asking for you, Maguire. I'll take you to the hospital. Miss Rossini, that black and white you'll see on the street. Officer's name is Costa. He's got direct radio contact with the clubhouse. Anyone calls you on the phone to give you trouble, you tell Costa right away."

Maguire shrugged off the blanket and folded it. "I'll be back," he said to Honey, hugging her.

"I'm counting on it," she replied.

At the hospital, they passed Peach in her starched white uniform. She winked on her way into a patient's room. "I caught that," Ferndale told Maguire. "You couldn't get a date to save your life for all these years I've known you. Now you got girlfriends stashed all over town. I count three including Simone over at the coffee shop."

"Santa Claus came after all," Maguire replied.

"Wish he'd fill my stocking like that, Maguire."

They found Stoffleman pale and suffering under a pile of bandages and tubes. Maguire hardly recognized his editor except for the ugly battle scar on his left cheek. His glasses, cracked and bent, sat next to some pill bottles on the shelf above his bed. Both his eyes were black and the lids nearly swollen shut. A swath of white tape covered his nose. When Stoffleman attempted to smile through puffy lips, Maguire noticed some of his teeth missing.

"Think this is bad, you should see the other guys," Stoffleman whispered, attempting a predictable joke.

Ferndale leaned over Stoffleman. "Word is you landed a few punches but four against one ain't good odds. You can bet we'll find these mugs," he said.

Maguire felt sick. "You look like hell, boss. When did this happen?"

Stoffleman gripped the railings on the bed with a swollen right hand. "After midnight when we got the presses rolling. I left the *Bugle* out the front door like I always do. A man in shabby clothes stepped in front of me. You know, dressed like a miner who never saw a washing machine. He threw around some loose talk about the *Bugle* sticking its nose into private affairs. He wanted to know if I worked at the paper. These other men ease out of the shadows. They look like the kind of working-class stiffs who read the *Bugle*. I tell them I'm the editor, so if they have a complaint, I'm their man."

"They took you at your word," Ferndale said.

"I don't remember anything after that," Stoffleman said. "The doctor said they beat on my head. I evidently went down because they put the boots to me. Last time I hurt this much was when combat in Germany put me in sick bay. But never mind about that. Maguire, are you listening?"

"Right here, boss."

"Ferndale told me about your shootout at the Logan last night. You get down to the *Bugle*. Write a big-ass story for tomorrow's paper. Leave nothing out. Get the latest on the investigation from Ferndale here. Don Morgan's running the show in my absence. He knows the drill. I want it known that nobody intimidates the *Bugle* into staying quiet about a crime wave. When they see your story they'll know beatings don't stop the *Bugle* from publishing. Savvy? And tell Morgan, if anybody coasts while I'm gone, I'll kick butt from here to Sunday when I get back."

Satisfied, Stoffleman drifted off.

Ferndale smirked as he and Maguire left the hospital. "Think I'm tough on you? Stoffleman could ride herd on every soldier from here to Hitler's bunker."

"He already did, Duke."

Ferndale drove Maguire to the *Bugle*, briefing him on the way. Police had arrested five men, four of them Stoffleman's presumed assailants. All of them were Local 1235 members. The fifth man was Mack Gibbons. "He says to me, 'Don't nobody arrest no Cracker on Christmas,' " Ferndale said. "What do you call it when somebody talks like that?"

"Double negatives."

"I reminded him with a lick alongside the head that I ain't nobody. You ought to hear him howling in the jail. Cracker missing his Christmas dinner. Cracker going to whip every cop in Butte. Cracker kills men with his thumb. Cracker's head hurts. We're holding him on probable cause of running around behind one of these masks. Idiot as much as admitted it during our little talk at the mine. You heard it for yourself."

"You ate Cracker for lunch with that interrogation."

"You got a way with words, Maguire."

When Ferndale pulled in front of the *Bugle's* front door, Maguire finished jotting details in his notebook. He had taken note of Ferndale's best quote of the night, ensuring its publication in the morning: "This ain't trick or treatin' that's going on in Butte. These criminals hiding behind Halloween masks aren't coming around for candy."

Maguire stepped out of the car. "Where to now, Duke?"

"Back to the hospital to see Babe McGraw. It's Christmas, you know."

"You ought to propose to her before you're too damn old to remember how."

"Rare romantic advice from Red Maguire. Firing on all cylinders, ain't you? If you figure on getting in deep with Miss Rossini, remember she runs in a fast crowd of hoity toity high society types. How I see it, at least. You and me, we don't even iron our clothes. Simone might be more your style, Maguire."

"Thanks for the free advice, Duke."

Ferndale put his foot on the brake and shifted his car into drive. "Another thing, Maguire. Keep the door to the *Bugle* locked until we get to the bottom of this or you might find some unwelcome trash blowing in."

"I doubt we ever locked the doors in the history of the place," Maguire said.

"Start now," Ferndale ordered. "Check with me in the morning."

Maguire locked the door behind him and climbed the steep wooden stairs to the second floor. Morgan, a looming Scot with a red beard and a black necktie that hung to the swell of his belly, waved to him. Morgan had worked at the *Bugle* at least ten years. He was the night editor in charge of assembling stories and pages for the press. Stoffleman was the big dog in the city room. Morgan was a close second.

"We've got space on the front page for whatever you're planning to write," Morgan said. "Stoffleman called me earlier with marching orders. Didn't even sound like Clyde. Hell of a deal, that beating. Wish I had been there to give him some help. I was downstairs proofing pages off the press," he explained, almost apologetically.

Maguire went to his typewriter where he wrote:

"A police investigation into threats against Butte business owners widened Thursday after four men attacked the Bugle's chief editor and another assailant fired two rounds at the Bugle's crime reporter through the window at his hotel.

"The attacks came after Captain Harold Ferndale, the city's senior detective, questioned a union member in a confrontation at the Anselmo mine. That union member, Mack Gibbons, is now in custody in the Butte jail. Present at the questioning was Rusie Dregovich, president of Local 1235, the most powerful union in Butte.

"In addition to Gibbons, police arrested the men suspected in beating the Bugle editor, Clyde Stoffleman, who suffered extensive head and rib injuries. All the perps, Ferndale said, are members of Local 1235."

Maguire wrote and wrote until Morgan hollered from his desk that it was time to stop. "Deadline is coming faster than that slow train you're riding," Morgan said.

"You sound like Stoffleman."

Morgan took that observation as a compliment. "Clyde would settle for no less," the big man said.

Maguire handed over the eleven typed sheets to Morgan and went to the window. Christmas lights glimmered all the way down Butte Hill and onto the Flats. There's more to the story, much more, he thought to himself.

"After reading your story, nobody will doubt we've got a mess of trouble here in Butte," Morgan called to him, looking up from Maguire's story.

"Until we find out who's pulling the strings, it's about to become worse, much worse," Maguire replied.

~ 12 ~

'The Italian mafia'

Demands for money came the next morning. Honey Rossini called Maguire's phone at the *Bugle* from her jewelry store. "I'm hearing that some strange hustlers in suits want big money to make sure nobody gets hurt," Honey said, sounding distressed. "They take hundreds of dollars and warn against calling police or bad things will happen. People are afraid for their families, Red."

Maguire rubbed sleep from his eyes. He had spent a fitful night sleeping on a couch in a corner of the *Bugle* city room. It was lumpy and dusty. Nobody ever sat on that couch. He longed for another nap at Honey's house but knew better. Neighbors would talk. So would the cop who was parked outside her front door.

"So the bagmen are moving in. Ferndale told me it would happen. Did anyone come to your store?"

"Not yet, maybe because police are patrolling this block. Red? Many of our business owners can't afford $100. That's an entire week's profit at our smaller stores. I can't tell you who's getting hit because they swore me not to reveal their names. They're scared to death."

"Cops can't act if nobody reports this extortion," he said.

"They read your stories, Red. Nobody wants to wind up beaten or dead. Or place their families in the same danger. Please tell Ferndale what I heard. Tell him he can go to the bank with this information. And Red? Get to the bottom of this and fast, will you? Ferndale's good but you are better. And Red? Thanks for spending Christmas with me. I hate being alone."

When they hung up, Maguire slipped into his snow boots and pulled on his overcoat. He headed outside for the next big story. Back when he was a cub reporter, taking over the *Bugle* crime beat after the fabled Peter Sullivan died when the train ran over him, he put in an honest eight-hour day's work and went home to cook supper and read and listen to the radio. As he built a long list of sources for his stories, including Duke Ferndale, Maguire let his work consume him. He became accustomed to placing and taking phone calls at night. Crime knew no boundaries. Maguire spent most weekends trudging around crime scenes with Ferndale and uniformed cops. He also covered big fires. Murders came more frequently in warm weather, he came to understand, when people spent more time on the streets. Fires came in cold weather when stoves overheated. News came first.

He lived alone in a room with peeling wallpaper at a former hotel. No time in his life for romance. The envelope of notes and letters from women that he carried in his pocket remained pitifully small.

Maguire shrugged off his heartbreak as he walked to the police department. Someday Ferndale would retire his badge. To do what, neither man knew. Maguire dreaded the day Ferndale called it quits. Ferndale, Maguire's best source for news. Who then, Chief Morse? He talked the way he dressed, measured, meticulous, cautious. He lacked Ferndale's gift for revealing secrets. A good cop, even a tough one, Chief Morse, but not the type to make good copy in the *Bugle*.

Ferndale fumed when Maguire told him what Honey had said about the bag men. "Hired thugs, Maguire. That's who they are. Outside gunslingers like the mug who shot at you. I could tell at first glance he's not from around here. The dope won't tell us a thing. I ought to go box his ears."

"You're just the man to do it, detective."

Ferndale threw a couple of shadow jabs with his left hand. He winced at the lingering pain from the gunshot wound. "Still fast considering, ain't that right, Maguire?"

"I never doubted it."

"Your landlord put new glass in your window at the Logan yet?"

"Soon as I tire of the fresh air."

"Take a cop's advice. Stay away from windows, glass or no. I doubt this mug who took pot shots at you is a one-man show. Here's what I think, Maguire." Ferndale closed his office door and sat against the edge of his desk. He was back to wearing a shoulder holster. The leather strap on the holster crossed the very spot where the bullet tore through his shoulder.

"Don't quote me. You know the drill. Looks to me that the mine union is tied up with organized crime. I worked these streets long enough to know a local bum from an import. Something about that union guy, Dregovich, smells worse than a three-day-old tuna sandwich. Call it a hunch. First, we have these stupid threats on business owners, the type of nonsense Cracker would dream up, then strangers in suits showing up for the money."

"What's your hunch tell you about these strangers?"

"Might as well spill the official story, Maguire, and damn well confirm it before you put it in print. You never heard this from me, got it? A bulletin came in this morning from Chicago police. Some informant barked up the tree about organized crime messing with labor unions again but this time outside the city. Call me a dumb guy in Butte putting two and two together and hope it don't add up to three. It ain't a pretty picture."

"Organized crime? The Italian mafia?"

"You, being a Chicago rat, should know all about that, Maguire."

"I was eight years old when my old man moved us to Butte. Before that I couldn't find my way around the block."

"Still can't. What's with you Irish anyway?"

"Irish built Butte, Duke. When are you going to admit that?"

"More damn micks is all we need. Dublin Gulch and Corktown stuffed full of them. When I wore the uniform, I spent half my shift up there breaking up fights."

"I remember. I started some of them."

"Punk!" Ferndale grunted, waving Maguire out of his office.

Maguire waded down Granite Street to the Logan Hotel. Snow had drifted a foot deep on his floor near the broken window. Ice filled his sink. He dug the telephone from the snow and dialed his landlord, a wop named Nick. "Five bucks, Red, give or take. Comes outta your pocket, mister. I pay for natural disasters. You wanna have gunfights, you pay the damage. Five bucks and change. Add it to your rent next month. Yeah, I'll send a man over to put in new glass. Keep your powder dry, will ya? My building shot full of holes ain't worth nothin'. Tenants no good to me if they get a bullet in their head. Yeah, I read what you wrote in the *Bugle*. Hell of a mess going on here in Butte. Sure you don't want to hang some sheet iron over them windows?"

Maguire found his car buried in a snow drift. He noted with some satisfaction that nobody had flattened his tires. He drove to the hospital. Stoffleman, awake, looked more alert than the night before. A nurse stood over the editor, checking his pulse. "That you, Maguire? Can't see a cotton-picking thing without my glasses. Nurse, crank me up so I can see better, will you?"

Stoffleman grimaced as the bed moved. "Tough as it was holding the paper two inches in front my face, I read this morning's story, Maguire. Not bad. You might succeed as a *Bugle* reporter yet."

"Your attempts to humble me never change, boss. What's your doctor say?"

"To forget going back to work anytime soon. Hell of a doctor's report of my condition. Broken bones and some internal bleeding. Those boys who jumped me shovel ore for a living, I can tell you that. They had the punch of a piston behind those fists. It appears I left some teeth on the sidewalk, too. I ache from head to toe. I think I know how Harvey Addleston felt after what those two miners did to him in Finn Town. Maybe I understand a little more clearly why his daughter went after them, even if I don't agree with her methods."

Maguire stared at Stoffleman's beaten face. The purplish blotch around his eyes now covered his left cheek, engulfing the long scar from the war. He spoke through swollen lips.

"Where's Ketchul in all of this, Red? So he was at the Anselmo, playing peacemaker with the union boys to stop them from pounding you and Ferndale into dust. Tell me what you didn't write in your story."

Maguire remembered looking over at Ketchul's deserted desk on Christmas morning. Inside and outside the *Bugle* city room, people knew Ketchul as a respected no-nonsense newsman. He wrote his stories and left. Unlike his fellow reporters, he never talked about the story behind the story.

Maguire confided in Stoffleman about his suspicion that Ketchul owed something to Dregovich and the miners. "He threw it back at me that I'm too close to Ferndale and the cops and he's probably right," Maguire said.

"Knowing sources well, and having their trust, isn't the problem and both of you know what I mean," Stoffleman said. "It's when a reporter becomes beholden to them and does their bidding, trying to control how they look in print. Then comes real trouble. Never once did I think either one of you crossed the line. I'll tell you though, in my years at the *Bugle*, I've witnessed a few reporters succumb to that temptation."

"What's bothering you, boss?"

"That Ted hasn't written a lick about this big story despite my order to the contrary. He's being unusually stubborn about union involvement in this crime."

"He made that clear when he punched me in the face," Maguire said. He told Stoffleman what Ferndale had confided about possible mob infiltration of Local 1235.

"I've wondered the same," Stoffleman said, groaning as he shifted in the hospital bed. "Ted, he's been through hell and back in the Pacific. Maybe I understand him better than most people, even when I disagree with him. War veterans are complicated people."

"I've heard, boss."

"You're too young to know, Maguire. We never escape combat. We relive it. You wonder why I never sleep? Because I can't. Stuck in this bed, all broken up, brings it all back. For Ted, it might be the same when he sees two sides lining up against each other."

"Tell me, boss. Tell me your story."

Stoffleman groaned again. "Lord, don't let anybody ever kick your ribs. Maybe it's time, Maguire, time you knew." He exhaled. Maguire could see Stoffleman's pain was from more than the beating he took Christmas Eve.

"I was a foot soldier in Patton's Third Army when the Krauts pushed us back in Belgium. If you know your history, and I hope you do at this point in your *Bugle* employment, you remember that Hitler attempted to drive a wedge through Allied forces to stop our invasion of Germany.

Eisenhower sent Patton north to stop them. The fight that resulted was known as the Battle of the Bulge. That's the background, Maguire. Now, here's my story. Thousands of us swarmed into the fray. We had the wrong clothes for cold winter weather. It was a tossup what was colder, my fingers or the barrel of my M-1 rifle. Icicles hung off my helmet. We waded in snow drifts waist deep. Digging fox holes meant chipping away at the frozen ground for hours. The men who gave up died from shrapnel and wind chill. We argued which was worse, the Germans or the weather. We broke the German line on Christmas. Quite a gift, don't you think? It was a killing field, more than people know, with frozen men on either side throwing lead like nobody's business. When we crossed into Germany, taking cover behind our tanks, people fought with desperation. We shot down German soldiers like pigeons in a shooting gallery. Fighting was fierce. Never underestimate the will of resistance as people defend their homeland. Truman knew that about Japan before he dropped the atomic bomb.

"But for my personal story. My squad was hiking into Germany after we broke the German line in Belgium. I was a sergeant. Did I ever tell you that? I recall seven of us in that squad. New men replaced our casualties. It was spring. We were walking single file along a road, slipping in slush, when some Germans opened up on us. Our lead man went down. The rest of us slid into the ditch and fired back. We had no cover. I saw a head pop up and got a bead on him and fired off a round. Blood sprayed from his chest. We fired back and forth for five minutes or so until I told my men to stop shooting to save our ammo. We were too far away to throw grenades. Then I got the big idea to charge their position. We jumped up and ran. They shot two more of my men before we crossed the road. The four of us still on our feet ran right at their position, firing our carbines until we got on top of them. I counted five German soldiers dead. Until that moment it was just another battle.

"Suddenly there was a burst of fire from one of the Germans we thought was dead. A round sliced through my face, opening my cheek to the bone. It felt burning hot. Bastard nearly got me. I finished him off with a burst from my M-1. Then we got a good look at the Germans. They were boys, all of them. Eleven, twelve years old. The boy I shot from across the road had little pink hands. He had a letter in his pocket from his mother. His name was Rolf. He was younger than the rest, maybe ten. I think he stood up when we were shooting because he was scared and confused. We killed boys, Maguire, young boys who had no business shooting on a battlefield. Last night, when I fell asleep, I saw his face. It came to me in the dark. His eyes were big and round under that oversized helmet when I put a bullet in his chest. I killed boys, Maguire, no older than the kids who sell our newspaper on the street corners."

Stoffleman wiped a tear from his cheek. "I can't escape the nightmare, Red. The war ended nearly a decade ago. Still I'm haunted."

Maguire bent over his old editor, suddenly frailer than Maguire had known him. "You had no choice, boss. They wore the enemy uniform. They killed your men. They nearly killed you."

"Every one of us fights his demons. Ketchul survived Pearl Harbor with his life, true, but the guilt of killing other human beings and watching them die never goes away. I know this from personal experience. Who knows what burdens Ted's mind? Maguire, I will confess something else. I distrust Ted's reporting lately. He's hiding something, I'm convinced of it. Get to the bottom of it, will you?"

Maguire stood and pulled on his coat. "I know just the person who can help," he said. Stoffleman closed his eyes and drifted off.

In the hallway, Maguire encountered a nurse heading for Stoffleman's room. "Peach won't be back until the night shift," she said, winking at Maguire like she knew a big secret.

"Word gets around, I see," Maguire replied. "My boss just gave me an earful besides."

"The painkillers get his tongue wagging," the nurse said. "For the rest of us, it's the juicy gossip."

Maguire smiled when he thought about seeing Peach after dark. He asked for directions for Babe McGraw's room. After that, he planned to drive to a house of prostitution on Mercury Street. He kept that thought to himself.

~ 13 ~

'True confessions'

The nurse pointed Maguire in the direction of barroom cursing down the hall. "Babe's discharge can't come soon enough, between you and me, handsome. My name is Mary in case Peach loses interest," she said, winking.

He found Babe sitting up in bed, a white sheet swathing her bulbous form. She stopped her tirade long enough to take notice of Maguire. "I'm going to kick some sorry Butte ass if they don't let me out of this prison real damn soon!" she yelled toward the open door.

"Feeling better, I see," Maguire said to her.

Babe settled back on the bed. Daylight from the window fell across evidence of someone accustomed to bare-knuckle brawls.

"Ferndale told me about your shootout and how those boys roughed up your boss. What the hell happened to your face? Get in a boxing match with Duke, that old cuss?"

"I would look worse than this, Babe."

"I'm going broke, Maguire. A closed bar don't make no money. Ferndale promises to send every cop on the force to drink me out of inventory. Fact is, filling my place with dicks chases away miners. Them's my customers. Some of them boys have a beef with dicks. Hell, Maguire, you know that. They can chug beer in Babe's Bar long as they fork over jingle and take the fisticuffs outside. Some who don't get the picture, I teach who's boss."

"Like Mack Gibbons?"

"I read what you wrote about Cracker. Had enough of that little pecker. He better run when they let me outta here. I'll clean his clock but good."

"Did Ferndale say anything about the men who beat on you?"

"No witnesses. A hundred of them boys from the Hill could have jumped me. Maybe they got good reason now and then. That ain't no excuse. They dare to cross me, I will bust noses and anything else I can reach. They learn soon enough, them boys."

"They're coming for the money now, Babe." Maguire told her about the $100-a-week extortion demands.

"Bums won't get a penny out of me. Better damn well bring more than them four men next time. They'll take an axe handle alongside their head."

"I don't doubt they better run while they can," Maguire told her, squinting at the beaten face. He pulled a chair close enough to see silver in her teeth. "What are we talking about, anyway? You are no shy girl. They have no reason to rile you unless you have secrets. Nothing makes sense about putting an arm on you for dough. Know something else, Babe? This union man Dregovich shows himself too easy. Know what I mean?"

Babe winced as she turned to him. "Neck hurts like hell, Maguire. Stay in my line of sight, will you? Rusie Dregovich? He ain't nobody's pal, that man. You smell a setup, maybe?"

"Been writing crime too long in this town to think otherwise, Babe. Sometimes I get lousy ideas about big trouble. Sure, I bet next month's rent that all these two-bit jokers in masks take orders from Dregovich. What for? Only lonely men and fools lean into stiff wind."

Maguire left the hospital when Babe worked up another head of steam over being held captive. He drove uptown and ate lunch at the Silver Star as Simone fussed over him, refilling his coffee cup three times, and bringing him a generous plate of apple pie a la mode before he asked for it. "Just say the word, Red," she cooed in his ear before a customer called for service. He figured she wasn't talking about yet another coffee refill.

It was early afternoon when he stopped at the Windsor on East Mercury Street. The curved front of the three-story building impressed Maguire as a metaphor for the women inside. Most of them, anyway, except the likes of Big Bernadine who weighed in north of two-fifty. Men attracted to heft found plenty of it with her. By all accounts Maggie O'Keefe ran an orderly parlor house. She made sure the girls never "let themselves go," as she was quoted once in the *Bugle*. Maggie wanted her clients coming back for more.

A busty woman, still as a mannequin, stared at Maguire from a second-floor window. Even from the street he saw her ample cleavage. She stepped away when Maguire waved.

He knocked on the door and waited until a bruiser with black knuckles swung it open. Heavy velvet drapes blocked the afternoon sun. Maguire edged into the dim parlor, lighted with red bulbs under shag lamps, where he saw pairs of bare legs.

"Welcome, Maguire," came a silvery voice.

"That you, Maggie? Having trouble seeing in here."

"You know damn well it's me. Is this a social visit or do you have a few extra bucks wearing a hole in your pocket?" Women giggled.

"I'm hoping for a word with you, Maggie."

"As usual, I was hoping for more," she replied, mocking disappointment. "You do remember, Maguire, that we aren't the five and dime?" More giggles. "Follow me, Maguire. You know the way."

He followed her through a passageway to the back of the house, passing several doors on either side. Maggie's office had a carved mahogany desk fitting for a madam of her persuasion. A ledger with green lines lay open on it. Maggie saw Maguire taking it all in. "Try keeping the books in a place like this," she said, easing into a tall chair behind the desk.

Maggie wore her usual green satin dress. Her graying hair, swept into a bun, showed hints of its original fire orange. A black choker encircling her neck recalled Butte's earlier days in the red-light district. Outdated, but not a bad touch. Maggie looked every inch a madam but a worldly one. Maguire knew she commanded respect in Butte for her generous donations to charitable causes. She would never find membership in the Rotary Club, or earn a place on Mayor Ticklenberg's personal list of stalwart citizens, but her civic involvement discouraged attempts to close down her house.

Behind her, dolls outfitted in tiny pink and yellow dresses filled the floor-to-ceiling shelves. Some were of the Raggedy Ann variety, made of cloth, eyes sewn with thread. Others, miniatures of small children, beckoned to Maguire with open hands and stared at him with intense blue eyes. Maggie saw him looking.

"Ah, the dolls," Maggie said. "All the girls keep them. You would know if you came here once in a while for pleasure rather than business, Red. I inherit dolls whenever a girl quits the house. They took to calling me Maggie the Doll. Quite fetching, don't you think?"

"The nickname fits you well. How many do you have?" Crowded onto the shelves as they were, the dolls resembled schoolkids posing for a picture. They reached over shoulders, sat on laps, even hugged each other. Some of them had twisted lips and spit fire from their narrow eyes.

"Give or take a couple hundred, I imagine. That many girls never quit on me. No, men bring these dolls to their favorites. So I can see from your expression that this surprises you, Maguire. These dolls, they keep watch over me while I work. Some people think they get up and run around the house at night."

"They scare me," Maguire admitted.

"You don't strike me as a man who scares easily, Red. Don't let it get around that you're afraid of dolls. Not the kind that sit on shelves. You have a tough-guy reputation after all."

Maguire shrugged off his overcoat and hung it on a peg by the door. "I should be flattered that you know me that way, Maggie."

She offered him a cigarette from a silver tray. "Who doesn't, Red? My girls out there in the parlor quiver in anticipation every time you walk into my house. Here's the famous Red Maguire, a man with class, they say, a man who bathes and dresses like a gentleman and brings sophistication to this dirty dug-up city."

Maguire put a match to the cigarette and laughed. "The girls say all that, Maggie? I never underestimated your talent for sweet-talking a man into becoming a loyal customer."

"I didn't make it up, Red. Of course, you know I have a special appreciation for full-blooded Irish men. I look forward to the opportunity of showing you in person. On the house, for that matter."

"You make it difficult to say no," Maguire said, leaning a broad shoulder against floral wallpaper.

"A girl can hope," Maggie said. "It's clear to me, though, that you're here on business and I know why. I wondered how long it would take for you to pay me a visit."

"There's been trouble, Maggie."

"I read your stories in the *Bugle*. I also know about the Christmas Eve attacks on you and Stoffleman. What the grapevine hasn't provided me is the story behind that ugly bruise on your face."

Maguire told her about Ketchul punching him in the city room after they argued about miners wearing the masks.

Maggie lit a fat cigar and puckered two red lips around it, drawing the smoke deep. "Gets confusing keeping all the players straight, doesn't it? Now you come to the controversial Maggie O'Keefe for clarification. You know some people in this town would close my house in a heartbeat if they could prove I was stirring up trouble? Word gets out that I'm telling secrets and they close me down."

"We're talking on background, Maggie. No need to jam you up. Once again, I owe you."

Maggie smiled. "You're running up a deep debt at the Windsor, Red. I plan to cash in someday soon, and when I do, I don't want to hear any argument about it. Keep 9 East Mercury on your calendar."

Maguire eased the grip-end of the .38 from his pocket and placed it on Maggie's desk. "Here's how serious this thing is getting. This is the weapon I used to wing the mug trying to kill me. I guess criminals read the newspaper. Well, for my money, I intend to break this story wide open in the *Bugle*. So I ask myself, if Dregovich and his union buddies bring the muscle, who runs this extortion racket? I doubt Dregovich needs the jingle. Every miner on the Hill buys influence with that bohunk for certain shifts, certain jobs, certain mines, certain favors. You've heard?"

Maggie reached in a drawer. She pulled out a revolver similar to Maguire's and laid it on her desk beside his own. He could see it was loaded. "Proof I don't take anything for granted either, despite having two reliable bouncers working the floors."

She took another long puff from her cigar. "What I hear, Red, is that Dregovich isn't the end of the line, as you already suspect. That man is an operative. Think of a tree. You and Ferndale look at the branches when you should be finding the roots. Mack Gibbons is trouble, sure enough. I banned Cracker from the Windsor a few years ago when he punched one of my girls for making fun of his little thing. Cracker's the kind of fool who would carry out orders to wear a silly kid mask and rob people. The buzz around town is that he's one of the men who beat Harry Dalton at the Valley View gas station."

Maggie rubbed her eyes. "If Cracker commits crimes, Dregovich puts him up to it. Cracker is a branch on that tree. Dregovich is the trunk. As the boss of that union he's got enough men to keep Ferndale and the other cops guessing while this extortion racket gains speed. Those miners who beat up Babe McGraw and Clyde Stoffleman, nothing but more branches on the tree. Is this metaphor working for you?"

"Best I've heard yet," Maguire said, nodding his approval.

"We hear a lot of true confessions in this house. Men tell my girls everything. The girls compare notes between tricks. Those fillies are more sophisticated than people think. They read the papers. Gossip drifts over from the Dumas and Blonde Edna's down the street and other houses, too. This thing is bigger than anyone knows and soon will become a great deal more trouble for this town. Tell me, Red, what does a diligent news reporter do when he's trying to find the root of a serious crime story?"

"Dig deeper," Maguire replied without hesitation.

Maggie came around her desk to sit beside him. She reached out to take hold of his hand. "How old were you when you moved to Butte? Big enough to stand your ground?"

"I was eight. Boys in ragged coveralls beat me up the first day. It was the last time. My father showed me how to punch. Forget dancing around like some boys do, he said. Knock them down and put the boots to them. So I did."

"Good advice in Butte," Maggie said. "I came here when I was sixteen to work in the Copper Block around the corner. Like you, from Chicago. There's what, a good twenty years between us? Butte was a rougher place in those days. A big drunk man punched me, knocking me out. Another man threw me down the stairs buck naked. I never felt shame for what I do for a living but sometimes I have regrets. I see families with children and wonder what I missed. Those dolls behind me remind me every day."

Maguire squeezed her hand. "We Irish better stick together, Maggie."

"What I'm about to tell you, Red, never came from me. It's with more than a little irony that the current crime wave in Butte is coming from our hometown of Chicago. Maybe you heard that from Ferndale?" She didn't wait for Maguire to respond. "Somebody has the pinch on Rusie Dregovich. If word gets out that I told you, trouble will come for me. The muscle I have working for me is enough to toss drunks and abusers. My boys can't hold back professional killers like the mug who shot at you. You never heard this from me. Are we understood?"

"Maggie, you know..."

"Then find out if this is true. I'm hearing Dregovich does bidding for Tony Accardo."

Maguire's eyes widened. "The Mafia boss?"

Maggie nodded. "The girls hear that the mob infiltrated the labor unions. Easy money to them. When a bum like Dregovich mouths off that workers on the Hill deserve their fair share, Accardo's boys come a-knockin'."

Maguire saw fear in Maggie's eyes. He pulled her to him and kissed her on the lips.

"For old times, I presume," Maggie said to him. She handed him a tissue. "Wipe the lipstick off or you'll find yourself having to explain to Simone over at the diner."

"Word gets around, Maggie, although you must know I'm not returning her favors."

"Honey Rossini, now she's a different story, isn't she?"

"Is my life an open book, Maggie?"

"You tell me, Red. You're the one who comes to me for gossip, after all."

Maguire stood. He slid the .38 back into his coat pocket. "Honey, she's special," he told Maggie.

"Then you should be careful not to get too close to her until police shut down this crime wave. The goons will compromise you by going after her. You and Honey are as close to real celebrities as we have in this town. Everybody reads your tales of crime in the *Bugle*. Honey is upper crust, the belle of Butte, and would never consort with the likes of me. Trust what I tell you. Dregovich is smarter than he looks. You can expect he will do all he can to shut down your *Bugle* coverage of union involvement in this racket. You saw what those men did to Stoffleman. If Dregovich knows you're close to Miss Rossini he'll come for her."

Maguire patted the revolver in his pocket. "If they do, they'll have a fight on their hands, Maggie."

"This isn't kid stuff up in Dublin Gulch, Red. Watch yourself. That gunman who shot at you had no intention of sending a warning. He was trying to murder you. Put you on ice. Your dead body is of no use to me."

"You're a doll, Maggie," he said, winking.

"Nobody's putting me on a shelf just yet," she said, glancing at the dolls.

Melting snow filled the streets when Maguire drove away from the Windsor. He had to confirm the mob's presence in Butte, and fast. He never knew Maggie O'Keefe to lead him astray. She was right. The city was in serious trouble.

Back at the *Bugle*, Calvin Claggett lifted his sleepy head when Maguire walked into the city room. Maguire wondered how Claggett did it, writing about dead people day after day, week after week, year after year. His embalming job in the evenings was bad enough. Talk about a reporter knowing his sources.

"How's my favorite *Bugle* stiff writer?" Maguire shot his way.

"What a joker. Know how close I came to writing about you and Stoffleman approaching the heavenly gates?"

"That they were swinging wide open for us?"

"To the contrary, that they were slammed shut in your faces. Sorry to break the news prematurely."

"You're the man to know who pleases the higher authority, Calvin. Seen Ketchul around?"

"He stopped in two hours ago to file a story about miners sinking a new shaft at the Badger State. I guess he thought it was a big deal given the interest in open pit mining."

"Who cares about a shaft with all this other bad business on the Hill?" Maguire shot back, his jaw tense.

"Don't kick the messenger, Red."

Maguire went to his telephone to call Ferndale. The detective answered on the first ring. He sounded crankier than usual.

"The mayor burst in this morning breathing fire. He got wind of business owners paying off the thugs. Nobody admits doing it. Said he was going to can every cop on the payroll unless we put a lid on this thing in a week. Never seen him so mad. Ranted and raved about the *Bugle*. So far that old crank thinks your news tips come out of thin air."

"He'll never know the secret from me," Maguire said. "Got anything new on the Chicago connection?"

"A couple of legal dicks in expensive suits bailed out your shooter. Victim of mistaken identity is their line. My uncle's a frog, too. Got a name on the mug, though. Benjamin Doratelli, aka Bennie the Mule. If you saw his ugly puss you would know why."

Maguire scribbled in his notebook as Ferndale talked. "We're firm on that name, Duke?"

"Until somebody with a bigger brain than mine says different. Maguire?"

"Yeah?"

"It's time both of us watch our backs day and night. These men play for keeps. The Purple Rose Murders were local. Now these out of towners come butting in. We ain't got enough cops to cover all the possible trouble. We'll keep an eye on Irene Rossini because of all that fancy jewelry she sells, and we've got another cop watching the hospital, but I'm afraid you're on your own. Get yourself a box of ammo for that .38. The few slugs I gave you won't be enough to keep you on top of the dirt."

"Make sure you don't get shot, detective. I've got more stories to write."

"If I do, let's hope it's in the same place as last time," Ferndale said. "I need one good arm anyway."

Maguire hung up the phone. He should call Chicago, but first, he needed to check on Honey.

~ 14 ~

'Right here, boys'

She looked up with a start when he entered her store. A bell rang above the door. "You startled me. I haven't had a paying customer all day."

"Maybe because of the cop sitting in the black and white across the street?"

"Or your stories in the *Bugle*, Red. Masks, murder, mayhem, you name it. People should know, don't you think?"

"That's the point of newspapers, Honey." He shrugged off his overcoat. He took the piece out of his pocket and placed it on the glass display case.

"I told you, I don't like guns," she said. "What if a customer comes in and sees that? It was bad enough when you pulled it out at my house. It could go off, you know."

Maguire put the gun back in his pocket. "Jumpy, I guess."

"I don't understand what's happening to our town," Honey said, looking pitifully alone standing behind the lighted sparkling jewelry display. "It's creepy knowing how people are getting hurt because they won't give up their money. Since we talked this morning, I heard from another business owner scared out of her wits. A man walked into her store and stared at her from behind a mask."

"I thought they were done with that kid stuff. Wearing the masks, anyway."

"This one looked like Dracula. She's so spooked she will pay anything to make it stop."

Maguire pulled out his notebook. "Help me get to the bottom of this, Honey. Give me names."

Her red fingernails clicked on the display glass as she fidgeted. "You know I can't, Red. I would break confidences, just as you would if you revealed secret sources, know what I mean?"

"You're too smart for your own good," he said, smiling. He pushed the notebook into the same pocket that held the .38.

Honey came from around the counter. "Back here," she told Maguire. She walked to the back of the store, to the safe where she kept the jewelry, out of view of the window. Honey put her arms around Maguire's neck. "Tell me how this will end, Red. Please."

Maguire felt flustered. Honey's face was within inches of his. She was even prettier, if that was possible, up close.

"Are you talking about the extortions?"

"That, too," Honey said. Maguire was at least half a foot taller but she stood on her toes and pulled him to her. They embraced for a long kiss, their lips exploring, as Maguire pressed his open palms to the back of her red sweater. Honey kissed him deeply, not wanting to let go.

"I won't let anything happen to you," he assured her when she finally broke the kiss.

"I'll make the same promise to you, *Bugle* man."

The taste of Honey's lips lingered on his. "This city's blowing up. I need to find answers," he finally said.

"Isn't that the job of our police department?"

"I share as much responsibility, if my job as a crime newsman means anything." His eyes narrowed. "Don't go anywhere out of sight of that black and white. Those goons will lay low if they see a cop. I'm going back to the *Bugle* to write a story for tomorrow's paper."

"About what this time, Red?"

Maguire decided not to tell Honey about organized crime infiltrating Butte. Not yet. Not with night coming on. That would scare her even more.

He smiled at her. "When I know for sure, you'll read it in the *Bugle* in the morning. You've got my number, Honey." He pecked her on the lips and headed outside. The graying cop across the street, an older hand Maguire knew by the name of Harrity, gave him a knowing grin and waved. Maguire nodded his acknowledgement and walked the block to the *Bugle* offices. He locked the door behind him as Ferndale had encouraged. It pained him to do it. City rooms were public places where people come and go. Whatever fear he once had of working the streets in a dark city evaporated years earlier on the crime beat. Maguire knew death and grief. It lived with him.

He found a handful of reporters and editors working as dusk arrived outside the windows. Claggett, his mind dwelling with the otherworldly as always, hammered on his typewriter on yet another obituary. Davis, the young new reporter Stoffleman hired to cover City Hall after Antonio Vanzetti's murder, toiled over a story about a new ordinance for uptown parking. Ketchul banged away on his typewriter keys as if driving home a point. Maguire waved in Ketchul's direction, got no response, and walked over to Morgan at the editing desk. A pool of light fell over four grim men wielding pencils on tomorrow's news. Morgan, the big Scot, was doing his best to command the city room in Stoffleman's absence.

"Can we talk, boss? Privately?"

Morgan motioned Maguire to the meeting room across the hall and closed the door.

"Too many listening ears," Maguire explained.

Morgan took a chair. "We've never worried about that before, have we? Our city room is an open book."

"I no longer trust Ketchul," Maguire admitted.

Morgan nodded his understanding. "Nor does Clyde," he said.

Maguire told Morgan what he heard about the day's shakedowns of business owners and suspicions of the mob operating in Butte through Local 1235. That information came off the record, Maguire said, but from reliable sources. Nobody would be quoted.

"What would you write?" Morgan asked.

Maguire patted the bulge of love letters in his pocket. He felt more confident for doing so. He felt Honey's soft kiss on his lips. He saw Morgan staring at her lipstick, its evidence remaining on his mouth. "A story to raise the alarm that Christmas in Butte brought more than teddy bears and sleds. Enough to get us by until I can find out more about a Chicago connection."

Morgan looked skeptical. "Red, what if your sources are wrong?"

"They've never failed me yet, Don."

Morgan exhaled. "I suspect not. Here's what we'll do. Write your story for all it's worth. Run it over to Stoffleman at the hospital to get his take on it. Let me read it before you go. We might need to alert the Old Man before the presses run." Stoffleman said the Old Man worked in an upstairs office, but Maguire had never seen him.

As they returned to the city room they encountered Ketchul climbing the stairs from the street. "Stepped out for some fresh air," he told them.

Maguire returned to his desk and rolled a sheet of blank paper into his Remington. He typed frantically, drawing sudden accusing stares from Ketchul. Maguire ignored him. They had worked within fifteen feet of each other since the end of World War II. Neither man knew the other well. Ketchul kept a photo on his desk of his wife and young sons. They never came to the city room. The enigmatic Ketchul wrote a steady stream of stories about Butte's mining industry. More and more over the years they leaned toward the miners' point of view. Maguire recalled the moment when Stoffleman called Ketchul on his bias. "Those Company men can't tell a drill from a drift," Ketchul offered, reminding Stoffleman that the *Bugle* was known first and foremost as the working man's newspaper.

Maguire shook Ketchul from his mind. Time was short. He pictured an impatient Stoffleman, upright in his hospital bed, waiting for a look at his story. Maguire had finished most of it when he heard heavy boots thumping on the wooden staircase. Three men wearing masks burst into the city room. All of them were big men. Big enough as if Rusie Dregovich chose them himself.

Claggett, sitting closest, unlimbered from his usual hunch and took a deep puff from his smoldering cigarette. The first man grabbed Claggett's typewriter with grimy hands and threw it to the floor. Keys rolled away and the carriage wrenched off. Everyone jumped to their feet except Ketchul.

The man wore baggy bib overalls over a blue shirt darkened from sweat and mine dust. He hid his face behind a mask of a smiling, pink-faced, young girl. Maguire laughed. The man looked comical, even ridiculous.

"Where's Maguire?" he yelled in a deep voice. Maguire detected a Croation accent. The other two intruders, seemingly emboldened by the first, stepped farther into the city room. One of them knocked over a stack of newspapers near the door. He wore a mask of a mean cat. The third man tore a calendar off the wall for no apparent reason other than showing he was as disruptive as the other two. He had disguised himself as a skeleton.

In spite of himself, Maguire taunted them, feeling the grip of the .38 in his pocket. "Right here, boys. Send the girl over first."

In Maguire's line of vision, across the room, Morgan talked urgently on the phone. No doubt calling police. The first intruder edged toward Maguire, sizing him up. "Get ready for a pounding you won't never forget," the man growled. He crept past Ketchul, ignoring him. Ketchul continued typing as if nothing happened. The second intruder twisted the elderly Claggett by his necktie and slammed his head violently against the wall. The cigarette fell from his lips and his glasses slipped askew. Claggett, hurt and moaning, slid down the wall and slumped on the floor.

The man behind the little girl mask pulled a wooden club from his coat. He swung it in the air to make sure everyone saw it. "I a-going to fix you about them lies you put out about Butte's working men," he yelled in a slurred voice. "You gonna hurt bad, boy. We gonna make you squeal for your momma."

Maguire aimed square at the man's chest. Eyes blinked through the holes in the mask. Maguire's hand trembled but he pointed at the heart like Ferndale taught him to do. He pulled the hammer back with a click that echoed in the stricken city room. The cylinder rotated a bullet in front of the firing pin. The intruder hesitated. At that very moment, four ink-stained *Bugle* press operators from downstairs barreled into the city room. Each of them wielded a crescent wrench big as a baseball bat. The foreman, a rangy man Maguire knew only as Snuff, pounded his wrench on the wooden floor. "You boys want some teeth removed?" he shouted.

The press operators stepped toward the intruders. The two men closest to the door bolted and clattered down the stairs. One man cursed and fell, thumping to the bottom.

The intruder closest to Maguire swore behind his mask at Maguire's gun and turned to confront the approaching men covered with ink. When he attempted to swing his club, they swarmed him. Snuff smashed his wrench against the man's knee, knocking him to the floor as he roared in pain, and tore off his little girl mask. The man stared back with shock-open eyes from a white scarred face. They stood him up. Snuff clenched the man's oily hair with a black fist while the other pressmen pinned his arms back. The ugly man spit in Maguire's direction, exposing yellow teeth and a drool of chewing tobacco.

Maguire took three fast steps. He punched the mug in the gut hard enough to drive his stomach to his backbone. The man exhaled like a broken balloon. His legs wobbled and his head drooped as he shrieked for air.

"That's for hurting our talented writer of obituaries, a man twice your age," Maguire snarled. "Foolish move, as no doubt he'll be writing yours soon."

Ketchul stood, suddenly taking interest.

"Leave the man alone, Maguire. You've got no grounds for violence."

Maguire looked at Ketchul in disbelief. "Did you see what just happened here, Ketchul? I swear you did. Where were you in this?"

Suddenly Maguire felt like repaying Ketchul for the punch to the jaw. He lunged toward the labor reporter with a fist raised. Morgan stopped him just as Ferndale and two prowl cops hurried into the city room. "We caught the other two trick or treat clowns outside," Ferndale said. He saw the miner gasping in the clutches of the pressmen and smiled at the crumpled mask on the floor. "Cuff old cupcake there and throw all three goons in the clink," he told the uniformed cops. He retrieved the mask from the floor. "We'll keep this for evidence."

Morgan let go of Maguire's coat lapels. "Thanks for getting here so quick," Morgan told Ferndale. "You and our night crew downstairs. When Snuff and his boys came running Maguire here was itching to put a round in that loser. Clear case of common sense if he did."

While Ketchul watched, Davis and a few other men lifted Claggett to his feet. Blood soaked his collar. They helped Claggett to his chair where he slumped, his face paler than usual. "This man needs medical attention," Ferndale said. "I doubt he can walk out without help. Somebody find a medic." Morgan went to a phone. "What I can't figure," Maguire told Ferndale, "is how these men got inside the building. I locked the door behind me."

Ketchul spoke up. "Sure you did, Maguire."

"You went outside after I came in," Maguire said, pointing to him. "What's your role in this anyway?"

Ketchul sneered and put on his coat. He bent to his typewriter, ripped out a sheet of paper, rolled it up and stuffed it inside his coat. "You know better than to make unfounded accusations," Ketchul replied. He turned and charged out of the city room.

The ambulance crew came to haul off Claggett. He had taken a hard blow to his head. He also had an injury to his back where a coat hook on the wall had jabbed into him. While they loaded him on a stretcher, Maguire returned to his desk to write the rest of his story. He included the events of the evening, adding a description of the attack, and how Ketchul ignored it all.

When he finished typing, he handed the story to Morgan. "I don't know about casting blame on our own reporter, Maguire. Let the cops decide. On the other hand, everything you write here is factually correct as confirmed by my own eyes. Now it's Stoffleman's turn."

When Maguire arrived at the hospital, he met Peach walking to the front door to start her night shift. Snowflakes swirled around her smiling face under two big yellow lamps near the entrance. She kissed him on the cheek.

"You've got more business from the *Bugle*," Maguire said. He told her about the attack on Claggett.

"Red, this crime wave is filling up the joint. Butte will need to hire more doctors to keep up. The good news is that Babe McGraw should be discharged tomorrow."

"That ought to help settle things down," Maguire said.

"For the nurses, anyway," Peach said.

Stoffleman greeted Maguire's visit with his customary sarcasm. "You were never one to pay attention to deadlines, Maguire. Let me see the damn thing." He held out his hand.

"Glad you're feeling better, boss." Maguire forked over the story headed for the morning paper. It was at least a dozen sheets. Stoffleman fitted his bent and broken glasses over his ears the best he could. They sat cockeyed on his face but the editor paid them no mind.

"Don Morgan called, told me about tonight's social visit from the miners. Tell Ferndale I want the book thrown at Claggett's attacker. The man's in his sixties, for chissake."

"Good as done, boss."

Stoffleman held up his hand for silence. He read through the story quickly, then read it a second time slowly, scratching out some sentences with a blue pen. Maguire watched the expressions on his editor's bruised face as he perused the story. The damage to his cheeks and eyes had ebbed into pools of deep purple reminders of the beating he took. So many people lately carried the evidence of fists hitting bone. Altogether they were an ugly bunch, Maguire included. He avoided looking at himself in the mirror. He hoped the bruise from Ketchul's hard swing might be fading. Not ugly enough to stop Maggie O'Keefe from kissing him, or

Honey Rossini either. If people only knew that Butte's most famous madam and Butte's most famous glamor girl had kissed him full on the lips on the same day. Maguire smiled like a fool. Stoffleman, deep into the story, failed to notice.

Finally, Stoffleman looked up. "I deleted your mentions of Ted Ketchul. No point in airing our dirty laundry publicly. Not yet. We can agree that Ted's behavior tonight further suggests that he compromised himself somehow with bad people. Keep the story's focus on the crime and investigation. Ted will reveal his problems soon enough. As for rumors of organized crime, you know the drill, Maguire. Report, substantiate, document, investigate. I can help when they let me out of here in a day or two. Meanwhile, find somebody in Chicago who knows what's going on."

"I'm on it, boss."

"And Red?" Stoffleman handed Maguire's story back to him. "Stick close to Ferndale, my boy, when this scoop hits print. You and I both know the worst is yet to come."

~ 15 ~

'Assassins never miss'

Maguire returned to the Logan Hotel where he found melting snow and ice from the broken window before Nick fixed it. Heat from the old radiator filled the room. Maguire pulled the shades and braced a wooden chair under the doorknob. He threw a towel on the pool of water to soak it up. After wringing out the towel in the sink a few dozen times, Maguire decided he had mopped the worst of the water. The rest would leak into the abandoned lobby below. It was after midnight when he fell into bed. The neon hotel sign below his new window winked orange and black through the shades as he fell asleep beneath a wool blanket.

It was mid-morning when Maguire awoke to the faint sound of someone picking the lock on his door. He reached under his pillow for the .38. The lock clicked and the knob turned but the door jammed because of the chair. "C'mon in and taste some lead!" Maguire yelled.

Someone cursed. Maguire heard footsteps retreating down the staircase. From a crack between the shade and the window, he looked down on a man in a black suit and fedora disappear around the side of the building. Gun in hand, Maguire opened the door to the hallway. It was empty. A crumpled newspaper lay at his feet. Maguire shook it open. "Mob threatens Butte," said the banner headline in the *Bugle*. Below that, other headlines in diminishing sizes described the essence of Maguire's story:

Out of Town Criminals
Infiltrate Mining Union

**Well-Dressed Bagmen
Hound Business Owners
For 'Protection' Money**

Thugs Wearing Halloween Masks
Invade Bugle City Room, Rough Up
Paper's Long-Time Obituary Reporter

**Police Vow to Rid Our Streets of Thugs
Intending Bodily Harm Against Citizens**

*By Red Maguire
Bugle Crime Reporter*

The story followed.

Angry with himself for sleeping late, Maguire washed and shaved and drove to the police department. He found Ferndale throwing on his coat.

"Hospital kicking Babe out. I'll give her a lift home if she doesn't kill somebody first. Claims she's on the mend but that ain't the whole story. Hospital tired of Babe throwing bedpans. I might need to cuff her to calm her down. I done that a time or two until she started liking it."

"You can't keep her under lock and key forever, Duke. I saw her plenty mad and when she gets loose there will be hell to pay for somebody. I'm guessing whatever miners jumped her that night."

"Ride along if you want."

"Not on your life. If Babe's fixing to hammer heads, I'm staying out of the way. Besides, no need for me to interfere

145

with you two love birds. I'm headed to the *Bugle* to see where
we stand after last night's dance party."

"Suit yourself. Hell of a story you wrote in the morning
sheet. Call me later. Gotta run before Babe tears the place
apart. Thought I would get a statement from Claggett while I
fight her out the door. Old fart hardly made a lick of sense
last night. Kept blathering on about the dearly departed. He
might figure he went with them."

"Claggett goes about life with one foot in the grave and
prefers it that way," Maguire said.

Ferndale hurried to the parking lot. Maguire took his time
walking to the *Bugle*, detouring past Honey's jewelry store.
Her saw her pitching a sale to a customer over the glass
display case. He waved to Harrity, the cop parked across the
street, and cut past the M & M bar to the Hirbour Block.
Upstairs in the city room, Morgan sat pensively at his desk,
turning an unlighted cigar through his outstretched fingers.

"I hope enough of us remain to write the end of this story,
whenever it should come," he told Maguire. "Luverne reports
the switchboard burning red with the heat she's taking this
morning over your story. Half the calls are death threats.
Never saw anger like this in all the years I've worked for the
Bugle. Can you hear what Clyde would say about it?"

"That outrage is a lesser sin than boredom?"

Morgan lit his cigar. "Can't say I disagree. Nobody buys a
boring newspaper."

Maguire looked at Claggett's empty desk. "I can't recall a
time when Calvin wasn't sitting over there knocking out yet
another rosy picture of someone's untimely stroll to the
heavenly gates."

"The rest of us will pick up the slack until he's back on the
job, Maguire. Let's hope we don't end up writing each other's
obituaries." Morgan leaned back. The hinge creaked under
his couple hundred pounds and then some. "All that being

said, we both know that when we expose corruption, and crime, we can expect threats from people who don't want anyone to know they're involved in it. The Old Man called down this morning to say as much. A few advertisers pulled out of the paper. Hell with them. Several others commended you for shining light on what these criminals are doing to business owners. Your story is causing a sensation in Butte, that's for sure."

"Seems life is a barrel of trouble," Maguire said. "Especially now."

He walked across the hall to Luverne's windowless room. She handed him a fistful of telephone messages. "Sweetie, take it from this old gal, forget calling most of them back. I heard words I never knew existed and others I had forgotten. You would think old Luverne writes stories around here the way people hurl profanity at me. I tell them, leave the switchboard lady alone. Talk nice or take a hike down a deep shaft. I'm nobody's fool."

"Tell them to button up, Luverne. Nobody should blame you for the work we do in this joint." Maguire kissed her forehead beneath white curls manufactured at the beauty shop. She reeked of lilacs. Maguire wondered if she bathed in her perfume.

His phone rang as soon as he took his typewriter. He opened a notebook and reached for a pen in case anyone provided new insight about the crime wave. The first caller thanked him for raising the alarm. The second one condemned him for sounding it. On the third call he heard a familiar voice.

"Ya dumb or deaf, Maguire?" Rusie Dregovich barked into the phone.

"To the contrary," Maguire responded.

"Maybe a slow learner? Ya make our union look bad, real bad, in that rag ya call a newspaper. I told ya the other day the union ain't involved in no crimes in this town. Ya done and gone invited yourself a pile of trouble, newsboy."

"Mr. Dregovich?"

"Formal, ain't we?"

"Why did you send those men to bust up our city room? Who are the men stealing money from business owners? Who tried to break into my hotel room?"

"I ain't got a clue about youse troubles, Maguire, and ya know it."

"Some of these men belong to Local 1235. Are you denying that?"

"Ya make up lies, Maguire. Keep this up and ya can figure open season on the *Bugle* and ya. I got five hundred men on the Hill complaining ya wrecked their reputations. Them ole boys aching to shut ya up good, Maguire. Ya know who stops them? Rusie Dregovich. I ask myself for how long. My union runs this hill, Maguire. Time you understood I run this here show. Ya don't pay me no respect like Ted Ketchul does."

"And how is that?"

"Ketchul knows we ain't involved."

Maguire covered the phone and laughed.

"Bet you a Cuban cigar you're deceiving me about all of this," he said next. Dregovich went silent except for ragged breathing. Maguire pictured the giant's hulking frame at the other end of the line, his mighty fist encircling the receiver. Maguire was two hundred pounds of muscle. Dregovich was big enough to toss him like a mine timber.

"We have a union meeting tonight, Maguire. Come join us if ya have the guts. Bring some of those cop dicks if we scare ya. How about that washed-up pug Duke? Ain't nobody going to beat ya up. Not tonight anyway. Ya come see my boys and know the error of youse ways. Have Ketchul bring ya up. If'n youse not afraid."

"Don't think you can intimidate the *Bugle*, Mr. Dregovich. If you want to talk on the record telling your side of this business, I'm all ears."

Dregovich laughed. "Ketchul's doing that for us. He don't go around telling lies about the working men of Butte." The growly union boss ended the conversation with a click in Maguire's ear.

"Going for coffee, boss!" Maguire called out to Morgan.

"Better make that lunch at this late hour," the editor responded. "Just got off the phone with Clyde Stoffleman. We can expect him back in the city room tomorrow. He's got new glasses to watch us better and a bone to pick with everybody who fouled up while he was gone, so watch out."

Maguire pulled on his overshoes. "So in other words he's back to normal, Don?"

Morgan waved a dismissive hand. "Clyde was never a man to let a smashed face and two busted ribs stop him from printing another edition of the *Bugle*."

Yet another snowfall whitened uptown Butte as Maguire trudged to the Silver Star. He swung open the glass door and stomped snow off his boots. Simone escorted him to an empty booth. "Saved it for you, honey. You know how busy it gets when the lunch crowd shows up."

"How did you know I was coming over, Simone?"

"Somebody bet me a plug nickel, handsome." She handed him a menu. "Coffee, and?"

"Bacon and pancakes if not too late. I missed breakfast."

Simone spread pink-painted fingernails on the table with one hand while resting the other on her hip. She feigned a pose of confusion. "Oh dear, whatever is the lovely Simone going to do? The kitchen quit making breakfast at eleven. And what time is it now? Why, close to noon. The famous Red Maguire is running behind today. My oh my, what a dilemma for this girl."

Maguire started to speak but she held up her hand. "But wait! I spoke too soon. My watch is running fast. We have minutes to spare. Place your trust in Simone, honey. Your breakfast is coming right up."

Much to the recurring pleasure of every man in the diner, she skipped toward the swinging doors leading to the kitchen. "Homer!" she bellowed to the cook.

Maguire tapped the end of a cigarette on the table while he thought about Rusie Dregovich's offer. Going to an angry union meeting might get him shot. Somebody tried that already so what did it matter? Lost in thought, oblivious to the customers swirling around him, Maguire absent-mindedly slid the unsmoked cigarette back in his shirt pocket.

When Simone brought the breakfast plate, she kissed his forehead and slid a folded note onto the table. He flipped it open to find her lipstick puckered in a kiss. Beneath it she had written, "What you see is what you get." She winked when she saw Maguire's blush. She slid her fingers over his hand before heading to the counter to pour coffee for a row of impatient customers on stools.

Every few moments, as Maguire ate, he flipped open Simone's note. Flirts like Simone and Peach made life easy. He pocketed her note with the others. He tipped her and stepped outside. Thickening snow, falling in big glistening flakes, blanketed the sidewalks. Dark clouds gathered over the mountains to the west. Simone waved a sentimental goodbye through the big plate-glass window. Maguire felt good. His breakfast at the Silver Star was time well spent.

Back at the *Bugle,* he scribbled in his notebook for an hour, trying to piece together the puzzle. So what if Dregovich denied the union had anything to do with the extortion racket? It was plainly true to anyone who cared to look. He found himself distracted with thoughts of the curvaceous

Honey Rossini. When he telephoned her, she had just a minute to talk.

"Oh, Red, I was hoping you would call. I'm hearing these bagmen, as you call them, are putting the pinch on at least a dozen more business owners all over town. It's getting worse."

"And you, Honey?"

"Nobody has come to my door with Officer Harrity watching outside. However," and she paused, "a letter came in this morning's mail. It's crude, Red, made from letters cut out of magazines like in the detective shows."

"Read it to me, Honey."

"It says, 'Irene Rossini pay $200 a week or lose shiny jewlry. We say when and how.' Red, that's twice what they're extorting from other businesses."

Maguire jotted down the threat. "They're planning to slam you, Honey. Take that note outside to Harrity and ask him to show it to Ferndale."

"The thugs won't get a penny from me, Red."

"You might need to lay low until the cops fix this thing."

"I'm not running, Red. I started this jewelry store with three watches and two diamond rings on money my parents left me. They came from Italy. Did I tell you? My father knew the type of ruthless men who joined the mafia. He told me, 'Never bow to them, Irene, because if you do, they grab you by the collar and never let go. You will be beholden to them until you die.' "

"Grim warning," Maguire responded.

"My father, Cesare, he didn't mince words."

"Neither do you, Honey. Do you mind if I print the contents of this letter in tomorrow's story?"

"Why not, Red. How much worse could it get?"

"I keep asking myself," he said before hanging up.

His phone rang a few minutes later. He thought of ignoring the call but on a sense of duty reached for the receiver. "Maguire, *Bugle!*"

"Red Maguire? My name is Will James, crime reporter at the *Chicago Tribune.* I read your story about the mob and a protection racket arriving in Butte. It's all over the *Associated Press* and *United Press International* wires. Your story went national. Bad news travels fast, as we both know."

"What do you make of it, Mr. James?"

"Fits a familiar pattern, Mr. Maguire. Tony Accardo's organization has long arms. Authorities tried to stop the mob from infiltrating labor unions but with mixed results. The mob has too much muscle. Some of the police bosses in Chicago think Accardo's new tactic is to broaden the operation to industrial cities with strong labor unions. Hard to know for certain because, as you know, these people operate under a code of silence. Your story from Butte hit the mark this morning. It matches our suspicions that the mob is looking for sources of new money outside Chicago."

Maguire shifted uncomfortably in his chair. "Any cash stolen in Butte would be chump change by comparison. Why bother?"

"The payoff for the mob comes over time," James said. "The squeeze looks small at first but that's only the beginning. The mob deals in volume. As fear spreads, more victims come on board. More and more people fork over money. Protection rackets run pretty much how the mob controls liquor and gambling. Once the mob jams up the little guys, it starts owning the big guys. By that I mean city government, persons of influence. The duly elected."

"But why Butte, Mr. James?"

"Accardo's boys look for a toehold, some bold rube who will do their bidding. Accardo finds people who have a beef and works them with promises of wealth. In the end he drains them. If there's any strong suspicion in Butte that the Accardo organization turned Local 1235 to his benefit, as you report in today's *Bugle*, I'm reasonably certain the union will show its colors soon enough. It won't be pretty, but you already know that. Crime reporting never is."

"How long have you covered the mob, Mr. James?"

"On and off for thirty-five years. They beat me with fists, smashed me in the face with a bar glass, warned me of being tossed in the lake wearing cement boots, ran over me with a car, and threatened me with other creative means of death so many times I lost count. What about you?"

Maguire told James about the gunman outside the Logan Hotel.

"Must be some mug low in the organization looking to earn some stripes," James said. "Their veteran assassins never miss. Watch yourself because the Accardo bosses might send someone with better eyesight. These boys play for keeps."

Maguire told James he had lived in Chicago when he was a boy.

"You wouldn't recognize this town anymore," James said. "Sure, they put Capone away, but everybody knows Big Tuna and the Outfit run the labor and gambling rackets."

"Big Tuna?"

"Accardo. Big and ugly is how I describe the situation. Of course, that's the side of it I see day and night."

"I'm with you there," Maguire said. Before they hung up, Maguire jotted down a phone number for James at the *Tribune*. Maguire would want to know more about Tony Accardo.

All the talk about Chicago got Maguire thinking about his mother. He wondered if she was dead. Her drinking no doubt drove her to an early grave. He pulled the packet of letters and notes from his pocket, thumbing through them until he found the solitary page from his mother. "Dear Kieran. Lord knows how you got stuck with a mother like me." Maybe she sobered up, he reasoned. He pictured her living in a big house with a flower garden beside a picture window. She read books and magazines and daily editions of the Tribune and Sun-Times. She dreamed of Kieran. She wondered where he had gone.

Sadness hit Maguire with the force of a jackhammer. The real story turned out different. She ran away with a sailor. Their supposed love probably lasted until they drained a bottle of booze. Maguire then imagined the rest of the story:

The sailor beat her and took the last of her money. She had no home, no longer any family. Lily found herself on Skid Row on West Madison Street. She lacked the fifty cents to pay for space in a flophouse. She made friends with a toothless woman she met on the street. They were drunk when a couple of jack rollers stole their shoes.

Maguire looked again at the note Lily had left him all those years ago.

"You give me hope. I don't want to mess it up for you so I'm going away. Believe me when I say this is the most loving thing I can do for you. Love, Mother."

A tear dropped on the note once, then twice.

~ 16 ~

'I crack heads'

Ted Ketchul sauntered into the *Bugle* city room like big money. He smiled at Maguire for the first time in days.

"Word is you're joining me at the union meeting tonight, Maguire."

"If it's not hazardous to my health. I'm not so sure given the beatings and shootings of the past few days."

"Only if you wrongly assume these boys on the Hill have anything to do with that," Ketchul said, his smile fading.

Maguire caught the warning and let it drop. "When do we leave?"

They huddled with Morgan to tell him of the plan. He looked skeptical right off, his arched eyebrow telling all. If Ketchul noticed, he didn't let on.

"So you're going fishing in hopes of catching a big one?" Morgan asked. His question had a much different meaning for Maguire than it did for Ketchul.

"About the size of it, give or take," Maguire said.

The sturdy Ketchul braced his muddy work boot against Morgan's desk to cinch the laces. He never hesitated to get dirty on the job. Maguire admired that much about him, or had, but in the newspaper business "dirty" had two meanings.

"While Maguire's fiddling around, I have a story in the works that gives equal time to the union," Ketchul said, his fingers working at he talked.

Morgan, slow to rile, looked at him with narrowed eyes. "Do you mean to say you found proof the union isn't involved?"

"No more or less than Maguire here with his wild accusations that hit print this morning," Ketchul said. "I've been covering these miners since the war. I know every move they make. There's no evidence of union involvement in these crimes. I said so last week and I say so now. Rusie Dregovich went on record denying everything that's been said about Local 1235."

Morgan looked incredulous. "You're still taking his word for it, Ted?"

Ketchul tipped his head back, unleashing a defiant stare. "The union can't be held accountable for the actions of a few dumb guys. I'll write my story for tomorrow's paper. I'll come finish it after the chapel meets tonight."

Morgan raised both hands with fingers spread. "Hold off. Write it in the morning when Stoffleman's back in the house. We need full agreement on everything we print about these allegations."

Ketchul dropped his boot to the floor with a thud and stormed off.

"Maguire," Morgan whispered. "Do you think Ketchul unlocked the door to let those thugs into the city room the other night?"

Maguire nodded and whispered back. "Won't a slick poker player usually wait until late in the game to show his hand? Ketchul isn't playing with a full deck."

"An apt metaphor for this mess," Morgan said.

It was mid-afternoon when Maguire met Ferndale for a beer at Babe's Bar in Finn Town. They took a table off to the side. Battered and limping, Babe kept suds flowing to the miners crowding her bar. She took cash with her thumb and remaining finger on her left hand while punching triangle-shaped holes in the tops of beer cans with her right.

A few minutes later Babe slammed down two tall cans of Butte Lager in front of them. Beer sloshed onto the table. "That's a buck, Ferndale. And forget about them beers being on the house. Babe's got bills to pay. You boys keep the hardware out of sight. No use scaring away my paying customers."

Maguire attempted a joke. "You run your bar with an iron fist," he said, nodding toward Babe's finger-deprived hand.

"Last man who told me that, I say to him, 'You mess around in my bar and I beat you within an inch of your life. With both fists. Fingers or no fingers.' I done up and cold-cocked that spindly wretch of a miner when he made fun of me. Never saw him after that neither."

Maguire leaned away and held up his hands. "I've got no beef with you, Babe."

She went back behind the bar. Ferndale brought the beer to his lips for a gulp. He wiped foam from his mouth. "Babe's been loaded for bear since the beating she took. She figures it hurts her reputation with these men. The crowd here tonight tells me otherwise."

"Adoring fans is what I see," Maguire said.

Ferndale took another deep pull. He had something on his mind.

"Maguire, did I ever tell you how I met Babe McGraw?"

"You mean when your love affair started?"

"Careful, Maguire, or I'll cut Babe off her leash."

"Tell me, Duke. I can't imagine Babe any different from what I'm seeing right now." Maguire watched her reach across the bar to pull a miner face-first by the strap of his bib overalls. He wobbled on the tips of his boots as she shook coins out of his hand.

"I was a young cop in a prowl car on afternoon shift. I get a call about trouble down on Platinum Street about the time school quit for the day. I pull up and see two men flopped on the ground like yesterday's garbage. Out cold. This girl is standing over them. She was a short one, even then, built like a fireplug. I get out of my black and white. I see more fight in her. Wants to put the mitts to me. Not with me you ain't, I tell her. I ask her what happened. She tells me these mugs took a liking to her as she walked home from the high school. Pretty doll, all things considered, hair long and reddish and sassy eyes that make you stop and look."

"And you looked, Duke?"

"For a second or two, I admit. She tells me one man grabbed her while the other tore her blouse. Near as I could tell the fight was on that very second. I doubt those mugs could see out of their swollen eyes for a week. I found teeth on the street. One of the mugs told me when he woke up that she kicked him so hard in the nuts he doubted he would ever father kids. I'd been boxing for a couple of years by then. That girl could have held her own with the best of them. I asked the girl her name. 'Babe McGraw,' she said. You have a real first name? I asked. 'You hard of hearing? I said Babe,' is what comes back to me. I asked for identification. High school kids ain't got none, she tells me. After the ambulance crew hauled the men off to the hospital, I take Babe over to the school. The principal confirms her story. Junior class, sixteen years old. I drive her home in the black and white. She lived in the Cabbage Patch. I tell her go talk with her parents. To this day I remember her exact words. 'Don't have none.' What do you make of that?"

"Babe McGraw, Butte to the core."

Ferndale laughed. "She earned her reputation."

Maguire brushed his fingers over his jaw. "Look at her all broken up after that beating. She should be at home tonight sleeping it off. I doubt this is what her doctor had in mind when he sprung her loose from the hospital."

"The only thing he had in mind was the sweet silence that came after she walked out that door. That's what Peach told me. You gotta see things from Babe's point of view. This dumpy bar and that crowd of rough men over there is her life. She ain't got anything else."

Maguire looked over to where miners stood three deep, yelling and cussing, drinking away their thirst.

"You can bet Babe is watching every face in the joint, looking for those sad sacks who jumped her," Ferndale continued. "When she gets a line on them, watch out. I ain't never doubted that Babe runs these men."

Maguire took a deep swallow of the lager. "Then why would they pinch on her, Duke? Her being one of their own and all. I can't figure it."

"That's the great mystery, ain't it?"

Maguire asked Ferndale to join the party on the Hill that night. "Dregovich knows you're a boxing legend in this town. He said to invite Duke." Maguire finished his beer and waved two fingers in Babe's direction.

"There will be no punches thrown in that union hall. We ain't going to win a fight with them odds," Ferndale said. As usual, he promised to bring Jimmy Regan and two or three other big cops for window dressing. "What's the point of being there anyway? I'm dead certain we've got the line on the 1235."

"Powers of observation, maybe?"

"Powers of what? Talk English, will you?"

"Insulting the Irish again, Duke?"

"No better time than over beer at Babe's. Fair warning, Maguire. Keep your head down when we get up there. These boys get testy when they work up a lather. Watch out for the ones with a belly full of booze. They'll be looking for a round or two."

Maguire laughed. "We should take Babe. She'll give it to them."

"Don't tell her we're going. That doll will hear soon enough from the boys at the bar. Doctor told her no fighting for at least a week. She informed me on the ride home from the hospital that if she saw cause to take the axe handle to a miner's head, she wasn't spending seven days thinking about it. Babe ain't one to take orders."

"Sounds like Babe from all accounts," Maguire said.

"Something else you oughta know." Ferndale rubbed a hand over his bald head. "Some shyster in a double-breasted suit sprung the goons who are beating up your people. Looked straight out of an old gangster movie. Bail money apparently was no object."

"Sounds like the makings of something I write for tomorrow's paper," Maguire said, scratching in his notebook with a stubby pencil. "The *Bugle* won't go dark on this story, even for a day, but I've got to find real news. Stoffleman won't stand for more of the same and he's back in the morning. You got Babe riding you, I've got Clyde Stoffleman."

"Don't cry to me," Ferndale said. "Got my own problems. Now, here is a tip you can take to the bank. The FBI joined the case. Turns out J. Edgar Hoover don't like mobsters crossing state lines. Chief Morse wants it known. Call him at home for a quote. He expects to hear from you. Keep my name out of it. Stakes are high, maybe higher than those Purple Rose Murders. These dinks are trying to take our whole damn town hostage."

"If only the chief was as quotable as you, Duke."

Night swept over the Hill when Maguire and Ketchul arrived at the Anselmo mine in Ketchul's station wagon. A red ball rolled back and forth in the back seat. "How old are your boys, Ted?" Maguire asked, trying the friendly approach. He knew so little about the labor reporter.

Ketchul waved him off. "I don't talk family on the job," he said.

"I see you bought a new car, Ted."

"None of your business, Maguire."

A hubbub of voices greeted them when they entered the union hall. Hard men crowded onto rows of wooden benches facing the platform. Dozens more hunched against the walls. Men in the back stood on chairs to see over the ocean of union members in their brown and black work clothes.

Ketchul shouted in Maguire's ear. "This isn't all of them. The local has hundreds more men on its rolls. Most of the mines have an afternoon shift working underground. What you see here is mostly day shift. Stay back from the front of the room. The most aggressive men gather up there."

A few miners edged aside to give Maguire and Ketchul a place to stand. Ferndale and his three cops wedged behind them. Maguire could see the danger right away. If trouble broke out the miners would outnumber them fifty to one, maybe more.

A shaggy man with eyes like overheated light bulbs bumped into Maguire. His elbow swung into Maguire's ribs. Maguire raised a hand to strike him but Ketchul grabbed it. The man smiled mockingly through long crooked teeth and melted into the crowd.

"Don't fall for that," Ketchul said. "You swing at him and you'll give cause for five others to jump you. Most of these men have families and a sense of purpose and they give no trouble. The bad ones lost their manners years ago when they began hammering at rock a thousand feet down."

Maguire reached into his coat to feel his sore ribs. He sucked wind. Farther down, he touched the grip of the .38 for reassurance. He might need it before the night ended.

The room felt impossibly hot even before Rusie Dregovich shuffled onto the stage with his accident-injured limp and gaveled the meeting to order. Three men sat on either side of him. The union leader, standing behind a podium, dwarfed them. He wore a black floppy cap on a mammoth head that resembled an ore car. The cap fell over his left ear. The gavel looked like a toy hammer in his big fist. From where Maguire stood, Dregovich loomed bigger and meaner than he had a few nights earlier. A hush fell over the crowd. The leader's dark eyes scanned the assemblage until they settled on Maguire and Ketchul. Maguire sensed a shadowy grin pass over his bearded face.

"Ya there men in the middle, don't be saving room on those benches. We got brothers standing. Give them a place to sit." Dregovich waited as a couple dozen more miners squeezed onto the benches.

His deep voice rang through the long hall. "This here chapel meeting of Butte Local 1235 comes to order. This ain't no ordinary meeting neither. We got important business to discuss tonight. As most of ya know, our union is being unfairly accused ..."

Boos drowned out the booming voice. Dregovich held up his hand for quiet. "Hear me out, men. I got the floor. We got some people unfairly accusing our union of causing trouble down in the business district. We all know that ain't true." He paused as a few miners in the crowd yelled their agreement.

"Brothers! We got guests tonight. I invited them. Anybody who shows them disrespect, I crack heads. I ain't in the mood for lip. Over there," he said, pointing to Maguire and Ketchul, "are them reporters from the *Bugle*. Ya boys know Ted Ketchul, a friend to labor. Next to him is Red

Maguire, who ain't, who puts these lies in the newspaper. Now me and Maguire, we don't see eye to eye, but I told him to come tonight to see our local from the inside out. Nobody jumps him unless I say so." More booing. Some miners closest to Maguire shot him threatening glares.

Maguire felt a nudge in his back from Ferndale. The detective whispered in his ear. "The mug left a lot of room for error in that promise. When I say get the hell out of here, don't argue about it."

Dregovich gaveled the room to silence. "Standing behind the *Bugle* boys I see some of the dicks who go around cuffing our members in good standing. Give them no reason to wave badges in our chapel, brothers. This is our place, not theirs. Now, this ain't no ordinary meeting. We got us a problem. We ain't the trouble in this town. Butte's nothin' without us digging down in these holes. Without us this town would be nothin'. Ted Ketchul will be printing a story in the *Bugle* saying so. He's on our side." The union hall broke out in cheers.

Maguire leaned over to Ketchul. "You promised them a story, Ted? Stoffleman will flip his lid. You know as well as anybody that we can't take sides."

Ketchul whispered to Maguire dismissively. "Butt out, Maguire. We're the working man's paper, remember?"

Dregovich waved his meaty fists as he spoke. "Suddenly we got a new problem, brothers. Them Company hacks want to cut our wages. Costs too much to mine underground, they say. Running them ore trains to the smelter in Anaconda costs money, they say. That dollar an hour you make underground is too much jingle, they say. Them hacks want to cut twenty cents an hour from every man on the Hill. They want blood for the Company. They come to me yesterday and say, 'Rusie Dregovich, ya get your working men in line because there ain't no choice.' "

The room broke out in boos and catcalls louder than before. For the moment, miners had forgotten Maguire and the cops.

"Know what I told them Company hacks? Unions own this town. Never forget it." He paused again for wild applause. Maguire admired the giant's skill as an orator. His looming stature was plenty sufficient to boss the union men, yet he spoke with words that inspired them.

"We go home to shacks while those rich Company hacks prettify themselves in palaces on the West Side. It's us, brothers, who dig the copper and silver out of this hill. It's us, brothers, who lose arms and legs when the Company won't protect workers. It's us, brothers, who risk our lives in dark tunnels and inhale bad dust. It's us, brothers, who spend our hard-earned wages at businesses that Red Maguire accuses us of stealing from."

Dregovich let his words settle over the packed room. Maguire looked around. Miners covered in red dust edged closer to him. He pictured them underground, laboring in the drifts, blaming the Company for a hard life.

"Do we stand for this?" Dregovich roared. "I say hell no! Miners make other people rich while they pay us pennies for dangerous work. We have every right to own Butte. We produce the jingle that goes into other pockets. We make the rules. We run this city. Stand your ground, brothers. We take what's ours!"

The room broke out in chants of "Strike! Strike! Strike!" Miners stood on the wooden benches as they waved their fists and bellowed their anger. Dregovich faced them with arms crossed. He was the high priest of Butte labor and knew it. So did the hundreds of rowdy men in front of him.

Mack Gibbons staggered into Maguire's view through the tangle of bodies. "Cracker and these here boys got a bone to pick," he slurred. Maguire pushed him away.

Ferndale tugged at Maguire's coat. "Now!" he said insistently. They backed out of the room, squeezing through a throng of men who reeked of mine dirt and old sweat. One miner swung at Maguire's head. Jimmy Regan, close behind, knocked the man's fist away.

"Look at them chickens run!" somebody yelled. Maguire's last glimpse before stepping outside was of Ted Ketchul. His fellow reporter laughed at the ruckus. Nobody bothered him.

"What do you make of what happened in there?" Ferndale asked as he drove Maguire back to the *Bugle*.

"Dregovich wanted me to witness his power on display. From what I could see, there's no question of it. He was on the verge of turning that mob loose on us."

"All the bullets in these guns wouldn't be enough," Ferndale said.

Maguire felt his sore ribs. "I've got to find the miners who don't believe what Dregovich is saying. Clever that he riles up those boys with talk of losing money when he's the one taking it from them. He and the criminals in Chicago. I've got to find miners who will talk."

Ferndale pulled up to a stoplight. "Anyway, we've known for a long time that Dregovich surrounds himself with ruthless men. He keeps the good ones in line that way. You might find a few who will talk. Most ain't inclined because they're afraid."

"He's big enough and mean enough to give any man nightmares," Maguire said.

"Big men fall hard, Maguire."

~ 17 ~

'Teller of crime tales'

Red Maguire hurried to the *Bugle* to write his latest story. Morgan's eyes widened when Maguire told him about the FBI joining the investigation. "That's a significant new angle, all right," Morgan said, his eyes drifting to the clock. "You've got forty minutes, Maguire. Give it to me in thirty."

Maguire raced to his desk to call Chief Morse. "We'll keep it official for now, but yes, Ferndale was correct," the chief said. "I can't talk about details. This goes without saying but let me repeat that Butte citizens should know our police force will resist any outside interference from criminals. For that matter, crime committed by anyone who lives here. Law-abiding people who find themselves victims of crime should call police immediately."

"How many business owners are feeling the pinch from these bagmen, chief?"

"Verified, a few, but as you've reported in the *Bugle*, most likely several dozen. Makes me sick to think of our people surrendering their profits to these thugs."

Maguire said goodnight. He battered away on his Remington, slamming words onto the paper fast as he could think. Dregovich's warning about pay cuts for miners came to mind. Maguire walked over to Morgan.

"Ketchul hasn't said a thing about wage disputes, Maguire. The union would be under contract through next year. Stay away from that in your story. We'll ask Ketchul about it in the morning."

Maguire thought about going home to the Logan. Unlike the more fashionable Leonard, with its curving staircases and glass atrium, the Logan resembled a warehouse with windows in a shrinking Finn Town neighborhood. Company bulldozers had begun knocking down buildings standing in the way of the new Berkeley open pit. Someday, Maguire thought sadly, they would take the Logan. Like Sal the sweeper, the half dozen tenants on each floor mostly stayed indoors except when they walked to the grocery market down the block. It was their home.

Someday Honey Rossini's house in Meaderville would fall as well. It would vanish under a roar of heavy machinery and all of her childhood memories with it. Maguire called the operator. "Meaderville 2585," he told her. The phone crackled a few times until Honey answered. She sounded anxious.

"Oh, Red, it's good to hear your voice. Something strange has happened."

"Seems that's an everyday occurrence, Honey."

"That prowl car the cops put in front of my house? About an hour after the sun went down, the officer drove away. I haven't seen him since."

"He went to dinner maybe?"

"He disappeared three hours ago, Red. Suddenly my neighborhood feels dark and empty. I had hoped Martha next door would come home from Anaconda. The Christmas lights came off the gallows frames behind my house. I locked my doors but I admit it, Red, I feel scared. That telephone call this afternoon made it worse."

"What phone call, Honey?"

Her response came in a rush of words. "At my store. A male voice. He threatened me, Red. He said they are watching me. He told me they saw me with you. They saw us together at the Rocky Mountain Cafe. He said they will hurt you bad unless I pay up. I leave an envelope with $200 cash, five minutes after the next call, at a location they name. This month and every month. The man on the phone said if I tell anyone about this, they will know, it will be bad for me. And you. They want to break us, Red."

Maguire heard Honey's voice shaking.

"I'm heading straight to your house, Honey. Don't go outside."

"It will get worse if they see you."

"From my point of view it's already bad enough," Maguire told her and hung up. He pulled the .38 from his pocket and twirled the cylinder. Five bullets. Maguire reached in his desk for the box of ammunition he had bought. He loaded the .38 with a sixth bullet. He grabbed a handful more and dropped them into the side pocket of his suit coat. Morgan, across the room, heard the click of the weapon.

"You're playing a dangerous game but can't say I blame you. Get yourself shot and this story goes away and that's bad for the *Bugle*," he said.

"Or it makes the front page, Don. You will sell a ton of *Bugles* in the bars. Imagine the headline. Red Maguire, shot between the eyes by a mobster."

Morgan stroked his beard. "In that case, Maguire, make your deadline first."

Maguire arrived in Meaderville in under ten minutes. Cars crowded around the Rocky Mountain. He drove onto Honey's street. Houses on either side of hers, including Martha's, were dark. He parked his Pontiac near her front door. A few doors down, he saw someone pull aside a curtain for a hurried look. Suspicion knows no boundary, he thought.

Honey opened the door. She had tied a red scarf around her neck. Her earrings glittered under the porch light. "Always Butte's beauty," he managed.

"A man with a golden tongue, our newsman Red Maguire, teller of crime tales."

Honey took his overcoat while he pulled off his rubber boots. His leather shoes looked more scuffed that usual. He frowned at wrinkles in his slacks and the frayed ends of his shirt sleeves. Suddenly he cared about how he looked. Honey, as usual, dressed as if she had strolled off a magazine cover. He never tired of the image.

They embraced, briefly. Maguire breathed in Honey's fragrance.

"Are you worried, Red?"

"Fear is a reliable companion to common sense."

"Meaning what, word man?"

"Meaning I won't let anything happen to you."

They kissed, deeply. Falling in love with Honey Rossini meant putting her in danger, Maguire knew. He encircled her narrow waist with his strong arms. Nobody, he vowed to himself, would hurt Honey. She finally pulled away and led him to the couch. He set the .38 on an end table and threw off his suit coat. They sat, holding hands, smiling at each other.

"I feel like a schoolgirl," she said.

"You look like one in a grownup way," he told her.

"Can a girl confess without worry of being quoted in the *Bugle*, Red?"

"Try me if you dare, Honey."

"I haven't dated since my husband was killed in Korea because I felt guilty."

"Guilty for what?"

"For not knowing Frank better. For letting him die before we had made a life together. Being a widow left me sad and confused. People pity Gold Star wives. I hated feeling that way. I worked hard to overcome those feelings."

"The communists killed him, Honey. Not you. He died in combat. You can't change fate."

"When they told me he was gone I wondered what I would become ..."

"You became Irene Rossini, queen of the Butte SnowBall. Everyone in this town knows the striking Irene Rossini," Maguire interrupted.

"So you read the society pages of your newspaper? Your interests weren't limited to dead people in dark alleys?" Honey managed a smile.

"I've been accused of both," Maguire said.

"You know, Red, you really haven't said much about yourself."

"We were talking about you."

"Tell me, Red. For the first time since the telegram came about Frank I want to know about another man. Indulge me, please." Honey went to the armoire and poured brown liquid into a glass. "This will loosen your tongue," she told him. She poured a second glass for herself.

The shot of whiskey warmed Maguire. For as long as he remembered he drank mostly beer. Ferndale made sure of that. "I more or less raised myself," Maguire began, describing his father's accidental tragic death and his mother's abrupt early disappearance. "They were Sean and Lily. We were an Irish family living in an Irish neighborhood in Chicago. Our little house was one of many like it on our street. Like Butte, we lived close to one another, some of those houses just a few feet apart. Unlike Butte, we had no mountains or hills. Streets in Chicago went on for miles. I was too young to know my mother had boyfriends all over town. Those long streets would lead her to disappear for days to places unknown."

Honey nodded her expectation that he continue telling his story. She watched his eyes.

Maguire talked of his mother's drunken fits and his father's disgust with her. He told Honey of his birthday trip to the Cubs game that started splendidly but ended with his mother in the arms of a drunken sailor. He told of coming home from school to find his father loading the pickup truck with furniture, leaving his mother behind as they rolled west to a city named Butte. He told her that he never knew what happened to his mother.

As Maguire talked, the most painful moments of his young life came to him in vivid color. He saw his mother's sweet loving face contrasting with her swollen inebriated one. He saw his pale unmoving father at the wake, lids pulled shut over his unseeing eyes.

Maguire shed a tear as he finished his story. Honey held him.

"Oh, Red, I had no idea. What a sad life."

"Sorry to burden you with this, Honey. Everybody has their problems."

"I wanted to know, Red. You carry secrets. I knew that from the moment I met you." She reached over him to pull the chain on the lamp. The room fell into darkness. Maguire had revealed too much of himself. More than with Mary before he knew she was Nancy. Honey pulled him close, like a parent would hold a child, caressing her long fingers through his thick hair. He rested his head on her neck. Curves under her white sweater rose and fell with her breathing.

Maguire fought sleep.

"I forgot to call Ferndale," he whispered.

"Where did the police go?" she whispered back. Suddenly it hit him. He sat up and turned toward the window. From the darkened room, he glimpsed a car parked a few dozen feet behind his Pontiac. A streetlight behind the car silhouetted two broad-shouldered men, wearing hats, watching from the front seat.

"Who was the cop out front?" he said to Honey as he watched the car.

"He never came to the door to introduce himself like the others did. I didn't recognize him."

The driver of the mysterious car opened his door. He climbed out and rested his big body against the hood. A cigarette glowed red in the shadow of his face. Honey started to speak but Maguire held a finger over her lips. They watched as the passenger swung his door open. Both men looked toward her house.

"Red? What do they want?" Maguire felt Honey trembling in the dark.

"They're looking for me," he told her.

"Or my money. I'm not rich, Red. Despite appearances, I barely make it at the jewelry store."

Maguire leaned away from the window. "We won't give them a chance to find that out. Quick, into your coat and boots. They won't see us leave through the back door."

"I don't want them ransacking my family home, Red. I can't leave."

"They won't come inside right away. It's me they want. Hurry! We have just a few minutes while they look around to make sure the neighbors are sleeping."

Red led Honey by the hand into the kitchen, feeling for the doorknob, while she reached for her purse on the counter. They stepped into the frigid night air. Stars blazed in the sky. The crescent-shaped moon cast light across the backyard.

"They'll see our tracks in the snow, Red." Honey suddenly sounded composed, even defiant. Her gorgeous face looked strong and confident even in the weak blue moonlight.

"Not with what I have in mind, Honey." They broke a trail through the snow to a tall spruce tree at a schoolyard a block away. "Wait here for me in the shadows. Watch for my car. Hide if it's anybody but me. I won't be long."

"Red, won't those men have guns?"

He pulled the .38 out of his pocket. "Two can play that game," he said.

She handed him the key to her house. "Lock it, will you? Silly, I know, but still."

After Red kissed Honey he followed their tracks back to her house. At the risk of alerting the two men he stomped snow off his boots on the back porch, thinking of the fine rug in swirls of maroon and green in her living room. He entered the kitchen, locking the door behind him, and hurried a glance through the front window. The mugs stood closer to Honey's house. The smoker kicked his cigarette, probably his second or third, into the snow. It left a shower of sparks. Maguire burst out the front door. He pretended he never saw the men. His old Pontiac fired on the first turn of the key. He slammed the gear lever into drive and spun forward onto the icy street. In his rear-view mirror, he saw the men running for their car. One of them, the driver, slipped and fell. The other man fired at Maguire. A bullet clanged the Pontiac's front fender as Maguire turned the corner.

Ahead of him, on Meaderville's main street, cars went back and forth. Figuring he could confuse the mugs behind him, he pulled into an alley behind an abandoned house and shut off his headlights. Their bulky Oldsmobile roared past seconds later. Maguire figured them for out of towners. They had no idea about the rutted roads winding around the mines. He waited until he was sure they were gone before he drove around the Minnie Healy to a street that led to the school. Honey came running after he flickered his headlights a few times.

"Of all the nights to wear a dress," she said, smiling, when she slid in beside him.

"It's hard to plan for spontaneous adventures."

"Is that what we're calling this night on the town, Red? What happened to those men?"

As he pulled out of Meaderville, following back roads, he told her about his getaway. "They'll follow taillights every which way until they're so lost on our winding streets that they think they're back in Chicago. Those goons are no match for a couple of Butte lifers."

Honey moved across the seat next to him. "Feels like a date, doesn't it, Red? How come you never asked me out?"

"A newspaper gumshoe like me, asking out Butte royalty? I never had a chance with you."

"Now you know better."

Maguire braked the Pontiac to a stop on a hill in the McQueen neighborhood. Lights on all of Butte Hill twinkled to the south and west of them. The car idled, its heater blowing warmth, while they kissed.

"Maybe I am a teenager again," Honey whispered.

"No doubt the most popular one in Butte," he said.

"I had hoped so at the time. When I was a girl in pigtails, I was full of false hopes."

Maguire watched her brown eyes in the moonlight. "You can't go back to your house until we end this. I should have had better sense than to implicate you."

"If you remember, it was me who made the first move. What happened tonight, Red?"

"That cop in front of your house either was bought off or he wasn't a cop at all. That's why he left before those goons drove up. Ferndale will crack heads over this."

"Where do we go now?"

"I put my brain to work but you won't like it, Honey." She stayed quiet as he steered the Pontiac down the hill to Park Street and west to uptown, where he turned onto Mercury Street. They stopped in front of the Windsor.

"Red?" Honey asked, sounding more apprehensive than usual.

"Trust me, Honey. You'll be safe here."

She waited in the car while he went inside. Maggie O'Keefe nodded sadly at his suggestion. "Maguire, if word gets around that she's here she won't have a shred of reputation left. We both know that. Being dead would be worse, though, wouldn't it? She can use a bedroom in my private quarters upstairs where she can stay out of public view. Use the back stairs."

Honey fell silent when Maguire told her about Maggie's offer. "The mobsters won't know to look for you here," he reassured her. Maggie met them at the door. She reached for Honey's hand when they were inside. "I can imagine you're feeling the worst kind of worry about being inside my house, Miss Rossini. You will be safe here. My bouncers will make sure of it. All I ask is that you give me and my girls some air. You have cause to judge. And no, Maguire spends no jingle here, for the record, but he knows I'm someone he can trust. I'm fairly certain he thinks the same of you."

Honey managed a smile. "Thank you, Miss O'Keefe. I can't make sense of what's happening to my life right now. I ought to be celebrating the new year. Instead I worry about staying alive. What's the answer?"

"Red Maguire will find a way, and please, call me Maggie. We deal in first names here."

"And I'm Irene."

Maguire opened the door and stepped outside to the dark alley. "I'll be back," he said, somewhat grandly. "Never underestimate the power of the press."

~ 18 ~

'Feathering pockets'

Ferndale blew a gasket over the drama at Honey Rossini's house. When Maguire called Ferndale at home after midnight, waking him, the detective grumbled into the phone.

"You clear-headed, Duke? There's more."

"There always is," Ferndale said, sounding tired.

Maguire told him how the cop outside Honey's house drove away, leaving her unprotected, while two mugs arrived with trouble on their mind. "One of them with a heater took a wild shot at me," Maguire said, relating his getaway.

Ferndale, silent for a moment, unleashed a string of profanity. Maguire waited for him to calm down. "Dammit! You telling me that wop cop we sent up there is working with the mob?"

"I'm telling you it looked that way to me, Duke."

Ferndale huffed his anger into the phone. "My orders to the prowl crew were to post wop cops in Meaderville because they know how things go up there in the Italian district."

"The mob is full of wops," Maguire said. He heard rustling over the phone.

"I'm getting dressed to head to the clubhouse, Maguire. When I find out who pulled that cop from his assigned post, I'll kick some sorry ass from here to Sunday. I warned you against playing kissy face with that doll. Irene Rossini is a big name in this town. If the goons can take down the famous

Irene, the other business owners will fall like dominos. As for you, Maguire, they would just as soon shoot you for exposing their crimes in the *Bugle*. Give them any more looks at your sorry mug and I kneel over your remains like I do with all them other dead bodies. The two of you together make a big target for these criminals. My advice is that you lay low. This ain't a city that gives many second chances."

"If I hadn't gone to Honey's house she might be dead right now, Duke."

"Give her a big sloppy kiss for me," Ferndale said, and hung up.

Rossini's Fine Jewelry was hit overnight. Burglars tried to pop the safe but Ferndale, on a hunch, sent a prowl car to the store. When the cop shined his spotlight through the front window, the perps fled out the back door. Maguire was shaving at his tiny sink when he got the call. He had fidgeted all night, gripping the .38 and listening for footsteps on the staircase.

"They smashed the glass display case. We got there before they cracked the safe. They pulled it halfway out of the wall but never broke it open," Ferndale told him. "Now that you wrapped up your beauty sleep, where do I find Irene Rossini? She needs to hear about this."

Maguire told him about stashing Irene at the Windsor. "You got her hiding with the painted ladies, Maguire? Not bad, you damn mick. You think like a cop, I give you credit for that. Tell Miss Rossini we barricaded the alley door of her store to keep them out. And Maguire? That cop we posted at her house? Costa? He said he got a radio call telling him to prowl in Walkerville for the rest of the night. Problem is, that call didn't come from us."

"How can somebody use police frequency, Duke?"

"Yet another mystery, ain't it?"

"Seems we're neck deep in mysteries nowadays."

"You want another story, Maguire? Go see Babe McGraw. She opens her bar in the morning for miners who like to belly up before the afternoon shift."

Maguire slipped on a clean white shirt and dressed in the same rumpled brown suit he had worn for a week. He pulled a brown tie from his closet. He owned four of them. Brown was his chosen color. How frumpy and predictable he must look next to the gorgeous Irene Rossini. He wondered how she was faring, with no change of fashionable clothes, among the strange company at the Windsor. It was a fair bet she declined to borrow anything they wore.

At Babe's Bar, Maguire let his eyes adjust to the dim interior. The long room, stinking of spilled beer, felt as cold as the air outside. "Over here, Maguire," Babe called from where she mopped the bar.

"You teaching winter survival in here, Babe? Feels cold enough to freeze meat."

"I turn the heat down to forty degrees when I close the joint. Saves on my pocketbook and not cold enough to ice the beer or buckle the pipes. You here for a news tip?"

"You got one?"

"I hear talk. Men running at the mouth like nobody's business. So it's early this morning, right around closing, when two of them miners start up about Rusie Dregovich. Many of these men don't know up from down but these two, I give them credit for a brain. They know something, Maguire. They whisper to me if I know Red Maguire. They read your stories in the *Bugle*. They want to jaw with you. Trouble is, they're scared Dregovich will get wind and send them to an early grave."

Maguire scratched his phone number on a piece of paper and handed it to Babe. "We'll find a way to make this work." He studied the bruised bartender, who looked even more fearsome in the dim light. "Babe, shouldn't you be home in bed? You're a day out of the hospital."

Babe shot Maguire a look that could fry eggs. He held up his hands in a defensive motion. "Looking out for a friend is all."

"I ain't got time for nursery games, Maguire. We ain't friends neither."

"What about the four men who jumped you?"

"Them criminals stayed out of here last night, much as I could tell. That was the word among the drinking men anyway."

"Why not let Ferndale handle it?"

"Ferndale knows this fight is between me and them boys. A man who jumps Babe gets his jaw broken sooner than later."

"Never doubted it," Maguire told her.

Back at the *Bugle*, Maguire found Stoffleman walking stiffly around the city room. They shook hands. "Every time I sit, I feel like a corpse waiting for burial," Stoffleman said, eyes loaded with pain peering out from beneath his customary green eye shade.

"A corpse doesn't sit, boss."

"Thanks for the clarification, Maguire. I never cut you short on your talent for observation. Now, about this wave of labor racket crime. People are scared."

"Anyone who sees a kiddie mask on a grown man won't forget."

Stoffleman stared back at Maguire with steely eyes. The black frames on his new glasses gave him a strange professorial look. "Heard anything new about Ketchul?"

"Ted's in trouble is all I know."

Stoffleman looked satisfied. "We'll find out soon enough. I want a story for tomorrow that takes us to the heart of these crimes. If the cops can't get on top of it, we will. I count on you, Red, to get it done with or without Ketchul's help. To this point he's contributed nothing but silence anyway."

Maguire told Stoffleman about his conversation with Babe McGraw.

"It's time to take our town back," Stoffleman said. "End it now."

At that very moment, they heard Ketchul's heavy boots on the staircase outside the city room. The labor reporter went straight to his desk without acknowledging Stoffleman's first day back at work after the beating he took. Maguire thought Ketchul looked more harried that usual. He sat down and began pounding out a story on his typewriter.

Stoffleman shrugged and hobbled away. Maguire's phone rang. He heard Ferndale's gruff voice. "Meet me at the Silver Star in ten. Never slept a wink. I need coffee."

"Maybe beer at the M & M would suit you better?"

"Nah, you know my rule. Not before noon. I don't want to rile the chief."

Maguire found Ferndale waiting in the back booth, their usual place. He had taken off his frayed suit jacket. Other Silver Star patrons, seeing his shoulder holster and the gold badge on his shirt, gave him room.

"Feeling casual this morning, detective?"

"Hot under the collar is more like it. Fast as we arrest people, those shysters in fancy clothes spring them from jail. Don't care a lick about that damn Cracker Gibbons. Who I need is Rusie Dregovich." Ferndale fell silent as Simone approached with a full pot of fresh coffee.

"Morning, boys. I suppose you've read the news." She winked at Maguire in exaggerated fashion and laid a copy of the *Bugle* on their table. "Everybody in the joint is reading your story this morning, Red. We must be in serious trouble if the FBI had to come along." Maguire looked toward the counter where a row of breakfast patrons discussed the story.

"The heroic Red Maguire and the fearsome Duke Ferndale sitting right here in my restaurant," Simone swooned. She raised the back of her hand to her forehead for dramatic effect.

"You put on quite a show, Simone."

"Oh, Red, how good of you to notice. And Red? Remember I start work at six and leave at two, Monday through Saturday. Haven't I told you that? I know you're a man who pays attention to detail." She blew him a kiss as she walked away.

"That doll has it for you bad," Ferndale grunted.

"I figure her for a born flirt. I'll bet she talks that way to every man who walks into the Silver Star."

"Don't fool me, Maguire. You got dolls stashed all over town. When I was hauling Babe out of the hospital, we met Peach heading out to sleep off the night shift. She asks me about you. Makes those big eyes that dames show off when they feel all romantic. That bundle of love letters in your pocket will weigh so heavy you'll need a wagon to pull it around."

Ferndale stabbed at the *Bugle* front page with a chapped forefinger. "The chief said to congratulate you for getting the facts straight in this morning's story. That was after the mayor came storming in demanding answers we ain't got a clue about. He blew a cork even worse than last time. If he keeps that up they'll have him fitted for white pajamas over in Warm Springs. The chief, give him credit, sat the mayor down and walked him through our investigation from start to finish. I admit it ain't looking good. We got practically the whole department working on the case. The robberies stopped. Now the perps are aiming for people like you and me."

Maguire stirred sugar into his coffee. "You figure on breaking this thing wide open anytime soon without the FBI?"

Ferndale smiled. "I ain't got a clue, but when we do, you'll be the first to know. The chief would like nothing better than to get the word out that Butte police solved this crime."

"So would Clyde Stoffleman, who's back at work. He knows he's lucky he didn't wind up dead."

"Stoffleman and you and me," Ferndale said. "Cop or newsman, hazardous to our health, all the same. Don't get yourself shot."

"Advice you should take yourself," Maguire replied. They parted outside the cafe. Maguire turned in time to see Simone's come-on wave. She acted as if they had a secret between them. When he returned to the *Bugle* city room, he found Ketchul and Stoffleman yelling at each other. Ketchul clenched his fists like he wanted to fight. Stoffleman stood his ground. The old combat veteran had seen worse. Behind him, Morgan rose to his feet. The big Scot expected to keep them apart.

"That's the best story I've written in a year and you spiked it!" Ketchul bellowed. He pointed to the upturned silver nail on Stoffleman's desk. The nail thrust through several sheets of typing paper. A spiked story meant bad news for a reporter. It would never see print. Rarely had Maguire seen Stoffleman spike a story.

"It's not a legitimate story at all, Ted, and you know it. I told you a week ago to get to the bottom of union involvement in these crimes. You did nothing. Now you write a puff piece that exonerates the union without proof. Hardly a morsel of journalism in what you wrote, a damn fairytale, Ted. This brute Dregovich denies union involvement and you don't quote the police chief or anyone else who beg to differ? Where's the truth?"

Ketchul cast an accusing glare at Maguire. "That man there," Ketchul exploded, "writes story after story from the cops' point of view. Show me the truth in that? Rusie Dregovich has a right to be heard."

"No disagreement on the importance of telling Dregovich's side of the story, Ted. But that man is a prime suspect in this labor racket. So he denies knowing anything about it. Your story reads like you taking him at his word. Despite considerable evidence to the contrary, mind you. Look here." Stoffleman pulled Ketchul's story off the spike. He traced the typed lines on the paper with his finger.

"Dregovich said the police investigation is a hoax. 'Local 1235 has nothing to do with any crimes in Butte,' he said."

Stoffleman pulled off his eye shade. "Letting him deny it is one thing. He deserves a voice, yes. Where's the other side? The context of your story is a one-sided megaphone for Dregovich. Not a single comment from anyone who disagrees with him. Hell, Ted, it reads like Dregovich wrote it. What happened to the Ted Ketchul who covers labor in this town with a skeptical eye?"

Simmering, Ketchul poised to attack Stoffleman. Morgan stepped between them.

"Now I know what this paper stands for!" Ketchul bellowed again. "Don't give me that song and dance about the *Bugle* being a working man's paper. It's tired tripe, but worse yet, it isn't true."

Stoffleman refused to back down. "You know darn well what this paper stands for. We report news. We investigate wrongs. We don't deny facts that stare us in the face. We don't climb into anybody's pocket. We have sources we can trust but we don't get chummy with them."

Ketchul laughed. "Maguire and Ferndale practically go around holding hands."

Maguire stiffened. "Careful, Ted. Not true and you know it. I know where to draw the line."

"Keep out of this, Maguire. I gave it to you once and will do it again."

Maguire pulled himself up to his full height. If Ketchul tried to sucker punch him again he would feel the pain of a Dublin Gulch fight. "Speaking of holding hands, Ted, why did Dregovich promise to a roomful of miners you would write a story letting the union off the hook?"

"What the hell is this?" Stoffleman raged.

Ketchul suddenly recognized he was cornered. He changed his tone. "How do I get a story into print, boss?"

The man's attempt at conciliation failed to fool Stoffleman. "By doing what I told you several days ago. Work with Maguire. Get to the bottom of this story, wherever it takes you. Co-write a story for tomorrow. Include Dregovich's denial, by all means, but ask hard questions. It was clear to me, even when I was flat on my back in that hospital bed, that the cops have him boxed in. If he turns out innocent in the end, so be it, but prove it. Are you hearing me, Ted?"

Ketchul nodded and returned to his desk. Maguire noted his worried expression.

"And Ted? How come you let those thugs knock Claggett around the other night? The man's old enough and blind enough to sell pencils on the street corner, for chrissakes."

Ketchul shrugged. "It happened too fast."

"We stand up for our own," Stoffleman shot back.

***

Maguire soon heard from the miners Babe had mentioned earlier that morning. He answered his ringing telephone to hear a man speaking in a Welsh singsong voice. "Mese and another guy have a thing to say. Meet us at the yard at the

Travona mine in an hour. Ain't nobody around since it closed last year. We need your word, Maguire. Ain't nobody can know about this."

"You boys are safe with me," Maguire told him.

The intrepid crime reporter found the miners waiting in an idling truck behind the boarded-up head house. The thin man behind the wheel smoked a pipe. A much larger man wearing a slouch hat filled the other side of the cab. Maguire felt in his pocket for the .38. He had no love for rude surprises. The past week had been full of them.

Maguire rolled down the window in his Pontiac. "Hello in the truck!" he called. The men nodded and climbed out. Their denim coats flapped open despite the frigid winter wind. They defied cold like men accustomed to working outside. Gusts from the north swept sheets of snow off the gray buildings of the abandoned silver mine.

"Another storm coming over the mountain," Maguire told the men, both of whom had drooping mustaches.

The smaller one, puffing on his pipe, held out his hand. "Al Shukler. This here tall one is Big Danny Dawson. We work underground at the Badger State. Babe McGraw says we can trust you. That true?"

"Babe ought to know," Maguire said.

The big man spoke up. "We need to hear straight that if we tell you what we know our names never get out."

Maguire pulled the collar of his overcoat closer to his reddening ears. "You've got my word, boys. Step out of the wind, will you? I need to take notes on what you say but how about I leave out mentioning your names and any other identifying information. That fair enough?" The men nodded.

They stood close to the weathered wood of the mine's repair shop. Shukler spoke first in the Welsh accent Maguire had heard over the phone.

"We see your stories in the *Bugle*. We know things ain't right. These crooks are turning against their own people. Me and Big Danny, we're tired of it."

Dawson took over. "What's going on in Butte casts suspicion on every miner working on the Hill." His deep voice bounced off the dark buildings. "Truth is, honest men in Local 1235 want it stopped. Most are afraid of saying so. Anybody who defies Rusie Dregovich will never work in Butte again. The least he will do is blackball them from the union. We seen him arrange accidents that cripple men so bad they never work again. You saw what he can do. He ordered those beatings of your boys at the *Bugle*. Babe McGraw too. We don't know your boys but we know Babe. Ain't nobody in their right mind messes with Babe."

"No argument here," Shukler tossed out.

"Babe," Big Danny continued, "she kicks a few bucks out of her till for any miner down on his luck. She don't want to see any man come to the Hill with nothin' in his lunch bucket."

Shukler took up the tale. "Me and Big Danny, we deal on the square. Not so with Dregovich. That man is dirty and powerful and mean. No worry to him to take this city down with him. Everything you wrote about him is true as far as we know. We hear talk on shift about Dregovich being in deep with this Accardo fellow from Chicago. That ain't the half of it though."

The men paused for dramatic effect.

Maguire stopped scribbling with his pencil. He blew on his cold stiff fingers. "So tell me what," he said.

"Rusie, when he was a young man, most everybody liked him," Shukler said. "He was all for the union. When a man got stoked up from sickness or from getting hurt down the hole, Rusie would pull that man's weight. He'd tell the man to take five. Then he would do the work of two or three men in an hour. When the shift boss come around, every man got credit for a good day's work. I saw this with my own eyes. Worked with Rusie at the Anselmo when I was young. Trusted him then but saw the danger in pushing him too far. There ain't a larger man on the Hill. Rusie carries oil-soaked timbers on his shoulders like he done gone out for a Sunday stroll. Strength of a giant and mean like one too when someone riles him. Any man with the name of Dregovich ought to make you think. Anyone who dares cross him, look out."

Maguire raised his hand, palm out. "He's Russian?"

"Not Russian, Serbian," Shukler said. "One of the Serbs from Centerville. You know him when you were a kid?"

Maguire shook his head. "I had my hands full with the Irish in my own neighborhood."

"We don't hold it against you," Shukler said.

Finally sensing the cold, Dawson buttoned up his coat. "We thought Rusie was honest when we voted him as union boss back in '47. Got us better wages from the Company. Made mines safer. Then he started feeling his power. More and more of us thought he turned dirty. Al here, he knows."

Shukler jumped in. "Squeezing the Company for wages weren't enough for Dregovich anymore. He said we deserved to get rich off the city. Clever how he says it though. You heard him at the union meeting the other night. We saw you there. Dregovich will say over and over again miners deserve their fair share for digging rock. What he ain't telling people is that the jingle he's stealing from them store owners is feathering pockets of him and them gangsters in Chicago."

"How do you know for sure?" Maguire asked.

Shukler nodded at Dawson. The bigger man pulled three folded papers, covered with boot prints, from his coat pocket. They watched Maguire as he read them.

"My god," Maguire muttered. He followed the list from top to bottom with his finger until he found the entry, "Rossini's Fine Jewelry, Irene Rossini, weekly, $200." He shuffled the pages again and again, seeing familiar business names and amounts of money being extorted from them. Shukler, puffing on his pipe, pointed to the list.

"Me and Big Danny figure that's just the start. After they scare all the owners into paying up they squeeze their suppliers. I hear about these knockover rackets. Goons break people's legs and burn their houses when they don't play along."

"And send hit men to shoot at you," Maguire said.

"We done seen that in your *Bugle*," Dawson offered.

Maguire wiped the look of disbelief from his face. "How did you get this list, boys?"

Shukler squared up. "We tell you how, but you forget where you got any of this or we're dead men, sure as we're standing here."

"You have my word," Maguire said.

"The other night in the union hall," Dawson began. "You saw it. Full of men milling around, half of them drunk. Dregovich has these boys he calls his enforcers. That simple-minded Cracker is one of them. After these meetings, Rusie wades into the crowd with his enforcers. That's how he does it. Rusie shoulders people as a warning. Slams into them is what he does. Any men who make bad to Rusie, gives him lip, his enforcers work them over outside. Rusie, he don't like anyone pinching his style. I can name a dozen men who found out the hard way not to cross him."

"Get to the point, Big Danny," Shukler said.

"I see this paper fall out of Rusie's pocket. Right there on the floor with men walking over it. I put my boot on top of it. I wait a moment and reach down and hide it in my hand."

"Nobody saw you?" Maguire questioned.

"I wouldn't have a thing to say about it today if they did."

"You are telling me Rusie Dregovich is careless enough to carry this incriminating list around?"

Shukler pulled his pipe from lips somewhere under a drooping moustache. "Careless ain't the word, Maguire. He ain't got a care in the world. That beast is king of the Hill. The biggest. Rusie Dregovich thinks he's bigger than God our maker. If he knew we found his list, he and his thugs would break our fingers. It would get worse. Unless he kills us outright his boys will take jackhammers to our knees and elbows underground where nobody could hear us scream. It wouldn't be pretty."

Maguire shuddered at the picture in his mind.

"There's more," Dawson said. "That buddy of yours at the *Bugle*."

"You mean Ted Ketchul," Maguire said with resignation. He knew this was coming.

"That one. Everybody knows Ketchul. Friend of the working man. Exposes corruption in the Company. Fell in deep with Dregovich. A mile below ground, that deep. We don't know nothin' more than what we hear."

"What do you hear?" Maguire asked.

Shukler spoke. "Word is Dregovich pays Ketchul to ignore the rackets and lie about the union. Rusie ain't happy with Ketchul for not keeping up his end of the bargain."

"Which is?" Maguire asked.

"To print stories in the *Bugle* making this all go away," Shukler said.

Maguire thought of Ketchul's strange behavior in the city room. So Ketchul could be bought. He sold his soul to criminals. "He was an honorable man until this," Maguire said.

"Perhaps you don't know," Shukler said. "Rumor is that Ketchul has a boy with polio. Dregovich hooked him with payoffs. Lots of jingle to pay for medicine and doctors. Now it's too late for Ketchul to get out."

Maguire shook his head, saddened. He thought of Ketchul's shiny new station wagon with the red ball rolling in the back seat.

"The *Bugle* doesn't pay a lick but that's no excuse," Maguire said.

Shukler looked around the darkening mine yard. The storm over the mountain spit waves of swirling snow. "It's time to leave. Night watchman will be coming soon. Hard to think of the Travona gone silent. They say the Company's open pit will close all of our underground mines. Between that and Rusie Dregovich stealing all the jingle he can get, Butte's miners won't have a dime left to their name. Anyway, take that list, Maguire. Put it in the paper. Say what you want from what we told you. You don't know me and Big Danny. You never met us. You ain't never heard our names. You never speak them. We ain't young men but we ain't hoping for eternal sleep neither. If we have anything else to say we call you, not the other way around."

"Trust me on that," Maguire said.

"If we thought different we wouldn't be jawing," Dawson said. "Babe says trust Red Maguire, promises to shoot you if she finds out she was wrong."

"Never doubted it, boys." Maguire shook hands with the men. They drove off, their pickup trailing white exhaust in the dirty air.

He had a real story now. The list would blow the lid off the case. Real evidence of Dregovich taking over Butte. Evidence provable enough to send him to the state prison in Deer Lodge to crush rock or whatever a miner does in the joint. Maguire wondered if Ketchul had seen the list. Printing it would spell doom for the veteran labor reporter.

'Protect that girl'

Red Maguire hopped the stairs to the city room two at a time. Stoffleman was there. So was a sulking Ted Ketchul. "A minute, boss, in private?" Maguire whispered to Stoffleman. Hunched over from the pain of his broken ribs, the editor motioned Maguire to a back door. Stoffleman shuffled to the end of a dark hallway and fetched a key from his pocket.

"How long have you worked at the *Bugle*, Red?"

"Before the war when you hired me from Dublin Gulch, boss."

"Back then I wasn't sure you'd make it in this business. An orphan kid who took everything personally, wanted to fight at the drop of a hat, remember? You didn't know a lick about newspapering either."

"Why did you take a chance on me?"

"You were an unbridled colt but you had principles. I saw a disciplined workhorse someday. Time showed I was right."

Stoffleman fit the key in the lock and opened the wooden door to an odor of beer and cellar air. "I never brought you down here, boy? I note from experience that you prefer the M & M bar for your daytime drinking."

"How did you know, boss?"

"How do I know anything? By observation, of course. A quick glance out the windows of our city room to the M & M, being only a block away, presents the necessary evidence. Now, how well do you know your Hirbour Block history?"

Maguire followed Stoffleman down a narrow staircase. "Tallest building west of Minneapolis, they say, framed with steel. Home of the *Butte Bugle* for forty years. Landmark at the corner of Main and Broadway. Is there more?"

Stoffleman laughed. "Today I'm introducing you to one of the best-kept secrets in Butte. Everybody hears stories about secret tunnels leading to the parlor houses on Mercury Street. Most people have no idea where to find them. We have a few secrets of our own around here. This place, behind the barber shop downstairs, was a speakeasy during Prohibition. Still like that, a private club if you will. Oh, legal all right. When I talk of the Old Man being upstairs, I mean his office. The publisher of a newspaper needs a presentable place to meet select members of the public. The Old Man owns this little bar down here. One thing, Maguire." Stoffleman stopped in front of a second closed door. "What we're doing today is nobody's business but yours and mine. I bring you down here because it's time you knew. I trust you to keep this secret. Not everybody knows, especially Ferndale, because it's no place for cops."

Stoffleman swung the door open to a long windowless room bathed in yellow light from several wall lamps. A bearded man dressed in black scrubbed a polished wood bar at one end. Eight booths with curtains and high back cushions filled the rest of the room. Maguire, hearing murmuring voices, squinted to see in the dim room.

"Back here, Maguire." Stoffleman hobbled to an empty booth in the corner. "Keep in mind that even in a place like this, the walls have ears," he said quietly after they seated themselves. The bartender, a slender man with big ears that Maguire imagined had no trouble catching gossip, came to their booth. "Two draft beers, Sam," Stoffleman told him. Sam nodded and melted away.

"I had no idea, boss. Who are these people?"

"Just folks who want privacy. They dislike the public bars. In here, nobody pays attention to anyone else's business. We have a code of behavior. Ask no questions including last names. Don't tell."

"Like a secret society?" Maguire asked.

"Something like that I suppose. It's a place like any other but known to few."

"Is the Old Man in here?" Maguire asked. Sam brought their beers in frosted mugs. Stoffleman handed him a buck and waited until he left.

"Remember the code, Maguire. Not a place to jam anybody up. To acknowledge him, even if he were sitting next to me, would violate the code. Give me your word?"

Maguire nodded. "Now, Red, you want to tell me about something?"

After inhaling a swallow of beer, Maguire leaned over the table. "Boss, I have sources on the inside of Local 1235. They're dead men if I reveal their names." Stoffleman snapped to attention as Maguire divulged details from his conversation with the two unnamed miners. "They also confirm Ketchul's involvement, boss."

Stoffleman exhaled in exasperation. "I figured as much but hoped it wasn't true," he said. "Frankly, I tried to deny what was plain to all of us. Ted's been a reliable reporter for a long time. He earned my trust by getting the facts right and telling it straight. I should have known about his boy's polio. Ted shuts off his personal life like everybody else in our shop."

Stoffleman fell silent. His stern face, still swollen and purplish, reminded Maguire of better days.

"But first things first," Stoffleman finally said. "We print that list in tomorrow's *Bugle*. Keep names of individual business owners out of it. They have enough trouble on their hands. Sum up the numbers. How much total, whether some businesses get socked more than others. Reactions from the mayor, police chief, any business owner willing to go on the record. You know the drill, Maguire.

"Now for Ted. Bad as it looks, I'm not ready to give up on him. Once and for all I want Ted to show his true stripes. Either he works for me or he works for Rusie Dregovich. I will order Ted to interview Dregovich about the accusations you uncovered today. You go along to see what he does. If you need help, take Duke Ferndale and the FBI agent. The police have as much stake in this as we do. We know every story we print about this case increases the risk of violence. Until the cops get Dregovich in custody, and chase off Accardo and his gangsters, we stand at their mercy. Keep that gun handy that you carry around. When your new story hits print, you'll erase any doubt you're the biggest target in town."

Maguire smiled. "Nancy Addleston came a twitching finger away from putting a bullet in me. The hired gun from Chicago missed twice. Maybe I'm blessed."

"Or living on borrowed time."

"What is it about this town, boss?"

Stoffleman drained half his beer in one long gulp. "Long as I lived here, which is long enough, I've known Butte as having the complexion of a big city. People living here come from every country in Europe. We have more dialects that any other city in Montana. Right here in Butte you see the high life, with our performing arts theaters, and the low life with our whores and gambling houses. Butte's faded glory leaves me sad. For the most part the boom is gone. Gone, yet greed and corruption associated with riches coming out of the ground remains strong as ever. You know how the Company runs this town. That mining pit they're digging is the latest evidence."

"That and the crime that goes with mining. I've never been wanting for sensational stories to write, boss."

They stood to leave. Maguire caught a glimpse, through a drawn curtain on the adjoining booth, of a well-dressed couple pawing and kissing. "This also is a place for trysts," Stoffleman whispered to Maguire. "Remember the code."

They left the speakeasy and climbed the stairs to the city room. Night had settled on Butte. Maguire saw the glow of streetlights outside the dark windows. Ketchul had left. "We won't see him until morning," Stoffleman said, taking a seat beside Don Morgan at the editing desk. "Write your story, Maguire. Make it sing. I'm calling the Old Man to let him know it's coming."

Maguire had knocked out half his story on the battered Remington when Stoffleman appeared with a cockeyed grin. "The Old Man says great work, Maguire. He saw the merit in your story right away. He ordered five thousand additional copies on tonight's press run and fifteen newsboys working uptown street corners at dawn."

"Just like the old days, except they have school to attend, boss."

"Just like the old days, they don't care," Stoffleman said. "The Old Man's paying a nickel for every sheet sold. He wants to see tomorrow's *Bugle* in the hands of every living person by breakfast or I can stand in the soup line outside St. Vincent de Paul by lunchtime. His exact words."

"I've never doubted the Old Man even though I wouldn't know him on the street," Maguire said.

His story the next morning rocked Butte with screaming headlines:

Corrupt Union Unmasked

Secret List Shows Gangster
Holdup of 43 Butte Businesses

Extortion Racket Steals
$200 a Month Payoffs
From Unfortunate Owners,
Will Leave Most Broke

Newsboys lugged their heavy canvas bags of papers up and down the streets, waving the headlines to everyone who passed. Fights broke out as they jockeyed for the best corners. The boys returned to the *Bugle* again and again until they sold the extra copies. Maguire's story quoted Mayor Ticklenberg, who reminded readers that Butte remained open for business. Chief Morse, at the police department, issued an ominous warning that any organized crime threat to one Butte resident meant danger to them all. The FBI agent on the case, Wilbur White, declined comment.

Maguire's phone in the Logan Hotel began ringing when the first papers hit the streets at dawn. He rolled out of bed in his underwear and put the receiver to his ear. The first two callers grumbled death threats and hung up. The third caller, naming himself as a store owner, demanded to know who gave him the list of payoffs.

"Confidential. Who are you?" Maguire asked.

"None of your damn business."

Maguire cursed and slammed the phone down. When it rang again, Maguire almost threw it through his new window glass. Instead, Honey Rossini's nervous voice came on the line.

"Red? Have you forgotten me?"

"Send the white coats for me if I did, Honey. Are you safe?"

"I would say. Maggie O'Keefe fawns over me like her lost daughter. Well, maybe that's the wrong way to put it considering where you stashed me." Honey laughed at her joke. "Maggie let me use her phone. I need more clothes, Red. Hurry up and bring me some before Maggie dresses me in one of these frilly nightgowns the other girls wear."

It was Maguire's turn to laugh. "I'll picture that all day, Honey."

"So you didn't forget me after all."

"Hardly. But I imagine you don't want to joke."

"Red? Get me out of here. If word gets out nobody will understand, Red. Nobody. I'll lose my house, my business, my reputation. This will ruin me."

"Just a little longer, Honey. Did you read the *Bugle* this morning?"

"The house man, Buddy, brought me a copy with breakfast. He scares me, Red. That man never smiles. He's got a face of a thousand fights."

"If Maggie has Buddy looking out for you, you're safe from harm. Any man who crosses Maggie and her working girls can expect trouble. I remember when Buddy caught a rube cutting a paramour named Baltimore Kate and threw him out of a second-story window, glass and all. I got a hell of a story out of that incident. Try interviewing a perp who has missing teeth and a broken jaw."

Honey sighed. "Red Maguire, what a glorious life you lead. Crime newsman who never misses a beat or a broken body. Should I be worried, Red? Will this bruiser throw me out a window?"

"Nah, he'll protect you like a wall of steel."

"I read your story this morning, Red. Maybe you should hire Buddy as a bodyguard. You hide me in a house of ill repute while you run around Butte with no protection except that gun that might go off in your pocket. Your *Bugle* byline is out there for everybody to see. You put your name on stories about perps committing crimes. This Dregovich man, what if he comes for you?"

"Then I'll have another story for tomorrow, Honey." His voice sounded huskier than he intended, too full of mock confidence. He knew he was only trying to comfort her.

"You never quit, do you?"

"If I did, we'd never know the half of it in this town. Shining light into the darkness, that's what I do."

"How noble, Red. Bad enough that men are trying to kill you. And me. Before this trouble I lived a clean life. Did I tell you I belong to the library board? Soon we decide how many new books to buy when the vendors make their annual sales visit. Did you know I volunteer at St. Helena Catholic Church to help hungry parishioners? My parents took me to that church, you know, when I was a little girl. Irene Rossini, a citizen in good standing, now this. Oh Red, I worry about my jewelry store. I invested every cent I own in the place. If someone cracks my safe, why…"

Maguire slapped his forehead. "I completely forgot, Honey." He told her about the attempted burglary at her jewelry store. "Ferndale wants you to know it won't happen again."

Honey breathed her exasperation into the phone. "I've never been so angry in all my life."

After they said goodbye, and Maguire had washed and shaved, he headed for the police department. He found Ferndale holding his telephone receiver a foot from his ear while an angry woman raved at him. "Tell me, will you? What are you cops doing about this? I wanna straight answer, you bum!"

Ferndale tried to reason with the woman but finally hung up on her. "Another one of your dolls, Maguire? Meant to call you and dialed me by mistake?"

"In your dreams, Duke. I have my own problems." Maguire stood in front of the detective's desk.

"So I read this morning's paper. I bet Rusie Dregovich burped up his coffee when he saw what you wrote. Can I see that list you got on the QT?"

Maguire reached in his pocket for the folded paper. "Keep it if you want the evidence. I copied every entry into my notebook. Have you heard from any of those business owners?"

Ferndale scanned the list. "One or two is all. Thanks for this. Jimmy Regan will go jaw with all of them. Time for hiding is over."

"What about Dregovich? Can you bring him down?"

"If we catch him red-handed. I doubt we can prove this list came from him. Maybe if you tell me your sources."

"You know I can't."

"Worth a try to ask," Ferndale said.

Maguire told how he and Ketchul would be going to the Anselmo mine to confront Dregovich one more time.

"You begging for that brute to break you in two, Maguire? Want me to go along and bring some black and whites?"

"I thought so but I changed my mind. I don't want Ketchul blaming cops for crashing the party."

"That's a refreshing thought," Ferndale said.

Maguire swung by the Silver Star for coffee, hoping to see Simone, but a waitress named Charlotte said she had called in sick. He drank a cup, dropped a dime on the counter, and headed for the *Bugle*. He found his editor in a foul mood.

"About time!" Stoffleman barked from across the room. His eyeshade, fixed firmly on his forehead, showed

Stoffleman meant business. He came over to Ketchul's desk, where the labor reporter stared at the wall. Ketchul tried to ignore Stoffleman but the editor moved into his line of vision. "You two boys get up to the Anselmo today. Push Rusie Dregovich on the allegations that you, Maguire, reported this morning. Ask him straight out if that list is his. Ted, here's your chance to fold Dregovich's denials into a story you and Maguire will write for tomorrow's paper. Joint byline with all the trimmings, even if Christmas is a few days past."

Ketchul snapped straight in his chair. "You're pushing me too far, Clyde. I told you again and again, the union has nothing to do with this. How about you tell Maguire to write a new story correcting all the misinformation he reported this morning? I'm tired of his mistakes."

Stoffleman's eyes narrowed. "First of all, how do you know it's misinformation? Second, I told you a week ago to get on this story. Third, I run this shop. Button it and get to work." Stoffleman took a few steps toward his desk and stopped. "Fourth, why haven't you visited Claggett? The duffer's flat on his back at Silver Bow Hospital. You thought about going to see him? After you're done writing your story about Dregovich you can write obituaries until Claggett returns to work."

As Ketchul fumed, Maguire played out the series of events in his mind. Gunmen shooting at him. Harry Dalton from the Valley View gas station dead. Babe McGraw beaten, Stoffleman stomped, Claggett hurt in the city room invasion, and four dozen Butte business owners scared stiff. Honey Rossini in hiding, and Ketchul too, but for different reasons. Like Ferndale would say, "It ain't a pretty picture."

Maguire jotted a reminder in his notebook to weasel information out of FBI agent White. Ferndale said he was the only one in Montana. The rumor was that any agent exiled to Butte found himself on the bad side of J. Edgar Hoover, the power-hungry FBI chief in Washington. Maguire thought Hoover got it all wrong. Butte was a town where a good agent could make a reputation fighting crime, not to wither away for lack of it.

He looked up to see Ketchul standing at his desk. "Might as well get it over," the older man said in a tone of defeat.

Maguire looked at his watch. "Little early, isn't it? Won't Dregovich be working underground?"

"We'll take a ride below in the chippy hoist. I know where to find him."

"You want to go down below to Dregovich's kingdom, Ted? If he turns on us we have no escape."

Ketchul attempted a smile but his lips pulled back in a sneer. "What's your trouble, Red, scared without dicks around to protect you?"

"Hardly." Maguire tried to sound convincing.

Ketchul's eyes wandered over Maguire's suit. "Change into some working man's clothes, will you? Underground mining is no place for someone dressed like he plans to teach Sunday school. Meet me at the Anselmo at noon. We'll find Rusie working a drift on the 3,000-foot level."

Maguire had gone down a few shafts in his day but never as deep as where Ketchul planned to take him. They had worked together since 1946 on good terms. Now, a few days short of 1955, Ketchul might be intending to snuff Maguire for good. Maguire thought of the cavernous mine as a graveyard, Dregovich as its deacon, and tommyknockers howling their ghostly voices in the dark. "Quite a picture," he said aloud.

He returned to his room where he hung his suit in the tiny closet beside his bed. He dressed in a pair of overalls, added a button-up wool shirt, and threw on a faded blue jacket he hoped wouldn't leave him too cold outside or too warm underground. He flipped open the .38 to check for six live rounds, as had become his habit, before tucking it into his overalls and zipping his jacket to hide it.

A bitter wind chill settled over Butte. Maguire went outside to his Pontiac. It complained for a minute before the motor turned with a squeal from the fan belt. He waited until the heater spit warm air before turning east to Meaderville. When he parked in front of Honey's house, her neighbor Martha hailed him. "Mr. Maguire?" she called, her plump body half out her front door. A tornado of curlers decorated her graying hair. "Is that you? I didn't recognize you dressed like that."

Maguire returned her wave and walked over to her. "Where is Irene?" she asked him. "I read the papers when I got off the bus from Anaconda last night. The neighbors said somebody fired a gun on our street. If anything happened to that beautiful girl I would die." She let her emphasis on that last word linger.

"She's safe in a place where nobody can harm her, Martha. I will make sure nothing bad happens." Martha cocked her head in a gesture of wanting to hear more but Maguire pointed to Honey's house. "I'm taking some clothes to her. She'll tell you everything when she gets home. For now, trust me."

Martha waved her finger at Maguire. "You protect that girl, Mr. Maguire. Lord knows somebody should. I looked out for her since her parents died. An independent sort, she is, but never been in a lick of trouble." With that, she closed her door to the wind chill and vanished inside.

Maguire pulled the key to Honey's house out of his pocket. He clicked the lock open. He saw what he expected when he stepped inside. Someone had ransacked her house. Cold wind whistled through a broken window in the kitchen at the back of the house. Next to it, the door to the backyard stood partly open. Maguire closed it. He covered the window with a cushion from the sofa. "That will have to do for now," he said to himself.

The perps had scattered drawers and their contents in the parlor and bedroom. Honey's bed had been turned over. Her dresses, immaculate when she wore them, lay in a heap on the closet floor. A jewelry chest in a corner of the bedroom yawned open.

He had to admit he had seen worse, but still, the violation of Honey's home sickened him. Whatever cash she had hidden was gone. Jewelry too. He called Ferndale, whose bad day was getting worse.

"Don't figure me on having a job by tomorrow the way this thing is going. On my way. Don't jam me up, Maguire. You know better than to get your hands dirty before we dust for prints."

"I need to take a few dresses, Duke."

"What the hell, I knew it. You looked goofy in those suits anyway."

When Ferndale arrived with Jimmy Regan in a black and white, Maguire headed to the Windsor. He went around to knock on the back door. Maggie opened it first. "Last time a man came to my house with dresses I charged him a special rate," she said, squeezing an eye shut in a wink.

"You're hilarious, Maggie. How's your house guest?"

"Go upstairs and see for yourself, Maguire. She's in a mood, all right, being here where anybody might mistake her for one of the girls. No chance of that long as she stays in my quarters. I don't allow my girls and their men up there anyway."

Maguire kissed the madam on her forehead. "You're a dream, Maggie."

"You know how to charm a girl, Maguire. Too bad you aren't inclined for more. I wouldn't come out of retirement for just anybody."

"You know I can't sleep with sources, Maggie."

"Red Maguire, always the principled *Bugle* reporter. Go upstairs and see that beauty. She has a thing for you."

Maguire climbed the back stairs to the third floor. He found Honey reading a romance novel from the light of the window. "These stories aren't half bad once you get into them," she told him. "This one is about an actress who goes to Hollywood to meet her leading man."

"Surely the only place where you'll meet a man like that," he replied.

"Maggie has a room full of these novels. She said the girls read them when, you know, they have nobody to entertain. Do you think they aspire to a life beyond the Windsor, Red?" Honey put the open paperback book face down on the windowsill without waiting for an answer. She kissed him on the lips. "Where's your suit? Taking a day away from the *Bugle*?"

Maguire folded her dresses over a couch next to a frilly pink lampshade. Maggie's sitting room, lavishly decorated with paintings and expensive furniture, reminded him of her influential status in Butte. Maggie harbored too many secrets about important men.

"You'll want this," Maguire told Honey, handing her the framed photograph of her and her parents. She frowned at the cracked glass. When he told her about the burglary at her house, and her stolen jewelry, she cried.

"Most of that was my mother's. All gone?" Tears ran from her brown eyes.

"For now, I'm afraid. Ferndale is on it. The perps might be those two mugs watching your house or some neighborhood boys who saw a dark house and wanted to steal from you. Ferndale and his crew will find it, all of it."

Her crying stopped. "What really matters is that nobody shot either of us dead."

"I'm stupid for bringing this on you, Honey. I should have refused to put your name in the paper."

She tossed her head just as Maguire had seen Jane Russell do in the movies. Honey did it so naturally that Maguire doubted she was aware of how she mimicked the famous actress. "I fight my own battles. Sure, this crime wave is hard to laugh off. Nobody runs me out of my town, Red."

"Except to Hollywood?" he asked, trying to lighten the mood.

"Show me the train ticket and I'm off." She pulled back and looked at him. "Really, why are you dressed like that?"

Maguire told her about going to the Anselmo with Ketchul. Honey looked like she wanted to argue. Instead, she bit her lip. "If you wind up dead I'll never get out of here. Never mind that I won't get another date to a shootout."

"If I wind up dead, call Ferndale. He'll know what to do, even if it isn't the right thing."

They kissed again before Maguire noticed the time. "Almost noon, got to go." He thundered down the stairs, taking two steps at a time. At the bottom, where the door to Maggie's office stood open, she looked at him curiously.

"Sorry, didn't mean to alarm you," he said.

"Maguire, you know how many men come running from upstairs after they lose track of time with my girls? You'd think they were going to a fire."

"Honey's not any girl, Maggie."

"So I see, my lovestruck *Bugle* friend."

"I put you in a tight spot, Maggie. They're trying to get to her to crack me."

"Buddy won't let it happen. Remember that I keep my heater right here in the desk. In the event things get interesting I'll summon some dicks in blue to come mop up what Buddy can't finish. That is, if I can find an honest one." Maggie pulled herself to Maguire to kiss him on the lips.

"Two can play this game," she whispered before pushing him away.

~ 20 ~

'Ya deaf, Maguire?'

Maguire headed west down Granite Street toward the Anselmo. If Rusie Dregovich jumped him underground, he would pull out the .38 and start shooting. He hoped six rounds would be enough to stop the giant. Some people said he had the strength of a grizzly bear. Shooting Dregovich would bring trouble. Maguire pictured miners swarming out of the dark with shovels and pickaxes. Maguire knew it was a different world underground. Dregovich owned it.

He found Ketchul waiting inside the comfort of his station wagon. Ketchul barely acknowledged Maguire's arrival. He waved him toward the chippy hoist where a miner waited. "Billy will take us down," Ketchul said, his boots clomping as he boarded the metal contraption. Maguire followed. Billy handed them hard hats and cap lamps. "Can't see a foot in front of your face without them. Air ain't none too good neither. Hotter than a Saturday night down on Mercury Street," he said to Maguire.

Maguire caught a mocking look from Ketchul before Billy closed the cage and signaled the engineer on the bell to start it on a rattling descent into the dark earth. "You claustrophobic, Maguire? You like a casket lid staring you in the face?" His laugh mixed with the machine noise.

Maguire squeezed his eyes shut. He had feared tight spaces ever since his mother barricaded him in his bedroom closet during a drunken binge. He had come home from kindergarten class with a crayon drawing of her holding a liquor bottle. Lily destroyed the drawing in two malicious rips. She slapped him hard on the face, pushed him into the closet, bracing the door with his dresser. Kieran's father, working swing shift at the mill, wasn't home to intervene. Kieran felt brave at first. He made a game of feeling in the dark for his toys and games. He easily found his baseball mitt and hockey skates by touch. He had three boxes of games. Which was which? He reached inside each one to explore the pieces between his thumb and forefingers. He was halfway through the second box when he heard his gasping. The walls of the little closet held him captive. His body grew hot. Feeling panic, Kieran pushed against the door. It didn't budge. He pounded on the walls and called for his mother. His breath came in sudden sharp intakes. He grabbed wildly at the shirts and pants above him. They slid off the bent wire hangers and piled on top of him. He sank and cried. He fell asleep. Lily came for him late at night. She pushed him toward his bed with a warning never to color a picture of her again. "There's no need to tell your father about our disagreement, is there, honey? You be a good boy and Mommy will buy you ice cream."

Now, plunging deeper into the mine, Maguire heard Ketchul yelling as the noisy hoist passed flashes of light where men worked on the upper drifts. "Watch yourself when we get off the hoist! There's a million ways for a man to get hurt down here. One wrong step and you get a fast ride down so deep the devil can't help you."

The bell sounded. The hoist slowed and stopped. Billy opened the cage. Dust and an acrid odor of dynamite hung in the air. Men passed silently like black ghosts. Dim lightbulbs led the way into the drift. "Down there," Billy said, pointing into the darkness. "The boss man is down there."

Maguire followed Ketchul into the drift. Occasionally when he walked too close to the side his hardhat scraped against a shelf of rock. A train of ore cars passed them. The driver, his facial features unrecognizable under the harsh glow of his cap lamp, waved as he rumbled past. They walked for what seemed like a quarter mile before they found Dregovich working under electric lights. The union boss stood head and shoulders above the men around him. He braced a massive jackhammer as casually as most men wielded a shovel. As it pounded against the rock face, Dregovich's muscled arms and shoulders coiled like dock rope. Maguire cupped his ears against the commotion.

When Dregovich caught site of Maguire and Ketchul, he shut off the hammer and set it down. He glared at Maguire. "Ya ask for serious trouble coming down here, *Bugle* boy. First off, I warned ya not to put them lies in the paper. Ya ain't got no union card neither. Nobody comes into our mines without a card. Ya trying to bust our union, boy?"

Maguire eased back. He hoped he looked braver than he felt. His gun seemed useless. Before he could reach for it, Dregovich would pummel him with those beer-barrel fists.

"Here's your golden chance to tell me different, Mr. Dregovich."

The giant laughed. His booming voice filled the room of rock. A half dozen miners, peering from the shadows, quit work to watch. "I give ya every chance until now. Them stories you put in the *Bugle* paint me and my boys as criminals. If that ain't enough, Ketchul here failed us. That right, Ted? I give ya facts. I give ya jingle. You write nothing and let us twist in the wind? When I pay ya to tell the truth? How do we settle this do ya figure?"

Maguire heard Ketchul's trembling voice beside him. "I need time, Rusie, you know that. My editor back at the *Bugle* won't cooperate."

Dregovich surprised Maguire with his agility as he took a quick step forward and grabbed Ketchul by the shirt. The union boss lifted the muscled Ketchul until his feet dangled. "Co-op-er-ate?" Dregovich yelled. "Who side ya on, anyway, mouse? Need persuasion? You know I can give it to ya."

Ketchul's hard hat fell off as Dregovich tossed him backwards. Ketchul thrashed in muddy water before climbing to his feet. Ketchul was a tough man, Maguire knew, but Dregovich broke him. He broke everyone who defied him.

The giant turned on Maguire. "Ya want some of this, *Bugle* boy?"

"You tried more than once," Maguire replied.

Dregovich eased off. "Ya come down here to get our side of the story? Ya got more power to print it than this here girl Ketchul? Start askin' but ya try to play around with me, I'll kick your sorry Butte ass. I ain't in the mood."

"So I see," Maguire said, watching Ketchul grimace in pain.

"Get on with it, *Bugle* boy. This here place ain't some frilly newspaper. Men work down here."

Maguire pulled out his notebook and a pencil. "This is so I get your words right," he told the giant, who nodded suspiciously. "Did Local 1235 rob stores to scare people into paying up?"

"Nonsense!" Dregovich roared.

"Did you order members of your union to attack people to scare them off?"

"No!" he roared again.

"Did any members of your union attack people of their own volition?"

"Don't know that word," Dregovich said.

"Did they attack people without you knowing about them doing it?"

"Nobody does nothin' in this union without Rusie knowin' 'bout it."

"Did they attack people?"

"No."

"Did your men kill the owner of the Valley View gas station? Harry Dalton?"

"What the hell you talkin' about?"

"Is Local 1235 working with Tony Accardo's mobsters from Chicago to steal money from business owners in Butte?"

"Who's he?" Dregovich struck a defiant pose with his feet apart and his arms crossed. He reminded Maguire of a labor poster.

"Are you or anybody else in Local 1235 doing business with the mafia, organized crime, gangsters squeezing money from Butte?"

"Hell, no."

"What do you know about two times when men tried to shoot me?"

"Don't surprise me a bit to hear it."

Maguire tried a different tact. "So you are paying Ted Ketchul to write stories benefiting your union?"

Dregovich took the bait. "I ain't paying him a penny more. When a man wants jingle in his pocket he works for it. Nobody crosses Rusie. See here. Who makes the rich people in this town even richer? Miners underground, that's who. Down here in the dirt and dust digging out fortunes for them people who eat on fancy tablecloths. Look around at these here men. Ya see anybody here who ain't from Centerville or Corktown or grow up in the Cabbage Patch? We got rights, Maguire. Just because we ain't got manners don't mean we ain't going after what's coming to us. Ya tell people that, *Bugle* boy. Ya tell 'em the men who mine this Hill own Butte. Ya tell 'em Rusie Dregovich ain't got any idea about them crimes in stores."

Maguire wanted to hear his denial once more. "So you're saying that you, and Local 1235, had nothing at all to do with beatings of innocent people?"

"I'm sayin'."

"You're saying that you, and Local 1235, have nothing to do with extortion of business owners?"

"Throwing out big words ain't making ya any smarter, Maguire."

"Are you stealing from business owners?"

"Ya deaf, Maguire? I told ya we ain't involved."

"Does that list I printed in the *Bugle* belong to you?"

"Ain't my concern."

Maguire slid his notebook and pencil back in his pocket. He turned to Ketchul. "Questions you want to ask, Ted?"

"Nothing I don't already know," he said, sounding less confident.

Dregovich stepped close to Maguire. Stale beer breath roiled from his mouth. "I ain't giving ya jingle. Ya get this right or they'll change youse name on top of the story from Red Maguire to Dead Maguire."

"He's not kidding," Ketchul said almost involuntarily.

Dregovich glared at Maguire. He shoved him backward with a mighty open paw. Maguire reeled from the force of it. "Ain't nobody messes with Rusie," he roared again, and turned away.

Ketchul said nothing on the ride to the top. The chippy hoist emerged into a blaze of afternoon light and fresh air. Billy threw the gate open. Wind swept across the Anselmo yard. Maguire marveled at the difference between the hot dark underground and the frigid sunlit sheet of snow at the surface. Ketchul headed to his station wagon without saying a word. Maguire hurried after him.

"He bribed you, Ted. You took money to throw a story his way."

Ketchul whirled, laden with worry. "Nothing he wanted got into the paper, Maguire. Please, let it go."

"Ted, it didn't get into the paper because of Stoffleman. You tried. I never saw what you wrote but when Stoffleman read it he knew the game was up. Tell him that you took a bribe, or I will. Ferndale too."

Maguire thought he saw tears in Ketchul's blue eyes. He suddenly felt sorry for the labor reporter. "Expenses pile up, Red. I've got a boy with polio. Eight years old. You can't imagine the costs. You think I can save him on my wages from the *Bugle*? What Stoffleman pays me barely covers the rent."

"You should have told us, Ted. All of us, even Claggett, we could help you."

"None of you understand my desperation, Maguire. Yes, I got in too deep. That what you want to hear? You think I liked taking jingle from that thug? My son, that polio, it broke me."

Maguire squared up. He squinted in the bright daylight. "You've also got a new station wagon, Ted, a spanking new Chevrolet. What happened to you? Remember when you came to work at the *Bugle*? Straight out of the Navy, wasn't it? You had discipline and principles. Stoffleman bragged about you being the best labor reporter who ever set foot in a Butte city room. Now look. What have you done?"

Ketchul looked away. "Tell Stoffleman I'll be along," he muttered. He got into his car and drove away. Maguire watched him go. Ketchul was in trouble. Serious trouble.

Something occurred to Maguire as he turned the ignition key in his Pontiac. Only a man who understood death more than any other would know the answer. Only a man with enough nerve to ask personal questions during deep times of family grief and put it all in print. Butte had only one man like that. Calvin Claggett.

'Dregovich is lying'

Maguire thought of Peach when he arrived at the hospital. She was a lonely working girl like Simone, Butte all over. He checked his watch. It was mid-afternoon. Regrettably her night shift was nine hours away.

He found Claggett barely awake in a second-floor room at the back of the hospital. The old obituary reporter lifted his head when he saw Maguire. Claggett looked about the same as usual, Maguire thought, his usual being pale and haggard and near death.

"How's she go, Maguire? I thought you died," Claggett greeted him.

"You'll be the first to know, Calvin."

"No doubt of that, Maguire. I've got a backlog of bodies staring me in the face. Davis is the only reporter in the city room taking up the slack. Stoffleman tells me you're too damn busy writing about mobsters. Ketchul refuses. Those other reporters in the room, I don't have a clue what they do."

"Sports and society, that kind of thing." Maguire started to brush mine dust off his sleeves but thought better of it. Claggett watched him curiously through wrinkled eyelids.

"Why are you dressed like that, Maguire? On your way to a wake?"

"Could be, Calvin. That's why I'm here."

"Not a social visit, then?" The frail man tried to hide his disappointment.

Maguire told Claggett about his meeting with Dregovich underground and what the union boss said about Ketchul taking a bribe. Claggett, sensing he was being asked for his advice, pulled himself to a sitting position in the hospital bed. He looked small and shrunken against the sheets.

"Think back, Calvin. What man has more bragging rights to institutional memory in this town than you? You wrote what, thousands of obituaries? How many of those miners who died in accidents belonged to Local 1235?"

Claggett looked out the window. Maguire knew he was calculating.

"Can't put my finger on an exact number," Claggett finally said. "There was your old man. I remember that one well. Many dozens. Maybe hundreds."

"Do you recall the most common causes of death?"

Claggett held up a wrinkled spotted hand with fingers outstretched and began counting. "Falls for sure. Explosions. Fires. Collisions with machinery. Electrocutions. Big objects hitting men in the head. Those six."

"What did their families say, Calvin?"

Claggett smiled. He understood what Maguire was asking. Claggett knew more about death than anyone in Butte, maybe anyone anywhere.

"Those wives and brothers never got the facts on what happened. You could say they were suspicious, almost all of them, of how their men died. The Company never says much. We all know underground mining is dangerous work. Circumstances of their accidental deaths go to the grave with them. Nobody likes to admit what happened even if they know the truth. When I'm embalming with Arnie at the Forever More we ask ourselves why men die like this. They get hauled out of the hole all broken up, burned up, blown to pieces. We pretty up their faces and send them back below ground again. Terrible irony, Red, open to suspicion."

Maguire gripped the metal frame at the foot of Claggett's bed. "Suspicion, how? Maybe some of these men crossed Rusie Dregovich?"

"Speculation, isn't it? So little is known about these so-called mine accidents that anything could befall a man underground. Suspicion that the union never knows what happened. The union blames the Company. If any of these men died from being clobbered by another man, or from deliberate negligence, the truth is hard to come by. Proof is an elusive thing when death comes knocking."

"I'm worried about Ted Ketchul, Calvin."

Claggett opened the drawer beside his bed. "That woman with the orange hair took away my Old Golds. Nurses get in the way of a man smoking in the hospital. Anyway, that man Dregovich has a terrible reputation. He scares people to death. No small admission from an obituary writer, Red. You had better help Ferndale pin something on him before Ted arrives at the Forever More in a non-talking mood."

"You have a way with words, Calvin."

"We would put murder out of business if everyone remembered that in death as well as in life, let honesty prevail. Take it from an old man who wrote a graveyard full of these obituaries. Nobody hides their misdeeds forever. Anyone who thinks different better read up on history. This city is full of scandals, not all of them forgotten either."

Maguire pulled three cigarettes from his shirt pocket and handed them to Claggett. "I get your meaning, Calvin. And don't tell Peach where you got these."

"Got a thing for that lassie, do you boy?"

"Curious is all but there's another who suits me better."

Maguire left the hospital after Claggett vowed to return to the *Bugle* where he could smoke all day. "A man can't live without his Old Golds," Claggett said as they parted, afternoon shadows falling on the hospital.

Night settled as Maguire parked in front of the *Bugle*. Frigid wind from the north whipped down Main Street. He slipped on ice and nearly fell as he hurried into the warm Hirbour Block. Stoffleman, as expected, waited for him in the city room. "In here, Maguire," Stoffleman said, pointing to the meeting room across the hall. He brought Don Morgan along for good measure.

"Give me the headline first," Stoffleman said.

"Dregovich accused Ketchul of taking bribes. Ted didn't deny it."

Morgan hung his head and Stoffleman nodded, sadly. "Our suspicions confirmed then. Again. And I hoped I was wrong. Again."

Maguire told his bosses about the encounter with Dregovich and his bluffing that the union had no hand in the rash of recent crimes. He also told them about how Ketchul shrunk from Dregovich without asking questions.

"So it's what Ted said. The union denies responsibility. Believing what Dregovich said is true is yet another matter," Morgan said.

"Nobody disputes Dregovich is lying," Stoffleman said without hesitation. "Write this up for the front page in the morning edition, Maguire. Put your shoulder into it. Ted is washed up as a newsman. Nobody who takes a bribe can expect to work another day at the *Bugle*. Let's hope Ted walks in here to admit it to my face. I will call Ferndale to report this and run upstairs to tell the Old Man. If you boys think I have a hard heart, I'll tell you this. What a sad day for Ted's wife and sons and for Ted himself. Nobody admires dishonor."

Maguire, still dressed against the cold outside, went to his desk where he found a phone message from Babe McGraw. It came from Luverne at the switchboard. She wrote "urgent" at the top.

Babe answered on the third ring. The first shift had come off the Hill. Babe shouted to be heard above the noise at her end. "Maguire, I hear talk about your buddy at the *Bugle*. Ted Ketchul. Word on the Hill is that Dregovich plans to kill Ketchul. Maybe hurt him bad anyway. It ain't good any way you cut it."

Maguire hurried across the city room to tell Stoffleman. The editor nodded solemnly. "Trying to reach Ferndale. I hope it's not too late."

The story Maguire wrote consumed two full columns on the front page and two more inside the paper. He put Dregovich's denials at the top, following with grave skepticism from Police Chief Morse that Dregovich spoke the truth. Even the secretive FBI agent, Wilbur White, agreed to comment. "Local 1235 is being investigated for serious crimes and links to organized crime," he acknowledged.

Somewhere in the middle of Maguire's furious typing, Stoffleman handed him the spiked story Ketchul had written absolving the union of any guilt. "Use what's appropriate," Stoffleman said. Maguire snagged a few quotes and some background about the union for the new story. The rest of Ketchul's piece, he could see, was utter nonsense. It read like Dregovich had written it.

When Maguire finished the new story, he added Ketchul's name at the top in a sudden pinch of mercy. The new story, after all, did include some of his reporting. "By Red Maguire and Ted Ketchul, *Bugle* reporters," it read.

It would be Ketchul's last byline in the *Bugle* and one he never saw.

Late that night, cops in a prowl car found Ketchul hanging from a rail crossing above Butte near Walkerville. A rough hemp rope encircled his neck. The *Bugle* labor reporter twisted in the bitter January wind, coatless and lifeless, his new station wagon parked nearby.

"He ended it before they got to him," is how Ferndale broke the news when he appeared at Maguire's door in the Logan Hotel. They drove to the *Bugle* to inform Stoffleman. The editor knew why they had come even before they told him.

"You want to stop the presses, boss? Add the news of Ketchul's death?"

Stoffleman put the news before anything else. Now he shook his head in a rare display of empathy. "Have a heart, Maguire. Ted had a family. We need to tell his wife. Her name is Lou. Oh, lord, this is terrible. The Japs couldn't kill Ted. The union did, in a way. Is that a fair assumption, Ferndale?"

"Appears so, Mr. Stoffleman. I'll go see Mrs. Ketchul to notify her."

"We'll do it together," Stoffleman said, his tone softening. "You're sure he took his own life?"

Ferndale ran his fingers through the gray fringe around his head. "Positive. I was there when they cut down that rope. I know Ketchul on sight, even with ice on his face. Driver's license confirmed it. His wife reported him missing. Suicide, conclusive. Only tracks in the snow were his."

The three men piled into Ferndale's car. He drove to Ketchul's address on West Gold Street, where a porch light burned like a beacon. They sat there for a few minutes, none of them eager for the task ahead, for the finality of it.

"She doesn't need to know all of it, not tonight," Stoffleman cautioned. They walked to the house. Lou Ketchul, dressed in a pink housecoat, swung open the door. Her eyes went straight to Ferndale's badge. She collapsed when Ferndale told her Ted was found dead. Maguire caught her before she hit the floor.

~ 22 ~

'Bad side of our city'

"Tell me again why you don't arrest Dregovich on grounds of something or other?" Maguire asked Ferndale early the next morning over coffee at the Silver Star.

"Got to find hard evidence tying him to these crimes. I doubt I could even prove he wrote that list of payoffs unless I find a witness who saw him do it. You know as much," Ferndale said. He rubbed the dark circles around his eyes.

"I wonder if I know anything at all anymore," Maguire said. He barely slept. Lou Ketchul's screaming haunted him all night. They sat in the back booth, Ferndale facing the front window as he always did, Maguire resting the back of his head against the tall wooden divider between the booths. He struggled to stay awake.

"You and me both, Maguire. I've gotta say, your interview with Dregovich put him square in the middle of these crimes. No innocent man acts like that. I suppose I could arrest him for assaulting Ketchul in the mine. I would rather pin murder on the mug. We got Harry Dalton dead and buried but his murder case is still wide open. Chief's all over me like a dog in heat. Mayor too. One detective can't keep up with crimes in this town."

Maguire told Ferndale about his suspicion Dregovich had killed men in the mines. "Claggett tells me nobody knows for sure how men die underground. Is that how you see it?"

Ferndale yawned. "Tell me something new. Suspicion is my job, and yours. You know damn well we have a different city below the surface and one we can't patrol. Dregovich has a reputation as a mean skunk all right. Murders underground? Knock me over with a feather. Between you and me, I ain't got a way of proving what happens down there. A killer finds a dozen ways to fake an accident. Sure, I hear rumors. Getting to the truth is a different story."

Simone, unsteady on her feet and her face pale as a dinner plate, came to the booth to pour a refill. "Sorry, boys, that flu knocked me flat." She glanced at Ferndale. "Did the cops receive any reports that my boy Red here was flirting with other waitresses while I was gone?"

Ferndale smiled and began with, "I'd throw away the key..." Suddenly his face hardened. He tried to push Simone away. Maguire, not understanding, reached to steady her.

"Look out!" Ferndale yelled as an ear-hammering boom filled the Silver Star. Somewhere in the room, a woman screamed. Simone slammed face first against the wall. The glass pot of coffee she held shattered. Maguire caught a glimpse of a widening circle of blood at the base of her neck before she crumpled to the tile floor.

Another shot rang out. Maguire ducked just as a bullet tore through the wooden divider near his head. Splinters showered over him as he reached wildly for his .38. In his panic his hand went to the wrong pocket. As he fumbled, Ferndale whipped his service revolver from his shoulder holster as only a practiced cop would do. The long-barreled gun jumped twice in his hand. The booth filled with the acrid odor of gunpowder. Blood bubbled from his upper arm. Maguire slid out of the booth and rolled to the floor, landing next to Simone. He heard another shot that sounded far away. He caught a glance of a man in dirty clothes collapsing against a table. Silverware and a plate full of food flew everywhere as man and table crashed to the floor.

Then it was over.

Maguire saw customers shouting but the roar from deafening shots blocked their words from his ears. He turned to Simone. Her lifeless eyes stared at the ceiling. Spilled hot coffee left scorching red trails on her cheeks. Maguire wiped it away with the sleeves of his suit coat. He cradled her and ran his fingers over her face. Her blood felt thick and warm.

Ferndale slumped in the booth, service revolver still in his left hand, fingers of his right hand clamped over the torn flesh on his left arm. He set the gun on the table and pointed to the shooter. Maguire crawled over to the crumpled man who had a Porky Pig mask over his face. When Maguire pulled it loose, he saw that Cracker Gibbons no longer would haunt Butte. The distasteful little man had taken a round in the throat and another square in the chest. A gun of a caliber unfamiliar to Maguire lay beside him. Ferndale's third shot had missed, shattering the Silver Star's front plate-glass window, leaving only the letters "Si" intact.

Maguire heard sounds, faint at first, but they came in a rush as he regained his hearing. A sobbing waitress knelt over Simone. Customers cried out in panic. Ferndale tried to stifle a moan. Sirens wailed on the street. Maguire took off his necktie and cinched it around Ferndale's arm to stop the bleeding. The old detective watched him with sad eyes. At least four black and whites screeched to a halt. In a matter of seconds cops swarmed into the Silver Star, Chief Morse among them. He checked Gibbons for a pulse and shook his head as cops herded scared customers off the premises. Morse examined Simone and shook his head again.

"What the hell happened, Ferndale?"

"Man can't get a cup of coffee anymore," Ferndale started. "I'm sitting here with Maguire when I see a man pull a gun.

The girl got it first. Ain't got any idea about the chain of events after that. Know him?" Ferndale tossed his head toward the dead shooter.

"It's Mack Gibbons," Maguire said.

"Figures. Got panicky and sprayed bullets. A trained killer would walk to the table and plug us before we whistled Dixie." Ferndale exhaled and closed his eyes, like he wanted to sleep. Two ambulance attendants wearing white pants rushed into the cafe. The chief motioned to them.

"This man needs a fast ride to the hospital. Take a black and white with you so nobody messes with him on the way."

Morse then turned to the cops. "I want witness reports, I want evidence, I want photos, anything else you can find. Jimmy Regan? Make sure your boys keep gawkers away. Crack down on anybody sneaking a look at the bodies. Maguire, you see any of this?"

"Simone going down. Ferndale hit. My back was turned to the gunman."

"You knew the waitress?"

"Only when I came to the Silver Star. She had a tender heart. She didn't deserve this."

"Innocent victims never do," the chief said.

Later that afternoon, Morse called Maguire at the *Bugle*. Doctors proclaimed Ferndale in fair condition. "Duke, he's the toughest old bird I know, Maguire. You can print that. Beats me how he put that fool Gibbons down with an injured arm. Doctor says the bullet tore a hole but missed bone. The ornery cuss will hurt like hell for a few days. And that waitress? Her full name was Simone Hazel Andrews, date of birth November third, 1924. We notified her brother an hour ago. Shell shock from the war. Didn't show much emotion when we broke the news."

"Considering that, I'm guessing her job at the Silver Star was pretty much all she had," Maguire replied.

"And Maguire? I hate to speculate but I'll do it anyway. No doubt Gibbons had orders to take out both you and Ferndale. Unfortunately for Simone he got jumpy. Like Ferndale said, a gangster from Chicago would have left no doubt."

Claggett came back to work that afternoon. He shuffled to his desk, pushed his ashtray within reach of his typewriter, and began hammering the keys like he never left. Stoffleman went upstairs to talk the Old Man into publishing another *Extra*. It would hit the streets before dinner time.

"Forget the usual detached newspaper writing on this one, Maguire," Stoffleman said when he returned. "I want first person. Tell about the gunfight as you saw it and heard it. Leave nothing out. Claggett will find out more about the personal backgrounds of Simone Andrews and Mack Gibbons. You keep working the crime angle."

"Will do, boss."

"And Maguire? Good thing Gibbons failed to plug you. I don't need yet another job opening at the *Bugle*."

"You make me feel warm all over, boss. We lost what, three reporters to violence in six months? Mary Miller, Vanzetti, now Ketchul?" Maguire shot back.

"Like I told you when I hired you all those years ago, newspapering isn't for the faint of heart," Stoffleman said, worry creased into his face.

The story poured out of Maguire as he wrote furiously. He pounded on his Remington without a break. Even Claggett, normally lost in his world of dead bodies, showed his admiration with a thumbs up. Maguire continued writing, deep in thought, when his jangling phone interrupted.

"Maguire! *Bugle* city room!" He sat up straight when he heard Honey Rossini's frantic voice.

"Red! You're alive? We heard rumors that you and Ferndale and the waitress were shot dead. Maggie was told some crazy miner put a bullet in your head. Oh, Red!" Honey was close to screaming.

"I wasn't hurt, Honey. Ferndale took a round but he'll live. You heard right on Simone the waitress. I'll set the facts straight in the *Extra* this afternoon."

He heard Honey take a deep breath. "Two men came to the Windsor this morning, Red. Two men in dark suits. They asked about me and tried to come upstairs. Maggie pulled a gun on them. They defied her until Buddy and Junior trapped them and worked them over is how she told it to me. These men, they were strangers to Maggie. Not Butte men, outsiders. They know, Red. They know I'm here."

Maguire's mind raced. "You're seeing the bad side of our city all right."

"It hurts my eyes to look," Honey said.

"Wait for me. I'll come get you. Stay upstairs. You're in safe hands with Maggie O'Keefe."

"Do you Irish always stick together, Red?"

"In Butte especially, Honey."

Distracted as he was, Maguire plowed back into his story. He finished two hours later at about five thousand words. "Not bad for a cub reporter," Stoffleman threw at him. "Maybe in a few years you can learn to write twice that length on a critical story like this."

"Glad you're feeling better, boss."

"That, and I'm tired of these hoodlums trying to run our town," Stoffleman said, turning his attention to penciling changes into Maguire's story.

The presses roared to life at dinner time. The banner headline read:

Reporter Details Bloody Shootout

Waitress Killed, Cop Takes a Bullet
at Popular Uptown Restaurant

**Gun-Wielding Miner,
Known Butte Troublemaker,
Put Down for Good**

Stoffleman and Maguire went downstairs to watch the press belch a steady river of *Bugles*. The foreman Snuff, blue sleeves rolled to his elbows, pulled a handful of newspapers rolling off the press and handed them to Stoffleman. The ink felt wet to the touch. "You can thank Don Morgan for the crack headlines," Stoffleman yelled to Maguire over the noise.

Newsboys hawking from street corners sold all of the *Bugles* by dinner time. "You're making a habit of these sellouts, boy," Stoffleman told Maguire, sounding close to a compliment.

Story finished, Maguire rummaged through Ketchul's desk, searching for evidence of Rusie Dregovich's crimes as much as personal effects to return to his wife. Calvin Claggett slid his chair over to help.

"He loved his family. Of that there was no doubt, Maguire. Sad thing is, I worked next to Ted Ketchul for nine years but hardly knew him. It's a hell of a thing knowing people better in death than in life."

Maguire lifted his blue eyes. "Lately that is something we have in common, Cal. Thanks for your help with my story. So many people are dying it's hard to know which story to tell first."

"Welcome to my world, son."

Maguire reached into a drawer stuffed with used notebooks. He pulled out a handful of letters. "Look at this,

Cal." Maguire opened an envelope and started reading. Claggett did the same, scanning one page and then another. "Letters from war buddies, Maguire. A find like this is an obituary writer's dream. Listen to this one. 'You saved me, Ketchul, after the Japs blew open the hull with that torpedo. I caught shrapnel in the forward gun turret. Do you remember carrying me out of the line of fire? I'll never forget.' "

Maguire shook open a letter. "Here's another. Navy man from Philadelphia. 'I served with you for a year but never really knew you until Pearl Harbor. Nobody deserved the Navy Cross more than you. I remember to this day when it was pinned on your uniform. I owe my life to you. You are a good and honorable man.' " Maguire tossed the letter on the desk. "Ted received the Navy Cross? I never knew."

Claggett carefully replaced the letter he held in its envelope. "I imagine all the rest say much the same. How about I include some of this in Ted's obituary before we give these letters to his widow? People ought to know he was a good man and a good newsman for most of his time at the *Bugle*. Why did he turn?"

"His boy's polio did it, Calvin. Ted needed money. He took a little and then he took a lot and got drunk on the payoffs. Drunks make foolish decisions. Ted strung himself up to make sure we never know the extent of it."

"Dead men tell no tales," Claggett said.

Maguire reached again into Ketchul's desk. On impulse, he ran his hand along the bottom of a drawer. "Wait, there's more," he told Claggett.

He felt another envelope, taped out of view. Maguire tore it loose. Inside, he found five worn fifty-dollar bills and a note scrawled in pencil. "Tell my story or use this money to pay for your funeral. RD."

Maguire showed the evidence to Stoffleman and Morgan. "I would hate to see Ted's funeral financed with dirty money," Maguire said, as the other men nodded their agreement. He threw on his overcoat and stepped outside. A bitter windchill swept down Main Street. Maguire walked the envelope over to Police Chief Morse at the police department. "Doesn't take much imagination to know these initials belong to Rusie Dregovich, does it?" Maguire asked the chief.

Morse, frowning, pointed to a row of photographs on his office wall. "You know those men, Maguire. Butte's police chiefs that came before me. Some did a better job than others, but we remember all of them for keeping law and order in a rough town, or in some cases pretending to." The chief's shoulders sagged. In that moment, Maguire thought, he looked older than his fifty-two years. "What will history say about me? First the Purple Rose Killer, now a rash of deaths over greed. Mayor Ticklenberg asked me, just this morning, how I let so many criminals take over Butte. Hopping mad the FBI got involved. He asked me if that means our cops lost control of the investigation. No matter to the mayor that mob interference makes this a federal case as well as a local one. I doubt I'll be wearing this uniform much longer." The last time Maguire had seen the chief that despondent was when his daughter died in the traffic accident. Morse reached for the pink teddy bear on his desk. It had been her favorite.

"You can't be judged by a body count," Maguire said. "You didn't bring these crimes to Butte."

The chief turned to Maguire. Some of his customary resolve returned. "Ferndale showed me your list of business owners paying ransom. Every one of them denied doing it. Fear is a terrible thing. People read about the beatings and shootings and know it could happen to them. Count on us to nail Dregovich very soon. Count on it. You can help by solving this mystery, Maguire. With Ferndale down for the time being, it's quite possible you're the only one who can."

Back at the *Bugle*, Stoffleman pulled Maguire aside. "We're on the verge of blowing this story wide open, Maguire. I'm sending you to Chicago. The Old Man, tightwad that he is, sprung for a train ticket. You leave tomorrow morning on the North Coast Limited. Go see that reporter you know at the *Times* and find out about Tony Accardo's connection in Butte. Get the dirt on Dregovich that will stand up in court."

"I need to take Irene Rossini with me, boss. She's not safe in Butte."

Stoffleman lifted an eyebrow above his ghastly battle scar. "Everyone told you not to drag her into this mess, Maguire. What the hell, I guess everybody needs love." Stoffleman opened his wallet and pulled out three twenties. "This will buy her ticket. Call it money unspent in my own loveless life. Take that piece you carry around in case anybody gets wind of you two boarding that train. And Maguire? Come back soon or I won't have a wink of copy to print in this newspaper."

"You've got Claggett and Davis, for a start."

"Truth is, Maguire, nobody can hold a candle to the volume of words you write for the *Bugle*. Not even Claggett, bless his love for departed souls. Figure on three days in Chicago. Then you come back and write up a storm or else."

"Or else what, boss?"

"Or else I'll figure Accardo's mugs accomplished in Chicago what they couldn't get done in Butte."

Maguire called Maggie at the Windsor to tell her he would come to get Honey before dawn to catch the flyer to Chicago. "Don't leave your car at the depot if they're watching the trains, Red. I'll send Buddy to drive you."

"He doesn't talk much, that Buddy."

"That's because he's mute. It works out because there's no way he can tell anyone about who visits here."

"I owe you, Maggie."

"You always do, Red. You had better set aside a full month to pay up."

Near midnight, in a howling north wind, Maguire coaxed his Pontiac to a reluctant start outside the Logan Hotel. As the car groaned to life, he caught the flicker of a match across the street. A man's hard face flashed into view for a second or two. Criminals can't resist lighting cigarettes, Maguire thought, even when it means revealing themselves during a tail. He pulled into the street slowly, giving the impression he planned to turn left. Suddenly he whirled the steering wheel right and punched the gas. The worn rear tires spun on ice until they hit a dry patch of pavement. The eight-banger under the hood threw the car forward. Maguire caught the stalker square in his headlights. He very much resembled the man who earlier had tried to shoot him. The man stumbled away from the oncoming car, his eyes wide, his arm waving a gun. Rather than shoot he panicked and turned to run. Maguire braked and jumped from his car. He grabbed the mug as he struggled to escape through a narrow opening between the grocery and a hardware store. Gripping the man's overcoat, Maguire punched him twice in the head, putting his two hundred pounds behind the blows. The mug reeled and fell, tearing off his overcoat and pulling Maguire off balance to his knees. Free from Maguire's grasp, the gunman scrambled into the dark passageway.

Maguire watched the dark form disappear. He heard the man fall again and curse. There, in the glare from the Pontiac's headlights, lay the mug's gun. His coat stunk of cigarettes. Maguire reached into the pockets. They were empty except for a scrap of paper that read, "Logan Hotel, Granite Street, second story front."

Must be a dumb shooter to need a map, Maguire thought to himself. His fist throbbed. With some satisfaction, he knew the mug would hear birds sing for a week. He locked the gun in the trunk and searched the street for more trouble. A few locals watched him curiously. They were the usual rabble who prowled uptown streets late at night. One of them, a man in a red stocking cap, carried a snare drum that he beat with a stick when anybody interrupted his routine. Startled now, he pounded away.

At the hospital, Maguire found Peach in the dim hallway. She put a finger to her lips. "Every patient in the joint is sleeping now except for your friend Ferndale," she whispered. Peach led Maguire into an empty room and kissed him before he pulled away. He had Honey Rossini after all. Peach's lips tasted like peppermint.

"What did I do to deserve that?" Maguire asked when she finally let him go.

"Nothing at all, it seems," she said with some regret. "You'll have to work for the next one. That is, unless a criminal plugs you first. Red Maguire, how are you still standing?"

"It's the Irish in me, Peach."

"That's always the answer in this town."

"What's your nationality?"

"Don't ask me. I came from Dayton, Ohio. One mill town is the same as another, don't you think? Say, Ferndale's expecting you. That ornery old cop fights to stay awake. He swears he's going back on the job in a day or two. He keeps up this nonsense and he'll be flat on his back for a month. Just like the last time we had him in here all shot up."

Peach led Maguire to Ferndale's room. A uniformed cop sat outside the door. "Maguire," the man said, touching the bill on his hat. "Officer Sullivan," Maguire responded.

Ferndale's sallow face matched the beige walls of the room. His sunken eyes resembled pockets on a billiard table. Bandages swathed his left shoulder from his neck to his elbow. Wires and tubes trailed to a flickering machine in the corner. Ferndale looked bad but Maguire had seen him in worse shape.

"About time," Ferndale managed in a frail voice. "Beats me how I take a bullet every time you stir up trouble in the *Bugle*. Care to tell me how she goes?"

"Pretend you don't know me next time."

"Damn near bled to death. You know that? Two quarts low and change. Peach showed me the *Extra* you wrote, Maguire. Anybody say you made it up? Reads like fiction you dream up but I ain't got cause to say different. Turns out I blacked out half of what went on. Damn shame about the waitress. The round she took was meant for me. I saw that idiot Cracker shoot her. I go blank after that."

"You saved me and yourself, Duke. Maybe other people in the diner, too. The chief told me Gibbons had another loaded gun stashed in his coat. He got off three shots before you took him down. The first hit Simone, one hit you, and the third tore through the booth beside my ear. You put Cracker out of his misery with two slugs."

"Yeah, I read all that in your story. Surprised you remembered the details. People get jumpy in shootouts. Tend to fire every which way. Recall that bar shooting in McQueen what, five, six years ago? Perp has a bad day with the old lady, goes crazy over a spilled beer, whips out a piece and tries to plug the bartender."

Maguire finished the story. "And hit four other people instead. One fatal."

You read literature, Maguire?"

"I'll admit to it if you will."

"Then you know all about conflict between good and evil. Seems the world doesn't go around without a little of both. Or a lot. Take your pick."

"I figured you for reading dime novels over lager at the M & M."

"Then you ain't got a clue. I read enough of them big-shot books to know good versus evil ain't an isolated incident here in Butte. Yep, even me, a flatfoot on the beat. Now I ain't an educated man, as you well know, but listen, Maguire. I read a book by Hemingway, that one about the old guy in the boat fighting the big fish and neither gives up. Ain't that what goes on here in Butte? Me and you pulling one way, criminals pulling the other? Get my meaning?"

"You sound like a wise old man for once, Duke."

"Being all shot up gives me time to think I actually know something, Maguire. What's your next move?"

Maguire told Ferndale about the fight with the mug outside the Logan and his plan to leave on the early train for Chicago. As Maguire talked, Ferndale reached for his shoulder and grimaced. Red circles appeared on the bandage.

"Close the door, will you? I got something to say." After Maguire swung it shut, Ferndale spoke in barely a whisper. "They want the girl more than they want you right now. They figure if they kidnap Miss Rossini, they shut down what you're telling about them in the *Bugle*. Maybe even force you into writing love notes about the union that they paid Ketchul to deliver. The FBI man and the Chicago cops told me how these rackets go. After they get payoffs flowing, they squeeze anybody who stands in their way. By squeeze I mean measuring for a burial suit. That would be you and me at the top of the list. After they get control of the *Bugle* and the cops, they elect their own to run city government. Imagine Rusie Dregovich as mayor. That's where this thing is going."

Maguire leaned close to Ferndale to keep his words from Officer Michael outside the door. "You've got dirty cops?"

"Suspicions but no proof. Somebody in the clubhouse used radio dispatch to pull my cop off Miss Rossini's house. I find out who, lights out for that chump. You can watch if you want. Make a hell of a story in my book."

"Deal, Duke. Count me in. If my newspaper survives these hoodlums, that is."

Ferndale shook his head. "No, not that. Shutting the *Bugle* ain't what they want. In that case they would shoot Stoffleman dead instead of sending a few mine boys to beat him senseless. They want to use your rag to tell people Butte ain't a bad place after all. Forget the Company paper up the street that don't print a hint of controversy. That ain't the one exposing their crimes. The mob knows you got in deep with Irene Rossini. Hell, everyone knows that by now. Maguire and Rossini, you two ought to buy a billboard on the highway to Pipestone Pass. Put your kissy faces right out in public. Get her out of Butte, Maguire, but Chicago? Those mugs in cheap suits have better aim in their own backyard."

"Honey has a cousin there, Duke. What better place than under their noses?"

"You got guts, I give you that." Ferndale held out his left hand for a shake. "Hope to see you again, Maguire."

~ 23 ~

'She's in peril'

The temperature fell below zero, an hour before dawn, when Maguire stashed his Pontiac in an alley a few blocks from the Windsor. Nobody moved in the streets except for a panel truck with the words *Butte Bugle* painted on the side. The driver pitched bundles of newspapers onto the sidewalks. Soon, newsboys would arrive with jack knives to cut the twine and begin their deliveries.

Buddy, from the back door, watched Maguire approach the Windsor under a streetlight. Maguire found Honey bundled and waiting for him in Maggie O'Keefe's office. Worry clouded Honey's movie star face. Maggie stood behind Honey, gripping her shoulders.

"Take the back streets and watch for a tail," Maggie told Buddy, who nodded. He loomed big as a gorilla. Maguire wondered, briefly, if Buddy could take Rusie Dregovich in a fight.

Honey turned and hugged Maggie. "You're one of the most decent people I've ever met, Maggie. I'm sorry for ever judging you."

"In the end, none of us are all that different," Maggie said, embracing her.

Buddy drove them to the train station in an ancient black touring car he pulled out of a ramshackle garage behind the Windsor. He stood at the door of the depot, watching for trouble, until they boarded the eastbound train and left. His hulking form waved to them from the platform. Then they were gone, headed for a long climb over the Continental Divide.

Honey attempted humor. "Red, this isn't how I imagined our first date."

"I thought we had a first date for steak dinner at the Rocky Mountain Cafe on Christmas Day. That's how I saw it, anyway. We had another first date the night the mug put a bullet in my fender."

"I prefer first dates where the man hasn't been shot at. Then again, Red Maguire, you've added zest to my life."

Honey nestled beside him in the coach and fell asleep. She felt warm against him. Men stared at her when they passed in the aisle. "Take a good look at a real Butte woman," Maguire told one gawker, a slender bespectacled man with a white handkerchief sprouting from the pocket of his oversized suit coat. As the train crested the Divide and gained speed on the downhill tracks, a pink rim of light appeared on the horizon, soon changing to golden rays that stabbed through the windows. Maguire closed his eyes as the train rumbled and swayed. He lost track of when he had last slept.

Sometime in the afternoon, Maguire awoke, but only for a few seconds. Fatigue pulled him back into a dark canyon. He kept falling, losing his grip on sharp rock, surrendering to the lure of gravity. The canyon became a mine shaft. Bells rang as the chippy hoist plummeted past familiar angry faces. Cracker Gibbons. Rusie Dregovich. Men staring through eye holes in masks. Men in dark fedoras flashing bursts of orange from unseen guns. Anguished ghostly faces of his stricken colleagues Ted Ketchul, Antonio Vanzetti, Mary Miller aka Nancy Addleston. Sounds too. Ted's wife howling her grief at hearing of his suicide. A bullet smacking into Simone. The faint voice of Lily, his mother, calling his name. Deep in the dark, an *Associated Press* teletype machine, chattering a river of yellow paper full of news. Maguire on his knees, hearing Dregovich hammer rock, crawling in dirt while trying to cover his ears.

He snapped awake, unsure of his surroundings. Daylight filled the train coach. People all around him looked different than the passengers who occupied those seats before he fell asleep.

"Bad dreams, young man?" an old woman across the aisle inquired. A flowered scarf encased her tiny head. Purple glasses with a drooping neck chain reminded Maguire of a stern librarian at his elementary school in Chicago. The woman knitted furiously, pulling yellow strands of yarn from a bundle in her lap. "You were yelling in your sleep. You said something about falling down a hole."

Maguire ran a hand over his face. "Where are we?"

"Yes, I suppose you slept through most of the station stops. We crossed into North Dakota headed for Bismarck. I boarded in Billings myself. Going to see my granddaughter in St. Paul. She has a new baby girl. You didn't figure me for being a great grandmother, now did you, young man? Now let me ask..."

"The woman next to me!" Maguire cried out. "Where is she? Tall, wearing a red coat?"

The old woman stared back. "She sounds lovely, young man, but I think you're still dreaming. All alone over there since I came aboard this train. Anybody you know?"

Maguire jumped out of his seat. Except for Honey's purse, no trace remained of her. "Are you sure?" he demanded of the woman.

"Completely," she said with some indignation.

Maguire shoved Honey's purse into his coat pocket. His face hard as granite, his eyes probing every space, he rushed through the coaches and the dining car to the front of the train. No Honey. He tore back the other way until he reached the sleeper cars where he found a porter making a bed. "Ain't no woman like you describe back here," the man said, smoothing folds on a white sheet with hands brown as baked beans. "Go find the conductor, sir. He knows these things. Look for dat man in the black uniform who' walks all over this here train. He about somewhere, sure as rain."

Maguire nodded his thanks and returned to the coaches. He inspected every face as he worked his way down the aisle. No Honey Rossini among them. As he crossed the bridge between two coaches, he met the conductor coming the other way. Wind pouring through cracks in the shaking floor ruffled the man's graying handlebar mustache.

"I remember your woman," the conductor shouted over the clacking of wheels beneath them. "She left the train with two men in Montana. Not sure which stop exactly. Billings, maybe. One of our busier stations and too many passengers come and go. The woman in the red coat, well, what a beauty. Hard to forget. Something else, too, if it matters. She didn't seem none too happy in the company of those fellows."

Maguire heard himself yelling. "Why, if they hurt her, I'll..."

The conductor quickly comprehended. "Is this a law enforcement matter, sonny?"

"They kidnapped her!" Maguire burst out.

"We've got telegraph in the baggage car," the conductor yelled over the noise. He motioned for Maguire to follow. They walked through two sleeper cars to the train's last car, where a clerk worked at a wooden desk under a swaying yellow lamp. Surrounding him were stacks of brown Samsonites and gray canvas mail bags. "Tell me who you are, son?" the conductor inquired of Maguire.

"I'm Red Maguire, a newsman traveling to Chicago to investigate crimes being committed in Butte. I was escorting the woman in red, Irene Rossini, to a relative's home for safekeeping."

"You have a personal relationship with her?" the conductor asked, his eyes betraying envy.

"That's why those men took her," Maguire said, feeling more rattled than he could remember. "It's complicated, but trust me, she's in peril."

The conductor turned to the curious man at the telegraph table. "Frank, send whatever telegrams necessary to help Mr. Maguire. If someone committed a crime on the train, and by Mr. Maguire's judgment we have that very situation, we need to inform Northern Pacific. Take care of Mr. Maguire first. I'll compose a message for our bosses that we'll send afterwards."

Maguire grabbed onto a steel post as the train rocked violently on the tracks. Several suitcases tumbled onto the floor. "You get used to it, riding the rails like we do," said the conductor, who barely flinched. "Another thing, Mr. Maguire. We arrive in Bismarck in an hour. The depot has a public telephone."

The conductor rested a fatherly hand on Maguire's broad shoulder before retreating through the stacks of freight and personal belongings to the coaches rolling in front of them. Frank handed Maguire a pad of lined paper. Maguire quickly jotted a message. "To Clyde Stoffleman *Butte Bugle* stop. Companion kidnapped from train stop. Possibly Billings by two men stop. Wearing red coat stop. Please contact Chief Morse stop. Need urgent APB stop. Maguire stop."

Frank took the message without showing any reaction. He began tapping a series of dots and dashes on the telegraph key. Maguire pictured his message being received in Butte. The keys clicked again, this time on their own. "That's confirmation of receipt from Butte. I marked your message for critical delivery," the clerk said. "You can bet your man will have it within the half hour."

"The miracles of telegraph," Maguire muttered.

"Isn't that so? Someday, telephones on trains? Now wouldn't that be some invention?"

Maguire thanked Frank and returned to his seat. Without Honey, the train felt forlorn and captive. He checked his watch. The men who seized her had several hours' head start. It took no imagination to figure they were Accardo's men. Maguire felt rage. He would have plugged them with all six bullets in his .38. Three for each man.

As the North Coast Limited rolled to a stop in Bismarck, the conductor happened by. "Frozen brakes, Mr. Maguire. Figure on an hour's stop at least. You'll find the pay phone inside the station." Maguire scrambled off. Frigid air took his breath away. Men in coveralls carried heavy tools through great clouds of steam and exhaust as the train rumbled outside the depot.

Maguire found an empty phone booth. He closed the folding glass door against the hubbub in the depot and dialed the operator. "Placing an emergency call, collect to Butte, Montana," he told the woman who answered. The call clicked through three exchanges, one female operator handing off to another each time, until Luverne answered at the *Bugle* switchboard. "Red? What's wrong, honey?" she inquired after accepting the charges.

"Sweet Luverne, please get Stoffleman on the line and hurry. It's urgent."

"Right away, dear," Luverne responded.

Stoffleman picked up on the first ring. "Morse is all over it," the editor said without waiting to hear Maguire's voice. "Butte cops, Highway Patrol, police departments in Billings and everywhere else where these mugs might hide her. I talked to Ferndale. He got so worked up they had to tie him into the hospital bed. He said to tell you his aim is as good with his right hand as his left. Let's hope Miss Rossini doesn't change out of that red coat."

"I never should have taken her along," Maguire said.

"What happened, anyway? Give it to me straight."

"She was sleeping. Then I fell asleep. When I woke up she was gone. Maybe she went to the dome car or dining car when they grabbed her. I could have protected her if I hadn't nodded off."

"Given all that's happened it surprises me that you could stay awake at all, Red."

"I'm coming back, boss. I've got a loaded gun that says they better not harm her."

"I admire your bravado, but no. Think straight, will you? You have a job to do. You go gallivanting around Montana like a vigilante with a gun and a grudge they get what they want. Your voice in the *Bugle* goes silent. If you go off half-cocked, and they catch you, what then? Let the cops do their jobs. You do yours. Get to Chicago and find the damning evidence that links Dregovich to the mob."

"But we're talking about Honey Rossini, boss. Lately the woman of my dreams. I'm in love with her."

"So give her an engagement ring when the cops find her safe. You've got another, what, day on the train? Call me from Chicago. This is your moment, Maguire. Don't foul it up."

Maguire climbed back onto the warm train. Never in his life had he felt so low. Not even when Mary, or Nancy, plugged herself. Stoffleman was right. Maguire compromised himself as a news reporter when he fell for Honey Rossini. He was in the sunset of his thirties. He thought of Simone, her apparently loveless life bleeding to a cold death on a tile floor. He thought of the ever-beckoning Peach, what a doll. He thought of the striking Mary Miller, a blond charade who led him astray. As the train pulled away from Bismarck, Maguire reached inside his suit for the bundle of love notes. By now they were worn and crumpled. He pulled out the note he had received from Honey that first day he saw her at the Silver Star. "I wish to attend to a matter that's come to my attention," she had written in looping precision.

The train arrived in Chicago late that night. Passengers swarmed trains at Union Station. Frenzied adults, yawning children, piles of baggage everywhere. Beat cops in blue, nightsticks in hand, wandered through the crowd. The big clock, framed with gargoyles, showed six minutes to midnight. Maguire slipped into a bank of phone booths to call Stoffleman. After business hours, when Luverne hung up her headset and shut down the switchboard, she routed calls to the city room. Stoffleman sounded relieved when he heard Maguire's voice.

"I hoped they hadn't grabbed you, too."

"Let them try. I'm in no mood," Maguire said, feeling inside his coat for the gun.

"The cops haven't spotted Miss Rossini. I will lay money that the men who abducted her figured you would follow. I don't pretend to know what's on their minds."

"They could have saved time by shooting me on the train while I slept."

Maguire heard Stoffleman exhale. "Makes too much sense, doesn't it? Those mobsters apparently figure you are better off in their pockets than dead. That said, watch your back in Chicago. Let me say again that I've had my fill of burying *Bugle* reporters. Fair warning."

Hardly remembering anything about the city where he started his life, Maguire walked to a dump of a hotel on West Randolph Street. A dame in a torn pink dress and a man in a soiled gray suit made out on a ripped sofa in the lobby. She sat on his lap as he murmured to her drunkenly. Maguire watched the woman slip a hand inside the man's coat to steal his wallet. Maguire paid five bucks for a room that at least had clean bedding. He thought of Honey all night and hardly slept. Somewhere outside his window a gun belched two shots. Sirens wailed on the busy streets. Night noises in Chicago. Butte's no better, he thought.

In the morning he took a cab to the *Tribune* tower on North Michigan Avenue. "World's Greatest Newspaper," a banner in the lobby proclaimed. He took the stairs to the sprawling city room. A clerk at the counter went to find Will James. Maguire waited as she disappeared into a sea of desks full of editors and reporters. She returned a few minutes later with an older man who had a complexion the shade of old steel. James held out his hand. "I figured you would show up sooner or later, Mr. Maguire."

"I had no idea the *Tribune* was this big," Maguire said.

"The mission of journalism is the same no matter the size of the paper, wouldn't you agree?"

"That's the way I see it," Maguire said.

James led him past rows of newsmen and an occasional newswoman, many of them interviewing sources on the phone, to a stack of boxes far back in the city room. Unlike Maguire, James was slender and short, hunched but alert. His skeptical scowl came from years of police reporting, Maguire knew, as did his distaste for small talk. James got right to it.

"When we talked on the phone a few weeks ago I told you I was looking into evidence of Accardo infiltrating labor unions outside Chicago. I grabbed every document I could find. These are investigative records the cops seized in raids and so on. None of them came easy. Cops refuse to cough them up through official channels. I've got my sources on the inside as I'm sure you've got yours in Butte. You know how it goes."

"I know how she goes," Maguire said.

Maguire stared at the cardboard boxes full of paper. He counted fourteen. "What are your plans for this collection of lifetime reading?"

James cracked a smile. The *Tribune* reporter reminded Maguire of Stoffleman. Tough and resilient. "Eventually I'll write a series of stories exposing this latest crime and corruption. You ever see that movie, *The City That Never Sleeps*, that came out a few years ago? When I go to print with these stories, picture me as Johnny Kelly in that movie. Most eventful time in my career and you know what? I'll wish I had quit the newspaper business when I had a chance."

"I have similar thoughts but without wise guys like us who would report the news?" Maguire said.

"That's what haunts me night and day. So here you go. I read but a bit of this jumble. If you find proof of Accardo's connections in Butte, the story is yours to break. In return I want to use whatever you uncover when I write my own stories. Fair enough?"

"More than," Maguire said. James pointed to the whereabouts of his desk and walked away. Maguire threw his overcoat over a chair, laid his suit jacket on top, and rolled up the sleeves on his white shirt. Clattering typewriters and insistent voices interviewing on the telephone echoed in the long room. Maguire pulled a handful of papers from a box. He read police reports, private letters, even notes from the Accardo organization. Hours went by and soon it was lunchtime. He had found no mention of Butte. He bought a ham on rye sandwich from the cafeteria downstairs before tearing into more boxes. Later that afternoon, he found a sheet of numbers torn from a ledger. On the third row from the top, beside an entry that said "$5,000 weekly," was the name Rusie Dregovich.

~ 24 ~

'Where's the girl?'

Maguire called Stoffleman with the news. Conscious of long-distance toll charges, Stoffleman unleashed a string of comments over the telephone lines. "Is he raising that sum for Accardo? Or is that the sum he earns from Accardo for stealing from our city? Keep digging, boy. You're on the right track for sure. Nothing new on Miss Rossini but the chief stopped by an hour ago to tell me, confidentially, that the cops will tail Dregovich until they catch him making a wrong move. Ferndale left the hospital against his doctor's orders. Doubtful if he can shoot straight. He told me he'll be damned to miss the action. Pass along my thanks to that Chicago reporter."

James left for home at mid-evening. Maguire worked into the night. The *Tribune* city room fell mostly silent except for a couple dozen smoking and wheezing editors seated around an oval table where they wrote headlines. Two or three disheveled late-night crime reporters came and went. It was close to midnight when Maguire, feeling discouraged at finding nothing else linking Dregovich to the mob, hailed a cab to return him to his hotel. The cabbie's name was Al. "New in town, ya?" he inquired from the front seat. His curled ears, silhouetted against oncoming headlights, stuck straight out.

"Back for a visit but I'm a Chicago original," Maguire replied, hoping for a conversation.

Masks, Mayhem and Murder

"No kidding," the cabbie said, barely interested. He suddenly steered the cab onto a dark street. The tires whined.

"This isn't the way, bub. I'm in no mood for tricks," Maguire told him. He looked closer at the burly driver. The man wore a gray fedora and a heavy overcoat. He didn't resemble a cabbie at all.

The man's big ears twitched. He said nothing but leaned on the gas pedal. The cab raced past strip joints and third-rate beer joints. Maguire pulled the .38 out of his pocket. He pressed the tip of the barrel against the man's thick neck. "Stop now or I'll shoot and if you think I'm fooling it's your last mistake," Maguire hissed at him. For emphasis, he pulled the hammer back with a metallic click.

The cab slowed to the curb. "You make a poor impression of a cab driver, bud. Your name is Al like my name is James Dean," Maguire said. "Quit fooling. Stick your right hand to the dashboard and leave it there. Hand me the keys with your left like you've got a lick of common sense."

Wordlessly, the driver reached behind him with the keys. Maguire pushed the gun harder against the man's head. "Now the piece, Mickey Mouse, left hand again." The man drew a heavy pistol from his coat. Maguire grabbed it from him.

"Boss man ain't gonna like this, Maguire." The man spoke in a heavy Italian accent.

"So you know my name," Maguire replied. "Then you're one of Accardo's boys."

The man greeted that comment with stony silence.

"Where's the girl? Or you're an errand boy Accardo doesn't trust with information like that?"

The silence continued.

"Get out!" Maguire commanded. He slipped out the back door of the cab. The mobster eased reluctantly from behind the wheel. He was about Maguire's size but had a colorless

247

face resembling lumpy mashed potatoes. He was a night worker, all right, paid to break bones in the dark. "Back here!" Maguire commanded again. He opened the trunk. The man obeyed until he reached the back of the car. Just as Maguire expected, the man braced and swung a vicious hook. Maguire blocked the blow, taking a clip on the top of his head, before pivoting his hips to launch an uppercut to the man's ribs as Ferndale had taught him to do. The mug grunted in pain. "This is how we do it in Butte," Maguire said, swinging the butt of his .38 square into the man's face, knocking him cold. The mobster fell backwards into slush in the gutter.

Two bums emerged from the shadows. They rolled the man out of his coat and took his watch and wallet. "Don't forget his fancy shoes," Maguire told them. "I planned to take this mug for a ride but there's no point now. Help yourselves."

Maguire drove the cab to within a block of his hotel on Randolph and killed the engine. He locked the doors and side-armed the keys onto a two-story building with bars on the windows. He saw no suspicious cars lurking on the street. Upstairs in the hotel, he gathered his satchel, dropped his room key at the front desk, and walked six blocks before hailing another cab. He looked the driver over good before climbing inside. "To the *Chicago Tribune*," Maguire said. Once there he talked the night guard into admitting him into the dark city room. The presses had rolled to print the morning paper. All the night editors had left. Maguire switched on a light over the stack of boxes at the back of the city room. He pulled out a handful of paper and began reading.

Will James arrived soon after the sun came up. He found Maguire sleeping and shook him awake. Maguire told James about the cabbie incident.

"Good thing you had a piece on you," James said. "A few miles farther in that cab and that mug would have delivered you to a welcoming party of his associates."

"Look at this," Maguire said, suddenly aware he had fallen asleep clutching a legal filing. He handed it to James.

"You found a magic bullet in this criminal indictment?"

"Appears so."

James whistled as he read. "You sure did. Rusie Dregovich, mentioned right here as an accomplice in the Accardo organization's labor racketeering operation. I can't believe this filing escaped my attention."

"Well, you collected a lot of paper here, Will." Maguire stretched and yawned. "That's not all I found. An exhibit was attached to that indictment. It's a handwritten letter from Dregovich to some Accardo lieutenant named Petey the Gun Moretti."

"I know Petey," James interrupted. "He carries weight. I interviewed him a time or two. You want to be careful around that guy. The word in this town is that Petey orders hits like most people order an ice cream cone. Not the showy type who runs around with dumb blondes and five-dollar Cuban cigars. Petey operates with precision. Deadly precision. So what does the letter say?"

Maguire squinted the fatigue from his eyes. "Dregovich calls himself the Milk Man."

"How quaint," James said.

"What I get from his tortured prose is that he milks money out of Butte in hopes for a promotion, so to speak, in the Accardo mob. I'm no expert, but does a Serb have a chance in an Italian outfit?"

"About as much as you and me," James said.

"So what's his angle?"

"The Accardo boys will play Dregovich as long as he delivers. He could become king of Butte for all they care.

They want to bleed the cash. They probably give him, say, ten percent of what he brings in. They want five grand a week, he gets five hundred of it. You can bet none of the miners who do his bidding will see a penny of it. Easy money at first. The Milk Man will think they made him rich. The problem for him is, as you say in your stories, is that the mob will want more. The five grand becomes six, then seven, then they pinch him hard. So Dregovich and his boys scare a family hardware store into paying a hundred bucks a week for so-called protection. It seems too easy at first. Accardo sends a few foot soldiers from Chicago to work as bagmen and a few others to stalk you. Their presence throws fear into people all right. Nobody wants gangsters roaming their town. But the success of this racketeering depends on Dregovich. As long as he stays in the picture, it's a local operation. When the mob tells him to squeeze more money out of your city, he becomes desperate, more willing to kill to get what he wants. The mob will stuff him full of lies about how he's earning his stripes for a larger role in the organization. I can tell you, as a Chicago newsman who's covered the mob for thirty years, your Milk Man doesn't have a prayer for promotion. The mob only wants him to think so. Accardo has no interest in dirtying his hands in Butte as long as Dregovich does his bidding."

Maguire brushed a hand through his thick hair. "And if the cops take down the Milk Man?"

"If they do it soon, Maguire, they might chase Accardo away. The longer this trouble goes on, the more perilous it becomes, especially if Dregovich finds new sources of cash to send to Chicago. If the mobsters get some big money flowing, let's say they take over companies that run the mines, you can bet Accardo brings more than a few second-rate shooters to Butte. Now, for the Milk Man. If he fails, Accardo might well try to recruit a successor. Sure, Dregovich lacks sophistication. The mob could care less. What Accardo wants is a ruthless bully who bosses those miners with an iron tongue. If the Milk Man goes down the mob will find someone else with similar credentials."

Maguire stood and stretched. "Now that I've found proof of Dregovich's involvement, I'm headed back to Butte. Too bad it's not ethical to quote another newsman in the story I'm going to write. You know better than anybody how the puzzle pieces fit together."

"With one exception," James said, his gray eyes revealing a surprise. "You can't quote this man by name, Maguire, but you can take his testimony to the bank. He's a silent source of mine, a man close to the Accardo organization. You game?"

"Show the way," Maguire said.

They met at noon in an empty warehouse near the wharf. The wind was up as usual, sweeping sleet off Lake Michigan, while the cavernous old building creaked and groaned. Maguire shrugged deeper in his overcoat. He had forgotten the windblown chill of Chicago winters.

The source's mob name was Jimmy the Jowls. Flabby cheeks hung from a swollen red face that screamed high blood pressure and heavy drinking. Maguire looked him over. Blubbery, wide as he was tall, raspberry jelly poured into a worn suit that strained at the seams. Jimmy's eyes darted back and forth for no good reason Maguire could tell.

James had assured Maguire that outrage was Jimmy's only reason for telling secrets to newsmen. Not being a made man, a fully initiated member of the Accardo outfit, despite his years of service. Jimmy lived in fear that one of his associates would bump him off because he lacked sponsorship from a controlling member.

James nodded at Maguire, who explained the Butte situation to Jimmy as concisely as he could. Their breath rose in vaporous clouds. "So I'm wondering if you've heard of this man Dregovich?" Maguire asked.

Jimmy stared back through eyes swimming in his fat face. "I know the man. Big as Paul Bunyan ain't he? Got a mouth on him too. I seen him here in Chicago a year ago. Some of our boys brung him to lay out details for Butte. Big man but an easy score. He seen himself as owning your town. Throws weight with the wrong men. Don't know dirt."

Maguire scribbled furiously in his notebook to keep up.

"Hey!" Jimmy barked to James. "Our deal is no name."

Maguire raised his pencil. "That's our deal, no name, confirmed. I write down what you say to make sure I don't forget any of it."

Jimmy nodded his appreciation. "So this Milk Man ain't a wop, right? I got no love for bringing him or any other loser into the organization. He might be big enough to break fingers but he ain't a wop. Let's say I heard some talk about this place Butte. The Milk Man, he don't want nobody back home to know he's dealin' with Accardo. Talks about rights of working men in the mines. Them boys of ours, they tell him to shut his mouth and spit out the pork. They don't want no drama."

"Pork?" Maguire interrupted.

"Jingle. Money," Jimmy said, his jowls shaking. "Milk Man don't spit out the pork, he be hollerin' like a stuck pig."

James spoke up. "How do you know for sure, Jimmy?"

"Because Petey the Gun was in that meeting. Petey ain't there for window dressing, if'n you know what I mean."

"What worries you about all this?" Maguire asked.

"Ain't right to run rackets in some two-bit mining town three states away when we got prospects right here in Chicago. I got ideas. Big ones. This ain't it."

Maguire shook Jimmy the Jowl's fleshy mitt and rode with James back to the *Tribune*. "I can trust this man?" Maguire asked.

"As I said before, Maguire, he's dirty but he's never done me wrong. Jimmy's no climber but he's an insider and he's connected. Sure, he wants news coverage to turn his way and sometimes it does. Keep his name out of your story. I need silent sources like Jimmy and others like him to do this job. I'm echoing your own work, I presume?"

"To the letter," Maguire replied.

"Remember, you have a war over control of your city," James said. "Someone will win. Someone will lose. The question is, who?"

Maguire called Stoffleman from the *Tribune* city room. "Head back now," the editor commanded. "The Old Man said to forget riding the train. He'll spring for an airplane."

"I don't know, boss. Never been on a plane. I don't like the idea of being high off the ground."

"Life is full of miracles, Maguire."

***

The plane landed in Butte after circling the mountains three times to find an opening in a storm cloud. When he dared to look, Maguire saw the famous mining district's jagged and torn landscape from the air for the first time. He also noticed how the widening new Berkeley Pit threatened to consume neighborhoods. It had the appearance of a mouth opening for a scream.

Stoffleman waited for him at the airport. "I thought for sure the *Tribune* would hire you away, Maguire."

"I'm not ready for the big city. Too many killers running loose here."

"True, that," Stoffleman said, leading Maguire to a faded yellow Nash Rambler with a luggage rack on the roof. "Like my car? Bought it new in '50. Turned thirty thousand miles on the odometer this winter."

"Ever leave town, boss?"

"Not much point, is there? Not when we work for a daily newspaper. I told you that when I hired you, or did you forget?"

"I remember. Married to the job. You gave me little reason to forget."

"Splendid, Maguire. Now, get serious." Stoffleman glanced at his wristwatch. "Too late in the day to print another *Extra*. Load up the morning *Bugle* with every scrap of news you can find. Call the chief and the FBI as well. Ah, hell. You know the drill. I forget sometimes how long it's been since you were a dumb kid from Dublin Gulch."

"If you hadn't taken a chance on me to write those weekend police reports, I would be a dumb grown man sleeping up there in an old board shack coughing up my work underground, boss."

"You caught on how it works at the *Bugle*, Maguire. Back to that big story you will write for me. So you found the criminal indictment that names Rusie Dregovich. Why didn't the cops find it first?"

"Because it was right under their noses."

"I hope they appreciate you solving this case. They'll get the drift soon enough when they read the *Bugle* tomorrow."

"Know what bothers me, boss? If Dregovich is the Milk Man, he delivers. Isn't that what a milk man does? Who supplies the milk?"

"He probably thought the nickname fit him, Maguire. What are you driving at?"

Maguire turned on the seat to face Stoffleman. "Is he alone in this? The brain as well as the muscle? I never took the brute for a deep thinker, boss. Maybe someone else tells him what to do. Someone besides the mob."

"Another of your wild notions, Maguire, or do you have a name in mind?"

"Gut feeling is all, boss. I'm no detective."

Stoffleman shook his head. "In my book you're the best detective in this city. Even Ferndale and Chief Morse might agree. All the dirty looks thrown your way would seem to confirm it."

As Stoffleman steered down Broadway Street to the narrow Hirbour Block, its eight stories rising sharply above connecting buildings, Maguire nodded off. He had been wide awake since Honey disappeared off the train. Fatigue draped his brain like a warm blanket. Stoffleman slapped him hard on the shoulder.

"Stay awake, boy. I need you in full command of your faculties. I have some high-octane coffee brewing in the city room that will have you alert in no time."

"If you can pull the spoon out of it first," Maguire said. "I've got to find Honey Rossini, boss."

Stoffleman pulled to a stop outside the *Bugle.* "Write this story, Red. Then go for her. I'm entirely confident you'll find her before the cops do. Another thing, too. The funeral for Simone the waitress is Saturday morning. Ted Ketchul's wife wants a small private service, family only."

Maguire found a welcoming party in the city room. Morgan, Claggett and Davis offered their hands for a shake. An air of nervous anticipation hung over the room. Everyone knew Maguire was about to blow the lid off the Halloween Mask Robberies. The crime that embraced Butte was now much more than what that name implied, but it stuck. They also knew about Honey's abduction from the train. Maguire, the fool, was in love again.

His front-page story the next morning left no doubt about Dregovich:

By Red Maguire
Bugle Crime Reporter

"Butte's most powerful union leader, Rusie Dregovich, is named in an investigation linking him to notorious Chicago gangsters.

"Law enforcement records show Dregovich funneling as much as $5,000 a month, stolen from Butte business owners, to the Tony Accardo organization. A mob source close to the transactions witnessed Dregovich, in Chicago, making the deal. He calls himself "Milk Man," according to legal documents.

"Butte police and the FBI issued an arrest warrant last night for Dregovich, who commands Local 1235, the largest and most influential union on Butte Hill. Dregovich hasn't been seen at his Centerville house or the Anselmo mine for two days and remains at large, said Chief Donald Morse.

"Also missing is Irene Rossini, a prominent Butte jewelry store owner and socialite. Two unidentified men kidnapped her from an eastbound train.

"For weeks, thugs and misfits scared Butte business owners with beatings, robberies and threats from behind an assortment of children's Halloween masks. The wave of crime also led to a recent shooting in the uptown Silver Star cafe. Waitress Simone Andrews died as did her assailant, Mack "Cracker" Gibbons."

That morning, Maguire missed the sensation that rippled through Butte after the *Bugle* hit doorsteps and newspaper racks. He was deep in sleep in his room at the Logan Hotel when an urgent knock came at his door. He pulled his gun. Creeping cautiously in his bare feet, he yanked the door open to find Ferndale with his arm in a sling.

"I hope that piece is loaded, Maguire. I ain't much good with a gun at the moment. I think I know where Dregovich is holed up. He might have Irene Rossini. You game?"

"Soon as I pull on my pants, detective."

~ 25 ~

'What crime, Maguire?'

As Ferndale shuffled impatiently in the hallway, Maguire
threw on his clothes, pulled on his boots over a pair of wool
socks and dropped a handful of extra bullets in his pocket.
Nobody caught short in a gun battle lived to brag about it.

"You owe me one, Maguire," Ferndale said when they
scooted into his idling car.

"How's that? You should be flat in the hospital admiring
the back end of Peach on midnight rounds."

"Already done that. Got me nowhere."

"You don't look so good, Duke."

"I can steer the car, can't I?"

"Barely. Want me to drive?"

Ferndale pulled his sedan to the curb, nearly jumping it.
He moved over to make room for Maguire to slide behind the
wheel. "What I gotta say," Ferndale continued, "is that I'm
breaking the rules by knowing you might get yourself killed."

"Never stopped you before, did it? And since when do
you give a hoot about department policy? Or me getting
killed?"

"Hell, I don't know. Getting shot up makes a man think
funny."

"No more than usual, I suppose," Maguire said.

"All of Butte's gone crazy. I had to talk down Babe
McGraw last night. To hear her talk she plans to drive to the

Anselmo all by her lonesome and call out any man who did this town harm."

"If she's that riled up the miners might need help."

"That Babe, what a doll," Ferndale droned in a weak faraway voice. "Maguire, I ain't feeling so good." The Oldsmobile, Ferndale's private car, was outfitted with a police radio. He grabbed the mike clipped to his dashboard and asked Betty at police dispatch to advise the hospital. That done, Ferndale, his face drained of color, flopped against the door post. Maguire heard him moan.

"Hold on, Duke, we're almost there. Are you bleeding by any chance?"

"Something warm running down my rib cage," he mumbled. "I ain't no damn help to you at all."

"Tell me where to find Dregovich. I can recruit the FBI and the chief and every cop within fifty miles to go after him. Or, I can go myself."

Ferndale moaned again. His words came in a ragged whisper. "You're a lot of things, Maguire, but don't play cop. Get help. A cornered man is meaner than a junkyard dog. Now listen close before they haul me away. You got Dregovich on the run. I thought hard about where he might hide out. Then it hit me. He went where he could meet up with the gangsters who took Miss Rossini. She's now a hostage for a desperate man. He knows about an abandoned farmhouse near Whitehall. Not far from Highway 12. Before I got shot, I found a report from fifteen years ago. We chased Dregovich toward Pipestone Pass after he stole a car. County cops took over after he crossed the divide. Bear at the wheel. Good thing we never caught him. Pity the man who tried to throw the cuffs on him."

"The location, Duke. Hurry, here they come." Maguire pulled into the emergency entrance and saw the hospital door fly open. Two chubby nurses, rolling a gurney, headed for the car with a purpose suggesting they would take no prisoners. Maguire had a disquieting thought of Babe McGraw in white.

"Address on that old report is 112 Tobacco Root Road. West of Whitehall a few miles. House still standing when I drove to Bozeman a year ago. Two stories tall, covered front porch. That location is a hunch, Maguire, but a cop doesn't get far without thinking like a criminal."

"You told the chief about this house?"

"Naw, the chief thinks Dregovich is hiding in Butte in an abandoned building. He's got Muldoon and Regan and every other mick on the force looking."

"A search like that could take forever in an old mining town," Maguire said.

"Especially with the Irish in charge."

"How would a Scot know?"

The nurses yanked open the car door. Maguire helped them load Ferndale. The cop tottered on the edge of passing out. The drama grew inside. Ferndale's doctor chewed on him as a "fool with a badge" and "lacking enough blood that even Dracula would go away disappointed." Maguire took notes. Calvin Claggett would be interested in the doctor's quotes if Ferndale kicked the bucket. Claggett never missed a chance to dress up a person's obituary with a theatrical description of his final hours.

Maguire drove Ferndale's car back toward uptown Butte. Maguire turned the dial on the police radio to hear crackling dispatches sent to prowl cars. Cops were on the hunt for Dregovich and Honey Rossini all right. He heard the chatter as they searched streets winding around the mines. Maguire knew why Ferndale neglected to mention his suspicions of Dregovich's whereabouts to the chief. Maguire had a personal score to settle. Ferndale wanted to help him do it.

Maguire drove to the Logan Hotel, parked Ferndale's car, and started his Pontiac. He resisted a fleeting thought to notify Chief Morse. Maguire wasn't a cop, after all, but a newsman. He headed south off Butte Hill toward Highway 12 on the Flats. No matter if Dregovich tried to tear him apart. He would save Honey Rossini. He was a reporter in love.

The Pontiac roared between huge snowdrifts at the top of Pipestone Pass. As Maguire descended toward Whitehall, he thought about the mobsters who kidnapped Honey off the train. They would be handy with guns. With the gig up, they would shoot to kill. That is, unless they had abandoned Dregovich, the Milk Man, and headed back to Chicago. He was a marked man after all.

The farmhouse was easy to spot. Maguire found it a half-mile from the highway. Maguire saw a wisp of smoke rising from a chimney. He turned off the highway onto a snow-packed country road. He parked behind a grove of naked and gnarled cottonwood trees. His .38 and the extra bullets stretched his pocket. The air felt heavy, full of foreboding. Maguire suddenly wished Ferndale, veteran cop, was with him. Killing a man, even the Milk Man, meant blood on Maguire's hands. A trial would follow. Stoffleman might fire him. Maguire hated to die, too. Pulling a trigger meant taking a life. Or, in Honey's case, saving one.

Dark clouds blew over the Continental Divide. Snow swirled around Maguire as he raised his collar to the wind and began trudging through drifts. He pushed his cold hands deep into the pockets of his overcoat. He gripped his gun the way a child held onto hard candy.

Maguire crept as close as he dared. A lantern illuminated a large room. He saw a shadow cross the cracked window. When it moved, he ducked behind a tree. Rusie Dregovich appeared at the glass. The giant filled the window frame. He looked to the highway in the distance. When Dregovich turned away, Maguire hurried to the side of the sagging house. He slipped under the window just as Dregovich swiveled to look outside again. He must expect company, Maguire thought.

Maguire struggled with what do next. Taking Dregovich by force would require four men. Then it dawned on him. He was Red Maguire, *Bugle* crime reporter. There was always one more big story for tomorrow's *Bugle*. Stoffleman would be proud.

Maguire stood and walked to the front door. His snow boots clomped on the old wood steps of the porch. He knocked with his left hand as his right gripped the revolver in his pocket. Something fell over inside. "*Bugle* reporter Maguire, here to interview Rusie Dregovich," he shouted.

Dregovich swung the door open wide. Disbelief clouded his face.

"Why you here?" the man roared. He appeared ready to attack. Maguire, a good three inches shorter, stepped back.

Maguire knew Dregovich hadn't read about the morning's *Bugle* story that nailed his connection to Accardo. Abandoned farmhouses had no newspaper delivery. Maguire banked on the man's confusion and desperation to carry his ruse a little further.

"I've come for your side of the story, Mr. Dregovich."

"Maguire, how ya ...?"

"Know where to find you? Good newspaper reporters always have their connections."

Dregovich shifted in the doorway just enough for Maguire to glimpse Honey Rossini standing across the room near a fireplace. She had changed from the fashionable dress she wore on the train. Now she wore laced boots, brown pants, and a man's red-checked wool shirt that hung to her knees. Maguire thought of a lumber camp. Honey had pulled her hair into a loose ponytail. Even a bit disheveled, without lipstick and jewelry, she struck a pose he wouldn't soon forget. Maguire stared. This woman before him, somewhat a stranger, looked as beautiful as the other Honey he knew. Maguire blinked, searching for evidence she was the same Honey, and saw her red coat hanging on the wall.

"Who is it, Rusie?" Honey's sweet voice sounded flat and distant.

"It's that *Bugle* idiot who went sweet on you, Honey."

"Let him inside, will you?" she said in a commanding tone of voice.

It was Maguire's turn for confusion.

Dregovich opened the door wide, turned his back on Maguire, and went to Honey. She put an arm around him.

"Honey?" Maguire heard himself saying.

She spoke to him. "How nice of you to show up, Maguire. Knowing how you butt into everybody's business, being a victim of your intrusions myself, I expected you sooner rather than later. Did you enjoy your train trip to Chicago?"

Maguire felt his face turn to rock. He hoped his eyes didn't betray his true feelings. First Nancy Addleston. Now Honey Rossini. Ferndale had reminded him a million times how he fell for dames with dark secrets. He felt his eyes go wet. Wouldn't that be something, the *Bugle* crime reporter shedding tears in the company of a criminal and the woman who betrayed him?

"Honey?" he asked again. "Why are you here? How are you mixed up in this crime?"

"What crime, Maguire? I think you're dreaming."

"Porky Pig scared you at your store. I was there, remember? Mobsters came to your house. I was there, too. Tell me what this is about."

Honey stared at Maguire for a moment, her dark eyes simmering, before turning her shoulders to the warmth of the fireplace. He caught a quick glimpse of the room. Faded torn curtains and peeling wallpaper suggested it once was a family's parlor.

"Get on with it!" Dregovich growled. Maguire eased his hand off the gun in his pocket and opened his notebook to a blank page. The brute watched him suspiciously.

"Mr. Dregovich, you are clearly misunderstood. Set the story straight, will you? Did you have anything to do with Irene Rossini leaving the train?" Maguire held a pencil, ready to write.

"Ya done asked me questions down in the mine and printed lies," Dregovich spit out, pointing at Maguire with a thick finger.

Maguire squared his shoulders. "Here's your chance to tell me what's what, then."

"She left the train her ownself," the giant grumbled.

"You're saying no?"

"That's what I'm saying, Maguire."

"Did you have anything to do with Ted Ketchul's death?"

"That man Ketchul was weak. He tied the rope around his neck his ownself."

"Did you send Cracker Gibbons to the Silver Star to shoot Detective Ferndale?"

"Don't know nothin' about that."

"Is Local 1235 taking responsibility for the shooting death of Simone at the Silver Star?"

"Who that?"

"The waitress Gibbons shot and killed."

"Ain't got nothing to do with the union."

"Did you send your goons to beat up Clyde Stoffleman?"

"Got no idea what youse talking about, Maguire."

"Did your union boys beat up Babe McGraw?"

"Got no beef with Babe."

"Did you?"

"No."

"Did you send perps in masks to the *Bugle* city room to beat up people, including our obituary reporter?"

"No."

"Who attacked Harry Dalton at his gas station, resulting in his death?"

"Ain't got a clue."

"Did your men rob Rossini's Fine Jewelry with intent to steal from the safe?"

"Where?"

It was Maguire's turn to look smug. "You're cozy with the woman hugging you and you don't know she owns a jewelry store? The classiest one in all of Butte?"

Honey started to speak but Dregovich waved a huge paw to silence her.

"Already done answered youse questions that day in the mine. I run the most powerful union on the hill, maybe in the country, ya think of that? Don't know what juice ya think ya got, *Bugle* boy. I ain't got a thing to do with any of this."

"Then why do you call yourself the Milk Man?"

Dregovich flinched. Maguire saw it. "Well, Milk Man?"

"There ya go telling lies again, Maguire. Ya learn nothing from what happened to your buddy Ketchul?"

Maguire calculated. Dregovich could reach him in two broad strides. He dangled his right hand near the pocket with the gun. "So, Milk Man, if you're not involved in these crimes, why are you hiding out in this abandoned farmhouse with the woman mysteriously abducted from the train?"

Honey turned from the fireplace and took a step forward. "Abducted from the train, Maguire? A good newsman doesn't assume the facts."

Maguire watched her with narrowed eyes. "So you were in this all along, Miss Rossini. I should have known."

She smiled at his understanding. "Are you referring to your many broken hearts, Maguire? You have a sad reputation for letting romance cloud your judgment. Perhaps now you should write a story that leaves no doubt of Rusie's innocence in this matter, a so-called crime that you yourself contrived in the pages of the *Bugle*."

"How tender that you're on a first-name basis with this mobster," Maguire said. "You haven't told me, Milk Man, why you holed up here at the farm. Why not go back to Butte and show your face? Surely, since you are an innocent man with the lovely Miss Rossini on your arm, you should run for mayor. The election's coming up in the fall."

Anger flickered in Dregovich's eyes. Maguire was certain he saw the same signal that proceeded somebody being thrown down a mine shaft. He saw it when Dregovich tossed the stocky Ketchul like a rag doll.

Suddenly Honey's eyes shifted past Maguire to the door behind him. He heard a floorboard creak. A gun barrel pressed against his spine. A stubby man with sagging lips came around in front and hit Maguire hard in the gut. Then he felt a crashing blow from behind.

Maguire awoke in the dark on a cold wood floor. He tried to touch his pounding head. Someone had tied his wrists with electrical wire. It looped behind him, binding his hands tight to his body. Maguire rolled over. His hands and feet ached from the frigid air. His overcoat was missing. So was his gun. He heard men talking in an adjoining room.

"Should have killed the mug, Joey."

"Still can. He ain't nothin'."

Then came Honey's voice. "We need a hostage, don't we? Until we can clear Rusie with the cops and get back to business?"

Their voices dissolved into a murmur. Maguire's brain felt heavy. He drifted in and out. He saw his mother as if she were standing next to him. Lily wore a white top that resembled a sailor's tunic. She beckoned from behind cascading curls, hair red like his. "Mother?" he whispered. She winked and faded away.

So Honey was complicit in the crimes. Honey, who wore a mask of her own, a mask of sincerity that disguised her true intentions. Maguire loved her. Now she would watch him die. He became the fool once again, bending to a pretty face and a whiff of seductive perfume, cheating *Butte Bugle* readers of the truth. Irene Rossini, goddess of glitzy jewelry and *Glamour* covers, groveled with the likes of Dregovich and Accardo. Butte's snow queen was in deep with the mob.

Maguire felt bleeding on his head. His gut ached from the cruel punch. Being tied up in an unheated room in January worried him more. His ears felt warm from frostbite, his fingers numb. Clouds of his breath rose in the shafts of moonlight through a window. He shook violently. Soon he would freeze to death. He knew the end would take its sweet time at coming.

Sometime during the night the door banged open. Maguire thought he saw a ghost looming over him. The ghost seized him by his belt and dragged him to the warmth of the fireplace. A stranger with a mashed nose leaned over him. "He won't last an hour when that fire goes out," the man said. A second stranger, taller, stood away from the lantern light.

Maguire tried to sit up. He heard men laughing. He fainted and fell backwards. Daylight filled the room when he awoke. He was alone. The only sound was of wind whistling around the farmhouse. The fireplace had burned to ash. Maguire felt colder than the night before. He struggled to loosen the wire. The mugs who tied it around him were no amateurs. He looked around for Honey. He listened for her voice. She was gone.

Maguire heard tromping on the front steps. Dregovich and the mugs had come back to kill him. When the door swung open, he saw Duke Ferndale.

~ 26 ~

'Dizzy with a dame'

"You damned fool, Maguire. I told you not to play cop." Ferndale stood over him, holding his gun in his right hand. His left arm remained in the sling.

"Did Peach kiss your ugly mug and discharge you on your merry way?"

"If you're mad about it I'd say yes," Ferndale said as he holstered his gun and untied Maguire with his free hand. "As they were pumping blood into me the chief shows up. I ask him if he heard from Maguire. He says no. I knew right then you went rogue on us. I had to admit to the chief that I had a notion where you went. He wanted to know why I told you about this location and not him. Ain't never seen the chief that mad. Probably lose my badge over this. What the hell, I'm a tired old man."

Three other men wearing badges clamored into the room. One wore a blue Butte uniform. The other two, young Jefferson County sheriff deputies, wore brown. "Here's the posse," Ferndale said, waving to them. A big deputy knelt down to lift Maguire to his feet.

"Dregovich and Honey Rossini had two mugs with them," Maguire said.

"Way ahead of you, Maguire. We caught the mugs. Couple of them Chicago boys with cute names, Joey the Nose and Frankie Legs, the real deal. They confessed to taking Miss Rossini off the train. Clear case of kidnapping. They ought to share a prison cell over this, but fact is, some rich Italian lip with gold rings and pressed pinstripes will spring them by tomorrow."

Maguire wobbled. Ferndale braced him with his free arm. "Damn lucky they didn't snuff you right here, Maguire. They were the types all right. Left you to freeze to death looks like."

"Can't argue the point, Duke. Did they put up a fight?"

Ferndale laughed. "Never had a chance to find out. Caught 'em standing alongside the highway taking a leak. Recognized their clothed parts right away from the APB. We light the cherries on top to show we mean business. They got no hands free to pull their heaters. Easiest arrest ever made in Montana history. Asked if they could zip before we cuffed 'em. One of them pinched his manhood. Hilarious."

"Where's Honey?" Maguire asked in the morose way any jilted man laments a woman he thought loved him.

"Don't know, much as it pains you to hear it. The Chicago mugs in one car, Dregovich and Miss Rossini in another. Mugs refused to give a description of it. So we're looking for a big man at the wheel and a pretty woman as his hostage."

Maguire glanced sadly toward the fireplace where he had seen her standing. "She's no hostage, Duke. Sad truth is, she turned on me. Honey got me going all right. Had me believing she loved me. I come to save her and find her cozy with Dregovich. I should have known all along, Duke. I'm a damn fool."

Ferndale waved the other cops back outside. "Not the first time you got dizzy with a dame without knowing her, Maguire. Who would have figured a doll like that running with Dregovich and leaving you with a broken heart? If you wanna know, I hoped Miss Rossini wasn't playing you."

"Are you saying you had suspicions? Because I didn't."

"Detectives don't fall in love first and solve crimes second, Maguire. Yeah, I wondered about her motive. Look at this like a cop. Why was Rossini the only business owner willing to speak up? Other than Babe? Seemed curious that a looker like Rossini would draw attention to herself like that."

"She's a brave woman, Duke."

"Or she don't fear criminals. Ask yourself why."

"What about Porky Pig showing up at her store? The attempted burglary to steal jewelry from her store? The mugs at her house?"

"Ain't got easy answers, Maguire. Maybe she sees a big pot of jingle at the end of the rainbow. You tell me, lover boy."

"What now, Duke?"

"What do you mean, what now? Here you are with your head all bashed up and your feet about to turn black and fall off. Besides all that, you look like hell, worse than usual. Figure on a free ride in the meat wagon back to the hospital in Butte."

"Says the cop who nearly dropped dead yesterday."

"Ain't the first time, Maguire."

"Have a heart. I need to write the end of this story."

"Something tells me this has more to do with Irene Rossini than Rusie Dregovich."

"I'm not saying," Maguire said, looking away. "Where did they go, anyway?"

"I've got a hunch."

Maguire groaned. "Not this again."

"You interested or not?"

"You know I am. They took my gun."

"Never got a shot off, did you?"

"I figured the pen was mightier than the sword."

"A revolver would have worked better. You should have shot Dregovich and the mugs. If you repeat that I will deny saying it. Judges in Butte hate vigilante cops. At least some."

Maguire shuddered. "It's freezing cold in here since the fire went out. Did you find my coat? My letters? I've got my whole life in that bundle of letters."

"You mean your miserable tale of woe love life I've heard about long as I've known you?"

"Yes, that one," Maguire said. He went to the bedroom where he woke up in the middle of the night. There, crumpled in the corner, was his suit jacket and his overcoat. He searched frantically through the pockets. His letters were gone.

"Now I'm really mad," he told Ferndale.

"Then let's follow my hunch," the detective told him. They went outside where the three uniformed cops awaited orders. Ferndale advised them to prowl along county roads in hopes of catching trouble.

"You're a little out of your jurisdiction, Duke?"

"It's only twenty miles from Butte and who cares anyway?" Ferndale replied. "We got every cop in Montana searching."

Ferndale climbed behind the wheel of his Oldsmobile. "At least you had the common sense to hide the keys underneath the floor mat where anybody could find them."

"I can't figure out Honey Rossini," Maguire said. "What's her role in this anyway?"

Ferndale turned onto the highway. He pushed the speedometer needle to eighty-five, swerving past occasional patches of ice.

"Maguire, your problem is that you can't figure out dames, period. Guys like you and me ain't the kissy-face types. We got enough hurt without crying over deceitful women and we both loved a lot of them."

"You're talking about Babe as well?"

"I wouldn't go that far."

Maguire shook in his overcoat. "Can you turn up the heat in this jalopy before my feet fall off? I might need them."

"When did you last eat, Maguire?"

"Don't remember. Nobody showed me a menu back at that old house."

Ferndale reached over to click open the glove box. "Couple of candy bars in there. Bought 'em new last month. Help yourself."

Maguire peeled the paper off one and took a huge bite. "So help me understand, Duke. What if Honey Rossini flashes a gun? Do we shoot back?"

Ferndale reached under the seat. He handed Maguire his .38 Special. "The mugs we arrested stole your shooter. Good thing I found it before it wound up in the evidence room. After the chief fires me for fouling up this investigation he will fire me again for arming a civilian. And yeah, it's still loaded."

Maguire pocketed the gun.

"Make sure the chamber is empty or you'll be singing soprano and I ain't in the mood for a concert," Ferndale said.

"What's your hunch anyway?"

"They figure you for dead. Left you to freeze on that floor. That was the idea, weren't it? Put you out of your misery? No Red Maguire, no bad stories about them in the *Bugle*. You helped them along with that damn fool stunt you pulled. What I can't figure is why they didn't plug you and be done with it."

Maguire reached for another candy bar. "I realize we've had our differences, Duke, but why sound gleeful about them killing me?"

"Guess I should show mercy given your drooling state of mind over Miss Rossini."

"Not the first time I lost my way over a woman."

"Everyone in Butte knows, Maguire. Hell, it ain't front-page news. You might have lasted two hours tied up like that with the fire gone out. Then what? More beer for me at the M & M."

"What are friends for?" Maguire said.

Ferndale drove into Butte. Dark clouds hovered over the Hill. Snow swirled around the Oldsmobile. The two-way radio on his dashboard squawked. It was Betty, the dispatcher. "Here we go again," he said, as he reached for the mike.

"Captain Ferndale, come in. Base to Car 2."

"Ferndale, over."

"Man down. Shots fired. Reported location Logan Hotel. Two squads responding."

"Roger that, Betty. On my way."

Ferndale dropped the mouthpiece in its clip and flipped switches for lights and siren. People on the sidewalks stared as the Oldsmobile raced past them.

"Gunplay at my place?" Maguire muttered.

Ferndale stopped outside the Logan where Jimmy Regan waited on the sidewalk. He waved over Ferndale and Maguire. "You won't believe it, Cap. Come take a look."

They tromped up steep stairs to Maguire's room where a body lay heaved over an overturned table. Blood pooled around Rusie Dregovich's head. Maguire whistled his surprise. "What's he doing in my place? Where is Honey?"

Ferndale knelt to take a closer look. "Shot square in the face, boys. Small caliber left a pretty hole in his nose. As ugly dead as he was alive. One little bullet ended his misery."

Regan stood over the giant's body. "So them mobsters finished him off."

Maguire tipped his fedora back, slid his hands into the pockets of his slacks, and leaned against the wall. Ferndale knew the signal.

"You got a theory, Maguire? Spit it out."

The newsman stared a moment at the still body. "We know nobody put a bullet in the Milk Man at some other location and carried him up the stairs to drop him on my floor. Four strong men would struggle doing it. Besides, all that blood soaking into my cheap rug proves somebody killed him here. You can bet my neighbors heard the shot. Whether they paid attention is another story. We get a lot of gunfire around here."

Regan started to speak but Maguire whipped a hand from his pocket in a halting motion.

"So it went down like this, I figure. If Accardo's mobsters wanted to kill the Milk Man they could have shot him back at that farmhouse, or right after they kidnapped Honey Rossini."

Ferndale stood and winced at the pain in his shoulder. "It ain't no kidnapping if she's in on it, Maguire."

"I admit none of this adds up, Duke. Somebody packing heat persuaded Dregovich to come here. Shot him dead. Killed him in my room to pin his murder on me. This somebody had no idea I was tied up all night in Whitehall without my gun. No idea I had an alibi that you, Duke, could prove. That I had been away from my room in this no-account Logan Hotel since I left for Chicago. Honey Rossini didn't kill the Milk Man. *She knew I wasn't here.*"

Ferndale sank into Maguire's reading chair. He drew a shaky hand over his pale weary face. "Ain't too bad for an amateur Irish detective, Maguire. Now, about Miss Rossini. We all hope she's off the hook, but we can't deny she fell in pretty deep with Dregovich. Said so yourself, Maguire. Innocent people don't disappear from crime scenes."

"She hates guns, Duke. She told me."

"Don't mean she can't shoot one."

Regan patted the service gun on his duty belt. "I ask myself how a socialite like Miss Rossini could put down a man twice her size as he stood there watching her. If I was a'facing him three or four feet away I might not have time to draw my weapon before he broke me in two. Takes a lot of nerve, too. Every cop knows pulling the trigger on a man ain't no picnic even if he deserves it."

Just then Maguire heard commotion in the hall. His elderly next-door neighbors, Buck and Myrtle, peered into the room, staring at the body sprawled on his floor.

"Oh my!" Myrtle squealed, her cry sounding more curious than horrified.

"Did you hear anything?" Maguire asked her.

"Nothing. Me and Buck, we left for the clinic at mid-morning. He's got the con, you know. Lungs black as coal. Coughing all night, my Buck. You know how clinics are. We waited and waited. Did you shoot this man, Red?"

"Wish I did, Myrtle, but no. Sorry for the trouble. Seems I attract people with guns."

"Better than daytime television," Buck said. Myrtle nodded her agreement. Maguire led them to their door. He returned to his room at the front of the hotel to find Ferndale suddenly sounding more like a cop.

"Jimmy, get a camera up here to photograph the body before he goes stiff. Get some uniforms to help Arnie at the Forever More haul him away. Ask the other neighbors if they saw Miss Rossini. Me, I should tell the chief what we found here. He ain't going to like it. I ain't up to more excitement today the way this shoulder is throbbing. Maguire, you oughta get some rest but given that your room is currently occupied, I don't know where."

"I do, Duke. Say, you don't look good. Try not to fall over. Can you picture the *Bugle* headline? 'Butte boxing legend faints at the sight of blood.' Bad for your reputation."

"Ain't you the funny guy," Ferndale said.

Maguire went outside to find his Pontiac. It was gone from its usual spot beside the hotel. He remembered he had left it parked at the farmhouse. He trudged north on the Hill to Dublin Gulch. A haze of blue wood smoke hung over the neighborhood and curled out of chimneys on rooming houses and board shacks. Children played in the snow. It was Sunday, a day off from school. He came to the two-story building where Aggie Walsh lived. Four apartments on the first floor, four on the second. Irish in all. Maguire climbed the stairs and knocked on Aggie's door. It flew open to reveal the usual baking aromas. Aggie, swathed in her usual yellow apron tied around a blue dress, screamed her surprise.

"Red, me boy! You're alive, I thank God in heaven for the sight before me." Aggie gave him a mighty hug. The *Bugle* printed a story that you were missing. I called Mr. Stoffleman to ask what happened. That cranky cuss really does care for you, Red. Tell me what happened. Tell me all of it. Oh, look at you. Your clothes all dirty, your face tells me you haven't slept for a week, what's a mother to do, Red?"

"Feed this poor boy, Aggie?"

"Why, I have a meat pie coming out of the oven. Apple pie too. Take a chair, me boy." As she heaped a plate, he began the story for her, telling of his train trip to Chicago.

A flash of hurt washed over Aggie's face. "Did you find your birth mother in Chicago, Red?"

"Lily is lost to me, Aggie. You and I, we might not be blood, but you are my mother. That will never change."

She came around the table to kiss him on the forehead. "Me son, pity any man who tries to hurt you."

Maguire told her about finding Dregovich dead. He dwelled more on his crush for Irene Rossini than he intended.

"Aggie, I came for advice."

"So you're in love again," she replied. She leaned toward him, her arms folded on the table, afternoon light filtering into the warm kitchen. Aggie Walsh was as Irish as Kieran "Red" Maguire. If only his father had lived long enough to marry Aggie. If only Red had been born to her. If only.

"Irene Rossini, I call her Honey. That's her nickname. I quoted her in the *Bugle*."

Aggie nodded, not wanting to interrupt.

"If she's involved in this miserable affair she will go to prison unless the cops shoot her first...."

"How did you solve every other crime, Red? The Purple Roses Murders? All those others? Long as I've known you, coming on thirty years now, you let that sentimental part of you take charge when things go wrong. Why is that? Life has battered you, me son. When you were but a mere boy you fought for your respect in the Gulch. You lost both parents. Criminals shoot at you. Beat on you. Still you get up. And yet, well, sometimes you lead with your heart instead of your head. Your dalliance with Mary Miller nearly got you killed. You want Miss Rossini? Instead of proving she threw in with these mobsters, prove she's not. Find the missing piece to this puzzle. I tell you this, me boy. You stalk these dark streets and see nothing but sadness and despair."

"It's my job, Aggie. Crime never quits."

"That I understand, me son. You hope to save Miss Rossini? From herself? From mobsters? From the law? If you think Rusie Dregovich wasn't the end of it, then who?"

Maguire stretched out on Aggie's couch and fell asleep. He awoke in the dark. He found her in the kitchen kneading dough. "More baked goods, Aggie? Do you ever stop?"

Aggie waved a floured hand. "Pays my rent, Red. That and the money you send me each month. You know how it is, being alone. I remember when I started selling pies and breads up and down the Gulch. Children everywhere. They say someday our neighborhood will be gone. The Company wants to dig everything up, even our houses. How sad, me son. This is my home. And yours."

"Got to run, Aggie. I think I know who killed Rusie Dregovich." He kissed Aggie, shrugged into his overcoat, and stepped outside into a thick hail of falling snow.

***

Maguire saw a light shining in Lucky Finero's bail office in the back of a dark building next to Sundberg Plumbing and Electric. He opened a battered door on Galena Street and climbed the narrow staircase to a hallway where a single bare lightbulb hanging on a cord illuminated the peeling wallpaper. He pounded on the door. "Lucky, it's Red Maguire. You alive?"

Footsteps. The door swung open. Finero brandished his vicious glistening knife under Maguire's nose. "So if it ain't the crime-bustin' pretend cop from the *Bugle*. Hell of a deal, the ending to them Purple Rose Murders. C'mon in, Maguire, I hear you got yourself in another mess of trouble."

"Planning to cut off another set of ears, Lucky?"

"Not unless somebody comes in here demanding cosmetic work, Maguire. You game?"

"Doubt it would help me, Lucky. I came for advice."

The smaller man tossed the knife on his desk. "You want to know about Rusie Dregovich. Hear he wound up dead in your place at the Logan. You kill him?"

"Somebody else got to him first."

"Had dreams of being a wise guy, that Rusie. Heard that even before I read your story in *Bugle* about him being cozy with those Chicago mobsters. Streets have ears. Whatta you want to know, Maguire?"

"Who killed Dregovich?"

"I hear things, Maguire. I ain't inclined to say."

"Never stopped you before."

"Got my reasons, Maguire. You got yours?"

"I think I know who did it, Lucky."

"Then who? Better not be me unless you're fixin' to ditch them ears." Lucky reached for the knife.

Maguire spoke the name. Finero nodded. He penciled an address on a scrap of paper and handed it to Maguire.

***

Back at the Logan Hotel, where the "L" had long ago gone dark on the flickering orange neon sign, Maguire found the door open and Ferndale smoking at the window.

"Sorry for the break-in, Maguire. Can't sleep. Hell, can't make sense of any of this. Robberies, murders, mobsters, you name it. Now this big Serb dead. What a calling card, huh?" Ferndale, coatless, pointed to the blackening blood stain on the rug. His left arm of no use, his service gun holstered on his right hip, his words in ragged near-whispers.

"Let me take you to the hospital, Duke. Haven't you done enough?"

"I ain't solved a lick on this case, Maguire. Chief will tell you that. Probably fired me already far as I know."

"What do you hear from that FBI agent? Wilbur White?"

"Shoulda told you, Maguire. He ain't no help to us. Got drunk at the Board and Trade and spilled rumors about J. Edgar Hoover to a pretty woman. Then she and her accomplice boyfriend rolled the gossiping Wilbur in the alley for his wallet and wristwatch. Bet you never heard that one before."

"If being sent to Butte is punishment, I pity the man when Hoover is done with him, Duke."

"He weren't no use to us anyhow."

"Tell me again why you're not going back to the hospital?"

"Got to find Miss Rossini. Arrest her for murder and all these other crimes she committed with Dregovich."

"Except the killer is someone else, Duke. It was right in front of us all along."

Ferndale jerked his head around. "No mystery why you feel sore, Maguire. A sad man drains a bottle of liquor over a case like this. Maybe you swallowed one since I saw you a few hours ago? I sure as hell would if I stood in your shoes. You want answers? Hell, the corpse won't tell us. Somebody shut him up but good."

"Duke, you know as well as I do."

Ferndale snuffed out the cigarette in an ashtray on the windowsill. He turned to face Maguire, his eyes dark and twitching.

"Give me a name."

Maguire did and found himself socked in the left eye with such force he fell backwards. Duke Ferndale stood over him, right fist cocked, anger flushing his face.

"I thought you were a left-handed boxer," Maguire managed.

"Never said I couldn't hit with my right. Maguire, you damn fool. You can figure on a punch to the other eye if you're wrong about this."

"Once hurts bad enough and you know it," Maguire said, rubbing his face before staggering to his feet. He reached in his pocket and handed over the scrap of paper from Lucky Finero.

The cop heaved a sigh. "Let's go," he said, retrieving Maguire's fedora from the floor.

After some bartering over whose injury was worse, Ferndale handed over the keys to his Oldsmobile. "You can drive with your good eye considerin' the other is swelled shut, Maguire."

"You hit me with a jackhammer, Duke."

"Ain't nothin'. Back in my ring days I led with my right, slammed the other guy with my left. 'Cept my left ain't workin' too good right now."

They headed for Finn Town. "Ever hear of that Finn by the name of Karvonen, Duke? Tall, blond? Fell right in with the labor Democrats. Wore hockey skates all winter on the rinks. Came from Minnesota. Another eastern immigrant moves to town with big ideas about politics. Go figure."

Ferndale grunted. "Them Finns sure love snow and ice. Saunas too. If the Irish don't take over Butte the Finns will."

"There you go again, Duke."

"Sure could go for a cold lager if Babe is pouring," Ferndale said, waving Maguire to a stop at Babe's Bar. They found the place packed with miners. One of them stood on the bar to blow Babe a kiss as she hustled to pop the caps off beer bottles. "Get off my bar or lose a leg!" she shouted over the commotion.

Maguire and Ferndale took the only open table. Babe came over. "You look like hell, Ferndale. Maguire, you look worse. You see out of that eye, mister?"

"Two drafts, tall." Ferndale waved two fingers and dropped a fiver on the table.

"I close in ten. You jokers better drink up fast and get."

"What's the rush, Babe?" Ferndale asked.

"Not feeling good, that's what."

They drank up and left as miners dribbled out of the bar. Ferndale's Olds complained in the cold and then turned over. Maguire tried to read the scrap of paper from Lucky Finero. "No need. I'll tell you where," Ferndale said.

The sedan slid down a steep icy street. Several blocks later they passed the little house, did a U-turn, and parked a few doors up. An hour passed before they saw headlights. The approaching car, rumbling through the snow, stopped in front of the house. When they saw lights in the windows, Ferndale exhaled like a man at the end of his rope. "Good a time as any. Bring your piece, Maguire."

Ferndale knocked on the door. When Babe McGraw swung it open, her face showing surprise, Ferndale barged in.

"Where is she, Babe?"

Babe feigned a look of confusion.

"You know damn well, Babe. Irene Rossini." His voice came even and low.

"Get out of my house, Ferndale. Take the newsie with you. Ain't no Rossini here, you clueless dick cop."

A muffled cry came from a back room. As the cop and the newsman turned toward the source of it, Babe whipped an ugly black pistol from her coat pocket. She pointed it at one man and then the other. Maguire thought of Nancy Addleston and how tired he was of seeing the business end of a gun.

"Can't say I knew Babe was dirty for a fact," Ferndale said, almost whispering.

"She turned, Duke. They got to her. What was it, Babe? That beating you took set you on fire?"

Maguire took a step toward Babe. She trained the barrel of the gun on his chest. He saw the gold tips of the bullets in the cylinder. Her finger twitched on the trigger. "Easy, Babe. What are you doing mixed up in this anyway? No need for gunplay. Bring Miss Rossini out. She has no part in this."

Babe backed away, her eyes wide, her voice a disturbing growl. "Hands up, face the wall. I ain't gonna say it twice." They heard a door open and a rustle of clothing. Maguire sensed two people in the room. "Red?" came Honey's soft voice. Both men turned. She wore the same odd work clothes from the day in the farmhouse. Maguire saw a torn lip and blood dried around her nose. A vicious purple bruise stretched from her jaw to her right ear. Honey wobbled, her eyes teary, her hands tied behind her back. "Help me, Red, please," she implored. Babe grabbed Honey's hair with the hand missing three fingers and jerked her head back.

"Whiny bitch ain't she?"

Maguire wondered why he and Ferndale had walked into Babe's house without drawing their guns. Because they wanted to believe they were wrong about Babe? Now she had the drop on them.

Ferndale brushed his coat back to show his gun. "What's your trouble, Babe? This ain't your style. You and me, we go back a long ways. Put the gun down, Babe, we have something between us. What the devil is going on?" He sounded flat and despondent, not like Ferndale at all.

"This ain't about us, Ferndale. Sure, we had us some good times. I ain't got a good reason to regret any of it. Look at you and your buddy Maguire over there, two doomed men. Ain't any understanding of my lot in life. Dammit, I deserve something in this world. Something you two boys won't never understand. You think I get rich selling beer at my bar? Got no insurance, got no jingle in the bank, those hospital bills done broke me. Know what? Them working men showed me respect until Dregovich sent Porky Pig and his buddies to steal from me. Dregovich, he never understood them miners like I do. Them boys listen to what Babe says, except them four who jumped me. Dregovich wanted to take over Butte. Big man, big talk. When he fouled it up them mobsters came a'callin' to me. They say, 'Babe McGraw, this Milk Man double-crossed us. He ain't sufficient to run our operation. They hand me an envelope full of cash. Big money, boys. Enough jingle to pay off the mortgage on my bar. They say they ain't got use for Dregovich anymore. Too much trouble. They want him dead."

"So you killed Dregovich," Maguire said. "You delivered on the Milk Man."

"Good with words, ain't you, Maguire? Sure, I shot him. He weren't nothin' to me. Saw my gun and wailed like a baby. Blubbering fool begged before I put a round in his skull. Rusie, I put up with him until he sicced those miners on me."

Ferndale snorted. "So you murdered him over a beating?"

"Doubt you much care, Ferndale. They want me to run this town. I got a reputation, Ferndale. Ain't nobody who messes with Babe and gets away with it. Them miners, they listen to me. I got means now. Them boys in Chicago, they say I can own this town. They ain't going to let nobody take this away from me."

As Babe waved her gun for emphasis, Honey hung her head. Maguire wondered how many times Babe had struck the woman he loved.

He felt the beer rising in his throat. "How do you see this reckless scheme playing out, Babe? Trying to frame me for the Milk Man's murder? Nobody will believe I shot Dregovich in the Logan Hotel. I had an alibi, Babe. News to you? Ferndale knows. So does Honey. Why try to pin the murder on me?"

Babe leered a nasty mouthful of little sharp teeth. "Slow to catch on, Maguire? Sure, I helped you at first. You wrote them stories in the *Bugle* that gave Dregovich all the glory. I get to thinking, why not Ruby McGraw. My formal name will mean something in this town. But you get in the way with all your big shot questions and them stories you write for all of Butte to read. Wanna hear a confession? You scare me, Red Maguire. You ain't weak like Ted Ketchul. I needed to stop you before you figure me involved with those Chicago boys and print my name in the *Bugle*. Yeah, I talked Dregovich into breaking into your room at the Logan. Told him we would wait for you and Ferndale there. The dumb Serb never questioned my motive. The gunshot was loud enough to wake the dead. Ain't that who lives with you in that old heap of nothin' hotel?"

Maguire felt sweat trickling down his back. He knew what was coming.

"So you figured Ferndale would arrest me for murder. Then what?"

"Either arrest you for murder or I would shoot you myself. And then him," Babe said, waving the gun toward Ferndale.

Ferndale said, "Don't I know, Babe. I love you." Maguire saw Ferndale reach for his gun, but fumbled with it, his dominant hand being the left one in the sling. Babe yelled "Duke!" as she capped off a round. Ferndale bucked and fell.

Maguire heard himself yelling in the commotion. Honey screamed. Babe turned her smoking gun to Honey's head. He felt the chiseled grip of his .38 in his palm, the barrel rising as he took aim at Babe. His first shot slammed into her stocky thigh. She reeled and stared at him. He saw desperation in her eyes. She again lifted the gun to Honey's head. Maguire's second shot struck where Ferndale had taught Maguire to shoot, if he ever took a life, the only place he could be sure. Babe's gun clattered to the floor. She slammed over an end table, her legs askew, and went still. Blood pulsed from the hole in the center of her chest. Her eyes stuck open and vacant in the way a hopeless drunk passed out watching a bad television show.

The room reeked of gunpowder and fresh blood.

Honey fell to the floor.

'Nobody forgets Red Maguire'

Chief Morse, who arrived on the scene soon after the shooting, confiscated Maguire's gun for evidence.

"I ought to arrest you and still might," the chief fumed.

"I shot in self-defense, Chief. It wasn't vengeance and it wasn't an idle moment for a *Bugle* reporter on the crime beat. Babe intended to kill us all."

"Noted, Maguire, but a civilian using a police weapon in commission of a fatal shooting is a serious crime. At least it ought to be."

Nobody knew how Ferndale stayed alive on the way to the hospital. Babe's bullet hit him high on the left side of his chest. It tore open the gunshot wound from Cracker Gibbons and the previous ugly wound that Nancy Addleston inflicted, knocking him unconscious and rendering him cruelly close to death at the hand of the woman he loved.

Ferndale was out cold, sleeping off surgery early the next morning, when Chief Morse seized his detective's gun and badge. "I'll tell him later he's fired," the chief told Peach, who stood protectively over the older man. A half hour remained on her midnight shift. When the chief stalked out of the hospital, she followed.

"You can't do that!" she shouted at him, her orange hair riffling in the wind. She remembered the day those many years ago when the chief's young daughter came dead on arrival to the hospital. The chief begged the doctor and nurses to revive her. The doctor checked for a pulse and shook his head. Peach held the chief as he sobbed.

Now with Ferndale again all shot to hell, the chief raged. "This is none of your affair, Peach. My mistake for talking that way in front of you. Duke Ferndale, what a pain in the ass. You know that as well as I do. I can't have him and his newspaper buddy Maguire going vigilante on us."

"What would you do without them, Chief? They put an end to Dregovich and everything evil he did to this town. Maguire exposed his many crimes in the *Bugle*. Ferndale tracked him down like you paid him to do. Those two men caught Babe McGraw red-handed before more damage was done to this town. Look at your captain in there, shot to hell with nothing in the world to call his own except that badge you hold in your hand, and you fired him for doing his job. He isn't even awake to swear at you for doing it."

The chief looked indecisive, but just for a moment. "You've never steered me wrong, Peach."

Coatless, Peach shrugged against the bitter cold. "The battle's over, Chief. You've won." She pulled him close and kissed him on the cheek. Long a fan of Peach, he leaned into her.

They went back into the hospital together. When Ferndale awoke a few hours later, he found his badge on the table beside his bed and his service revolver in the drawer.

"Babe?" he called out, longing in his voice, before he fell asleep again.

***

Maguire wrote the story Butte expected.

Clyde Stoffleman hustled around the *Bugle* city room in his usual state of agitation, demanding that Maguire spill every detail from the shootings of Duke Ferndale and Babe McGraw. "I don't know whether to fire you or praise you, but for the moment I'll stand by the latter," the editor told Maguire as the clock ticked toward midnight.

"Might as well do both, boss."

"Next time, if you're going to shoot someone, damn well do it before deadline." Stoffleman frowned and walked away.

Maguire pounded the keys on his Remington. He poured out everything that crossed his mind. The Milk Man's murder. The mobsters. Honey as a hostage. Babe turned bad. Ferndale shot, again. Wayward miners willing to hide behind masks to scare merchants. The entire devious plot.

As Maguire wrote at his typewriter, Don Morgan, the night editor, hurried off with each finished page. "Off the floor in ten!" Stoffleman yelled across the room, meaning Maguire had ten minutes to wrap up the story. "The Old Man says we can hold the press for an hour tops. You foul this up, Maguire, both of us will be busting rock a mile down by noon tomorrow."

"Doing my best, boss!" Maguire yelled back.

"Give it to us in five, Red. Those union compositors in the back room need to set your story in type. The Old Man reminds us he pays them by the hour. They don't work cheap."

Still, the presses roared to life nearly two hours late. That was after a glowering Snuff, the foreman, appeared in the city room with ink-stained hands on his hips to hurry things along. Morgan's headline filled the top third of the *Bugle* front page:

Deadly Gunfight
in East Butte

The *Bugle* sold out in record time that morning. Stoffleman convinced the Old Man to publish an *Extra* by supper with further details of the Halloween Mask Robberies. "The name doesn't do justice to the magnitude of these crimes," Stoffleman told Maguire. "How about Masks, Mayhem and Murders?"

And so it was. Maguire spent the morning gathering new details with assistance from obituary reporter Calvin Claggett.

"Should I assume you find yourself in seventh heaven in moments like this?" Maguire called over to Claggett.

"Admirable wordplay, Red, but I can't deny it. I hear we get a joint byline in the *Extra*. Both of us *Bugle* stiff writers. How does it feel, Maguire?"

"You mean staff writers, Calvin?"

"I mean stiff writers and you damn well know it."

***

Simone's funeral came on a stormy day, like every other day in Butte that winter, on a day when the sky swirled with dark clouds.

Maguire expected a small ceremony. Instead, it seemed all of Butte turned out. Stoffleman and Morgan came, as did the hunched Claggett, seeking as much an obituary for the city's latest wave of crime as for the passing of a popular uptown waitress.

Arnie Petrovich at the Forever More accomplished his classic restoration of Simone to an appearance resembling her living self. She lay in the casket in her Silver Star uniform, her apron tied around her waist, her order book clasped in her wrinkled white fingers. Her brother, mute and head bowed, sat in front of her casket in a wheelchair.

All the Silver Star regulars came. So did Mayor Ticklenberg, Police Chief Morse, dozens of business owners and a few hundred Butte folks who never knew Simone but read about her murder. An attack on one Butte resident meant an attack on them all.

And Honey Rossini.

***

The morning after Maguire shot Babe, he drove Honey home from the emergency room in Ferndale's Olds.

Babe's punch to Honey's pretty face had blackened her right eye and fractured her cheek bone. Her glamorous good looks took a vacation. Maguire knew it was a temporary condition. Nobody put Honey down for long.

"I suppose you wonder," she said after several minutes of icy silence.

"You were hugging a crook, Honey."

"I can't pretend to know how that looked to you, Red."

"I can't pretend how sorry I am that it went this far."

Honey sighed. "That we fell in love, Red? You and me?"

"No, I mean that I dragged you into this hell and nearly got you killed, that's what. Babe came a second away from ... well, what's the use of talking about it anyway?"

"Red, please let me tell you what happened back in that awful farmhouse, when those men tied you up and left you for dead."

Maguire nodded. Betty from police dispatch came across the two-way radio on the dashboard. The M & M bar called for officers to break up a drunken fight involving beer bottles and somebody's ham and eggs from the restaurant counter at the other side of the room. Maguire looked at his wristwatch. Still morning, but life goes on in Butte.

"It was the worst time of my life," Honey continued. "Those men, Joey and Frankie, saw right away that I was fooling Dregovich. I only wanted to keep him from killing me, Red. From killing you. I thought we had a chance until they got the jump on you. After they tied you up in the bedroom, they became desperate and mean, pacing with guns in their hands. They said they would shoot me if I tried to help you. Joey tied a rope around my neck, like a noose. When I complained he pulled on the rope until I gasped for breath. Dregovich never said a word to stop him. I think he was afraid of those men. They told him they shot anyone who crossed them. They said it was nothing to them to shoot us all. I could tell they were unhappy about how things were going."

Maguire pulled in front of Honey's house. They went inside before her neighbor Martha saw them. Honey wanted to hide her bruises.

"She won't take kindly. Oh Red, look what those criminals did to my family home."

"I'll help you clean up. How did you end up with Babe?" Maguire said, pushing to hear more. They tossed off their coats and went to work.

"We left the farmhouse in Dregovich's car. He was in a foul mood, worse than before. I was hungry and tired and scared. When we got back to Butte, I saw a policeman in a black and white. I waved for help. I remember nothing after that. When I woke up my face felt numb. I hurt all over."

"He punched you when you signaled the cop."

"I was in a cold cellar, tied to a chair."

"Babe's house," Maguire said. "I guess we'll never find out how she crossed paths with Dregovich after you arrived back in Butte. All we know for sure is that she killed him. Babe McGraw and Rusie Dregovich folded to greed, the foundation of most crimes, and once they smelled easy money, they felt no guilt at killing for it."

"Neither of those people should be confused with clear thinkers, Red."

Honey reached in her pocket. She pulled out the precious photograph of her as a little girl, standing with her parents in their Easter clothes. She squeezed her dark eyes shut. A tear wandered down her cheek as she traced the cracked glass with her fingers.

"Glass comes cheap, Honey. The photo looks fine."

She fell into his arms. They were a pair. Exhausted, dirty, beaten. And, in love. Honey tucked her head into the big Irishman's neck.

"On a better day, let's pose for another," she whispered.

***

Then Honey told him the rest of it.

When Maguire fell asleep on the train, she napped beside him with her red coat pulled over her like a blanket. She awoke when the conductor announced a half-hour stop at the depot in Billings. Cold air blew into the coach when the porter opened the door. Honey stepped into the aisle and slipped her coat back on. She went outside to the landing with the thought of walking back and forth to stretch her legs. Strangers, men in dark suits, appeared on either side of her. "Holler and you're dead," whispered one of them. Honey later discovered his name was Joey. They led her to a brown car, Joey at the wheel, and turned west toward Butte. Neither man talked. Honey, wedged between them in the front seat, feared what they intended to do with her.

They rode for fifty miles on the highway before the taller man introduced himself as Frankie and offered her a cigarette from a red package. Two hours later they pulled into a trashy motel on the outskirts of Bozeman. It appeared abandoned from the outside, Honey had observed, which explained why it was otherwise empty. The men bound Honey's hands and feet and stashed her in an adjoining room with flowered curtains and a matching bedspread that had never seen a washing machine. The room had no phone. Honey slept fitfully on top of the bed, wrapped in her coat. The next morning, after she ate a breakfast of day-old donuts, Rusie Dregovich came into the room. He leered at Honey from head to toe, cut loose the clothesline rope binding her, and left. His odor of oil and sweat lingered.

"Ain't she a looker?" Honey heard Joey say through the paper-thin wall.

They spent two days holed up in the motel. During the second night she pressed her ear to the wall and heard a conversation about her fate.

" ... kill the broad," someone said in a low growl. "What's the use of her?"

A deeper voice, presumably Dregovich's, came to her defense. "I need her to find Maguire. Stay off her."

"We take our orders from Chicago, not some oily miner," Joey said.

"You gonna pay for that," Dregovich told him. "I got hundreds of union members who do what I tell 'em."

"We got hundreds and all of them pack heat and break kneecaps," Joey replied.

Frankie spoke up. "How you get in deep with Mr. Accardo anyway?"

"He knows I own Butte," Dregovich said.

Joey again. "Then what we doing holed up in a two-bit motel with a broad that oughta be in movies in hopes of catching a newsie so you can shut him up? That add up, ya think? Put a bullet in their head and be done with it."

A chair scraped and Dregovich spoke again. "Maguire will write anything I want now that I have his girl. That joker will tell all of Butte about the great man Rusie Dregovich leading the workers to take charge of what's theirs. I will tell them people how it is, ya wait."

"Ya ain't got a brain, Milk Man," Joey said.

"You small-timers better watch your mouths. You ain't running this show."

"Ain't that a fact," Frankie said. "Thing is, our bosses ain't gentlemen like us. Watch your back, Milk Man. Size don't matter in our business."

"If you don't like it, get lost. Accardo sent you to help me."

"This ain't what the boss had in mind, Dregovich. You should be in Butte raising jingle for the cause. He ain't seeing the cash you promised. The boss, you make him unhappy, figure on him makin' some adjustments to your general welfare. Hear me, Milk Man? This here chasing around is what you call a side show. We come here for the circus, get it?"

Honey fell asleep. Sometime in the night Frankie nudged her awake. "We gotta go, doll. Cop nosin' around with the manager. Go to the car. Milk Man getting antsy."

They went to the deserted farmhouse near Whitehall. Dregovich struck a match to a heap of brush in the fireplace. The three odd men stood around arguing. Honey sensed their growing desperation. Dregovich, she could tell, began to admit his serious mistake. His pursuit of Maguire had taken him far astray from his principal purpose of fleecing Butte.

"I oughta plug the broad," Joey said in front of her. Honey could see Dregovich warming to the suggestion. The arguing continued until Joey and Frankie stormed out of the house with a vow to drive back to Chicago.

"Them boys won't get far. Too many cops. Now I take over," he said, staring ominously at Honey. She knew he had no gun, nor did he need one. He would beat her to death. She decided to humor him to save herself.

Honey told Dregovich they could run away together. She remembered Jane Russell in the movie *Fuzzy Pink Nightgown* when she pretended to fall in love with her kidnapper. Honey put on her best acting performance.

"Now it's just you and me, Rusie," she told the lout standing before her.

"Don't be gettin' no ideas," he said, wary and interested at the same time.

"Forget Maguire, Rusie. He made a mess of everything. I watched you from afar so many times and asked myself why we couldn't be together."

"You talk nonsense," he grunted.

"Here we are, finally, even in the worst of conditions. You and me, Rusie. We don't need Maguire. That man is dead to us now. No need to run away. Let's go back to Butte. Like you say, you own that town. Can you imagine what a pair we would make, working together? I know how to make money. Lots of it."

She stepped close to Dregovich. Wrinkling her nose, she grabbed onto his bib overalls and hugged him. He pushed her away. "I heard a car door," he said, walking to the window. He stared into the falling snow for a minute before turning to Honey, chewing tobacco dribbling from his coarse mouth.

"What a pair we'd make," he echoed.

Then Maguire knocked on the door. His ruse to trick Dregovich might have worked if Joey and Frankie had continued down the road to Chicago.

***

Even with Rusie Dregovich and Babe McGraw dead, rumors of mob influence in Butte hung in the air like old smoke. Maguire telephoned Will James at the *Chicago Tribune*.

"I hear from my reliable source Jimmy the Jowls that Accardo gave up on Butte. The city gave him too much trouble. You, Red Maguire, broke him."

"Nobody dares to mess with Butte, Mr. James. At least from the outside."

Maguire heard a laugh over the telephone line. "I'm a believer. Show me around if I ever come to your city. Keep your heater handy if things get rough."

"The police chief took it away. I'll get another."

"Say, Mr. Maguire, you should know that the *Tribune* published your stories in full, under your byline, ever since you cracked this case. Why Butte when you could work here? I encouraged my editors to hire you. Hundreds of thousands of readers in Chicago saw your stories. Why not make it official?"

It was Maguire's turn to laugh. "People like to shoot at me, Mr. James. Makes a guy feel at home here in Butte. I have a good reason for staying here. It doesn't involve gunplay."

"So you fell in love, Mr. Maguire. She's worth it?"

"After a strange week, I'm back to thinking so."

"If anything changes, call me. I could use your help at this newspaper. After dark, Chicago becomes a boiling pot of misfits."

"Apt description of Butte even before the sun sets," Maguire said.

"One thing, Mr. Maguire, and take me seriously. Accardo never slips away like a lamb. You can bet he won't forget. Dregovich was a hard case, and so was McGraw, but if the mob wants back into Butte they will find another person like them to do their bidding. Your fine city has too many dollars rolling around. Watch your back, my friend. These mobsters despise newspapermen. You and me, we find the bodies they want to bury. What's more, we tell everybody about their vice in print. The mob hates newsmen as much as cops."

"Fair warning, Mr. James. When I get done writing about these crimes nobody in Butte will find good use for a Chicago mobster."

"But nobody will forget Red Maguire," James said before hanging up.

Including Lily.

Soon as Maguire hung up the telephone, Luverne, from the switchboard, handed him a letter postmarked from Chicago. A woman's careful cursive on the envelope, different from the typical death threat, compelled him to tear it open. It began:

"Dear Kieran, I saw your stories in the *Tribune* about the trouble in Montana. Please read all of my letter before you throw it away." He skipped to the bottom of the third page. "I am ailing and must see you soon. Lovingly, your mother."

Maguire placed the letter back in the envelope and slipped it inside a drawer to read later. Shaken, he thought of how Lily's letter felt like a betrayal of his doting adopted mother Aggie Walsh.

"So many years, why now?" he whispered.

Red's vague memory of first grade, his only one, involved a Valentine card he received from a classmate named Carlotta. She lived across the alley and up three doors from his little house. "I love you Keran," she wrote on the Valentine. No matter that she had misspelled his name. He took the Valentine home to show his mother. She smelled of that awful brown liquid she poured from a tall bottle she kept in the cupboard. Lily laughed. First grade boys had no business chasing girlfriends, she slurred in what his father called her "evil voice." She tore the Valentine into pieces and tossed the scraps into the trash can under the kitchen sink. Kieran followed Carlotta home from school a few more times. She never looked back.

Talk about the Chicago mob lingered until Maguire's next story appeared in the *Bugle* relating Accardo's withdrawal from Butte. Then the talk vanished as sudden as it had arrived.

Members of Local 1235, eager to restore the union's reputation, elected Al Shukler as their new president.

Maguire never disclosed that Shukler was his secret informant. The Welshman telephoned Maguire at the *Bugle* to say he and other new officers put a bounty on miners who robbed business owners of their money. "We suspect we'll find more than fifty hoodlums in our ranks willing to follow Dregovich to his grave, and if they don't own up to their crimes, they damn well might. You quote me on that, Maguire. These dark times of cringing in fear are over."

A few days later, when the coroner released Babe McGraw's autopsy, Maguire read it with shaking hands. Taking a life left a man feeling despondent, regardless of circumstances. Just as Ferndale had described so many times.

Maguire's first bullet tore through the femoral artery in Babe's thigh. She would have died within minutes from that wound, but minutes too long. Crazed and desperate, Babe still had the strength to raise her gun to Honey's head. Maguire didn't hesitate. His second shot pierced Babe's heart. Death came sudden.

***

At the cemetery, Honey Rossini pressed against Maguire, her arm through his. They watched two thin men wearing earmuffs lower Simone's casket into the icy ground. Honey reached into her purse. "You'll want these," she said, pulling out the letters and notes Maguire held together with the red rubber band. "No, I didn't read them, Red, so don't worry. I knew they were private."

"Where did you find them, Honey?"

"I saw that creep Joey come out of that room with the bundle in his hand. He was going to burn them to get the fire going again. I distracted him with an old magazine I kept rolled up in my coat. I told him it would light much faster."

"One of your glamor magazines."

"What symbolism, my dreams of Hollywood turning to ash."

"Nothing is forever, Honey."

"Says the man who survived certain death."

"So you couldn't save me, but you saved my letters?"

"Oh, Red. I'm so sorry for how I talked to you back at the farmhouse when you came to rescue me. It was a foolish gamble to distract that beast Dregovich from killing us. Will you forgive me?"

"I already did. You had him believing you, Irene Rossini."

"Call me Honey, remember?"

"I'll call you anytime, Honey."

"Something's on your mind, Red. What is it?"

"How close we came to winding up like Simone. Like all the others I write stories about, the ones who died in violent crimes. My job is to make sense of the mayhem for readers of the *Bugle*. Until the other night my weapon was a typewriter, not a gun. I killed her, Honey. What have I become?"

Honey kissed him on the cheek. "A newspaper detective who solves crimes. You care about people, Red. Only a good man does that. Judge yourself by saving my life, not by ending the life of my attacker."

"You help me see what I didn't understand, Honey."

"What does that mean, Red Maguire, chronicler of crime?"

"That the next story I write for the *Bugle* needs to tell so much more than people dying from gunshots in the night. History will remember this winter's chain of events as a dark chapter, all right, but the story tomorrow is a tale of triumph over greed, of love over fear. I see it all now. No criminal owns Butte. This city belongs to everyone."

Honey leaned up to kiss him. "Our city, Red. You and me and Butte."

They walked past the tombstones, clutching each other close, as the mighty mine gallows frames on the hill watched over them.

###

Masks, Mayhem and Murder is my second Red Maguire mystery novel. The first is *Mystery of the Purple Roses*. Both stories take place in the legendary mining city of Butte, Montana, in 1954 and 1955. Maguire reports crime for the *Bugle* newspaper.

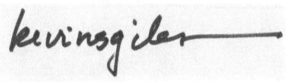

Website: kevinsgiles.com
Email: kevin@kevinsgiles.com
Free newsletter signup: green button at kevinsgiles.com
Facebook: facebook.com/kevsgiles/
Twitter: @kevsgiles
Amazon profile: amazon.com/Kevin-S-Giles

Also by Kevin S. Giles:

Nonfiction:
One Woman Against War: The Jeannette Rankin Story
Jerry's Riot: True Story of Montana's 1959 Prison Disturbance

Fiction:
Mystery of the Purple Roses
Summer of the Black Chevy

To order: https://booklocker.com/

CPSIA information can be obtained
at www.ICGtesting.com
Printed in the USA
BVHW070919240621
610369BV00005B/24